UNTIL THE SUN

CHANDLER MORRISON

This is a work of fiction. All of the characters, organizations, and events portrayed in this novel are either products of the author's imagination or used fictitiously.

Until The Sun Copyright © 2019 by Chandler Morrison

ISBN: 9781639510481

Published by Death's Head Press, an imprint of Dead Sky Publishing, LLC
Miami Beach, Florida
www.deadskypublishing.com

Cover by: Sam Wolfe Connelly

ACKNOWLEDGMENTS

For their contributions to the publication of this book, and for their steadfast support and encouragement, the author wishes to thank the following individuals: Jarod Barbee, Patrick C. Harrison III, Monica J. O'Rourke, James Lee, Lisa Marie, Sarah Ruth, Kelsey Burke, and Tracy Applegate.

The Devil pulls the strings which make us dance;
We find delight in in the most loathsome things;
Some furtherance of Hell each new day brings,
And yet we feel no horror in that rank advance.

—Charles Baudelaire

PROLOGUE

GOOGLE TELLS YOU THAT you're going to die at 7:06 AM.

You grip the balcony's railing and look to the east. Miles of suburban wasteland stretch out beneath you. Downtown Cleveland shimmers on the horizon, its dagger-like buildings menacing over the skeletal fingers of the barren black treetops. To the north, Lake Erie is a pane of black glass glittering beneath the amber sky. From it a cold blast of November wind swoops inland and bites into your bones, but you do not shiver.

You check your phone, nearly dropping it from your trembling hand. It's 7:05.

One minute.

One minute to sunrise.

One minute, and *poof*, there goes the neighborhood.

No. Not the neighborhood. Just you.

Your eyes burn from the light, to which they've become unaccustomed, causing tears to stream down your face. They're not *real* tears, though. They're not the kind of tears you shed for Mara or Justine, for Quincey, or for your parents. *Those* had been tears. No, there's nothing emotional tied to the briny fluid dampening your cheeks. It's a biological response to an unfamiliar agent, perhaps one of the last natural components remaining in your no-longer-human body.

A body that will be reduced to ash in less than sixty seconds.

Your skin prickles with pained discomfort, pleading for you to retreat back into the mansion, back into the safety of the dark's welcoming embrace.

It is a plea that falls upon willfully deaf ears.

You pull back the hood of your jacket, turn your face up to the brightening sky, and wait for the sun to take you.

PART 1
– THROUGH
DARK GLASSES

CHAPTER 1
– VARNEY &
FRIENDS

1

Blood.

Everywhere.

You look around the living room. Your gaze is stoic. The man sits slumped in the armchair, his jugular punctured. His skin is pale like card-stock, his body withered. A spilt bottle of Bud Light lies next to him on the carpet.

The woman is on the floor a few feet away, face-up, a similar stab wound in her neck. She's as white and shriveled as the man. Her arms lay perpendicular, like a crucified Christ.

You blink hard. Once, twice. Three times. Your initial thought had been that you were dreaming, slogging through the horror of that endlessly recurring nightmare that's haunted you for over a year, but the details are wrong. You know that dream. It's always the same. Not even the most minute of differences have ever been evident.

This is different.

For one thing, there's not as much blood. There's a lot of it, but not as much as there always is in the dream. Not as much as there had been the night you'd walked downstairs for a glass of milk last summer. The sight that your tender fourteen-year-old eyes had beheld that night had been far more gruesome than this.

Your eyes shift to the dining room, to the three figures that stand staring at you with evil pink-toothed grins, unmoved by your presence. That's different, too. There shouldn't be anyone else here. It's always just been you and the corpses.

The three mysterious figures are all dressed in black. Two boys and a girl, none of them appearing to be much older than you are. The first boy, standing in the middle of the trio, is tall and thin. He has hair like shoe polish, slicked back tightly over his scalp. He's wearing pleated black pants and a dark woolen coat that's matted with blood. His mouth and cheeks, like those of the other two, are smeared and spotted scarlet.

The second boy is even taller than the first. His auburn hair is pulled into a loose bun, and his face is scruffed with a patchy attempt at a juvenile beard. His shirtless torso is garbed in a black vest adorned with dozens of pins of varying sizes, each bearing the name of an obscure indie band. His tapered charcoal jeans cling to his thin legs.

The girl is alluring in a dangerous kind of way, with skin as treacherously ashen as fentanyl and long hair dyed daisy-petal white. Interwoven through her cascading tresses are fine strands of gold, like a drizzle of butterscotch stirred into a bowl of vanilla ice cream. She's wearing a crop-topped silken blouse that hangs off of one shoulder, tight leather hot pants, and ankle-length metallic leather boots that glitter and sparkle in the moonlight. Her nails are long and pointed, each of them painted ebony and imprinted with a white pentagram. Her navel is pierced with a long jewel ending in a diamond-encrusted inverted cross. There are crisscrossing lines of grayish-pink scars up and down her forearms.

Each of them is wearing a pair of dark Ray-Bans. The ones worn by the boy in the vest have circular lenses, like the kind John Lennon had popularized in his heyday, and the other boy has Aviators. The girl is wearing Wayfarers, which incites a smarting pang in your heart that conjures up memories of better days.

All of them are wielding thin, pointed daggers that gleam in the moon rays that pour in from the shattered dining room window.

You should probably run, but you don't.

Even when the girl starts toward you, you remain rooted in place. Not by fear, but by fatalistic choice.

"Wait," says the boy in the pea coat. The girl stops. "This kid just came down from his bedroom to find his dead parents, yet he looks utterly indifferent. He should be screaming and pissing his goddamn pants. It's not as fun when they aren't scared. Why aren't you scared, kid?"

"They weren't my parents," you answer. "They were my foster parents. I hated them."

"What happened to your real parents?"

"Also dead."

"Interesting. Well, now *you're* about to die. *That* should scare you."

"It doesn't."

He exchanges a brief glance with the other boy and then asks, "How old are you?"

"Fifteen."

The boy tilts his head, stroking his chin. The girl turns back to him and says, "No."

"He's the right age," the boy answers. "Fearless, disaffected. No family ties."

The kid with the man-bun says, "We really don't need..."

"I like him," the other boy says. "There's something about him that's intriguing. Ambrosio would like him, too, I think."

"You're the one who's going to talk to him, then," the girl tells him. "If he isn't pleased, you're taking the heat for it."

"That's fine. I'm not concerned. Tell me, kid...would you like to live...*deliciously?*"

"You stole that from a movie," you say.

He shrugs. "So what. It's fitting."

"I don't have much desire to live at all. Deliciously or not."

The boy snickers. "Yes, I think you'll fit *right* in. Listen, introductions are in order. I am Varney. This loser next to me is Mircalla, and the pretty lady is Erzsebet. Speaking on behalf of all of us, we are emphatically pleased to make your acquaintance."

"Those aren't your real names," you say.

"They didn't used to be, no. But they are now."

"What are you?"

"You know what we are." He licks his dark crimson lips and gestures to the bodies in the living room. "Now, are you coming with us, or not?"

You look at the girl, who winks at you and then removes a grape-flavored Blow Pop from behind her ear, unwrapping it delicately before inserting it into her mouth and sucking on it with exaggerated sensuousness. Mircalla takes a fidget spinner out of his pocket and twirls it absently.

You glance once more at the carnage in the living room. "Fine," you say, running a hand through your hair. The girl is eyeing you the way a fat kid appraises a stack of syrup-drenched pancakes, and the uneasiness this arouses within you clashes oddly with the stirring warmth in your adolescent loins.

"Atta boy," Varney says. "First things first, though. We need to clean ourselves up. Could you be so kind as to direct us to your washroom?"

You point down the hall. You're eyeing Erzsebet's legs, and she knows it, but you don't care.

"Right, then," says Varney. "We'll go make ourselves presentable, and then we'll be on our way. Have you anything you need to pack?"

You think for a moment, then shake your head.

There is nothing.

There hasn't been anything for a long time.

2

They lead you out into the humid August night, where a black Rolls-Royce Phantom is parked at the curb. Erzsebet opens the rear suicide door and gestures for you to enter. She climbs in after you. The back seat is wide and spacious, and the leather upholstery seems to mold to your form.

Varney slides behind the steering wheel and turns the ignition. A small, ceramic black skull with diamond eyes hangs from the keychain. When the car whispers to life, the stereo switches on and track one of *Eat Me, Drink Me* pours from the speakers. You almost roll your eyes.

Erzsebet is sitting cross-legged, her back against the door, staring at you from behind her sunglasses. You try to ignore her. Mircalla is still spinning his fidget spinner. The car glides down the suburban street, flashing beneath street-lights. Varney looks in the rearview mirror at you and says, "You're awfully quiet, kid."

"I don't really know what there is to say."

"Don't you have questions?"

You look out the window at the houses that haunt the street. They're all the same. One after another, you pass by them, and it's almost like you're not even moving. "Why don't you have fangs?" you ask.

The three of them laugh. "Common misconception based on myth," Varney answers. "Not all of the legends line up. The sun thing is real. Eternal youth. But no fangs."

"Got it," you say.

"Overall, not that much changes between life and death," Erzsebet says. "Not when you become as we are. You feel pretty much the same. I mean, shit, I still *menstruate*, even."

"Oh, yes, she certainly does," Varney says, looking at you in the mirror again over the tops of his sunglasses, a deviant twinkle in his eyes.

"I had thought that would stop," Erzsebet goes on, looking crestfallen, "but no such luck. It's a small price to pay for eternal life, though. And at least I'll never have to go through menopause."

Mircalla turns to look at you, his lips pursed. "You seem pretty unfazed by all this shit, man. I mean, fuck, when Varney and Erzsebet took me in and explained everything, I was like..." He makes exploding gestures with his hands on either side of his head and emits the appropriate sound effect.

"You haven't really explained anything."

"Dude," Mircalla says, "we're fuckin *immortal*. How does that shit not blast you into No-fuckin-way World?"

You shrug and look back out the window. "I guess I'm just hard to impress."

"Maybe you're right, Varney," Erzsebet says. "I think Ambrosio *is* going to like him." She presses a button on the door, and the seat-back between you folds down, revealing an ashtray and a little slot with a pack of Kools and a gold Zippo in it. Engraved on the lighter's surface are the words "FUCK CAPITALISM." Erzsebet lights one of the cigarettes and then holds the pack out to you. You shake your head. Upon exhaling her first drag, she erupts into a sudden paroxysm of wet, violent coughs. Tears stream out from beneath her sunglasses. Her white cheeks redden from the exertion.

You consider making a snarky comment about her apparent inability to handle tobacco, but instead you ask, "Where are we going?"

"Chatterley," Varney responds. "Ambrosio has a mansion there. That's where we stay."

"Who is Ambrosio?"

Erzsebet, seeming to have recovered from her fit, leans forward with a grin and says, "Ambrosio Cotard. He is our *Sire*."

Her tone is hushed and conspiratorial, and there's a faint trace of a lingering wheeze beneath her words. "He made us what we are. We don't see him much. He lives at the top of the house, on the sixth floor."

"Big house."

"*Very* big," Erzsebet says.

Something occurs to you. "What about my house?" you ask. "Or, my foster parents' house, whatever. It's a crime scene. It's a mess. The police will find you."

They all laugh again, more emphatically this time. "Ambrosio takes care of that," Varney says. "It's a nonissue."

"How? How does he take care of it?"

"We don't know," Erzsebet answers. "We think he might know people. Gangsters, or something. Someone who specializes in that type of stuff."

"I think there's magic involved," Mircalla says.

"Could be," says Varney. "Wouldn't put it past him. He is all-powerful."

"You talk about him like he's God."

More laughter from the trio. "No," Erzsebet says with a wide grin. "He's something much worse than that. Something much better."

CHAPTER 2 – THE PENNY DREADFUL TOUR

1

THE VICTORIAN-STYLE MANOR TO which they take you bears far more resemblance to a castle than it does a house. It looms ominously at the top of a high hill, enshrouded in curling wisps of fog and sneering condescendingly down at the neighborhoods below it. Its face is pitted with black windows that make you think of a spider's sleeping eyes, ready to spring open at any moment. Sharp spires stab at the overcast night sky. The huge wooden front door sits in a dark alcove beset by two wide pillars. A rampart-lined balcony juts out from the westernmost tower, and for a second you think you see a figure standing there, but a cloud of fog passes over it, and then it's gone.

"This all feels very cliché," you mutter to Erzsebet as the car begins its ascent up the long, winding driveway.

She smiles and runs her tongue over her still-pink teeth. "Ambrosio *invented* the cliché," she answers. She crushes her cigarette out in the ashtray. The filter is smeared with red smudges.

"Will I meet him tonight?" you ask.

She shrugs. "Probably not. Varney will need to speak with him, first. He needs to get approval for your, um, *induction*."

"And if he doesn't get that approval?"

"Then we'll eat you," she replies matter-of-factly.

You nod and look back out the window. "Cool."

"Even if he does approve, he won't turn you tonight," Varney says. He comes to a stop at the top of the driveway and throws the car into park. "We'll have to take you hunting with us a time or two, first. Just to make sure you've got the stomach for it, so to speak. And there will be a test, of course. You'll have to prove that you're one of us."

You very much doubt your ability to pass any such test. Instead of bringing this up, you ask, "What do you do during the day?"

"Sleep, mostly," he says. "But if we don't feel like doing that, we just do normal shit. Play video games, watch movies, read, have sex."

"And smoke weed," Mircalla interjects.

You look from Erzsebet to Mircalla to Varney, then back at Erzsebet. "All three of you have sex with each other?"

"Immortality has a way of erasing the boundaries of traditional sexuality," Varney explains. "When the three of us unite in carnality, we are no longer male and female. We are simply...*each other*."

Mircalla nods emphatically. "Besides," he says, "when I was alive, I didn't consider myself to be a male. It's too restrictive. I hate how society is constantly trying to put a label on everything and shove everyone into a category, you know? I fuckin hate that shit. Openness and expansion, *that's* the kind of shit *I'm* into."

"What did you consider yourself to be, then?"

Not missing a beat, he answers in a coolly pragmatic tone, "A non-binary genderfluid two-spirit pansexual."

"Right on," you say.

Varney shuts off the car, and the three of them get out. You follow suit. The night feels colder than it was when you'd left your house. You shiver and look up at the balcony where you thought you'd seen the figure, but there's still no one there.

Erzsebet comes around and slips her arm through yours, making you jump. "Come on," she says. "It will be dawn soon. If we're out here when the sun comes up...well, *poof*, there goes the neighborhood."

"Not the neighborhood," you say as she guides you up the cobblestone path that leads to the front door. "Just you guys."

Varney claps his hands from behind you and says, "Ah, but what is the neighborhood *without* us? What is *anything* without us?"

"The same as it is with you. Immortal or not, the world goes on with or without you in it."

"No way, man," Mircalla protests. "It's all connected. Everything. We all make a difference in everything we do."

You've reached the front door. Varney walks up and slides a skeleton key into the lock, and then pushes it open.

2

The foyer is lit by a huge chandelier that somehow hangs suspended from the high ceiling without any visible anchor tethering it in place, as though it's floating in midair. Candles glow from shimmering sconces along the hall that leads into the parlor. The gothic aesthetic borders on caricature, and you keep expecting a bat to fly out from one of the plentiful shadows.

"I must now speak with Ambrosio regarding the potentiality of your induction," Varney tells you after closing and locking the front door. "Mircalla, Erzsebet, would you be so kind as to show our guest around?"

"Yeah," says Mircalla. "We'll give him the penny tour."

"Give him the penny *dreadful* tour," says Varney. The others laugh, but you again find yourself resisting the urge to roll your eyes.

Once Varney has disappeared up the spiral stairs, Mircalla and Erzsebet first take you down into the basement. Or, as they refer to it, "The dungeon." Before seeing it, the cheesiness of the moniker made you want to groan. After descending the impossibly long flight of stairs, however, your dismissive attitude changes. It *is* a dungeon, lit only by torches and constructed of dark red stone. Manacled chains are affixed to the damp walls. There's a quartet of empty, rusty-barred cells, as well as a handful of angry contraptions that you can only assume to be torture devices.

"We haven't used any of this stuff," Mircalla says, answering the question you never would have dared to ask. "But it's cool to have it here. You never know when you might need it."

"Maybe we'll need it for *you*," says Erzsebet, lightly poking you in the ribs. There's a disconcertingly dark mischief behind her playful smile that makes you shudder.

They take you back upstairs and continue their tour in a giddy-but-disorganized fashion, escorting you up and down between five of the house's six floors with haphazard randomness. Erzsebet will say, "Let's show him such-and-such, next," and lead you up to a room on the fifth floor, then Mircalla will insist you go see this-or-that on the third floor, after which Erzsebet will remember something else on the fifth floor she'd wanted to show you. Twenty minutes into it, and you're panting for breath.

They seem to focus on the gimmickiest of the mansion's fixtures. There's a miniature movie theater that comfortably seats fifteen viewers in reclining leather chairs, and a library of leather-bound first editions down the hall from it. One room is filled with arcade games, pinball machines, a pool table, and a bowling lane. Another room has both a jacuzzi and a glassed-in sauna. There's even a red-painted room decked out with an endless supply of sadomasochistic sex equipment; of this, Erzsebet says, "Ambrosio calls this room 'the only good thing that came from that atrociously-written *Twilight* rip-off.'"

For every room they show you, there are at least two that they'll walk past without mention. The doors to these unacknowledged rooms are always closed, and there are a few from which you think you hear muffled, indiscernible noises. You don't ask about them.

Once they finally conclude that they've shown you everything of note, in respect to the house's interior, they take you out to the back yard. A tall brick wall topped with barbed wire encloses the vast lawn. The ankle-length grass needs to be cut, and a few patches of weeds have sequestered themselves in stolid isolation. Toward the back of the yard is a small greenhouse that Erzsebet refers to as "the Savage Garden," which apparently contains a wide collection of poisonous plants. On the other side of the wall is a three-car garage that houses Ambrosio's additional vehicles. According to Mircalla, these consist of an Audi A7 with a custom engine, and a vintage Plymouth that none of them touch based on Ambrosio's assertion that it's "sort of haunted."

Having some unpleasant familiarity with hauntings, you're about to ask him what he means when Varney strolls out of the house with his hands in his pockets and a smile on his face. "Ambrosio has approved of my decision to spare your life, for the time being," he says to you. "That doesn't mean you're off the hook, mind you. I've been wrong about things before. Not often, but it's happened. Don't let this be one of those times, kid."

"Okay."

He turns to Mircalla and says, "Come with me, there's something we need to discuss in private. Erzsebet, can you take it from here?"

Erzsebet eyes you in that weird, hungry way of hers and nods.

"Capital. We'll reconvene later." He goes inside with Mircalla, leaving you alone on the deck with Erzsebet. You suddenly feel very self-conscious.

"You look tired," Erzsebet says. "And rightfully so. Come on, I'll take you to one of the spare bedrooms."

"I don't feel tired. I don't think I'll be able to sleep."

"You're just riled up. I can give you something for that."

You swallow, thinking of Dr. April Diver and the cabinet full of medications you'd left behind at your foster parents' house. Whatever happens after tonight, you'll never have to take any of those godforsaken things again.

With that in mind, you decide that one pill to help you sleep really isn't that big of a deal.

3

Upon waking the following night, you find yourself in a huge, unfamiliar bed, in an equally unfamiliar bedroom. The curtains are drawn, and the only light present is that which is cast by the numerous candles placed around the room. Rolling over, you look at the clock on the nightstand. It's just past eight PM.

Your head swoons when you get up, and you have to sit back down on the edge of the bed to keep from falling over. Whatever had been in the pill Erzsebet gave you had been stronger than you'd expected. Your joints are stiff and creaky, and your brain feels like it's submerged in murky pondwater. You don't remember going to bed, nor do you remember undressing yourself; you're wearing only your undershorts and socks. You look down at the scar on your chest and wonder if the others had seen it.

Next to the clock is a black leather Michael Kors wallet, an iPhone, and a pair of black-and-gold Ray-Ban Clubmasters. You pick up the wallet, rubbing your thumb over the "MK" monogram, and then fold it open to examine its contents. You're startled to see a driver's license with your picture on it, purporting you to be twenty-two years old. The picture is the same one that appears on your school ID.

Also tucked in the wallet are a black American Express card and a thick wad of bill notes. You count the money and come up with 600 dollars in twenties and tens.

Erzsebet materializes in the open doorway and says, "Rise and shine, kid."

The wallet drops from your hands, and you feel your cheeks redden at your near-nakedness. She herself is wearing a long black dress with a plunging neckline and a slit up the leg. It makes you think of the time you beat off to a still from *Elvira: Mistress of the Dark,* earlier this summer. She isn't wearing her sunglasses, and the sight of her eyes paralyzes you. Their color is a scorching shade of bright chartreuse, and they're vibrant to such a degree that they appear to glow. You shiver as you feel them appraise you.

"Wicked scar," she says. "What's it from?"

You press your hand to it with an instinctiveness that's almost protective, the way pregnant women tend to brace their hands against their stomachs when standing in crowds. "It's...a long story," you tell her, suppressing images of purple eyes and deadly cake knives.

Erzsebet comes over and sits down beside you on the bed. Her proximity makes your pulse quicken. You can feel the heat coming off her warm body, and the subtle scent of her perfume fills your nostrils. "Well, I've got time," she says. "Nothing *but* time, actually. *All* the time in the *world.*"

"Maybe another day," you say. "Where are my clothes?"

"Oh, I pitched them. If you're going to hang with us, we can't have you looking like you shop at Target."

You elect not to tell her that your foster mother, who had purchased your clothes for you, was actually more of a Walmart shopper.

"We've got *loads* of clothes in the dressing room down the hall," Erzsebet says. "Come on, I'll show you." She takes your hand and pulls you up, leading you out of the bedroom and down the long, wide corridor. She stops in front of a tall door and opens it on a massive room filled with more clothes than a person could wear in a lifetime. You walk forward, only somewhat aware of your agape mouth, looking around at the crammed maze of chromium garment racks, the shoes lining the walls and cluttered around the floor, the hat trees and the gaudy accessories piled on innumerable shelves.

All of the clothes...every last shirt, coat, dress, and pair of pants...all of the shoes and headwear and gloves and scarves...all of them are black.

"If you can't find anything, there's more in the closet," says Erzsebet, indicating a walk-in closet that's twice the size of your bedroom back at your dead foster parents' house. She points to a tremendous wooden bureau with two dozen drawers and adds, "And there's fresh underwear and socks in the dresser. All designer, of course. Nothing from Target."

"All of this is Ambrosio's?"

"All of it is *ours*. Ambrosio says that what belongs to him, belongs to us. This is a socialist household. He's our own personal Bernie Sanders."

You run your fingers along the sleeve of a tweed jacket, pinching one of the silver buttons near the cuff between your thumb and forefinger and examining the intricate craftsmanship. "Where does he get it all?" you ask.

"Who knows. It was all here when I moved in."

"When was that?"

"Oh, a little over a year ago, or so. Give or take. I don't pay much attention to time, anymore. All that matters are the hours of night, from dusk till dawn. One night at a time. Anything outside of that is just extra."

Mircalla abruptly appears behind her and puts his arm around her shoulders. "Whoa, that's a gnarly scar, dude. How'd you get it?"

"Saved a puppy from a burning building."

Both Mircalla and Erzsebet laugh, and then Erzsebet says, "You're gonna have to tell us *eventually*. You can't go around sporting something like that and expect people not to ask questions. But for now, go ahead and get dressed and then meet us downstairs. We're just about to have breakfast."

A chilly tremor passes over the surface of your skin. "You're going to...eat someone?"

Erzsebet tilts her head confusedly, studying you with her glittering eyes, and then she laughs. "No, goofball, we're not going to eat anyone. Not yet, at least. Maybe later tonight, but not yet. We still eat regular food, too."

"Thank fuck for that," Mircalla says, grinning at you. "What point is there in living forever if you can't take some pizza and brewskis to Poundtown or hit up a Denny's after a long night of getting fucked up on booze and blood? Now, Erzsebet, how long are you going to make Varney and me wait on those waffles? They aren't gonna make themselves, and *we* sure as fuck aren't gonna make 'em, either."

Erzsebet lightly elbows Mircalla in the ribs. "One of these days, I'm gonna make the two of *you* cook for *me*," she chides him.

"Oh, I'll cook something *right* up for you, honey bunny," Mircalla says with a lecherous wink. He ruffles Erzsebet's hair and grabs her ass, and she laughingly pushes him away.

Watching them, it doesn't seem possible that these are the same kids who unflinchingly murdered your foster parents just last night. Their playful, lighthearted interactions don't jive with the *modus operandi* of what you'd expect from bloodthirsty monsters. These can't really be the creatures you'd found in your kitchen with the spoils of their kill smeared all over their faces. These are *kids*.

"We'll catch you downstairs," Mircalla says to you. He gives Erzsebet a soft spank on their way out of the room.

You spend a good ten or fifteen minutes perusing the endless stockpile of clothing. Most of it is too extravagant and showy for your taste, so you settle for a plain black T-shirt, a zip-up hoodie, jeans, and sneakers. Before going downstairs, you stop back in the bedroom to retrieve your new possessions. After putting the phone in your jeans pocket and the sunglasses in the pocket of the sweatshirt jacket, you open the wallet again and look once more at the photograph of you on the fake ID. Your cold, hard eyes stare back at you from the glossy plastic card. You know it's you, but it doesn't feel that way. It looks like someone else. It *feels* like someone else.

More than anything, you want it to *be* someone else.

4

Downstairs, you go into the kitchen and find an empty box of Eggos lying next to the industrial-sized toaster. Yellow crumbs are sprinkled across the countertop like confetti. A bottle of Jim Beam Devil's Cut, also empty, is lying on its side.

You follow the sounds of cheery voices and laughter into the dining room. The long wooden table has twelve chairs set around it, but Varney, Erzsebet, and Mircalla are sitting next to each other at the end closest to the heavy-curtained window. You sit down across from them, not saying anything and feeling awkward and out-of-place.

"Want one?" Mircalla asks you with his mouth full, spearing a waffle on his fork and holding it up. He has five others on his syrup-slathered plate.

You shake your head.

Erzsebet is nibbling daintily from her own waffle, sans-syrup. "Are you sure?" she asks. "I'm actually a pretty talented cook." Varney and Mircalla nod in emphatic agreement. You don't detect any irony in her voice.

"I'm...sure you are. I just...don't feel like eating."

"A drink, then?" Varney asks. The three of them have tall tumblers filled with dark amber whiskey next to their plates. Mircalla's glass has a Krazy straw in it. "The JB is all gone, but we have a plethora of alternative options in Ambrosio's liquor cabinet."

You shake your head again.

Pursing his lips, Varney says, "You aren't some sort of teetotaler, are you? We three are champions of hedonistic indulgence, and it wouldn't suit us to have a prude in our midst."

"I'm not a teetotaler. I just still feel kind of dizzy from that pill."

Varney's expression softens. "Ah, yes, I forgot. Erzsebet mentioned that she gave you some Ambien. Don't worry, the dizziness will pass." He takes a last bite of waffle and then pushes his plate away, lighting a cigarette. "So, kid, tell us...what's your story?"

"I don't have one."

"Bullshit. You wouldn't be here if you didn't have a story. It was no coincidence that we came across you last night. Ambrosio doesn't deal in coincidences. There has to be *something* that connects us. I asked him, but he played coy. He likes to do that. He says he prefers it when people figure things out for themselves. Cigarette?" He holds the pack of Kools out to you. You start to decline but then decide that you do want one, after all. It's been a long time since you smoked a cigarette. You had never much cared for menthols, but you consider that old adage about beggars and choosers and take one anyway. You lean across the table so Varney can light it for you, and then sit back in the chair and let the smoke fill your lungs.

"I grew up here in Ohio," you say after a moment. Your brain is buzzing from the nicotine. The unpleasant dizziness caused by the Ambien is replaced with a lightheadedness that borders on euphoria. "In Villa Vida, just down the street from where you found me. But then my parents got murdered so I was sent to live with my aunt and uncle in Los Angeles. That...um, that didn't work out, though, so I came back to Ohio and got put in foster care. That's it. That's my story."

"Hold on," Mircalla says, swallowing a mouthful of food and then putting his knife and fork down. "Your parents were *murdered?*"

"Yeah."

"When? Who killed them?"

"Last May." You don't want to answer the second question. It will open you up to getting cornered into a long dissertation. Still, you suspect they'll pester you about it until you spill, so you do. "Sterling McPleasant," you say.

The three of them react as expected, letting out a "*Whoooaaa*" in unison.

"Well, fuck *me*," Mircalla says. "The dude says he doesn't have a story, and then he goes and tells us that his mom and dad were killed by the Mudhoney Monster, himself. That's some righteously wild shit, man. You know he's, like, the most notorious serial killer since Ted fuckin Bundy, right?"

"He's not that famous," you say. "No one in LA knew who he was. I don't think many people outside of Mudhoney County knows who he is, actually."

"Is he the one who gave you the scar?" Erzsebet asks quietly.

"No. That was...someone else."

Her voice even quieter, lowered to a conspiratorial whisper, Erzsebet says, "Do you think what they say is true? That McPleasant is still out there, out *here*, somewhere in Mudhoney?"

"I know he is," you answer ruefully. "I used to think I was going to find him and kill him, but I gave up on that idea."

"Why?" the three of them ask at once, in a chorus of horrified bewilderment.

"Because it's stupid. If the cops can't catch him, how could a fifteen-year-old kid?"

"*Well*," Mircalla says, lighting a cigarette of his own and blowing smoke up at the ceiling. "You sure as fuck lucked out by meeting us. Don't you agree, Varney?"

Varney nods, showing his teeth in a rapacious smile. "Oh, yes, you're *very* lucky, indeed. If things pan out with you and us, I think it's quite safe to say that you'll be in a *much* better position to fulfill your quest for vengeance."

"Why do you say that?"

"*Because*, dude," Mircalla answers for Varney, "you'll be fuckin immortal."

CHAPTER 3 – THE DUDE ON THE UNICYCLE

1

AFTER BREAKFAST, VARNEY SUGGESTS a trip to the bar, an idea of which the others vigorously approve. Erzsebet announces that she's first going to shower and change, and Varney says he'll join her. As you listen to them scramble up the staircase, you picture the two of them naked together under the steaming water. It fills you with an unwelcome flood of jealousy.

Mircalla remains at the table with you, smoking in silence and watching you with curious eyes. When you're no longer able to bear the awkward quiet, you say, "So, uh, you guys don't have any responsibilities at all? No school, no work, nothing?"

Chuckling, he replies, "Responsibilities are for the living, dude. The dead are the only ones who are truly free." He pauses, considering the statement. "Shit, that sounded pretty good. Like something Varney would say, or even Ambrosio."

"Yeah. For sure."

"Why do you ask? You gonna miss going to school, or something? If you are, you're fuckin SOL, man. From here, you're either gonna become one of us, or become our dinner. Either way, no more school for you."

"No. I'm not going to miss it. The other kids liked to hit me."

Mircalla's eyes light up. "Dude, *same*. High school was the fuckin *worst*. I was always getting my ass beat."

"I'm sorry to hear that." Your voice is flat, but you mean it. The majority of your first and only year in high school had been a nightmare, and one you would wish only on a handful of people.

"Nah, dude, it's cool. It all worked out. If I hadn't been bullied so much in school, I never would have met Ambrosio. Every last beating pushed me closer and closer to immortality."

He's looking at you in a way that suggests he wants you to ask him to elaborate, so you do, and he does.

2

"Like I said, I got beat up a lot in high school. Like, *a lot*. And it wasn't even my fault. It was all because of Dilara Beckford. She was this bitch I was dating in ninth grade. She was *sort of* hot. Really big tits. But she had the wide hips and thighs of someone who's going to get super fat before she hits twenty-five. She was fuck-able enough at the time, though, so I was cool with banging her, and she wasn't too annoying to be around.

"Her brother, though...*he* was hot. Very dreamy. He was a poetry major at Baldwin Wallace. Well, one thing led to another when Dilara went out to get pizza one night, and we ended up fucking. Guy had the stamina of a racehorse, and that's what got us busted. If he'd been like the other guys I'd been with and blown his load after a minute and a half, everything would have been fine. But after fifteen minutes he was still hammering away at me. We never heard Dilara come in.

"As I'm sure you can imagine, it didn't go over too great with her. She blackened both my eyes and gave me a pretty bad concussion. Fuck, that girl could throw a punch. But she didn't stop there. She told *everyone*, and that shit spread like fuckin colon cancer.

"Now, this was Villa Vista, and you know how conservative that town is. They don't like gay kids too much. I tried telling them I *wasn't* gay, that it was more complicated than that, but this was a few years ago. Back then, people still thought there were only two genders. We didn't have a word for non-binary genderfluid two-spirit pansexuals, yet. You were either a guy or a girl, gay or straight. And if you were a guy who liked boning other guys, that made you gay. Even if you liked boning chicks, too.

"I had thought the whole mess would blow over, eventually, but it didn't. It just got worse. All the way into eleventh grade, I was getting my ass whupped left and right. They were never fair fights, either. It was always at least three on one, usually more. Not that I would have done that great in a fair fight, anyway. Yeah, I was tall, but I was awkward. I had no control of my limbs. They just kind of flailed around aimlessly, no matter what I told them to do.

"So, there I was, getting beat up all the fuckin time and generally hating my life. Someone started a rumor that I had AIDS, so nobody would fuck me, either. No girls *or* boys. I was like a fuckin leper. High school was a very lonely time for me.

"In the middle of my junior year, though, something happened. There was this kid, Emir Vathek. He was one of the cool kids. Played basketball, fucked bitches, *et cetera*. He was never an outright dick to me the way most kids were, but he was never nice, either. We had a couple of classes together, but he acted like I didn't exist. Until one day, when he approached me with *the proposition*.

"He came up to me after Ms. Carathis' English class and was like, 'Yo, bro, it seems like you get beat up a lot.'

"And I was like, 'Yo, bro, great detective work.'

"And he goes, 'I can help you, dude. The reason you get beat up is because people know they *can* beat you up, because you always lose. What you have to do is *win* a fight. All you gotta do is win one, and then you're set. If you show people you aren't gonna take any more shit, they'll back off. I'mma help you do that.'

"That should have been my first clue that something was up. There was no reason this kid should want to help me. I was nothing to him. But I was desperate. I still had a pretty fresh throb in my head from when a few kids beat the shit out of me with tennis rackets a couple days before. So, I figured, why not? It sounded better than any ideas I had, which pretty much just consisted of either running away or killing myself. I was a *seriously* miserable kid. All that isolation and torment can really wear on a dude, and I was at the end of my fuckin rope. Kids used to joke that I would end up becoming a school shooter. What people didn't know was that it had crossed my mind more than a few times, and the ones who joked about it were the ones at the top of my kill list.

"When I asked Emir what his plan was, he said, 'There's this freshman kid who's even more of a loser than you are. Real tiny, major dork. You could destroy him. Thing is, he *thinks* he's tough. He's extremely aggressive, always spouting off at the mouth. What I'm gonna do is tell him that you've been talkin shit, and that you want to fight. He'll totally go for it. All *you* have to do is show up and take him down. I'll invite a handful of people as witnesses. *Specific* people, who I know will talk you up and tell everyone how you fought like a champ and beat his ass.'

"Looking back, there were *so* many red flags. Why would anyone think I was tough for beating up some nerd who was smaller than me, right? And who were these 'specific people' who had any interest in making me look good? Literally *everyone* in the school thought I was the biggest fuckhead since...I don't know, some other fuckhead.

"Those were the questions I should have asked, but I didn't. I was too excited by the idea of not getting beat up anymore. I basically was just like, 'Fuck yeah, sign me up.'

"He told me to be at the soccer field at dusk the following day, and I told him I would be. I even *thanked* the asshole from the bottom of my heart for his generosity. And you know what that fucker did? He put his hand on my shoulder, smiled, and said, 'Don't mention it, dude. I got your back.'

"The next red flag came when I showed up at the soccer field the next night. Emir's 'handful' of 'specific people' turned out to be, like, thirty fuckin kids. Bad sign. But when I walked up to Emir and was like, 'Dude, what the fuck,' he said that it was cool, not to worry about it. He said a bigger crowd meant more people to back up my badass story. I was skeptical, but I was already there, so I couldn't back out.

"I looked around at the crowd for someone who matched Emir's description of the 'tiny dork,' but everyone there was someone who either *could* kick my ass, or already had. I asked Emir where my opponent was, and he pointed at the parking lot.

"This kid on a bicycle was riding up to us. I use the word 'kid' loosely because he was more like an ogre. He wasn't quite as tall as me, but he was fuckin *huge*. Must have weighed at least three hundred, maybe three-fifty. I don't know how that bike didn't fall to pieces beneath him.

"I looked over at Emir and was like, 'Dude, what the fuck?' He just shrugged and said he might have exaggerated a little when he said the kid was tiny. Fuckin prick.

"The way I saw it, I really only had one choice, and that was to try and beat him. If I pussied out, I'd just keep getting my ass kicked. But if I managed to win the fight, I would look like an even bigger hero for being able to take down Jabba the fuckin Hut, right? I figured that maybe I could use his weight against him, or something.

"The kid waddled up and was like, 'Yo, heard you been talkin shit,' and I was all like, 'Yo, uh, yeah.' That was pretty much the extent of our conversation. So, we got in our fighting stances, and we're kinda circling each other, and then I hit him. Punched him right in the jaw. Before that, I'd never punched anyone. I'd always got taken down before I even had a chance to swing. But let me tell you something, it didn't feel like I thought it would. It looks so easy in the movies, but that shit fuckin *hurts* in real life. I looked down at my hand and was all like, 'Fuck, I can't believe how much that fuckin hurt.' When I looked back up, the kid's face was deep red. It looked like his head had turned into a cherry, like those old Gushers commercials. He was so fuckin mad. Practically had steam coming out of his ears.

"And then he charged at me.

"Now, in a situation like that, every dude likes to think he'd be a hero, right? That he'd see this giant brute come running at him, all blind with rage and open to a frontal attack. He likes to think he'd uppercut him or kick him in the balls, or something. Or that he'd at least dodge out of the way and then hit him from behind. Yeah, that's what he thinks. That's what *I* would have thought, before that day. But the fact is, when you see a giant blob of pissed-off flesh come barreling at you, you've got one instinct, and that's to run.

"And that's exactly what I did. I turned and I fuckin *ran*.

"Well, I tried to, at least. I didn't get far. Maybe a step and a half before he tackled me with all his weight and started wailing on the back of my head with his fists, yelling 'Tap out, motherfucker! Tap out! Tap out!'

"And you know what I did? I tapped the fuck out.

"I gotta give the dude credit, because he at least let up when I surrendered. Just got right off me, hopped on his fuckin indestructible bike, and rode off. I can't say the same for the others. At least a dozen of them, probably more, all crowded around me and started kicking me and laughing like goddamn hyenas. Fuckers. Bludgeoned me up so bad I passed the fuck out.

"When I woke up, it was full-on night. I just laid there for a while, looking up at the stars and hating myself and my life and everyone in it. Then I pulled myself up and started to walk home. I moved slow, because it felt like every part of my body was broken.

"I hadn't even made it halfway across the school parking lot when Ambrosio appeared. Of course, I didn't know who he was, but I definitely knew he was *somebody*. I mean, it's not that often that you see a dude on a fuckin unicycle come riding up to you in the middle of the night. Plus, he was wearing a cape and a gunslinger-style Stetson hat pulled low over his face, and you know that anyone who's dressed like that in suburban Ohio has a fuckin story behind him.

"He rode up to me and said something like, 'Looks like you took quite a beating back there.'

"I wasn't in the mood to get heckled by some douche in a Halloween costume, no matter *what* his story was, so I told him to get lost. He had other plans, apparently. He kept riding in circles around me, so I was like, 'Dude, what the fuck?' And as he was going in those circles, he started to talk.

"He said his name was Ambrosio, and he knew how miserable I was. He knew I hated everyone, most of all myself, and that I'd been handed an unfair lot in life. He knew I was always getting beat up. He said he also knew that I wanted to die and that I wanted to kill. And he said he could give me both of those things, but that the death he would give me wouldn't be the end. That he could give me *un*death and, with it the power to kill anyone I wanted until the end of time, and *beyond* then, even. All I had to do was prove that I wanted it as badly as he thought I did.

"Pretty crazy stuff, I know. But the dude *was* riding a unicycle, and how many people have you seen ride a unicycle? I hadn't seen any, so I figured that maybe this dude was telling the truth. And he sure seemed to know a fuck-ton about me that he didn't have any way of knowing. I'd never told anyone about my fantasies of suicide and murder. I didn't even have a fuckin diary.

"Figuring I didn't have anything to lose, I was like, 'Yeah, I'll bite, what do I need to do?'

"Instead of answering, Ambrosio put his fingers in his mouth and whistled. As soon as he did, a car came shooting out of the darkness and drove right up to us. A blond guy with sunglasses got out and opened the back door, and I realized I was supposed to get in. I looked at the unicycle dude and he was like, 'Dude, get in the car. My assistant will take you where you need to go.' So, I was all like, 'Cool, whatever,' and I started to walk over to the car. But then Ambrosio rode in front of me and handed me a dagger and was like, 'Dude, you're gonna need this.'

"Even before the blond guy pulled up to Dilara's house, I knew that was where he was taking me. I just knew. And I was totally cool with that, because she'd been number-fuckin-one on my kill list ever since she started running her whore mouth about me and her brother.

"There was a bunch of cars in the driveway, so I figured she was having a party. I could picture them in there, laughing about my latest ass-beating, talking about what a loser I was. I got out of the car and started stomping up to the house, ready to bust in there and fuckin hack up anything with a pulse. But then I looked up and saw Dilara in her bedroom window. She must have just gotten out of the shower, because she was naked and had a towel around her head. By then, she'd put on a good twenty pounds since freshman year, and I couldn't help but think I'd dodged a bullet by getting out from under her when I did. Ha, get it? Out from under her?

"Anyway, her house had these creepy vines going up the front of it, which had always been convenient when I was dating her because I could climb in through her window so we could fuck, without her parents knowing I was there. Well, that night those vines were convenient for a whole different reason.

"I was no longer in pain. The adrenaline probably flushed it all out, so it was easy for me to climb up the house and slide the window open. She'd gone back into her bathroom, and I could hear the hair dryer running.

"Feeling more self-confident than I ever had in my life, I threw her bathroom door open, grabbed the hair dryer from her, and wrapped its cord around her neck before she even had the chance to scream. Then I dragged the bitch over to the tub, bent her over it, and used Ambrosio's dagger to cut her fuckin head off.

"It wasn't as easy as it looks in the movies, but that dagger was sharp as *fuck*, so it wasn't that hard, either.

"When I went back into her bedroom, Ambrosio was sitting on the bed, smoking a cigarette. He told me I'd performed as he'd suspected I would, and then he asked me if I was still interested in his offer. I was like, 'Dude, why the fuck wouldn't I be?' so he made me fuckin immortal right there in the bedroom of the girl who had ruined my life.

"Afterward, I felt like a million fuckin bucks. I also felt like killing some shit and drinking some blood, so I headed downstairs to fuck shit up. Ambrosio went out the window to wait outside with the blond dude.

"It turned out it was Dilara's parents who were having the party, so it was just a bunch of boring grownups drinking wine and eating cheese and crackers. There were seven or eight of them, and I sliced them all up and drank their blood with a smile on my fuckin face. Then Ambrosio and his douchey friend took me back to the mansion and introduced me to Varney and Erzsebet. They welcomed me with open arms and explained everything I needed to know about immortality, and then the three of us fucked. It was great. For the first time in my life, I was a part of something. And this might sound gay, or whatever, but that was really all I'd ever wanted in the first place."

3

"That's...quite a story," you say once he's finished.

Mircalla frowns. "You think I'm lying, don't you?"

Shaking your head, you say, "No, no, I don't. I swear." Again, your voice comes out sounding flatter than you'd intended. You really *don't* think he's lying. With everything that's happened to you over the past year, there isn't much room left in your mind for doubt. In fact, you think that if you told him even half of the events that had transpired over that time period, it would be *he* who suspected *you* of lying.

Before anything more can be said of the matter, Varney and Erzsebet reappear. The skin on both their faces is flushed pink, possibly from the shower but probably from something else. "My friends," Varney says, grinning and spreading his arms wide. "Let us make haste, for the night is calling to us, and we alone have the answer it seeks."

CHAPTER 4 – MUDHONEY'S GOT TALENT

1

WALKING INTO THE BAR with Varney & Co., you feel both coolly urbane and absurdly pretentious. Clad in black, with your sunglasses affixed to your face so as to match the gothic conceit of your companions, you can't help but suffer from a certain degree of awkward insecurity.

On the flip-side of the same token, however, their air of superiority has the infectiousness of a cold sore. It is this attitude that ultimately prevails over the former, in spite of the fact that you're significantly underdressed in comparison to the other three. Varney, with his top hat and elegant Victorian apparel, looks like he stepped right off the page of a penny dreadful serial. Erzsebet has changed into a leather corset ornamented with gold chains and buttons, and a lace miniskirt over fishnet stockings. Mircalla is attired in a slightly more casual fashion, with jeans and an Alien Sex Fiend T-shirt beneath a long leather jacket.

He has a spike-studded leather choker around his neck, and matching bracelets on both his wrists.

Even with your group's glitzy aesthetic, none of the other patrons acknowledge your entry; they all appear to be too drunk or stoned or both to notice anything other than their substances of choice and those within immediate proximity to them. Most of them look like they've crawled out from toxic waste dumps and backwoods trailer parks.

Excepted from this general description are a few groups of misfits who look as out-of-place as your own quartet. Crammed into one booth is a handful of prehistoric, overweight spinsters who probably should have been committed to retirement homes sometime back in the 80s. Seated one booth up from them is a trio of pretty college girls wearing cheerleader uniforms that sport the Baldwin Wallace Yellow Jackets' logo. At the slope-surfaced billiards table is a foursome of young punks who look like they got lost after performing in a high school production of *Grease*, chain smoking cigarettes and pausing to comb back their hair after every shot.

The bar itself, appropriately named the Bad Seed, is a shithole befitting of its clientele. Everything is coated in a smeary sheen of perma-grime. The stale air stinks of beer, puke, weed, and tobacco smoke. On a small stage over the empty dance floor, a haggard waif of a woman is finishing a bad karaoke rendition of "Crazy on You." The microphone sounds tinny, and its shoddy voice amplification fades in and out on a touch-and-go basis. A circle of cigarette butts and empty beer bottles is scattered around the woman's feet, like a sacrificial offering. The young, wasted-looking guy at the DJ booth watches her with bleary, red-eyed disinterest, smoking a crooked joint and sipping a bottle of Milwaukee's Best Light.

"It isn't exactly glamorous," Varney says, apparently sensing your disgust, "but it possesses a certain charm, don't you think?"

A mouse-sized cockroach scuttles across your shoe and disappears into a hole in the floor. At a table toward the back, a stringy-haired girl is preparing a shot of heroin.

"Totally," you say.

As a heavyset guy in a tracksuit takes the stage and begins sputtering his way through CCR's "Bad Moon Rising," the four of you walk over to sit down at the bar. You grimace down at its dull wooden surface, which is plastered with sticky rings of long-dried condensation. The bartender is a tall, gaunt man with shoulder-length black hair and skin like drywall. He's dressed in a suit, sans tie, with the top four buttons of his white shirt unfastened. When you all sit down, he pours a double shot of Bacardi into a finger-smudged glass and sets it down in front of Varney. He then fills two chipped mugs with beer from the tap and gives them to Mircalla and Erzsebet. With a sideways nod of his head, he gestures at you and asks Varney, "Who's the new kid?"

"A potential addition to our group. His fate is still up in the air." He lights a cigarette, and the bartender places a heart-shaped ashtray on the bar in front of him. Beams of refracted light from the dim bulbs overhead play upon its burnt-ochre glass, making its reflected image in Varney's sunglasses dance like fire.

The bartender stares at you with hazy, washed-out eyes. "He old enough?" he asks Varney, not releasing you from his gaze.

Varney snorts and tosses back his drink. "Don't act like you give a shit."

You start to reach for your wallet so you can present your fake ID, but the bartender shrugs and holds out his hand for you to shake. The sleeve of his jacket rides up a few inches, and you spot track marks on his wrist. "I'm Nick," he says. "Your friends are trouble. Gonna end up in the ground or behind bars any day now."

You shake his hand while Varney says, "Oh, fuck off, Nick. You've been saying that ever since you met me. And yet, here we are over a year later, and neither I nor my counterparts have fallen victim to any such fate."

"Give it time," Nick says with a twinkle in his murky eyes that hints at an unnerving knowingness. You think of Varney's comment about your fate still being up in the air, wondering how much Nick *does* know.

"*Hope you got your things together*," Tracksuit screeches from the stage. "*Hope you are quite prepared to die.*"

"What do you drink, kid?" Nick asks you.

"Just a beer is fine. Thanks."

Nick looks around for another glass. When he can't find one, he takes a half-empty mug from a recently-vacated space at the bar a few seats down, dumps out its contents, and refills it. After plucking a long strand of hair from the top, he puts it down in front of you with slipshod gracelessness. The beer within sloshes violently, and foam bleeds over the mug's cracked rim.

Mircalla is watching Tracksuit shakily deliver the last lines of the song, his voice cracking on every third word. "Fuck, Nick, you let anybody go up there and make a fool of themselves? That shit is just *cruel*."

Nick takes a cigarette from behind his ear and lights it, leaning against the bar. "What the fuck do you expect, *Mudhoney's Got Talent?* You might have your head stuck too far up your ass to notice, but this is the Bad Seed, not the fuckin House of Blues. Why don't *you* go up there, instead of sitting here playing Simon Cowell?"

"Maybe I fuckin *will*," Mircalla snaps. His tone is harsh, but he's smiling good-naturedly. He drains his beer in several long swallows and then saunters up to the DJ.

Chortling, Nick says "This'll be interesting."

"Don't write him off yet," Erzsebet says, taking a sip of beer and then dabbing moisture from her lips with a damp napkin. "We've got some tricks up our sleeves. All *you've* got up *your* sleeves are holes."

Nick gives her the finger.

The CCR song ends and Tracksuit gets off the stage, weaving back over to his booth. No one applauds. Mircalla replaces him behind the microphone, kicking a beer bottle out of his way. You, Erzsebet, and Varney swivel on your stools to watch. Mircalla taps the microphone twice with his forefinger and then says into it, "This one goes out to my fellow creatures of the night."

"Oh, brother," Nick groans, taking a swig from the Bacardi bottle before refilling Varney's glass.

A raucous beat roars out from the stereos, and Mircalla begins to sing.

2

What ensues is nothing short of extraordinary. The reedy quality of the microphone vanishes and its sound becomes clear and sharp. Mircalla's voice is thunderous and perfectly-pitched, almost godlike. He recites the words with confident precision, even though there's no cue monitor. His body shifts and grooves with the rhythm, as though the music were as much a part of his physical form as his own limbs.

All of the slurry conversations among the inebriated bar-urchins abruptly terminate. Drunken musings die midsentence deaths, their unfinished words hanging forgotten in the air with an irrelevance equal to that of the smoke clouds that share their space. Before Mircalla has gotten halfway through the first verse, he's assumed sole ownership of every bloodshot pair of eyes in the room.

You glance behind you at Nick, whose open-mouthed expression of disbelief makes his face look like the mask from the *Scream* movies.

"Damn," you say, leaning over to Varney. "He's pretty good."

Varney winks at you and raises his glass. "That, my friend, is what immortality sounds like."

The effect Mircalla has on the audience continues to escalate. Two by two, droves of drunken duos start getting to their feet and shambling toward the dance floor like a legion of zombified animals boarding an Ark to hell. The greasers desert the pool table and walk in the direction of the cheerleaders, who blush and giggle at their approach. Instead of stopping at the girls' table, the greasers bypass them and march up to the old women at the next booth over. With strikingly gentle chivalry, they help the women to their feet and lead them onto the dance floor. The cheerleaders observe this anomaly with infuriated envy before begrudgingly allowing themselves to be accosted by three portly old men in sweat-stained work shirts.

By the time Mircalla has finished the second verse and segued into the chorus, there isn't an occupied seat in the house save for the two upon which you and Varney sit. Even Erzsebet has taken to her feet; she's climbed on top of the bar and is dancing with devil-may-care abandon, her heels clacking on the wood as she nimbly sidesteps glasses, bottles, and crumpled napkins. When she catches you watching her, she beams at you and extends her hand. You decline her invitation with a diffident smile and polite shake of your head while you force yourself not to look up her skirt.

Varney takes off his sunglasses and stares at you with his dark blue eyes steeped in stern disapprobation. "My friend, when the most beautiful girl in the bar offers you a dance, it is not only impolite to refuse, it's *fucking retarded*."

You swallow and look out at the mass of twirling, jiving, and gyrating couples on the dance floor. You look at Mircalla, alive behind the microphone in a way you had, until now, thought impossible for a human being, immortality be damned. Finally, you look back up at Erzsebet, her whole being overtaken by the spirit of the music and mirth of the moment. She extends her hand again, and this time you take it.

You've never been much of a dancer. In fact, you can't remember *ever* having danced before, with the possible exception of one or all of the numerous unremembered, drug-fueled Hollywood parties to which Mara had dragged you with semi-frequent regularity, and at which anything could have transpired. Thus, your initial steps atop the bar are boundlessly uncoordinated. Much to Nick's graciously unspoken, but blatantly visible chagrin, your maladroit feet knock over every beverage container that Erzsebet had so skillfully avoided. Several of them shatter on the floor.

Then, something happens. Whatever has come over the rest of the bar's patrons suddenly takes you into its arms, as well. All of your self-consciousness falls away, sliding from your person and dripping off the bar to form unseen puddles on the floor amid the broken glass and cigarette butts. In its place, a lone seed deep within you sprouts and expands ever outward, its leafy boughs filling you with a prodigious sensation of ease and comfort. It is a feeling you can recall experiencing only one other time in your life. It had been last fall, driving up the coast with Mara and singing along to the Kinks, and you...

No, you think to yourself. *I can't let myself go there. I swore to myself that I wouldn't, so I won't. There is only this, here, now. And this, here, now...this might be the answer to everything.*

When you left Ohio and were sent to Los Angeles, you arrived there broken and devastated. For a time, Mara and her friends had glued you back together, reconstructing you into something far more remarkable than the meek child you'd been prior to, and immediately following, your parents' murders. But when you left a short time later and returned to Ohio, you came back empty. On the surface, and perhaps even a layer or two beneath that, you're still the same person Mara had built. The difference is that there's nothing inside of you. The life she'd breathed into your lungs has long since been extinguished.

But this...here...now...*this* may very well be exactly what you need to resurrect that *joie de vivre* that you had accepted to be a permanent fixture of the past, and never anything more.

It may very well be exactly what you need to resurrect *yourself*.

And it may very well be Erzsebet who holds the key.

Electrified by your newfound confidence, your legs adopt a life of their own and your dancing becomes elegant and effortless. You whirl and dip Erzsebet with natural fluidity, your steps timed to the beat without the slightest influence from your brain. In contrast to the song's lyrics...something to do with not feeling "quite right" and there being "something in the air tonight" ...whatever *is* in the air tonight is, in fact, making you feel *just* right. The words of the song attribute the described sensations to "the way she's lookin at me," and *that* sounds about right. You might not be able to see Erzsebet's eyes behind the lenses of her Wayfarers, but you can *feel* them, and that's more than enough to make you...

3

"Well, la-dee-da, look at Casanova."

The voice wrenches you from your musical trance, drowning out all of the other outside sounds. Everyone in the joint disappears, except for you and the kid sitting at the end of the bar. His face is hidden in shadow, but you know who it is.

Standing alone on the bar, surrounded by darkness, you take a step forward. In the silence, the sound of your shoe peeling off the sticky surface of the wood is as earsplitting as a fireworks finale.

Fireworks.

You shut your eyes and see hundreds of sparkling explosions erupting over downtown Los Angeles, a blinding spectacle of every color imaginable. Mara is with you, and you're in the back seat of her Corvette. She's saying something you can't hear. You start to ask her what she said, but then the fireworks all become purple until their flaring bursts make one enormous violet flame over the city, a flame that grows and grows until it consumes everything and it's all you can...

You open your eyes, and you're back in the deserted bar. The shadow boy leans forward into the light, and it is, of course, Quincey Conrad's face looking up at you.

If you can call it a face.

It's really just a gruesome dent cluttered with the smashed remnants of his eyes, nose, and mouth. His glasses, their lenses shattered and their frames crooked and bowed, seem to be precariously glued in place by dried gore. When he opens the hole that used to be his mouth, a rush of blood and teeth comes pouring out onto the bar in front of him. He glances down at the mess and then shrugs at you. "Sorry, that was gross, I know."

You take another step forward. "Are you dead?" you ask. "Did you die?"

"Ha! Wouldn't *you* like to know. Well, come to think of it, maybe you really *don't* want to know. You probably don't give a fuck, either way. After all, you sure as hell didn't wait around to find out what happened to me. Nope, you just turned tail and took off, as soon as shit went bad."

"It didn't just 'go bad,' Quincey. It was fucked. Everything was really, really fucked."

"Yeah, it was, but that's when friends are supposed to stick with each other. You just fucking *bailed*. Didn't even tell Rebecca or Ianthe where you were going, either. Shit, you could have *at least* stayed for Justine's..."

"Quincey, I'm *sorry*. I'm...I just...Mara..."

"Oh, save it. 'Mara this,' 'Mara that,' 'Mara knick-knack paddy whack.' Everything was always about Mara, with you. You know, I always thought you were a cool kid, right from the start. We all did. All of us really, *truly* cared about you. Shit, I think Justine was probably *in love* with you, or something in that ballpark. But when everything went to hell, you did a bang-up job of proving that Mara was the only one *you* cared about."

"That's not true. I loved all of you. I still do."

"Yeah. It sure seems like it. You up and bounced, and now you're dancing on the bar with your new friends like you're Charlie motherfucking Chaplin."

"I couldn't stay, Quincey. I had to come back. I had to. You have to understand."

"Oh, I understand, all right. I understand that you're a selfish, cowardly douchebag." For all the cruelty of his words, his tone doesn't quite match up. There's no reproach in it; there's only pain and sorrow. He sounds like a kid trying to hold it together enough to tell off a traitorous friend who's been hooking up with his crush. The words themselves do sting, but it's his delivery of them that really drives the barbed harpoon into your guts.

"Quincey, *please*, I..."

You blink, and he's gone. The bar becomes as it was, and you're still dancing with Erzsebet as if nothing had happened. Not a beat missed, so to speak. When the song ends and Mircalla steps away from the microphone with a flourishing bow, you take your own bow before Erzsebet, kissing her hand. Inwardly, you're still reeling from your encounter with Quincey's ghost (if it *was* a ghost; you still aren't even sure if he's actually dead), but outwardly, you're cool as a cucumber. You feel detached from your actions, like you've been subbed out of your own life and left to watch on the sidelines as the relief player runs circles around everyone else on the field, succeeding in all the ways you failed.

After you and Erzsebet retake your seats, you look compulsively over at the end of the bar, part of you certain that Quincey will be there. He isn't. The only person at that end of the counter is a miserable-looking drunk guy with faded blond highlights in his shaggy brown hair. He's scribbling in a spiral notebook. His wasted eyes meet yours for a second, and you're hit with a stab of *déjà vu*. He looks jarringly familiar, and you're almost positive you've met him somewhere before, but you can't remember where or when. While you're trying to figure it out, Mircalla rejoins your group to the accompanying cries of exultant praise from your friends and the handful of groupies who have followed him back here like puppies desperate for their master's approval. This breaks your concentration, and the man at the end of the bar is forgotten.

As is Quincey, along with the tragedies that had befallen you in LA. The memories will try to resurface again, as they always do, but for the time being they recede into the background.

For the time being, there is only this.

Here.
Now.
This.

CHAPTER 5
– BEREFT
IN DEADLY
BLOOM

1

THE HOUSE IS QUIET when you wake the next night, after a day of refreshingly dreamless sedative-sleep. The others must still be in bed, because when you go downstairs there aren't any indications that Erzsebet has yet toiled away over breakfast preparations. You decide you want some air, so you slip out the back door and onto the deck.

It's almost ten o' clock; the night is young but dark, and the humidity weighs on your body like molten lead. You're thinking about how you want a cigarette when you see a shadow moving inside the greenhouse (the "Savage Garden," Erzsebet had called it). Based on past experiences, you have every reason to fear mysterious shadows moving about in the night, but nothing about this one strikes you as ominous. Shedding the sweatshirt jacket and tying its sleeves around your waist, you walk down the wooden stairs and cross the lawn over to the greenhouse.

You'd expected it to be oppressively tropical inside, but it's surprisingly temperate. The interior seems larger than it does from the outside. The cool, damp soil feels rich and natural beneath your bare feet. The vast assortment of deadly plants is artistically arranged in such a manner as to give one the impression of being in an entirely wild ecosystem. If it weren't for the foggy glass encasing the area, you'd think you were in an actual South American jungle, not the back yard of a mansion in the suburban Midwest.

As you advance farther into the greenhouse, its size seems to multiply with the dizzying confusion of a funhouse mirror. Pushing through a dense patch of brightly-colored foliage, you come upon Erzsebet. She's sitting on a bench beneath a miniature tree, one that's maybe seven or eight feet tall, that has red and yellow flowers sprouting along its boughs. In her hand is a purple bell-shaped flower. She examines it with solemn affection, rolling its stem between the pads of her thumb and forefinger. When she senses your presence, she looks up and smiles.

"Sorry," you say. "I don't want to, um, intrude, or anything. If you..."

She shakes her head and moves over on the bench, patting the space beside her. Not without hesitation, you sit down nervously and clasp your hands on your lap.

"On the nights when I wake up before Varney and Mircalla, I like to come in here," Erzsebet says. "It's a good..." She's interrupted by a short, weak cough that escalates into a belabored fit of wheezing and hacking. When she's recovered and caught her breath, she acts as though the fit never happened and resumes speaking. "It's a good place to come and think. To remember." She looks fondly around at the lush flora. A gigantic black moth flutters over, and when Erzsebet lifts her hand, it perches upon her knuckles. The two of them share an intimate gaze before it takes off with a tremendous flap of its bat-like wings.

"What do you think about?" you ask, realizing too late that such a question could be considered prying. You bite your tongue, wishing you could snatch the words out of the air and stuff them back into your mouth.

If she's put off by the inquiry, she doesn't show it. Her response is light and casual. "Oh, all kinds of things, really. But the past, especially. And my mother." Her mouth twitches downward just so when she says this last bit. "I wonder what she's doing and if she's okay. Sometimes I think she's probably better off now that I'm gone. Other times, I worry that I may have ruined her when I left. When I disappeared." She fingers the flower petals thoughtfully, her expression unreadable.

"Why did you leave? What happened?"

She looks up from the flower and meets your eyes. The dazzling green sparkle of her irises is paralyzing. "Ambrosio happened," she says.

"He's the reason you left?"

"Not exactly. But he's the reason I stayed away. And in the end, I guess he's the reason for everything."

2

"I was pretty much your typical goth chick in high school. Black everything, heavy makeup, angry music, shallow look-at-me cuts on my arms...the whole shebang. I had one friend. She was this depressive, angsty bitch named Lois with a shaved head and dozens of really awful tattoos that her twenty-six-year-old junkie boyfriend gave her with a homemade rig. People called her 'Lois the Witch' because there were a lot of rumors...and most of them were true...about her experiments with pagan witchcraft. Everyone hated us and, looking back, I can't say I really blame them. We were weird and mean and stuck-up.

"My dad died when I was really young, and my mom was basically Mildred Pierce. She worked two waitress jobs that barely covered the rent on the shitty double-wide we lived in at a trailer park on the outskirts of Pottstown. She tried hard, and she loved me. I was too self-obsessed and stupid to realize it then, but I do now. I should have treated her better. She was hardly ever around, but when she was, I treated her like garbage. She really tried to connect with me and to establish some sort of mother-daughter bond, but I wasn't having it. On her rare nights off, she would try to convince me to let her take me to a movie or out to dinner or whatever. I always told her to fuck off because all I wanted to do was sit in my room cutting myself and masturbating to *Antichrist Superstar*.

"One Friday night, Lois's boyfriend got us into this show at a dive bar in downtown Philly. The featured act was a Bauhaus cover band from North Carolina called Stigmata Martyr. They weren't as good as they thought they were, but that wasn't important. What was important was the lead singer.

"His name was Dorian Wolfenbach. He looked like what you'd expect any goth rock front man to look like: tall, skinny, pale, with wild black hair and runny eyeliner. Nothing special. But when the band opened their set with 'Telegram Sam,' the way he moved on the stage was electrifying. If you thought Mircalla was good, and he *is*, you should have seen Dorian. He might as well have been Jim Morrison. They closed with 'She's in Parties,' and that was when he noticed me. His eyes met mine, and they stayed there for the whole song.

"When it was over, I went to the bar and waited for him to come. I knew he would, and he did. He didn't say anything. He just took me by the arm and led me out to his van and violently fucked away my virginity. He was in his early twenties, but he didn't ask how old I was. I was a few months shy of turning sixteen.

"That night, I left with him and his three bandmates to join them on their tour. I didn't even say goodbye to Lois.

"We travelled all around the eastern half of the country for the next couple of months. They booked their gigs at random, not caring if it made sense geographically. There was one week where they played in Delaware, Tennessee, Maryland, and Indiana, all in that order. When they weren't performing, we were driving. We stopped rarely, and never for very long. But I was having the time of my life.

"Well, for the most part, anyway. Dorian could be kind of a dick sometimes. I wouldn't say he was abusive, because he never raped me, and he was always very apologetic after every time he hit me. And he could say some pretty nasty shit, but he usually apologized for that, too.

"It was in New Orleans that things went bad. The band was playing at a goth bar in the French Quarter called Christian's. While they were setting up, I went outside to smoke a cigarette. I was gone for less than ten minutes. When I came back inside, I went backstage to the green room and found Dorian fucking some girl while the other three guys stood around and watched. The girl couldn't have been any older than twelve or thirteen. Dorian saw me come in, and he actually *winked* at me as he was thrusting into her.

"I didn't cry. Something inside of me told me that I was supposed to cry, that I was supposed to be sad and hurt and heartbroken, but I wasn't. I was mad. So very, *very* mad. Like a dog that a kid keeps poking with a stick.

"I sat at the bar for a long time, drinking myself stupid. I didn't even notice when the band came on and started playing. It wasn't until much later, toward the end of their set, that I finally looked over at the stage. Seeing Dorian up there, singing 'Bela Lugosi's Dead,' filled me with so much hatred that I couldn't stand it. I couldn't get the image of him fucking that little girl out of my head. I was afraid I would do something stupid, like run up to the stage and start beating the shit out of him with the microphone, so I went outside.

"I knew something was off right away, because the street was almost completely empty. There should have been a bunch of crazy drunk people all over the place, but it was a total ghost town. Except for...get this...an ice cream truck.

"It was parked on the street right across from the bar. It was old and white and had rust on the bumper. Stuck to the roof was a big plastic ice cream cone that had huge black eyes and a creepy grin. Painted across the side in cursive purple letters was, 'Ambrosio's Confection Connection.'

"As soon as the door to the bar had slammed shut behind me, the long metal window on the side of the truck slid open. It was too dark for me to see the person in it, but I knew *someone* was there. And I knew he wanted to talk to me.

"I was pretty drunk, and when I get drunk, my coordination gets shot to shit and gravity starts kicking my ass. But for some reason, when I walked over to the ice cream truck, my steps were steady and straight, and my head was clear. I had forgotten all about my anger and hatred. All that mattered was the man in the truck.

"Even when I got up close, I still couldn't see him. He was almost completely hidden in shadow, not much more than an outline, but I knew he was beautiful. And for all that darkness, there was a light, too. I couldn't see it, but I could feel it. He had a light within him that I wanted to be a part of. I wanted to curl up in that light and never leave.

"He called me by my name...my *birth* name, of course...and it didn't seem weird to me at all that he would know it. *His* name, he said, was Ambrosio. He told me that he knew I was angry, and that I *should* be angry. He said that it was wrong of Dorian to offer me the kind of freedom from real life and responsibility that I'd always wanted, only to turn around and betray me.

"I agreed, though I would have agreed with anything he'd said. He had a voice like maple syrup. He pronounced every word with such caring tenderness, like each sentence was a beloved child he'd raised and nurtured. I kind of figured he was hypnotizing me, but I didn't know if it was on purpose. I didn't care.

"Then he said, 'I can give you more freedom than that back-water swamp rat ever could. Come with me, and I'll give you the *world*.'

"I said yes, and I asked what I needed to do.

"He said that he didn't want much from me. All he wanted was to know that I would be his, and his alone. That I would be willing to cut ties with my past so I would be free to join him on an endless future. That I would do anything for him.

"I said yes a second time.

"What he did next took me by surprise, to say the least. He reached his pale hand out of the darkness to hand me an ice cream cone. Only, when I took it, it *wasn't* ice cream. The cone felt like it was made of dead skin, and sitting on top of it was a huge scoop of shit. There were little white worms crawling through it.

"I squeaked and jumped back, dropping the shit cone on the ground. I looked up to ask him why he'd done that, but the window slid shut before I could say anything. When I looked back down at the ground, the shit cone was gone. In its place was a dagger.

"When I went back inside, the lights were off and everyone had left. Even the bartender was gone. I didn't know how that was possible, because I didn't think I'd been outside for more than five minutes, but I didn't care. I had a one-track mind, and the bar's emptiness just made my mission that much easier.

"Dorian was alone in the green room, admiring his reflection in a glass pitcher of beer. He glanced up at me when I came in, grunted, and then went back to ogling himself. That casual disregard made all my rage come bubbling back, full force. I didn't waste time giving a dramatic speech, or anything like that. I just went over to him, grabbed the beer pitcher, and broke it over his head.

"His scream had more anger in it than pain, and that gave me a lot of satisfaction. I wanted him to feel how I felt. I wanted my betrayal to be his own.

"He shoved me onto the floor and jumped on top of me, but I still had the knife. I stabbed him right below his rib cage. He howled and fell onto his back, and then *I* got on top of *him* and just started stabbing him and stabbing him and stabbing him. I stabbed his face, his neck, his chest. Then I started slashing, slicing him up into bloody ribbons until he didn't even look like a person anymore.

"I didn't stop until a hand caught my wrist and gently lifted me to my feet. It was Ambrosio, and seeing him there in the light confirmed everything I knew to be true. He *was* beautiful, more beautiful than any angel that ever could have existed in even the most fantastical of make-believe stories. He smiled at me, and I knew I was home.

"I can't tell you about how he turned me, because that's something that you'll find out if he decides to do the same for you. But he did it right there over Dorian's dead body. There, in the back of a rinky-dink bar in New Orleans, I became immortal.

"When it was done, I heard laughter and footsteps from the hall, and I remembered that the other bandmates were still out there. I don't know where they'd been when I was killing Dorian, but they were coming, and I figured they wouldn't be thrilled to find their lead singer dead by the hand of his underage girlfriend.

"Ambrosio winked at me, told me that I knew what to do, and then stepped back into a shadowy corner of the room just as the three guys came in through the door. Their laughter got stuck in their throats as soon as they saw the mess, and the wide-eyed way they looked at me was kind of funny. Even if they'd tried to run, they wouldn't have made it far. I was too fast. I felt like a superhero. I cut them down in a matter of seconds and then drank their blood until my stomach felt like it was going to burst.

"When they were all dead, Ambrosio swooped me up and carried me like a baby back to his ice cream truck. He was always like that with me...very gentle, always treating me with reverence and respect. I tried to get him to make love to me, but he wouldn't do it. He actually seemed offended by my advances.

"We left New Orleans and drove until the sky started to lighten, at which point he parked at a rest stop and covered up the windows so we could sleep the day away. Once night fell, we drove the rest of the way to Ohio. He left the ice cream truck at a junkyard just outside Cleveland, saying it had outlived its purpose. He had this hot young blond guy come pick us up and take us back here to the house. I don't know who the blond guy was or what his relationship is with Ambrosio, and I haven't seen him since.

"Ambrosio introduced me to Varney that night, who'd been with him for a couple of months by then. He brought Mircalla to us about a month after that. And then, a year or so later, we found you.

"Everything Ambrosio promised me has come true. Perfect freedom, perfect happiness, a complete escape from the horrors of world...he delivered all of it in spades. He'll do the same for you, too, if he deems you worthy. And you know what? I think he will. No, I *know* he will. You're one of us. I can feel it, and I think you can feel it, too."

3

You wait a few moments after she's finished, and then you ask, "Do you really think that? A couple nights ago, you seemed pretty hellbent on...eating me."

"Oh, I'm still not *horribly* opposed to that idea," she says, but the way she affectionately tickles you under your chin with her pointed fingernails is indicative that there isn't much, if any, truth to that statement. "In all seriousness, there's just...something about you, I guess. Not just *you*, but the...the *circumstances* surrounding you. There's a reason that things happen. There's always a reason. I don't know what yours is, yet, but I'd like to find out. Even more than I'd like to eat you."

"I..."

She puts a finger to your lips. "Come on," she says, standing up and pulling you to your feet. "Varney and Mircalla will be up soon, if they aren't already. Tonight, we're going hunting."

CHAPTER 6 – FOX FOOD

1

YOU ALL PILE INTO the Phantom, with Varney and Mircalla up front and you and Erzsebet in the back. As Varney races out of the driveway and takes off down the dark, silent street, you ask him, "How do you choose your victims?"

Varney frowns at you in the rearview mirror. "'Victims' is such a strong word, and a substantially inaccurate one, at that. I prefer the term 'meals.' The thing is, no one we kill is a victim of anything. Most of the time, our meals are very, very bad people who deserve any and all befoulments that may befall them. *Sometimes* we'll select one based solely on convenience and opportunity, but that's rare. And even in those cases, it still..."

"It's just the fuckin circle of life," Mircalla interjects, turning around to look at you. "It's the food chain, dude. The bigger animals eat the smaller ones."

"*Precisely,*" says Varney. "When a fox eats a worm, do you feel *bad* for the worm? Is the worm a *victim?* No. It's just food. That's all."

Mircalla looks at Varney. "Dude. I don't think foxes eat worms."

"Foxes *definitely* eat worms. Erzsebet, Google what foxes eat."

Erzsebet pulls out her phone and says aloud as she types, "What...do...foxes...eat." She waits for it to load, and then reads, "'Foxes are omnivores and eat small mammals, birds, reptiles, frogs, eggs, insects, *worms*, fish, crabs, mollusks, fruits, berries, vegetables, seeds, fungi, and carrion.'"

"I don't buy it," says Mircalla, shaking his head. "That's fake news."

"My foster parents...was there some sort of moral reason that you killed them? Or were they just worms, too?"

The vulpine smile Varney gives you lends credence to his metaphor. "They were merely worms. We had just left the bar, and we were quite thirsty, so we drove around looking for a random house to hit. Erzsebet was actually the one who picked your house when she saw the address on the mailbox."

"How do you pass up something like 666 Barlow Lane?" Erzsebet says. She grins at you, lights a cigarette, and then expels the first drag in a series of short, harsh coughs. "It was too perfect, and I don't believe in coincidence any more than Ambrosio does."

"That's not the real address," you tell her. "It's six-six-*one*-six Barlow Lane. The 'one' came off and my foster dad never painted it back on. He kept saying he was going to. There were a lot of things he said he was going to do."

"Either way," Varney says, "it's still *far* too much of a coincidence to be called a coincidence. You can only cry coincidence so many times before you just sound ignorant."

"Coincidences are fake news," says Mircalla.

"Stop saying that," says Erzsebet. "It's a major trigger for me. It makes me think of that pussy-grabbing orangutan."

"I'm *making fun of* the pussy-grabbing orangutan. I'm *mocking* him. It's...shit, Varney, what's the word I'm looking for?"

"Tongue-in-cheek?" Varney says absently, pulling onto 480 and gunning the accelerator, heading east.

"Yeah, tongue-in-cheek, that's it."

"I don't care *what* it is," Erzsebet says. She has the expression of someone who's been sucking on a piece of sour candy. "I don't like thinking about him."

Snickering, Mircalla says, "Oh, lighten up. That fat fuck is never going to get elected, anyway."

"He better not," says Erzsebet. "Or sunlight and staked hearts will be the *least* of our worries."

No one says anything to that. You're too far out-of-touch with current events to even know who this "orange orangutan" is, and you'd just as soon keep it that way. Instead of asking for them to explain, you ask Varney, "Where are we going? Are you hunting someone specific? Or more worms?"

Varney's fox-grin returns and he says, "Oh, the guy we're going after tonight is certainly a worm, but he's a very *specific* worm. Tonight, our meal shall taste of justice and retribution. Tonight, we kill Donald Raymond."

"Who's Donald Raymond?"

"Dude," says Mircalla, "he's the cop who fuckin shot Theodore Christoval."

"Okay. But, um...who's Theodore Christoval?"

"*Dude*. How do you *not* know about Theodore Christoval? Did your foster parents keep you under a fuckin rock, or something?"

"Basically. I wasn't allowed to watch TV or go on the internet. Or have a cell phone."

"Well, you've got one now, so Google that shit. C-H-R-I-S-T-O-V-A-L. And 'Theodore' has an 'e' at the end."

You take the iPhone out of your pocket and do as instructed. After clicking on the first link that pops up, you skim the article while Mircalla and Erzsebet watch you expectantly. You can feel Varney glancing at you in the mirror. When you reach the end of the page, you look up and say, "It says here he was a convicted felon with three previous arrests, and that he pulled a gun on the cop."

"Give me that shit," Mircalla says, snatching the phone from you and scrolling up to the top of the page. Then he snorts and says, "Oh, no wonder. If you're going to get your 'news' from websites like *this*, you're going to get nothing but lies." He hands the phone back to you with a disapproving shake of his head.

"It was the first site in the list of results. And I don't think they can lie about arrest records."

"Dude, they can lie about fuckin *anything*."

"What about the gun?"

"First of all," Varney says, "it was a *toy* gun, and he didn't even point it at anyone. And even if he *did* have an arrest record, which is debatable, the cops wouldn't have even *known* about it if they hadn't pulled him over. Does your fake article say *why* the cop *claimed* he pulled him over?"

You look back down at the screen and read aloud, "'Christoval was pulled over for a routine traffic stop after exhibiting suspicious behavior.'"

"That's the key phrase, right there," says Erzsebet. "You can call *anything* 'suspicious behavior.' It's just an easy excuse that cops use to carry out their twisted agendas." She flicks her cigarette out the window and starts sucking on a lollipop.

Varney merges onto 71 and heads south. "Where does this guy live?" you ask him.

"In Melvin, naturally. The White Privilege Capital of Ohio."

You think it would be pretty safe to say that about most of the towns in Mudhoney County...Chatterley and Villa Vida, in particular...but you keep this sentiment to yourself.

Everyone is silent the rest of the way there. A few minutes after getting off at the Melvin exit, Varney turns down a residential street and shuts the headlights off. "It's official now, lady and gents," he says. "Fun fact for the day: turning off one's headlights is viewed as premeditation in the eyes of the law."

"Fuck yeah, shit just got *so* real," Mircalla says, flashing an eager smile that makes him look even younger than he is. It's the smile of a child preparing to open a Christmas present, not the smile of someone who's about to commit murder.

Varney creeps the car along the curb and comes to a stop in front of a long white house. There's a wooden sign in the shape of a police badge hanging from the porch that reads "BLUE LIVES MATTER." A black line of dead, out-of-season Christmas lights is snaked around the edges of the roof.

"How are we going to get in?" you ask, hoping you sound casual. Your pulse has quickened, but not as much as you feel like it should.

Mircalla reaches into the pocket of his leather jacket and pulls out a tool resembling a Swiss Army knife. He holds it up and unfolds it, revealing six blade-like objects of varying sizes and serrations. "Lockpicks," he says. "It's easier than you'd think. I watched a couple YouTube videos and got the hang of it pretty quick."

"What if he has an alarm system?"

"He won't."

"How do you know?"

"I just *know*, dude. Fuck, man, you ask a lot of questions."

Knowing you should shut up but unable to help yourself, you ask one more. "Why did you break in through the window at my house, if you could have just picked the lock?"

"Because we *felt* like it," Mircalla says through gritted teeth. "Not everything has to have Some Great Meaning, dude. We saw your foster parents sitting in the living room so we decided to fuck with them by throwing a fuckin rock through the window. That's it."

Great Meaning or not, you'd be a cold corpse with a stomach full of Drano right now if not for that rock going through the window, but you don't think this is worth mentioning.

Varney kills the engine and then he and the others get out of the car. After an abbreviated moment of halfhearted hesitation,

you get out, too. You feel a curious fusion of alarm and relief at
your relative lack of panic and anxiety. The logical part of your
brain tells you that you should be much more resistant to this
excursion; there is *some* trepidation, no doubt, but there isn't
quite enough of it. Other than a slightly accelerated heart rate
and an indistinct fluttering in your stomach, your homeostasis
is almost entirely unaffected by your acquaintances' witchy intentions.

Maybe, you figure to yourself, you've just been through too
much shit already. Maybe you've seen too much and done too
much to fall prey to normal fight-or-flight human responses.

You think of your parents, and of Sterling McPleasant. You
think of Mara, of the Grinning Man, of Captain Howdy. Dis-
torted bodies, sharp-toothed smiles. Blood clouds in a swimming pool. A knife piercing flesh. The look of life leaving the
eyes when you...

"Dude, you comin, or what?"

Snapping out of your reverie, you realize you're still stand-
ing by the car and the others are already halfway up the lawn.
Mircalla is staring at you with acerbic impatience. Varney and
Erzsebet turn around and mimic his expression.

You grumble an apology and follow them up to the door.
Mircalla gets it open in less than thirty seconds. No alarm
sounds.

Varney lifts a finger to his lips and says in a voice imitating
Elmer Fudd, "Shh, be vewy, vewy quiet." Erzsebet cups a hand
over her mouth to stifle a giggle as she follows Varney inside.
Mircalla goes next. You enter last, shutting the door behind you.

2

Walking into the living room, you're greeted by the warm
tangerine glow of an artificial fireplace. You hear the man snor-
ing before you see him. He's lying on the couch, a lumpy and
formless shape beneath a motif-style afghan. He looks to be in
his early forties, and his face is round and soft. His salt-and-pep-
per-hair is shorn down to a stubbly buzzcut that matches the

three-day growth on his cheeks and neck. Even in his slumber, dark lines of exhaustion stand out around his eyes as prominently as a football player's grease paint. He doesn't look like a murderer, but then again, your new friends don't really look like murderers, either.

Drawing his knife, Varney tiptoes over to the sleeping cop. Mircalla and Erzsebet do the same. You stand back with your shoulder leaning against the wall and your hands shoved deep in your pockets, observing them as they look hungrily down upon their victim. Their *meal*.

Varney nudges the cop, holding the tip of the knife inches from his doughy mug. The cop stirs and snorts but does not rouse, so Varney smacks him on his deeply-creased forehead with the back of his hand. This makes the cop jolt awake, and he sits up to find the points of three silver daggers hovering in front of his face.

"What the fu...?"

"Officer Donald W. Raymond," Varney says, elevating the tone of his declarative voice. "You have hereby been summoned to appear before the devil's court to answer for your crimes. Consider this your subpoena to *The People vs. Donald Raymond*."

Raymond, his face flushing with anger, attempts to stand. Varney hisses and shoves him back down, pressing the dagger against the hollow of the cop's throat. "I advise you not to do that, Mr. Pig. We, *the People*, shall have *order* in this *court*. And in case you haven't noticed, you're not dealing with unarmed kids tonight."

"You're dealin with fuckin immortals," says Mircalla.

"Who have weapons," Erzsebet says.

"*Real* weapons," says Varney. "Not toys."

Raymond stares up into Varney's sunglasses. "You don't scare me, kid. Put that thing down before you hurt yourself. You and your..."

Varney pulls his arm back and slashes Raymond across the face. An angry red gash appears on his cheek, and a curtain of blood spills down his neck, staining the sweat-yellowed collar of his white undershirt. He grunts but does not scream.

"See," Varney says, "here's the thing. *I* know how to use my weapon responsibly. *You* go around shooting kids just because you..."

THUMP.

You and your friends look down the dark hall in the direction from whence the sound had come. Raymond doesn't, but his already-pale face blanches further and his neck goes rigid. Varney looks down at him with a half-grin and says, "Sounds like we're not alone. Who else is here, Mr. Pig? Is there a *Mrs.* Pig we should know about?" He inclines his head at the plain gold band on Raymond's left ring finger.

"No. There's no one. It's just me. No one else is here."

"Are you *sure* about that, Mr. Pig? Because if you're lying, I'm going to find out. I'll huff and I'll puff and I'll blow your house right the *fuck* down until I find whomever it is that you're not telling us about."

"I swear. There's no one else here."

Keeping his gaze trained on Raymond, Varney says, "Mircalla, go check the bedroom."

As Mircalla stalks off down the hallway, Raymond changes his tune and appeals to Varney with stammering promises of all the money and drugs he could want, claiming to have full access to the evidence room at the police station. "Just please don't kill me," he begs. "Anything you want, I swear. Just name it and it's yours. We've got drugs in there you've never even *heard* of."

You wonder if he has Captain Howdy, and the thought sickens your stomach with green revulsion.

"I don't care *what* you have, Mr. Pig. *We* have enough money and drugs to make your evidence room look like a kid's coin bank by comparison. A kid's *piggybank*, actually." He snickers. "No, we don't need nor want anything that you..."

"Hey, Varney, look what I found!" Mircalla emerges from the hall with a plump but pretty-faced woman with two curlers in her hair, one on either side of her head. He has his knife pressed against the small of her back. In his free hand he's holding the policeman's utility belt. "Not only did I find Mrs. Pig, I also found *Mr.* Pig's toys."

"*Don*," Mrs. Pig whines. "What's going *on*? Who *are* these people? What's going on? *What's going on?*"

"Shut up, bitch," Varney snaps. "Now, Mircalla, do me a favor and toss that belt to Erzsebet, would you kindly?"

Mircalla does as he's told, and Erzsebet catches it with one-handed ease.

"Good. Tell me, Erzsebet, would there happen to be a Taser gun on that belt?"

Erzsebet examines the belt and then draws a small pistol-shaped object from its holster. "This?" she asks, holding it up.

Varney glances at it and nods. "That would be it, yes." Looking back down at Raymond, he says, "Okay, Mr. Pig, it's time for the question that I've just been *dying* to ask you ever since I heard about your trigger-happy debacle with poor young Theodore. Are you ready? Are you going to answer truthfully? You *better* answer truthfully, because I *hate* liars."

Raymond doesn't say anything. The blood streaming down his face and neck seems to have quickened its pace.

"I'm going to give you the benefit of the doubt and assume that your silence is a 'yes.' All right, here we go. Court is now in session." He clears his throat. "Did you, Officer Donald W. Raymond, have that Taser gun, or another of its nature, on your person at the time of Theodore Christoval's death?"

Raymond still doesn't say anything, but if looks could kill, Varney's brains would be all over the living room.

"In the interest of consistency, I'm going to again take your silence as a 'yes.' So, since we agree that you did indeed have the Taser on your person, it can *also* be agreed that you had the option to use nonlethal force to incapacitate Mr. Christoval at the moment you felt threatened, as opposed to putting *six bullets* in his chest. Seeing as how you elected to do the latter, we can syllogistically deduce that you deliberately murdered Theodore Christoval in cold blood. Am I correct in this reasoning?"

This time, Raymond responds with a feral growl, one so savage and animalistic in nature that it makes your hackles rise.

Varney, on the other hand, is unperturbed. Contrarily, his face lights up and he exclaims, "Ladies and gentlemen of the jury, it seems our defendant has entered a 'Not Guilty' plea! This...just...got...*interesting*. Honestly, I was hoping that was how you would plead, because I am an honorable man and I want to ensure we eliminate *every* shred of reasonable doubt before sending you to the gallows."

"Don, make them *stop*," complains Mrs. Pig. "*Do* something."

Paying her no mind, Varney says, "Now, Mr. Pig, seeing as how the odds *do* appear to be insurmountably against your favor, I'm going to throw you a bone. Let's posit, if only for the sake of argument, that there is the possibility that maybe your Taser gun is defective. I suggest this because it's the sole reason I can think of that would compel you to use your firearm. If your only means of nonlethal defense wasn't functioning, then I could *hypothetically* be persuaded to believe that deadly force *might* have been your only option. After all, when you've got a kid who's holding...not *pointing*, but *holding*...a *toy* gun, it's *perfectly* reasonable that you'd feel *so* threatened that you had to react with *any* means necessary. That being said, Erzsebet, would you be a doll and..."

Erzsebet doesn't wait for him to finish. Dropping the belt to the floor, she grips the Taser gun with both hands and fires. A tiny barbed electrode bursts from one of the chambers, a fine silver wire unspooling behind it. It hits Raymond on the bloodied side of his neck. His jaw clenches, his eyes roll back in his head, and he falls twitching onto his side.

Mrs. Pig starts to scream, but Mircalla slaps his hand over her mouth and puts the knife to her throat. "Easy, bitch," he whispers. "You don't want to be found in contempt of court, do you?"

Looking happily down at the convulsing man, Varney says, "*Well*. It looks to me like it works. Nevertheless, I believe there are *two* chambers, and while *one* of them works, maybe the other one..."

Again, Erzsebet complies before Varney even gives the order. She squeezes the trigger, and a second electrode shoots out and strikes Raymond not two inches from where the first one did. This time, the convulsions are worse. Mrs. Pig tries another scream, but the sound is nary more than a muffled groan against Mircalla's palm.

"Tsk, tsk, tsk," Varney says, shaking his head. "Mr. Pig, as far as I can tell, your Taser gun seems to be in *fine* operating order. Do you know what that means? You don't look like you're in any condition to answer, so I'll just tell you. What it means is that we have, I think, eliminated the existence of reasonable doubt. And what *that* means is that all of the evidence before us indicates that you killed Theodore Christoval in cold blood. Alas, that's not for me to decide. This is America, after all. We have procedures, and we're going to follow them." He turns to the side and looks at the other occupants of the room. "Jurors, what say you?"

"Guilty," Mircalla says.

"Guilty," Erzsebet says.

They look to you. You know the outcome of this is going to be the same, irrespective of your answer, but you surprise yourself with the level of unwavering calm in your voice when you say, "Guilty."

"That's three guilty verdicts," says Varney, "but we still have one more juror, and her voice is just as important as any." He points his dagger at Mrs. Pig. "Juror Number Four, what is *your* verdict?"

Mircalla takes his hand off her mouth, but when all she does is start to wail for help, he puts it back.

Varney tsks again. "My, my, I fear we may be faced with a hung jury. That won't do, not at all. Mircalla, remind me, how do we deal with hung juries?"

Mircalla cuts Mrs. Pig's throat.

"Ah, yes, I knew it was something like that," Varney says, his mouth a cruel smirk as Mircalla sucks the blood gushing from the woman's neck. He turns his attention to Raymond, who still hasn't roused from his state of not-quite-consciousness. His eyes are fluttering, and intermittent spasms attack various parts of his body. Varney hoists him back into a sitting position and says, "Well, Mr. Pig, there you have it. Justice has spoken, and it is now time we serve it that which it so hungrily craves. Erzsebet, will you help me do the honors?"

"With pleasure," says Erzsebet, dropping the Taser and joining Varney and Raymond on the couch.

Raymond doesn't react when Varney and Erzsebet each cut one of his wrists, and he remains unconscious even when they begin to drink from him. You watch with wide-eyed fascination. In and of itself, the act of the blood-drinking seems highly erotic for the three of them. Their faces, contorted as if in orgasm, stir up memories of surreptitious late-night trysts between you and...

No. None of that. Euphoric recall never got you anywhere.

Mircalla, who had fallen to the floor with Mrs. Pig so he could drink from her in leisure, is getting to his feet. Something appears to be wrong with him. He's clutching his stomach, and the orgasmic expression on his face has become one of pale-green biliousness. Staggering a few steps toward the hall, he stops, braces himself against the wall with his arm, and then bends over to expel a profuse torrent of red vomit.

"Holy shit," you say. "Guys, I think something is wrong with..."

Now Erzsebet is getting off the couch, only to fall to her hands and knees and puke up the blood she'd just taken in. After a moment, Varney does the same. You observe this horrific scene with rapidly mounting panic. For a second, you consider reaching into your jeans for your phone so you can call 9-1-1. You recognize the notion for its absurdity before your fingers even slip into your pocket. What are you supposed to say? "Hello, operator, my friends just murdered two people and basically sucked them dry, and the blood doesn't seem to be sitting too well with them"?

Varney is the first to finish. He stands up, daintily dabbing his mouth with an embroidered handkerchief procured from the inside of his tailcoat, while Erzsebet and Mircalla cough up a few last strands of stringy red bile. When he sees the horrorstruck look on your face, he laughs. "Nothing to fear, this is all par for the course. It's part of the ritual. Comes with the territory." He lights a cigarette and grins at you.

"This is...normal? You always throw up after you drink someone's blood?"

"Yes, I'm afraid so. What we are...it goes against nature. Even though we're no longer human, our organic selves rebel against that very concept. The human body is very complex. It's programmed for the trappings of life, not *immortal* life. Ambrosio says it took years for his body to adjust to immortality. He doesn't have to drink blood anymore, of course...he's lived for so long that he doesn't even crave it now...but in the beginning, when he *did* need it, his body fought him quite severely."

Warily eyeing the spots of bloodpuke on the carpet, you say, "So, that's what I have to look forward to if Ambrosio decides to turn me? Puking my guts out every night?"

Mircalla belches out one final spatter of Mrs. Pig's blood, wipes his mouth with the back of his hand, and then says to you. "Nah, dude, it's so fuckin worth it. The feeling you get when the blood first hits your tongue...shit, there's nothing like it. A little barf session is a small price to pay, for real. Besides, it's not *every* night."

Erzsebet is getting up now, but she doesn't seem to have recovered with the same rubber-band-speed that the other two have. Upon standing, she has to sit back down on the couch. Her breathing is heavy and shallow.

"Are you okay?" you ask her.

She nods, using the afghan to mop sweat from her forehead and blood from her lips. "Yeah, all good. Just a little out of breath." She smiles at you before being overtaken by a coughing fit that makes her heave up another few mouthfuls of bloodpuke. You watch this with a furrowed brow, fidgeting with your hands and wanting a cigarette.

"Anyway," says Varney, seeming not to be at all disturbed by Erzsebet's stunted recuperation. "Now that we've..."

A sound rises up from a room down the hallway. It's quiet at first, and then raises in volume and intensity. It is an unmistakable sound, one as easily-identifiable as a ringing bell or the flick of a zippo, though much less pleasant. That traditionally-connoted unpleasantness, though, seems to be lost on Varney; instead, it brings a horrible smile to his face.

"Do you lads and lass hear that?" he says, rubbing his hands together like a supervillain musing over his plans for world domination. "Do you know what that sounds like to me?"

No one says anything.

"It sounds," Varney says, "like dessert."

3

You're very quiet on the ride back to Ambrosio's. Seeing your friends kill the cop and his wife had affected you very little, overall. Maybe it was because Varney's brand of moral vigilantism was convincing enough to accept, or maybe it's really as simple as pure desensitization as a result of the other horrors you've experienced prior to this night. What happened at the end, though...that had been a little much.

As if reading your mind, Varney looks at you in the rearview mirror and says, "You look a trifle distraught, kid. What's troubling you? Was it our dessert?"

"No. Nothing's troubling me. I'm good."

Not buying it, Varney says, "Tell me, do you know about Wesley Parker?"

"Just stories. I was, like, three years old when it happened."

"But you know the gist of it, yes?"

"Yes."

"Do you know what he said his reason was for killing all of those little kids?"

"He said they were going to grow up to be bullies and assholes, or something. And he said the devil helped him."

"Correct. And while even *I* think that killing a classroom of kindergarteners with a nail gun and a dumbbell is a bit extreme, his head was in the right place. Well, mostly. The part about the devil always sounded to me like some schizophrenic bullshit, but that's not the point. The *point* is, he truly believed he was doing the world a favor. He believed he was acting in the interest of a greater good. I tend to agree. Most kids *do* grow up to be bullies and assholes."

A montage of sneering faces suddenly whirls through your head...Felix Clerval, his cunty sister Agatha, Bill Beaufort, Walton De Lacey...if someone had killed them when they were little, it would have saved you and a good many others a great deal of suffering. "Yeah," you say, "I guess. But..."

"You saw what an asshole that cop was," Varney continues, cutting you off. "Do you *really* think that any offspring of his would turn out to be any better? Had we left that blubbering little bundle of joy in its crib, what do you think would have happened? It would have grown up to win the Nobel Peace Prize?"

You can't think of anything to say to that. Once again, the logic behind his alternative moralism is proving to be surprisingly sound, in its own offbeat way.

"Plus," Mircalla says, "that little fucker was *delicious*."

"Like veal," Erzsebet agrees, nodding.

Like veal.

CHAPTER 7 – VARNEY'S FEAST OF BLOOD

1

ARRIVING BACK AT AMBROSIO's house after Donald Raymond's trial, the four of you spend the rest of the night getting stoned in the living room and listening to the Cure, waxing philosophic about government conspiracies and the natures of life and death. You don't contribute much to the conversation, preferring mainly to just listen and nod in the right places. Occasionally, you'll even find yourself laughing. It isn't the kind of loose, liberated laughter to which you became accustomed in LA, but it's laughter, nonetheless.

Sometime around three AM, after a long bout of silence in which you all just float on pleasantly subdued clouds of weed-induced euphoria, you sit up from your reclining position on the couch to light a cigarette. You look at Varney, who's sitting on the other side of the room in an armchair. Locks of his black hair have fallen out of place, and he's shed his jacket and waistcoat. The sleeves of his shirt are rolled up to the elbows, and his dark eyes are shot through with crinkly red lines. "Varney," you say to him, "what's *your* story?"

Erzsebet and Mircalla, who are both lying on the floor, sit up and look to their leader with eager eyes. "Yeah," Mircalla says. "You still haven't told us how *you* met Ambrosio. You know our stories. When are you gonna tell us yours?"

"We've been trying to get him to give us his origin story ever since we met him," Erzsebet says to you. "He always plays the 'dark and mysterious' card."

"Which is getting *old* as *fuck*," says Mircalla. "Come on, dude, spill it."

Varney straightens in his chair, his eyes flitting back and forth between you and the other two. His smile is cagey. "Well," he says, "I *suppose* I could tell you. But with the mystery gone, how do I know my value to you folks won't depreciate?"

"Oh, shut up," says Erzsebet. "You know we love you. That's not contingent upon some silly self-perpetuated mystique."

At her use of the word "love," something in Varney's cool expression softens. If you'd blinked, you'd have missed it, but it's unmistakable. A warmed tenderness becomes visible in his face, the look of an approval-deprived child whose father just told him he was proud of him. Then his usual wryness returns, and he's as cool as ever. "My story is a very personal one," he says, "and the life I led before I met Ambrosio is not something I see as relevant. However, if it is truly so important to you, I shall tell you my tale."

2

"Unlike you blokes, I was always the cool kid. I grew up right here in Chatterley, and there wasn't a kid in this town who didn't want to be me or fuck me or both. Ever since I was a lad, I *ran* the schoolyard. I was a kindergarten kingpin before I even knew how to count. All the teachers were afraid of me. They thought I was too smart, too cunning, too charismatic. Once, when I was in second grade, I overheard one of them tell the school librarian that she thought I was the antichrist.

"My peers, on the other hand, adored me. No, that's not the right word. They *worshipped* me. And not just the ones my age...even the older kids saw me as something akin to a god. When I was ten, I lost my virginity to my sixteen-year-old babysitter. She was a cheerleader. Then I went behind her back and fucked her boyfriend. She was so devastated that she killed herself.

"By eleventh grade, I'd fucked three teachers and the assistant principal. Oh, and the guidance counselor. *And* his wife. They were both cheating on each other with me, and as far as I know, neither of them ever found out. The fellow's wife had a mean streak of melodrama, and *she* probably would have killed herself if she'd known her hubby was banging me in the locker room after school.

"Do forgive me, I realize that the three of you had some rather unfortunate high school experiences, but honesty is something I greatly value so I'm not going to lie just to make you guys feel better about yourselves. The simple fact is, I had a grand old time in high school. If there was a party worth being at, I was there. And it was only ever worth being at *because* I was there. I could turn the lamest *Dungeons and Dragons* pizza party into a Gatsby-esque affair just by stepping in the door. Good times just seemed to follow me everywhere I went. Some people took to calling me 'the Magician' because I could make excitement and fun appear out of thin air. Come to think of it, I really ought to have played up that moniker a bit more than I did. Maybe learned some card tricks, or something.

"Alas, not *everything* was perfect. I'm quite aware that the portrait I'm painting of my life may seem *too* idyllic to be true, so allow me to assuage such doubt by assuring you that my human years were not without complications. The trouble was, I had a *wretched* family. My father was a bigshot CEO of a lucrative textile company, and my mother was a financial analyst. I had two brothers...one older and one younger...both of whom were utterly useless. My younger brother, Henry, was retarded. I mean, he was *actually* retarded. Full-on Down's syndrome, to the max. The drooling idiot was a waste of air since he took his very first breath. My older brother, Charles, wasn't much better. He wasn't *technically* a retard, but he was about as dumb as a regular person can get before crossing the threshold into Downy territory. Still, he had a full ride to CSU on a football scholarship, so he was my parents' pride and joy. Henry was their second-favorite, on account of the alleged fact that he was 'special.' And me? I was just their precocious middle child, whose social proclivities sometimes caused them minor degrees of embarrassment. Like, for instance, when my mother discovered I was fucking three of the women from the book club she hosted at our house the first and third Saturdays of every month.

"In the end, I suppose I can't complain *too* much, because it was my shitty family that ultimately led me to Ambrosio.

"My parents' deplorable treatment of me reached fever pitch one fateful night when they sat me down and told me I needed to get a job. My father said he was cutting me off, and that I needed to learn how to be a responsible adult. Have you ever *heard* such an unfathomable load of bullshit? I was a six-teen-year-old kid who'd never done anything wrong, and my holier-than-thou CEO dad tells me I have to get a *job?* The nerve of it *enraged* me. Well, believe you me, I gave the bastard a piece of my mind. Amid all the shouting, the retard got upset and started crying. That fat, soap-brained baboon was always crying about something or other, and my mother would fawn all over him every time. That night, the only way she could get him to calm down was to tell him I would take him to Walgreens to get some Raisinets. *That* shut the little shit up *right* quick. It was like she'd flipped a switch. One second, he's bleating and crying like a colicky infant, and the next he's grinning like a...well, like a *retard*. Fucker *loved* Raisinets.

"Naturally, I protested with the utmost vehemence, but it did no good. My father said if I didn't take Henry to Walgreens, he would ground me for an entire *week*. I couldn't let *that* happen, because I had plans to fuck his secretary that very weekend, and that was an appointment I did *not* want to miss. So, I took the retard to get his stupid candy.

"Afterward, I didn't feel like going home right away, so I drove to Lake Erie. It was almost eleven on a Wednesday night, so there wasn't anyone there. That allowed me to freely smoke a bowl on a bench while the retard stuffed his face. I'd wanted to leave him in the car, but he started crying again, and that was the last thing I needed.

"I had pretty much calmed down by the time I heard a car pull up. My initial reaction was one of panic, because I of course assumed it was a cop. My day had already been shot to shit, so what better way to end it than to get caught smoking weed in the presence of my retarded brother?

"It wasn't a cop car, though, as I'm certain you've already guessed. It was the Rolls-Royce. It was the most beautiful car I'd ever seen, and that remains true to this day. Nevertheless, just because it wasn't a cop didn't mean it would be someone who approved of what I was doing, so I made to leave. But then the car door opened and this blond guy with sunglasses and a fake tan got out and opened the rear door. Three guesses who emerged from the back seat.

"He was wearing a long black robe and a hood that hid his face, but I could immediately tell there was something special about him. *Truly* special, not special in the way Henry was special. He had this dark, mysterious aura about him that didn't seem human.

"He walked over to me and introduced himself as Ambrosio. I tried to play it cool and act like I didn't give a fuck who he was, but I was too transfixed by his presence to maintain the guise of aloofness for very long. I knew I was in the company of something that transcended the laws of the physical world. I knew he had power beyond my wildest imaginings. And somehow, I also knew that he could *grant* me power of near-equal measure, if he so desired.

"He didn't waste any time in getting to the point. He told me he knew who I was and what I was looking for. Now, there was nothing extraordinary about his knowing who I was, because *everyone* knew who I was. But what I was *looking for?* Even *I* didn't know what I was looking for. I hadn't really known I was looking for *anything*, really. At least, not until he told me.

"He said he could relieve me of responsibility and the burden of my abhorrent family. He said I would never have to grow up. I would never have to get a job or toil my life away adulting with other miserable adults. I would never worry about bills or healthcare or car insurance. I would never have to worry about anything at all.

"Under any other circumstances, I would have laughed away his Peter Pan shtick and told him to go fuck himself. But I didn't. I don't know how, but I *knew* he was telling the truth. I hadn't the slightest doubt that he could grant me all of those promises, and then some. So, I said, 'What do I have to do?'

"He then proceeded to tell me that power requires sacrifice, but that the sacrifice need not be my own. I merely had to prove that I was willing and able to do things that most others would not. And that was *all* he said. He didn't give me any explicit instructions on exactly what that entailed, but he didn't have to.

"While I'd been palavering with Ambrosio, Henry had found a large rock and was using it to etch nonsensical symbols in the sand. Without so much as a shadow of hesitation, I walked over to the retard, took the rock from him, and bashed his brains out with it. All it took was one strike, but I probably hit him a good twenty or thirty times. It was a tit-for-tat thing, just making up for all the head trauma he'd caused *me* over the years.

"When it was finished, I went back over to Ambrosio. Even though I couldn't see his face, I knew he was pleased. To be quite honest, I don't think he'd expected me to do what I did. Not with such abandon. I'm really not sure that had even been what he'd had in mind. Either way, it satisfied him, and he turned me right then and there.

"The instant power I felt was nothing shy of intoxicating. I was so delectably encumbered with willful violence that I could scarcely breathe. The bloodlust wasn't so much something I *felt*, but something I *was*. It was a thirst that had become a part of me, and I of it. And I knew it *must* be sated.

"Ambrosio must have seen it in my face, because he took the keys to the Rolls from the blond guy and gave them to me. 'Go do what you need to do,' he told me. 'My assistant and I will dispose of your car.' Then he looked at the mess in the sand and added, 'And your brother.' He took a pen from the folds of his robe and wrote an address on my arm. The address, as I'm sure you can guess, of the very house in which we now sit. He told me to go there when I'd finished with my business. The last thing he did was hand me a dagger.

"There are no words that can even approach accuracy when describing how it felt to drive that car for the first time, but I *can* tell you that I did not drive it in the manner one should when leaving one murder scene to go to another. I didn't just speed; I *flew*. I tore through every stop sign, every red light. I don't remember what song was playing on the radio, but I know I yelled along to it like I was a revivalist preacher in the deep South performing fast-talking healing rituals on a hot Saturday night. Newly-dead as I may have been, I'd never been more alive.

"I whipped into the driveway of my house and left the car running. I opened the front door just a tad, then kicked it wide for dramatic effect. My father was sitting at the kitchen table with his laptop, and I went straight to him with the biggest shit-eating grin you *ever* did see. I remember this part very vividly. He looked up at me and started to say something, probably intending to ask what had taken so long and/or where the retard was, but I spoke first. I said to him, 'You know, Father, I've always thought you were a rather pathetic creature, but tonight really sealed the deal for me, in that regard. Do tell me, if you would, *just who the fuck you think you are*. Oh, I *get* it, you're a highfalutin CEO bigwig, but what does that even *mean?* What does a CEO even *do,* besides sit around answering emails and counting his money? For someone like *you* to lecture someone like *me* about responsibility is so absurdly ironic that it leaves the realm of comedy and ventures into Sophoclean *tragedy*. You should be *ashamed* of yourself. You don't know what *real* work is. All you know how to do is boss people around. People like you are *exactly* what's wrong with this country. You're a plague. A parasite. You're little more than a deer tick on the flank of what was once a great nation. Worse than that, though, you're a nuisance to *me*. And I. Am. *So*. Over it.'

"He was starting to stand up when I drew Ambrosio's dagger and stabbed him right in the jugular. And let me tell you something, I *smelled* the blood before I saw it. Right before it shot out of his throat like Old fucking Faithful, the metallically sweet aroma filled my nose and set my entire body on fire. I fell upon him at once, pushing him to the floor and sucking his wound like a malnourished piglet at its mother's teat. I drank him *up*, and it was *delicious*. I could feel myself growing stronger with every swallow. I felt like I'd been transported into some Alice-in-Wonderland DMT-dream. The whole world faded from my perception. There was only me and the blood.

"When my father's deathly well had dried up, I was left wanting more. I was *desperate* for it. I had just slurped every last life-drop from the old man, but I was still absolutely *parched*. But then, with all the convenient timeliness of a dinner bell, my mother entered the kitchen just as I was getting up and wiping my mouth. She clasped her hands to her cheeks and did a praiseworthy impression of a throwaway female victim shrieking her lungs out in a B-horror movie. She didn't scream for long. I grabbed the toaster off the counter and swung it around at her by its cord. It hit her in the side of the head and knocked her out cold. I cut her wrist and made a lovely meal of her, drinking her in quiet solace.

"After my parents had been effectively dispatched, there was still the matter of Charles, the golden child. Going upstairs to his room was no easy task, because by then I had a few gallons of blood sloshing around inside me. I knew I was going to have to act fast, because he was bigger than me. *Much* bigger. He was built like your garden-variety gym rat, six-four and two hundred fifty pounds of roided-up muscle. If I didn't get the jump on him, he'd overpower me without even having to try.

"I needn't have worried. When I opened his bedroom door, he was asleep on the floor in front of his TV with an issue of *Sports Illustrated* lying open to an ad for Axe body spray. Appropriate, given that he went through that shit faster than a fat guy with IBS goes through toilet paper after a late-night trip to Taco Bell. He called it his 'shower in a can'.

"This seemingly irrelevant detail is actually crucial to my story, because it was Charles' body odor that nearly ruined everything. All that blood was not sitting well in my stomach, and the first whiff I caught of his gym-sweat brought me dangerously close to vomiting. That would have inevitably wakened him and left me defenseless, but through some stroke of good fortune, I was able to keep it down.

"I'll never forget the way his eyes sprang open when I cut his throat. As I knelt over him, he looked up at me with this puppy-dog face that was full of confusion and betrayal and fear. You can't scream with a sliced throat, but he tried. Oh, did he try.

"His blood tasted foul. I suspect it was from the steroids, but I can't be certain. Either way, I forced myself to drink it. *All* of it. I was no longer thirsty, but it felt imperative that I do it. There was a ritualistic quality to the whole affair. All my life, my family had been sucking the life out of me. It was only right that I repay the favor as my final act in my old life.

"Once he was dead, I stood and prepared to make my leave, but my body had other plans. When I rose to my feet, I was overtaken by dizziness and an excruciating nausea. I ran to the bathroom, knelt at the toilet, and starting puking up my family. There was so much blood, and it came so fast, that the toilet started to overflow no matter how many times I flushed it. By the time it drained what was in the bowl, I'd already replaced it with double the amount. In minutes it was seeping over the edges, so I moved to the tub and emptied into it the remains of my stomach's pilfered contents.

"I don't know how long it took, but when it was finally over, I felt *amazing*. I left the house with a spring in my step, and with an unburdened heart I drove to the address Ambrosio had written on my arm. I didn't even need to use a GPS. It was as if there was a beacon guiding me there. Knowing what I do now, I suspect that isn't utterly out of the question. I think that beacon was always there, waiting for me. It wasn't until I closed my mortal eyes and first looked upon the world with my *im*mortal ones that I was finally able to see it. And what a glorious sight it was, indeed. What a glorious sight it *is*."

CHAPTER 8 – FRANCES BANNERWORTH

1

IT'S JUST PAST MIDNIGHT when you leave the house the next night. Varney doesn't want to go anywhere loud, citing a desire for a "chill night," so he drives to the Metroparks and posts up at Ellis Lake. It's unusually cool for late August, even considering the time of night and the natural temperature drop near the water. The lake, if you can call it that...it's more of a large pond...is glass-flat and tar-black beneath the overcast sky.

The four of you smoke cigarettes in the sand, sipping from the Four Lokos that Varney bought from the Marathon on the way here. Mircalla lights a joint, but you decline when its rotation reaches you. You're still buzzed from a strong cocktail Erzsebet served you earlier back at the house, and you don't feel like getting too fucked up.

You haven't been there long...maybe a half an hour, tops...when a red Mustang pulls into the parking lot and comes to a stop a dozen or so yards away from the Rolls. It still has the paper dealer tags, the expiration date scrawled in orange marker.

"Fuck," Mircalla says. "Why do the fuckin townies always have to show up and ruin our fun?"

You raise your eyebrows over the lenses of your sunglasses and say, "Townies?"

Mircalla ignores you and says to Varney, "You think we should bail?"

Varney drags from his cigarette and then from the joint. He takes a swig of Four Loko. "Maybe. Not yet. They might just leave." A sliver of moonlight stabs through a broken cloud and bounces off the lenses of his Aviators.

The Mustang doesn't leave. Its headlamps blink off, and then two shadows emerge from it. They stand by the car and appear to confer for a minute or two, and then they start walking toward you. When they're about thirty yards away, they sit down in the sand, huddled close together. The darkness and distance prevent you from being able to see them in detail, but you're pretty sure it's a male and female.

"I don't think they're leaving," Mircalla says.

Varney sighs, taking off his hat and running a hand through his hair. "They're waiting for *us* to leave. They probably want to fuck, or something. But *we* were here first, so *we* aren't going anywhere. Give it a few more minutes and they'll skedaddle, just watch."

After a few minutes, the couple does indeed stand up, but they don't skedaddle. Instead, they start making their way over to your group.

"We should go," you say to Varney, trying not to sound as uneasy as you are. You have a queer feeling that something bad is going to happen. It could be your imagination posing as intuition, or it could be based purely on the empirical knowledge of Varney's relative sadism.

"Hold up," Varney says calmly, getting to his feet. "Let's see what they want, first."

You, Erzsebet, and Mircalla stand, as well, falling into formation behind him. The four of you are arranged in a sort of arrowhead, with Varney at the point, like a flock of migrating geese.

As the couple comes closer, you deduce that they're probably a little older than you, most likely the same age as your companions, but the details of their faces are still too concealed by the darkness for you to be certain. They stop a stone's throw away from the four of you, holding each other's hand with intertwined fingers.

"Good evening, sir and madam," Varney purrs. "Are you quite lost?" You shudder and look at Erzsebet, who smiles in a way that you suppose is meant to be reassuring, but it doesn't work. She palms you a cigarette, which you take and light with trembling hands. Something definitely feels wrong.

The boy folds his arms over his chest and says, "Yeah, look, not to be a dick, or anything..."

Varney holds up a finger. "Now, my dear fellow, when one starts a sentence with 'not to be a dick,' it more often than not is a rather sound indicator that the utterer is, in fact, about to be a dick. So, before you continue, please be advised that neither I nor my friends respond well to dick-ish behavior."

"Whoa, fuckwad, easy on the threats. Me and my girl just want some alone time, you follow? So, how's about you and your freaky little goth friends beat it and go listen to Hawthorne Heights and sniff some glue, or something, 'kay?"

"We don't listen to Hawthorne Heights," you hear yourself say before you can stop yourself.

"Or sniff glue," Erzsebet adds.

"I actually don't mind Hawthorne Heights," Mircalla says.

The boy starts to respond, but then the girl says, "*Wait* a second, *hold* the phone." She walks closer, pulling the boy with her. The moon peeks out from the clouds again, illuminating the couple in a band of pale silver light.

The girl is sort of almost-pretty in a dull, Midwestern kind of way. An Ohio 6, a California 3. She has freckles and mousy brown hair. Her cutoff jean shorts reveal the long, muscular legs of a soccer player or a track runner. The boy is tall and built like a swimmer, with broad shoulders and a wide chest tapering down into a narrow waist. His small, beady eyes are set too close together.

There's nothing tremendously striking about either of them, but for some reason, Varney's coolly poised posture goes rigid. You aren't positive, but you think you even hear him gasp.

Staring wide-eyed at Varney, the girl exclaims, "*Frances?* Frances *Bannerworth?* Holy shit, I *thought* it was you." She shakes her head disbelievingly, her lips playing at a toothy shark's grin.

"I...I am unfamiliar with this name of which you speak," Varney replies. He holds his head high, but the haughty self-assurance has left his voice. "You appear to have mistaken my identity for that of another."

The girl snorts. "Oh, Jesus, still talking like you've got a nineteenth-century stick up your ass, huh?" To the boy, she says, "Babe, this is *Frances*. He used to go to my high school. I swear to shit, you'll never meet a bigger creep in your life. He asked me to Homecoming freshman year, actually. It would have been cute if it hadn't been so p*athetic*. Poor little guy couldn't even make a sentence. You woulda thought he had a throat full of Legos, the way he kept choking on his words. I tried not to laugh. Really, I did. I tried *very* hard."

"Th-That never h-happened," Varney stammers. "You're th-thinking of s-someone else."

"Hang on," the boy says. "Is this the kid you told me about who almost got expelled because they found kiddie porn in his locker?"

"*Yes!*" squealed the girl excitedly. "That was *him!* They were gonna send him to juvie, but the little creep claimed it wasn't his and they couldn't prove otherwise."

"IT *WASN'T* MINE!" Varney shouts. "I mean...it wasn't *me*. You've got the wrong guy. I don't know who Frances is but I'm not him. I don't know who you are, either. I've never seen you before in my life, and I *certainly* never asked you to Homecoming." He looks over his shoulder at you, and then at Mircalla and Erzsebet. Cocking his thumb at the girl, he says, "Can you *believe* this libelous strumpet? *I* never asked *anyone* to Homecoming. Girls asked *me* to Homecoming. I practically had to beat them off with a stick." He tries to force his quivering lips into a smile, but the result is pitiably contrived.

The girl crows with snide laughter. "Is *that* so? Because *I* seem to recall you getting rejected by *five other girls* after me. And those are just the ones I *heard* about."

The boy looks Varney up and down and says, "If he dressed anything like he does now, it's no wonder. Fucker looks like he's on his way to the train convention, or something."

Varney, his voice still broken and feeble, says, "That...what? That doesn't even make *sense*."

"Whatever happened to you, anyway?" the girl asks. "For a while, we all just figured you killed yourself. That's what we hoped, anyway. But then we heard your whole family just up and disappeared without a trace. Did they get sick of having to live with a freakazoid baby-fucker?"

"Shut up. I don't fuck babies."

Erzsebet steps forward, her clawed fingers splayed at her sides. "Listen, bitch," she says. "You've got three seconds to fuck the *fuck* off before we eat you and your fugly boyfriend for dinner. I'm not even a *little* bit kidding."

The boy chortles. "You're gonna *eat* us, huh? You hear that, babe? The emo slut is going to *eat* us."

"One," Erzsebet says.

"Oh, puh-*lease*," says the girl with a roll of her eyes. "The only thing Frances eats is toddler pussy."

"Two."

"I kinda want to kick these kids' asses," the boy muses to the girl. "I mean, just for the fuck of it. How long do you think it would take me to bring them all down? Five seconds? Ten, tops? I think I..."

"Three."

There's a blur of movement to your left. A streak of silver slices through the air. Mircalla's dagger, thrown by its owner with admirable precision, embeds itself between the boy's eyes. He goes down in a hugely unspectacular fashion, crumpling into a heap in the sand like a marionette with cut strings.

Before the girl can register what's happened and react accordingly, Varney lunges at her. Putting one hand around her waist and cradling her head with the other, he dips her as one would a ballroom dance partner and sinks his teeth into her throat. He shakes his head like a dog with a chew toy and tears away a sizable chunk of flesh, which he spits into the sand. Shoving her to the ground, he puts his palm over her mouth to stifle her screams while he drinks from her neck.

Once she's gone limp, Varney stands and turns around to face you and the others. The moon has returned to its hiding place behind the clouds, so it's too dark to know for sure, but you think you can see a single tear escape from behind his sunglasses and roll down his ghostly face. "She was lying," he says quietly. "Those things she said...they weren't true. She was a liar."

At first, no one says anything. Then Mircalla walks over to Varney and puts his hand on his shoulder. "We know, dude," he says, and then pulls Varney into a tight hug. "We know."

Erzsebet walks over and joins them, putting her arms around them both.

You look down at your cigarette, which has gone out. After staring at it for several long seconds, you drop it into the sand and join your friends' embrace.

You don't know how long the four of you stand there. Minutes, an hour, who knows. All you know is that you feel like you're a part of something, whatever that may be. You don't know if it's good or bad, but it's something, and you haven't felt like that since you left Los Angeles. It isn't the same feeling, but it's close.

You could stand here forever, you're sure of it. Or, at the very least, until the monstrous sun comes up and immolates your friends, their flames swallowing you up with them. It wouldn't, you think, be the worst way to die. It would, as a matter of fact, be quite poetic. But then Varney starts to cough, and he has to pull away so he can go puke up the girl.

2

When you get back to the house, the four of you are silent as you go inside and ascend the stairs together. But as you make to get off on the second-floor landing so you can go to your bedroom, Erzsebet grabs your wrist and leads you up to the fifth floor with the others. You follow them down the hallway and into the bedroom the three of them share.

Standing in a circle by the bed, you all look at each other. The silence, which had moments ago been cold and distant, is now warm and evocative of things to come.

Erzsebet begins to undress.

Then, so does Varney.

Then Mircalla.

Finally, you do, too.

What occurs next is dreamlike and feverish, a frenzied collage of blurry photographs taped together to form an impressionistically pornographic mural. As it happens, you feel more like a voyeuristic observer than an active participant.

You watch as Varney kisses Mircalla, and as Erzsebet kisses you.

As the four of you fall upon the bed in a writhing knot, like a tangle of snakes.

As partners swap and positions shift...Varney behind Mircalla, Erzsebet atop you; you behind Erzsebet and in front of Varney, who's in front of Mircalla; you next to Erzsebet with Mircalla's head between your legs and Varney's between hers.

As Varney's head comes up with his mouth and cheeks red with menstrual blood, and as Mircalla licks it off him.

As Erzsebet's cries become your cries, and Varney's cries become Mircalla's, until four voices become one...a voice that is thick and guttural, infused with all of the horror and ecstasy that comes both with life, and with its unnatural and unending counterpart.

As barriers between worlds melt into a slimy concoction of blood and sweat, semen and saliva.

As monsters become lovers.

As fear becomes comfort.

As death becomes life.

As all of this happens, you watch.

And as you, too, become something else...something not quite opposite of what you were before, but *almost*...you realize this *is* where you're supposed to be. That maybe coincidences *aren't* real, *nothing* is random, and perhaps whatever is watching over you really *does* have your best interest at heart.

It is a good feeling.

3

When it's over, you're lying between the unconscious bodies of Varney and Mircalla, with Erzsebet asleep on top of you. For dead things, they provide immense warmth. Snuggled there among them, you could almost make the claim that you've never been so warm in your life.

Almost.

But not quite.

There had been one who was warmer. Only one. One who gave you more warmth than, you know, you'll ever again be able to capture.

And as you drift to sleep, you let yourself think about her. For the *first* time in *quite* some time, you let yourself remember.

Not just her, but all of it.

You remember all of it.

PART 11 –
SOME
FURTHERANCE
OF HELL

CHAPTER 9 –
THE GRINNING
MAN

1

YOUR REAL PARENTS DIED almost sixteen months ago, on May
3rd of 2015. Following their death, the Ohio courts sent you to
Los Angeles to live with your aunt and uncle and their daughter.
All ancestral records attached to your name indicated that they
were your only living relatives.

From the start, you knew that you would one day return to
your home state on a trailblazing path of fiery vengeance. That
errand, perhaps being one of a proverbial fool, would take place
far earlier than you anticipated upon first moving to California.
You lacked any prophetic intuition that so often seems to be a
conveniently plot-advancing trait of tragic young individuals in
tales bearing a resemblance to yours. You couldn't have known
that your time in LA would be shockingly short-lived, nor could
you have fathomed the cataclysmic event that would serve as a
catalyst to your bleak homecoming following your short stint
among the blond, tan angels in the city bearing their namesake.

Neither aunt nor uncle seemed pleased to take you in, but you saw them so infrequently that it didn't much matter. They would have been within their legal rights to refuse, but your cousin eventually told you, "My dad told me he fucked your dad over pretty bad, once. I guess he felt like he owed him something."

Your new guardians were both studio executives for one big movie company or another. They lived in a spacious, ultramodern house in Silver Lake at the apex of the steep hill that was Occidental Boulevard, overlooking Sunset. There was a gym, a fully-stocked bar, two tanning beds, and a fish tank teeming with exotic aquatic creatures that stretched the length and height of the west wall of the parlor. The backyard pool was tended by a teenaged Mexican boy who leered lecherously at your over the tops of his smudged sunglasses whenever you crossed paths with him.

You did a fair amount of leering during your time there, as well, though not at the pool boy, and not with the same lewd garishness. That was what you liked to believe, anyway. Later events would prove that your covetous gaze may not have been as clandestine as you'd thought.

The object of your infatuation was Mara, your sixteen-year-old cousin. She was as so many other California girls are known to be: smooth-skinned and slim-hipped and bright-eyed, with a tan complexion and a smile that shone with orthodontic perfection. Her long, dark red hair was banded with yellow-blonde streaks. She always looked casually bored, like she was too cool to be moved by the lavishness of the lifestyle into which she'd been born.

You had discovered the bottomless rabbit hole of Pornhub earlier that year, and the cliché of the hot stepsister (which was essentially what she *was*, you rationalized) was not lost on you. You would find LA to be a fairyland of clichés, a sprawling metropolis of stereotypes and tired movie tropes.

During the first month, you didn't notice much of anything. Even your cousin's alluring sexuality escaped your notice at first, only to be discovered at a later date when the California sun finally started to penetrate the dense haze of forlorn grief and emotional desolation. In those early days following your parents' deaths, the images from the ghastly scene in your childhood living room constructed an ever-present tapestry that had not yet restricted itself to the quiet darkness of your dreams. It hung before your wakeful eyes just as vividly, if not more so. Everywhere you looked, you saw blood and brains and haphazardly scattered viscera.

While the identity of your parents' murderer had been resolutely confirmed, the only picture the police had of the culprit was over twenty years old. It had been taken when the killer was a child, plain-looking and nondescript, save for a shock of orange-red hair that could have easily been dyed since then. Hence, every male stranger was a suspect in your eyes. You were constantly fighting the urge to seize the shoulders of random passersby and shout, *"Was it you? Did you kill my mom and dad? Was it you?"*

That was how you met the Grinning Man.

2

It was a late night in mid-June, a little over a month since your parents had been killed. Your aunt and uncle were at a party in Bel-Air. Mara might have been with them, but you didn't know for sure, nor did you really care. The comings and goings of your new family failed to register. Life was hazy and malformed, like a badly damaged photo reel on an old projector. You constantly felt like you were blinking in and out of existence.

That particular night, you'd descended Occidental and turned west on Sunset, walking nowhere. You noticed only the faint shadows and outlines of your surroundings. The expensive cars careening down the street, shining under the light of the streetlamps and neon storefronts, sounded distant. They revved their engines and bounced over potholes, their horns blaring as they zipped around one another, but it was almost as if some Great Being had turned the volume down to a nigh inaudible murmur.

It was hot. Your phone said it was 106, despite the fact that the sun had sunk into its sub-horizon slumber hours earlier. A simmering breeze, rank with the stench of exhaust and garbage, swirled up from the ever-busy boulevard.

Even the heat, for all of its nagging insistence upon claiming your attention, felt far away.

You hadn't walked for long, though, before you *did* notice something that brought you out of your fugue and sharpened everything into focus. Your sneakers ground to a halt on the pavement.

A man was staring at you.

And he was *grinning*.

It was an awful grin, stretched too wide across his face, in a manner that was frighteningly cartoonish.

He was maybe fifteen yards away from you, standing motionless outside Floyd's 99 Barbershop. There was an Albertson's shopping cart poised next to him, like an animal at rest. A purple sheet was draped over it, obscuring its contents. He was holding a cardboard sign that read, "AND SURELY THE BLOOD OF YOUR LIVES WILL I REQUIRE; AT THE HAND OF EVERY BEAST WILL I REQUIRE IT, AND AT THE HAND OF MAN (Genesis 9:5)."

He wore a torn oxblood sport coat over a stained and holey black T-shirt that read "JESUS SAVES" in loud yellow letters. His faded jeans were in a shredded state of disrepair that matched his ruined jacket. His stark white cowboy boots, however, were oddly untarnished. The polished leather glittered and gleamed in the oppressive light of the night.

Everything in you screamed that you should turn around and go back to the air-conditioned house, away from this terrible man and his hellacious grin.

But another part of you, a *louder* part of you, couldn't help but wonder, *Is this him? Did this man kill my parents?*

The man's impossible smile seemed to widen even further.

You walked forward.

As you drew nearer, with cautious slowness, you noticed his eyes. The irises were such a deep shade of midnight that they were almost indiscernible from the vacuous black holes of his pupils. They remained locked with your own, and when you came to a stop a couple of yards away from where he stood, his smile seemed to normalize. Its absurd size and wicked shimmer at once morphed into something warm and pleasant and friendly, as if its previous visage had been a lingering image from a mostly-forgotten dream.

There was something odd about his skin, too; like his teeth, it was too white. Smooth and pore-less, it cast the severe lines of his strangely handsome features in the hard mold of a Grecian statue. Its surface seemed to produce a fluorescent luminosity, like an ultraviolet lightbulb.

His hair was the color of strong coffee and appeared too clean to belong to a man of homeless destitution. It was longish but not unkempt, swept back off his forehead in a casually tousled fashion.

He looked like an actor playing the role of a stereotypical hobo, costumed appropriately (save for the peculiar boots) but still waiting for the makeup artist to apply the finishing touches of authenticity.

Putting his sign down on top of the shopping cart, the man said, "I didn't kill your parents."

The hot breeze became suddenly glacial, cutting savagely through your bones. It reminded you, with a sting of bitter melancholy, of the February winds off Lake Erie. An icy sweat broke out on the nape of your neck and slid coolly down your back.

"I know, I know, you weren't expecting that," said the Grinning Man, turning his palms up and tilting his head to the side in a gesture of mock sheepishness. "I just thought we should get that bit of unpleasant suspicion out of the way right off the bat. Besides, I wasn't sure you would have had the balls to ask."

"I would have asked," you blurted with angry defensiveness. And then, "If you didn't kill them, how do you know about it?"

The Grinning Man rolled his eyes and said, "Don't be daft, kid. I know *everything*. Well, *almost* everything. I never quite could get the hang of calculus." The timbre of his voice had a light, regal elegance to it. It had none of the garbled, slurry gruffness of the disturbed and drug-addled vagrants that skittered along the streets and alleys of Los Angeles like plague-ridden rats. It was more the voice of an aristocratic dandy, full of aloof amusement and mischievous delight.

Your eyes narrowing with the very suspicion the Grinning Man had allegedly attempted to eradicate with his inexplicable profession of innocence, you asked him in a flat tone, "Who are you?"

The man's eyes shone like molten onyx when he said, "Why is everyone always *asking* me that? There was a time when I was so immediately identifiable that a fucking blind man could have recognized me in a dark room from fifty feet away. Funny how fleeting fame can be for even the most infamous."

So, he *was* an actor, you deduced. You had never been much of a cinephile, though, so you figured your failure to pinpoint his identity was not unreasonable.

Procuring a pack of Dunhills from his jacket, the Grinning Man drew a cigarette from the square red box and then snapped his fingers, which were abnormally long. A bright orange flame erupted from between his thumb and middle finger, and he raised it to the end of the cigarette. He made a fist and the flame disappeared.

Startled, you took a half step back and asked, "How did you do that?"

Taking a deep drag from the cigarette, the Grinning Man waved his hand dismissively and said, "Oh, that's nothing, just a cheap parlor trick. A bit flashier than pulling a quarter out from behind your ear, though, wouldn't you say?"

Growing irritated with his trivially vain antics, you asked again, "How do you know about my parents?"

He rolled his eyes again. "That's a boring question. You can do better than that. Ask me something *real*."

Your agitation steadily mounting toward enraged intolerance, your eyes switched to the shrouded cart beside him. "What's in the shopping cart?"

He looked mildly taken aback for a moment, and then he grinned again. "*Now* we're getting somewhere," he said. "But that's information I'm not yet willing to divulge. Maybe some night in the future, but not this night."

"You're wasting my time," you said in a low, throaty tone that was almost a growl. Your hands curled into crude fists, your fingernails biting into your sweat-slickened palms.

The Grinning Man snorted. "Is that quite so? You're a fourteen-year-old orphan who's home alone on a Tuesday night. What could you *possibly* be doing, or *planning* to do, that is being impeded by my interference?"

Your first thought was to ask him how he knew your age, or that you were home alone, but you decided against doing so almost immediately. If he knew about your parents, there was no reason he shouldn't know everything else about you. Thereby, instead of challenging him with more questions, you just stood at rigidly tense attention, waiting for him to make the next move.

"Look, kid," he said with the cigarette clenched between his pearlescent teeth, "I want to help you. I'm *going* to help you."

"Why? How?" After a brief pause, you added, "You can't, anyway. No one can."

"Oh, Jesus, spare me the angsty wrist-cutting emo shit. Stop listening to Hawthorne Heights. Yeah, your situation kinda sucks, but it's nothing extraordinarily apocalyptic. Shakespeare isn't toiling away his afterlife writing your life story. Believe me, I'd know." That eel-like grin alighted upon his face once again, and his preternaturally black eyes burned through the blue-gray tendrils of smoke curling up from the glowing tip of his cigarette.

"I don't listen to Hawthorne Heights," you said. "And I haven't read anything by Shakespeare."

"Really? Not even *Macbeth*? Well, no, I suppose you wouldn't have. They usually don't teach that until high school, and you haven't experienced *that* particular nightmare just yet. You start ninth grade in, what, late August?"

You nodded.

"Well, you really ought to stop moping around and try to enjoy these last couple months of summer while you still can."

"You don't know that it's going to be a nightmare for me," you said. You were veritably confident in the sentiment that it wouldn't be one thing or another. You didn't have the energy to care about what high school might be like, and you had no credible evidence that such a sentiment would change.

The Grinning Man sniggered and flicked his cigarette into the street. "Oh, you poor, naïve child. High school is a nightmare for everyone, in one form or another. And you're not nearly as unique as you think you are."

Before you could answer, he gave you a final wink and then strode away with his shopping cart, whistling a Rolling Stones tune.

CHAPTER 10 – PICKLED FETUSES

1

THE FIRST REAL CONVERSATION you had with Mara happened on a hot Friday afternoon, a few days after you met the Grinning Man. You were sitting at a burnished oak table by the pool out back, shaded from the sun's scorching rays by a gaudy umbrella fashioned out of bamboo, straw, and palm fronds. You didn't know how long you'd been sitting there, watching the still water in a half-conscious daze with your back rigid and your hands folded on your lap, but you knew it had been a long time.

When Mara came out of the house and walked down from the deck over to the chaise lounge beside you, you hardly noticed her. Then she peeled off her tank top and stepped out of her frayed denim shorts, standing before you in a sky-blue bikini like some bronze goddess straight out of a libidinous male fantasy. Tilting her head to the side, she undid her ponytail and shook out her long mahogany hair, the blonde highlights sparkling in the sunlight like tongues of ravenous fire. As she began to lather herself with sunscreen, you felt the beginnings of a burgeoning erection. Inundated with guilt and self-disgust at your incestuous lechery, you shifted in your seat and crossed your legs.

You averted your gaze just as she looked up, but you could feel your face blooming with a flush of shame and embarrassment. You hoped the shade of the umbrella prevented her from seeing the color in your cheeks. If she did notice, though, she didn't say anything. She just regarded you with a passive stare, hinted with just the slightest trace of what might have been curiosity. She then unfolded a towel and spread it over the chaise, lying down upon it and tilting her face toward the sun.

The two of you sat in silence for a duration of time that surely could not have been as long as it had felt. You were finally summoning the will to get up and go inside when she said to you, "I Googled you. I wanted to read about what happened to your parents. It's some wild shit."

You looked over at her and met her gaze, which was cool and hard but not unkind. You tried to think of something to say, but her sudden forwardness had disarmed you, so you remained wordless.

"That dude who killed them, Sterling McFuckface, or whatever. The Mudhoney Madman, they call him, right? Did you know he has his own Wikipedia page? It talks about you in it, too. You're, like, Wikifamous."

"The Mudhoney Monster," you corrected her. "Sterling McPleasant. Yes, I know about the Wikipedia page." You didn't tell her that you'd read it hundreds of times, along with everything else about McPleasant that you could find online.

Lighting a cigarette, Mara asked, "How are you holding up?"

You looked back at the water and didn't say anything.

Acknowledging your silence with a sympathetic nod, she said, "Yeah, dumb question. Sorry."

You opened your mouth to tell her that it's okay, not to worry about it, but what came out instead was, "I'm going to kill him.

Someday, I'm going to go back to Ohio and I'm going to find him and I'm going to kill him."

She laughed with hollow humorlessness. "Sounds like the kind of shitty action movie my dad makes. Maybe if you pitch the idea to him in twenty-five words or less he'll give you a producer credit."

"I'm not interested in anything like that," you said mildly.

She laughed again. "If that's true, you're living in the wrong town. And *definitely* the wrong house."

"I don't have anywhere else to go. I didn't have a choice. This is where they sent me."

Shrugging, she said, "Well, you could do a lot worse. At least you didn't get sent to some hicktown in Tennessee, or something. Or, like, *the Valley*." She shuddered as though a spider had crawled across her shoulders.

"I won't be here forever. All I want is to go back, find Mc-Pleasant, and kill him."

She took a drag from her cigarette and then sipped her mimosa as she exhaled smoke from her nostrils. It fogged up the glass and escaped over the rim, collecting in a noxious cloud of alcohol-tinged carcinogens over her head before dissipating in the dry, hot air. "That shit will poison you, you know," she said. "I see it happen all the time. I mean, *your* case is kinda different, but the core of it is the same. People so consumed by resentment and grandiose desires that it pickles them like...like, I don't know, like those fetuses you see in jars at weird museums."

"It isn't the same. I don't want fame or fortune or my face on a billboard. I just want to kill the guy who killed my parents. I don't think that's grandiose."

"It's *a little* grandiose."

You didn't reply.

"Look," she said, capitulating. "I'm not saying you're not going to do it. I've seen weirder shit happen. I mean, fuck, I know this fat kid with *horrible* teeth who became an overnight YouTube sensation when he took a video of himself snorting

Pixy Stix while reading *The Cat in the Hat* into one of those voice-changer thingamajigs. He just got offered a lead role on Chuck Lorre's new sitcom. Signed a seven-figure contract. So, like, if *that* shit can happen, I guess your whole *John Wick* thing isn't all that crazy."

"Who's John Wick?"

"It's a movie. You haven't seen *John Wick?* Jesus. Okay, never mind. Anyway, when are you going to do it? As in, when do you plan on going back?"

"I don't know. I'll know when it's time."

Mara nodded, shrugged, and drained the rest of her mimosa. She took a final drag from her cigarette and stubbed it out on the ground beside her before dropping it in the empty glass, which she set down next to the suntan lotion on the little table beside her. "Fair enough. In the meantime, though, you should get out and, like, do shit, you know? Sitting around and wallowing in misery isn't going to make you feel any better, and it won't get you any closer to killing Mr. Mudhoney McDouchefuck, either. I can take you to some parties, if you want. Probably get you laid, too. My friends will eat you up. You've got this doe-eyed innocent look that chicks totally dig."

You really didn't want to go to any parties, nor did you want to sleep with any of her friends. You told yourself you didn't want to sleep with her, either, but you couldn't make yourself believe it. You wondered if *she* would eat you up. You wondered if *she* dug the doe-eyed innocent look.

You told yourself it didn't matter, you didn't care *what* she dug.

You couldn't make yourself believe that, either.

"Are you a virgin?" she asked.

The question made you bristle like a frightened cat. The last thing you wanted to talk to her about was sex. You shifted in your seat again and cleared your throat, trying to decide whether or not you should lie. You were never a great liar, though, and you figured she would see through it, so you just said. "Um, well...yes. I am."

"I can take care of that for you." She rolled over on her stomach and undid the straps of her bikini, baring her bare back to the sun. Her head was turned away from you, her cheek flat against the chaise, for which you were grateful; it gave you the ability to press hard against your groin in a feeble attempt to suppress your erection without her seeing. Her words hung in the air in much the same way as the smoke had hung above her head like a toxic halo. *I can take care of that for you*. It was a statement laden with promise and innuendo, even though you knew that wasn't how she'd meant it.

As if to affirm this, she said, "I'll introduce you to my friends as 'my cousin whose parents got murdered'. It's a major panty-dropper." Now she *did* turn her head to look at you, lifting herself up on her elbows just a little. It was enough to make visible the sides of her breasts, but not enough to expose them completely. "Hey," she said, "would you mind putting lotion on my back? There's never anyone around to do it, so I always end up getting burnt. But now *you're* here, so you might as well make yourself useful." She smiled when she said it, softening what may have otherwise been a somewhat harsh statement, considering the dry tone of her voice.

You were trying not to think about all of the Pornhub videos you'd seen that started off with scenarios eerily similar to this one. Your mouth was dry. You swallowed thickly, making your throat click so sharply that you almost jumped. "Sure," you managed to say, even though your erection had not subsided. She would see it if you stood up, and she would surely never talk to you again. You could picture her reeling back in disgust, pointing at you and calling you an incestuous creep.

But then she turned away, cupping her hands over her breasts and sitting with her back to you. "Don't put too much on, though. I still want to get a tan."

Getting timidly to your feet, the fabric of your shorts tented tautly around your shamefully half-erect cock, you said quietly, "You're already tan."

"One can *always* be tanner, kiddo."

You walked over to the little table beside her and picked up the lotion. Your hands were shaking with a severity more commonly associated with Parkinson's than with girl-induced anxiety, and you nearly dropped the bottle when you fumbled open its cap and squirted the thick white substance into your palm. Rubbing it into your hands, you got on your knees and began to massage the lotion onto your cousin's back.

Her smooth skin was warm and lightly glazed with sweat. The abrupt sensation of your cold touch made her shiver and arch her back just slightly, and she let out a quiet, bashful giggle. You started between her shoulder blades, your hands making slow, sweeping circles over the hardness of her bones and muscles. Seemingly of their own accord, they then moved up to her neck and over her shoulders before slipping back down and running along her sides. For what you hoped was an imperceptible moment, they lingered on the spot where the hard ridges of her ribcage gave way to the softer flesh of her waist. Finally, they traced over the iliac crests of her pelvis and then slithered back up to where they'd started.

Fifteen seconds, tops. That's how long that little ritual took to complete. But when you pulled your hands away, you felt like it had been hours. It took a confounding amount of resolve not to reach back out and pull her to you. You could picture yourself, with sickening clarity, kissing the back of her neck and sliding your hands up her stomach, gently removing her modest hands from her breasts so you could seize them and squeeze them and...

No, you told yourself firmly. *Enough.*

Mara looked over her shoulder at you, her crystalline blue eyes meeting your own and seeming to search them for something.

You held her gaze for a few seconds and then looked away, afraid of what she might find there.

"Thank you," she said. Her voice was hushed and sensual. You risked another glance at her and again became trapped in the steely indigo light emitting from her eyes. Your faces were so close that the slightest forward motion of your head would bring your lips together. Terrified your body would betray you and do exactly that, you kept your neck rigidly stiff and didn't breathe. Biting her lower lip softly, tantalizingly, she explored the depths of your eyes for a second or two longer, and then lay back down on the chair with her head once more turned away from you.

You released the air from your lungs in silent, staggered bursts. When you were reasonably sure the power of speech had more or less returned to you, you said, "I have to, um...I have to go inside. I'm going to get...um, I think I'm going to take a nap."

"Okay," she mumbled thickly, sounding like she was already drifting off to sleep, herself. "Sleep tight, don't let the monsters bite."

2

The sentence gave you pause, but only for a jaggedly fractured moment. Then you were bounding inside and clambering up the stairs to your bedroom, where you threw yourself onto your bed and began to masturbate furiously. Your hand was still lubricated with the slick concoction of Mara's sweat and suntan lotion. You tried to conjure up images of starlets and *Playboy* centerfolds, but there was only Mara.

In seconds you were gritting your teeth as your pelvic muscles clenched pleasurably, barely giving you enough time to grab a Kleenex and stifle your groans with your pillow before you were spurting hot globs of semen in a gushing stream you thought would never end. When at last it did, you wept breathlessly into your pillow until you were overtaken by a stern, domineering slumber that rendered you comatose until the following dawn.

If any monsters bit you in your sleep, you would have never known.

CHAPTER II – PEDIGREE

1

THE NEXT NIGHT FOUND you lying in bed, staring at the ceiling. Its ethereally white perfection unnerved you. No cracks, no paint bubbles, nothing so much as a scratch to indicate that it had been made by human hands. It made you think of the Grinning Man's skin.

There came a knock at your door...two short, delicate raps. You sat up straight, imagining the Grinning Man standing in the hall with his shopping cart parked beside him, its unknowable contents stirring beneath the purple sheet like an unspoken threat.

"Come in," you heard yourself say, though you hadn't intended to say it. Over the brief course of two long heartbeats, you were certain you'd just invited something evil into your bedroom. But then Mara appeared in the doorway, wearing ripped, low-riding jeans and a short, midriff-exposing white T-shirt. Her hair, aflame atop her head like a cozily-lit hearth, fell with effortless splendor over her shoulders.

"Come on," she said. "I'm meeting some friends at Café Tropical. I already told them you're coming, so you're not allowed to blow me off. I won't be made into a liar just because you want to lie around moping all night."

Your mouth formed the word "okay" and your throat emitted the appropriate sound to give it life, though both actions occurred of their own volition. The very thought of socialization made you sick to your stomach. Still, Mara was going to be there, and that was all that mattered. You comforted yourself with bittersweet lies, insisting with stubborn obstinacy that you merely liked the fact that she was being friendly. You remained steadfast in your refusal to acknowledge to yourself the fantasies to which you had masturbated the previous afternoon. You wouldn't even allow yourself to think about those fifteen sensuous seconds on the patio, and the intimate look the two of you had shared immediately afterward.

Swinging your legs over the edge of the bed, you got up and followed her into the hallway, down the stairs, and out into the muted scarlet glow of the darkening dust.

Café Tropical was a small and unassuming coffeeshop at Sunset and Parkman, right across the street from where you'd met the Grinning Man. When you and Mara walked down Occidental and turned onto Sunset, you were overcome with a heady sense of *déjà vu*. You almost expected to see the homeless magician standing outside Floyd's again, making fire dance between his fingers, or perhaps pulling a bouquet of black roses from his sleeve and offering them to Mara with a dramatic bow and a flash of his comic book grin. He wasn't there, of course; the only person at the corner was a wild-haired old woman walking in tight circles and muttering to herself. She had a red bottle of MD 20/20 in one hand and a thick blue book in the other. Occasionally, she would stop and leaf through the pages, holding it so close to her face that her nose mashed against the yellowed paper. Then she would snap the book shut, shaking her head as if in disgust, and chug down a hearty mouthful of the wine. She glared hatefully at you and Mara as you walked by.

2

Inside, Mara led you to a table in the corner occupied by four other kids...three girls and a boy...all of them Mara's age or a little older. The girls were pretty in a very California way; their skin was flawless, their hair luscious, their designer clothes hugging their trim figures. The boy was short and wiry, with springy corkscrews of curly black hair and huge Prada glasses perched high on his nose.

They all smiled at the sight of Mara, hugging her and air-kissing her, the girls excitedly squealing over her outfit and makeup and hair. You just stood there, trying not to feel and look awkward but knowing you were failing.

Mara introduced the first girl as Justine, a popular Instagram star. She was small but shapely, and had full lips and big almond eyes. She had the coppery tan complexion of a newly-minted penny, likely afforded her by a pricey membership at a high-end tanning salon. Her long hair was the color of a starless night sky. When you held out your hand to her, she ignored it and hugged you, kissing your cheek and taking your chin in her hand, examining your face and tracing a fragile finger over your eyebrows, proclaiming you to be "such a *darling*."

Rebecca had a luxurious mane of intricately-curled hair and skin like cocoa powder. Her breasts seemed too large for the rest of her and strained against the tight fabric of her striped tube top. Gaudy silver hoops hung from her earlobes, and her neck was encircled with a gold-plated Egyptian necklace. She, too, hugged you, and the embrace carried with it a pleasant aroma of clove cigarettes and expensive perfume.

The third girl, Ianthe, was the tallest of the group, with angular features and wavy blonde hair reaching down to her waist. Her demeanor was passive and reserved. She shook your hand with cold stiffness, offering a demure smile and nodding her head subtly. A series of ornate bracelets jangled on her wrist.

The boy introduced himself primly as Quincey Conrad with a weak handshake and a half-bow. The somewhat predatory nature of his hawkish face was betrayed by his perpetually astonished eyes, made even more so by the Coke-bottle thickness of his spectacles' lenses. There was an open notebook on the table in front of him, the lines crammed with swooping cursive. Adjacent to the notebook was a worn, dog-eared Radcliffe novel whose title was obscured by the deep white creases in the flimsy paper cover.

Hooking an arm around your shoulders, Mara stayed true to her promise by proudly proclaiming, "This is my cousin. His parents got murdered so he's living with me and my parents now."

Both Justine and Rebecca clapped their hands over mouths fallen agape, and then they both simultaneously pulled you into another hug, this one tighter and more protracted. Quincey's eyes bugged out even further, giving his face an absurdly lemur-like quality. Only Ianthe remained unmoved.

"No fuckin *way*, dude," Quincey said, closing his notebook and leaning forward with his hands clasped upon it. "Like, *how* were they murdered?"

"*Quincey!*" Justine scolded, tossing a crumpled napkin at him. "You can't *ask* things like that." She and Rebecca pulled you down into a chair and sat on either side of you, each of them holding one of your hands and petting your arms. The sensation of their gleaming acrylic nails gently grazing your skin gave you goosebumps.

"It's cool, he's not weird about it," Mara said, sitting down at the other side of the table. "Google the Mudhoney Monster. He's some whacko serial killer who goes around raping and murdering people in Ohio. He's the one who did it."

"Why do they call him the Mudhoney Monster?" Ianthe asked. "That's a stupid name."

"He does all of his killings in Mudhoney County," you told her, trying to sound patient. "And he's a monster."

"Did they catch him?" Justine asked.

You shook your head.

Raising her eyebrows with irritating skepticism, Ianthe asked, "How do they know it was him, then?"

"The police said it matched up with all of his other killings. And he took their fingernails. He always takes his victims' fingernails."

"Could have been a copycat," Ianthe said, and Mara shot her a look.

"No," you answered, your voice flat but vaguely annoyed. "The cops are the only ones who know about the fingernail thing. They leave that part out when they talk to reporters." You met Ianthe's taciturn stare and added, "So they can rule out copycats."

She opened her mouth to say something else, but shut it and looked away when Mara regarded her with another pointed glare.

"Jiminy *fuckmas*," said Quincey, his eyes glued to his phone as his thumb made intermittent swiping motions on the screen. He whistled through his teeth and shook his head. His glasses twinkled in the bright blue radiance of the backlight. "I found some crime scene photos. This is some seriously gnarly shit."

Rebecca grabbed the phone from his hand. She took one look at the images splayed across the glass and put her hand over mouth again. She thrust the phone back at Quincey, her face twisted in revulsion. "You poor thing," she cooed to you, caressing your arm again. Then, lowering her voice, she asked, "Did you...did you, like, see them? Your parents, I mean. Did you...um..."

"I found them."

"Oh...my...*gawd*," Justine said.

"Listen," said Ianthe, "I'm sure he doesn't want to talk about it. He's probably been forced to talk about it plenty."

You looked down at the table and didn't say anything.

Quincey set his phone face down on the Radcliffe book and straightened his glasses. "Yeah, she's right, let's come off it. This is the kid's first impression of us. I don't want him to think we're a bunch of weirdo murder groupies. So, um, what school are you going to go to here?"

"He'll be with me," Mara answered for you. "At William Marshal."

"Right on," said Quincey. "I graduated from there this year. I skipped a grade." He said this with a kind of pride that wasn't quite arrogance, but it was close.

"Do you all go there, too?" you asked the girls.

They shook their heads. "Justine and Rebecca go to Hollywood High," Ianthe said. "*I* go to *FSHA*." She pronounced it "fish-ah," and her tone *was* arrogant.

"How do you all know each other?"

"Parties, and shit," Quincey said. He suddenly brightened. "Oh, *speaking* of parties, we're having a little *soiree* at my parents' cabin in Topanga next weekend. You and Mara should totally come." Leaning forward, his lips twitching into a grin, he reduced his voice to a low whisper and said, "I'm gonna try and score us some Captain Howdy."

"What's Captain Howdy?"

Quincey looked around to make sure no one else in the café was listening. "It's this crazy new street drug my friend told me about. The name comes from Linda Blair's imaginary friend in *The Exorcist*. The one who turns out to be the demon. Apparently, this shit does something funky to your joints and makes you able to contort your body in all sorts of weird ways. My friend swears up and down that he twisted his torso a full hundred and eighty degrees. He said he could pop his arms in and out of their sockets at will. No pain." He lowered his voice even further to a pitch that was almost inaudible. "He said he watched a chick crawl up the wall like a spider."

"Bullshit," scoffed Ianthe.

Quincey shrugged, indifferent to her cynicism. "I don't know. Could be nothing. Could be *something*. You guys in?"

Before you had the chance to answer noncommittally, Mara said, "We'll be there." She bestowed you with a warm smile, and that was all it took. You would have followed that smile into the darkest depths of oblivion, if that's where she decided to take you.

At that vulnerable point in your life, though, you were so taken with her beauty and charm that you were wholly certain she would never lead you astray.

You were wrong.

Her intentions had never been malicious. You know that, and had always known that. She had never intended for you to get hurt...for *anyone* to get hurt.

But she was aboard a haunted ship charted for no uncertain destruction, and you were her faithful first mate.

Looking back, you really aren't sure you would have done anything differently.

CHAPTER 12 – CAPTAIN HOWDY

1

CAPTAIN HOWDY CAME IN the form of a bright purple powder that seemed to possess its own self-contained light source. It glowed through the clear plastic of the little baggie in which it was sealed. When Quincey held it up for you to see, the first thing you thought of when you saw it was the purple sheet that covered the Grinning Man's shopping cart. It filled you with an ominous sense of foreboding apprehension, but you ignored it.

"Do you snort it?" you asked Quincey, pinching the baggie between your thumb and forefinger and leaning in to examine it. The bizarre luminosity emanating from the tiny granules hurt your eyes.

"You can snort it, smoke it, or cook it up and shoot it. We're going to snort it, though. Smoking it would stink up the place. There's no way any of us are going to put a spike in our veins, either. That shit is for junkies."

You nodded in agreement. Back in Ohio, the news was always awash with reports of the dizzying numbers of addicts falling victim to the ravenous opiate epidemic, and you had no desire to join their ranks. You didn't know if Captain Howdy was of the opiate family, and you didn't ask. Something told you, though, that mainlining it would be as bad or worse as shooting up a dose of the elephant-tranquilizer-laced smack that was killing Midwesterners with brutal efficiency.

The rest of the group sat around the cabin's airy, high-ceilinged living room. You went over and sat by Mara on the loveseat, the five of you watching Quincey pour the contents of the baggie onto the triangular glass coffee table. He took a black AmEx card out of his Louis Vuitton wallet and carefully racked the miniature mountain of powder into six lines. He then produced a fifty-dollar bill and rolled it into a tight tube. Holding it up, he said, "All right, ladies and germ, who's first?"

"*You* first," sneered Ianthe. "This was *your* idea, Scarface. It's *your* party."

"Whoa, don't shoot," Quincey said defensively, holding up his hands. "I was just trying to be courteous, but whatever, it's chill." He bent over the table and hoovered up the first line with a quick, clean snort. He immediately fell back against the couch with a convulsive jolt. For a split second, his pupils flashed so vibrantly violet that it looked as though he'd shot purple death rays from his eyes.

Chest rising and falling rapidly, his gaze floated around the room as if following the path of some invisible floating specter. Then he looked at all of you, from one to the next, lingering a bit longer on Rebecca. "You *guys*," he said in a voice so deep and gravelly that it sounded like someone or something else was speaking through him. "This is off the fuckin *hook*."

"I'm next," said Justine, jumping up and prancing over to the table on giddy tiptoes. She picked up the rolled-up bill and snorted her line. Her reaction was much the same as Quincey's; she jolted and her eyes flashed purple, then she sank into a kind of wonderstruck daze, looking around at things that weren't there. She returned to her armchair and curled up in it, smiling like an amused infant.

It was like that for Rebecca and Ianthe, too. Even the latter girl was visibly overcome by a warm bliss that looked out of place on her face, which had, until that night, seemed frozen in a perpetual perma-scowl.

When only you and Mara remained, the two of you exchanged a glance. Hers was excitedly anticipatory, but yours was anxious and apprehensive. "I'll go first," she said, putting her hand on your thigh and squeezing a little. Then she took your wrist and led you to the table, where you both knelt before the last two lines. She snorted hers without hesitation. The resultant flash of abnormal color in her pupils seemed to last longer than it had for the others. Her eyes shone with the otherworldly luminescence for almost two full seconds before blinking out, at which point she fell back onto the carpet and stretched out her limbs while grinning rapturously. "Do it," she said. "It's heavenly." As it had been with Quincey, her voice was not her own. It was husky and earthen, the sound of brittle dead leaves and dry mud breaking beneath a boot heel.

When she looked at you, though, it was all Mara. Now that the spooky purple light had gone, her clear blue eyes were the same ones that had pierced your heart and whisked it away on that first day by the pool. Seeing her lying there with those eyes looking up at you, her body a treasure trove of sensual delights, you would have done absolutely anything she told you to do. Her tank top had ridden up on her torso, exposing her flat, tan midriff and the diamond piercing in her navel. Her hip bones poked subtly out from above the waistband of her denim shorts. You could make out the outline of her bra beneath the thin cotton of her shirt, the breasts within it rising and falling with slow irregularity.

"Do it," she repeated.

So you did.

2

At first, it was like you'd snorted a dusting of molten crumbs gathered from the core of an active volcano. The powder lit your nasal passages ablaze with an ensuing pain that was unlike anything you'd ever before experienced. That was just for a tenth of a second, though, if even that long. As soon as the drug hit your brain, the entire world exploded in an apocalyptic purple flare that eradicated everything that ever was or had been or would be. The universe itself melted away from the heat of the explosion. The very essence of life shriveled up and died as the fabric of reality went up in magenta-hued tongues of flame.

And it was beautiful.

Next, you were falling. Falling through the blackness left behind by Captain Howdy's blazing holocaust of fiery annihilation. It seemed there may be no end to the fall, and you were okay with that. You would keep falling for the rest of eternity, and that would be just fine.

But then the fall was over, and your eyes were opening upon the cabin from which you'd been so violently transported mere seconds ago. As everything fell back into focus and reality pieced itself together like a child's jigsaw puzzle, you were flooded with an incalculable sense of release. Everything...absolutely *every-thing*...was going to be okay. Nothing mattered except for where you were right then and there, lying on the carpet next to Mara in some rich kid's house in the canyons, and everything was ever so lovely.

And then shit got weird.

A song began to drift lightly through the air, soft and hushed at first, then steadily rising in volume. It was a woman's voice, and she was humming. There was no musical accompaniment, no instruments...just humming, pure and melodic and discon-certingly eerie. A frigid chill washed over your skin and made every follicle of hair on your body stand on end. After it had gone on for a minute or so, you were certain that nothing in the world could be so terrifying as that humming.

Until the voice began to sing.

The words crawled into your ears like centipedes and coiled around your brain. Though the lyrics were in clearly-articulated English, for some reason you couldn't process what they meant. The woman might as well have been speaking in some ancient evil dialect. Maybe she was. Maybe it wasn't English at all. Just the simmering hum of evil disguised to sound like the listener's native tongue, even though the listener would be inexplicably unable to decipher the words.

Whatever the case may have been, you knew you couldn't let it go on. You had to find the source of the song and make it stop, so you sat up, wiping sweat or tears or both from your eyes and...

Ianthe was standing in the center of the room, her shoulders hunched, her head bowed. Her hair fell down in tangled cascades that obscured her face. Her hands were warped into ungodly shapes, her twitching fingers sticking this way and that like the legs of a dying beetle.

Slowly, she lifted her head.

Her twisted hands rose to her face and parted her hair as though she were pulling a pair of curtains back from an open window.

Her irises blazed purple. Not a flash, this time...a steady, simmering glow. She was smiling, too, but the smile was all wrong. It was like the Grinning Man's smile, but somehow hers was even worse. It was a closed-lipped smile that stretched the span of her entire face, starting at one earlobe, swooping down along the length of her jaw, and reaching up all the way to the other ear.

The woman's voice was droning on, repeating the same haunting lyrics that you were still unable to comprehend. You wanted to scream but your voice had abandoned you, so you silently hoped and pleaded and prayed that Ianthe wouldn't open her mouth and reveal whatever awful things might be within it.

But hoping, pleading, and praying had never done you any good in the past, and that night wasn't any different.

Ianthe's lips parted and her smile swallowed up the entire lower half of her face.

You told yourself that what you were seeing wasn't real. It was the drugs, surely. Just the drugs. Her teeth weren't black and long and pointed. They didn't curve up out of her charcoal gums like fishhooks. Her mouth wasn't oozing a purple slime that dribbled down her chin and dripped onto her blouse.

Just the drugs. Just the drugs. Just the drugs.

It wasn't the drugs.

You opened your mouth and made another attempt to scream, but all that came out was a hoarse whistle. Ianthe's fanged mouth opened wider and she let out a booming laugh that made the walls tremble.

Then she began to dance.

Her movements were fluid at first, her body rocking back and forth and her arms waving slowly about her in tandem with the rhythm of the woman's voice. After a few chords, however, her movements became jerkier. Her limbs contorted into impossible angles. There simply weren't enough joints in the human body for her to twist into the shapes that she did. With loud, wet crunching sounds, her arms bent into zig-zags and her knees buckled inward on themselves, though she remained standing.

And she kept dancing.

And she kept laughing.

Justine suddenly emerged from behind the armchair. She was bent completely in half at the waist, with her palms on the floor behind her heels. Her upside-down face grinned at you with the same enormous sharp-toothed smile that Ianthe was wearing. She scampered over to you, her contorted body roiling with high-pitched giggles. When she drew near, you were able to summon enough energy to crabwalk backward until you bumped into a wall. Justine mercifully didn't pursue you, and you drew your knees to your chest and tried without success to blink everything away and return to the euphoria you'd felt when the drug had first begun to take hold.

You spotted Quincey in the corner, standing with his nose to the wall. Every so often his spinal column would shift drastically, pitching his torso to one side or the other with a loud *crack*. It sounded like he was crying.

Rebecca was on the floor in front of the loveseat. She'd pulled her legs up over her shoulders so her feet pressed sole-to-sole behind her head. Her palms were planted firmly on the carpet, holding her entire body aloft so that no other part of her touched the floor. She slowly craned her head to look at you, her joints popping. Her smile was identical to Ianthe's and Justine's.

You looked over to where Mara had been just moments ago, petrified of what you might see, but she wasn't there. You whipped your head around, your eyes scanning the room for signs of her, but there were none. You were alone with the...

And then all four of the others were surrounding you, standing only inches away, bending down over you and laughing or screaming or singing or humming or whatever it was that they were doing. Over the deafening sounds coming from their titanic fang-lined mouths, you could still hear the voice of the woman with pitch-perfect clarity.

As their faces drew closer to yours, their putrid breath assaulting your face, your body and mind gave up. Unconsciousness leapt up from some unknowable depth and seized you in a coldly comforting embrace, pulling you farther and farther into the dark.

Just before your eyes swung shut on the nightmare, you thought you saw something in the peripheral field of your vision. Something with red-and-blonde hair. Something that might have been Mara.

Something that was crawling up the wall like a spider.

CHAPTER 13 – PLAYING YOUR CARDS RIGHT

1

You woke up several hours later, a not-unpleasant pulse beating between your temples like a tribal drum. Your mouth was dry. Your joints ached.

The others were sitting in a crowded circle on the floor, playing cards and passing around a joint. They were cheerfully at-ease, laughing and chattering with joyous unrestraint. So far as you could tell, they all looked normal. No aberrant contortions or purple eyes or mouthfuls of fangs. Timidly, you got up and walked over to them.

Seeing you approach, Mara and Justine smiled and scooted aside, making a space for you between them. You sat down, your shoulders touching theirs. Your eyes flicked from person to person, inspecting everyone's face to assure yourself that they were no longer monsters.

"Man, you were *out*," Quincey said, glancing at you and then looking back down at the fan of cards in his hand. "Like, *coma*-style out." He placed two cards face-down on top of the other cards in the center of the circle and said, "Two ones."

"BS," Ianthe said, not lifting her eyes from her own cards.

Quincey grimaced spitefully at her, looked around at everyone else, and then sighed and picked up the entire pile of cards. The others laughed and clapped. They offered to start the game over so you could join, but you shook your head. It continued with docile nonchalance, occasionally inciting more roars of laughter whenever someone was caught in a bluff or when an alleged bluff turned out to be true. You weren't really paying attention.

Finally, you cleared your throat and said, "Listen, um, guys...what happened to you?"

Everyone fell silent and looked at you. You felt hot roses blossom upon your cheeks. Averting your gaze and looking down at the pile of cards laid out on the floor, you said, "When you took the Captain Howdy. What happened?"

"Pure, utter, *indescribable* ecstasy," said Rebecca, closing her eyes and receding into serene reverie.

Ianthe nodded and said with her trademark blandness, "Yes. It really was quite nice."

"Ten out of ten," agreed Justine. "Would recommend."

"But...you...you turned into..." You couldn't make yourself finish the sentence.

"Into *what?*" pressed Ianthe, her frigid gray eyes burning through you.

"Monsters."

The silence came again, lasting longer this time. They looked at you, looked at each other, looked back at you. Then they burst into laughter. Everyone except Mara, who was looking at you with such a level of concern that you felt a strange sense of guilt and embarrassment.

"What do you mean?" she asked. Her wrist had slackened, tilting her cards out and giving away her hand should anyone elect to look. The others were watching you too intently to notice, save for Ianthe, who was attempting to surreptitiously sneak a peek. Scowling at her, you gently took Mara's hand and pushed it up closer to her chest, once more shielding her cards from Ianthe's prying gaze. You weren't sure why you were so perturbed by her endeavor at cheating, but the thought of anyone wronging Mara in any way...no matter how trivial or childish the affront...made you sick with the imprudent fury of an overprotective older brother.

"It...I guess it doesn't matter." You kept your eyes lowered, your cheeks still aflame. "It must have...it was a dream."

Ianthe snorted and said, "Can someone say 'buzzkill?'"

The look Mara gave her could have cut glass, and now it was Ianthe's cheeks that burned. She muttered a halfhearted apology and looked down at her cards.

"Four fours," Justine said, putting down four cards. No one challenged it.

"I want to do it again," said Rebecca. "Quincey, doll, do you have any more?"

Quincey shook his head. "Nah, it's hard to come by. I think I can get more, though. Three fives." No one challenged that, either.

"Make sure you get enough for me, too," Ianthe said, picking up a card.

Justine picked one up, as well, and said, "And me. I want to do it again, too. That shit was *lit*."

Mara looked at you and said, "We don't have to do it again if you don't want to."

You shuddered inwardly at the thought of doing Captain Howdy again. You could see in Mara's eyes, though, that she *did* want to, and you knew you were fated to do anything she did, and all too willingly. "It's fine. I'll do it again."

"Yeah, he's chill," said Quincey. "He probably just had a bad trip. Happens to the best of us."

Mara looked at you for a moment longer, perhaps trying to find some trace of dishonesty in your eyes. Apparently satisfied with whatever she saw...or *didn't* see...she smiled, nodded, and said to Quincey, "Okay, count both of us in for next time, then." She glanced down at her cards. She had three left. She successively met the eyes of each member of the group, then placed them facedown and said, "Three sixes."

You looked at Ianthe. She frowned and said nothing.

"B-fucking-*S*," Quincey said.

With a sternly impassive expression, Mara turned the cards over, one at a time.

Six.

Six.

Six.

"I thought Jews were supposed to be good at cards," Rebecca teased as Quincey mournfully picked up the pile of cards and added them to his already-overflowing hand.

"You're thinking of barbecues," Ianthe said.

"Savage," Justine said.

Mara got up and went over to sit on the loveseat, taking her cigarettes from her purse and lighting one. You almost followed, but thought better of it. Best not to look like a lovesick puppy in front of your new friends. Especially after making a fool of yourself by confessing your silly drug-induced hallucinations. And *most* especially when the object of your affection happened to be related to you by blood.

After putting down three purported sevens and taking a quick selfie, Justine said to you, "Sweetie, *darling*, would you be a dear and grab us some beer from the kitchen?"

Not looking up, Quincey drew a card from the pile and said, "There are some six-packs in the fridge. Get the Heineken, not the Bud."

You nodded, got up, and went to the kitchen. After withdrawing the two green cardboard carriers, you nudged the refrigerator door closed and turned around to see Mara standing by the sink, a few feet away. You nearly dropped the beer.

"Are you sure you're okay?" she asked.

You nodded and swallowed the nervous saliva that was collecting at the back of your throat. "Um, yeah, totally. All good."

She took a step closer. "What did you see?"

"I don't remember."

She did that searching thing with her eyes again, and you could almost feel her in your head, flipping through your thoughts the way a desk clerk goes through a file cabinet. You tried to make yourself unreadable, closing off your mind and willing into existence a mental roadblock on an invisible, derelict street.

"It will be better next time," she assured you, with a tenderness that made you want to pull her into your arms and weep into her shoulder. "Maybe just, like, don't do as much. You snorted a pretty big line."

You hadn't thought your line looked any bigger or smaller than the others, but that wasn't relevant because you knew she knew that. "I'll be fine," you said.

She dove back into your eyes and tried to look around some more, but when she came up with nothing, she just gave you a little smile and said, "Okay. But if you change your mind, I won't be upset." Then, her tone lightening, she added, "Come on, let's go get wasted. Justine is *totally* going to fuck you."

You flinched. "What...uh...what makes you say that?"

"She *told* me, dummy. Rebecca wants to, too, but Justine called dibs. I'm pretty sure even Ianthe is hot for your dick, but she'll never admit it. Get her drunk enough, though, and her whole Ice Queen act melts away and she turns into a complete horndog. Play your cards right tonight and you could probably bang all three of them."

"I wasn't playing cards."

She laughed and gave you a light, playful shove on the arm. The sound of that laugh and the feeling of her hand upon your arm drove you wild with desire. Attractive as her friends were, you didn't want any of them. You wanted her, *only* her, forever and ever. Standing there alone with her, you forgot all about the fact that she was your cousin. You forgot about *everything*...even your parents and the Grinning Man and the Mudhoney Monster. There in that kitchen, in the house in the canyons, so far from the rest of the world that it might as well not be there at all, there was only Mara. And by forsaking all of that knowledge and the practicality that came with it, you felt the shackles of social acceptability fall away from you like a reptile's molted skin. You took a step toward her, falling hopelessly into the wintry blue pools of her eyes. You felt your grip on the beer carriers loosen.

You'd made up your mind. You were going to kiss her, consciously damning to hell everything that might ensue as a result. You took another step toward her, and then *she* did the same. You were almost touching. You started to let go of the beer so you could raise your hands to...

"*Are you two fucking each other in there, or what?*" shouted Ianthe from the living room.

The universe snapped back into focus with such abruptness that you thought your ears might pop. You and Mara both took two simultaneous steps back, looking toward the sound of Ianthe's voice. Then you looked at each other, and she smiled. You thought she might have been blushing, but you couldn't be sure; it was equally possible that it was your imagination, because you *also* had thought that you'd seen her crawling up the wall not too long ago.

Grabbing your wrist and leading you out of the kitchen, Mara said, "Come on, kiddo, let's get you laid."

2

Justine made her move on you right after Rebecca took Quincey into the bedroom down the hall. The latter two had started kissing and groping each other shortly after a bottle of Patron had been added to the equation. There were empty beer bottles everywhere, and an ashtray stuffed past its brim with cigarette butts and roached joints. Having drunk only two beers and a meager shot of the tequila, you were the least drunk of everyone. Mara, too, had imbibed less than the others. She was reclining on the loveseat with her feet kicked up on its arm, scrolling through Facebook and smoking a cigarette. Ianthe had drunk the most, downing drink after drink with somewhat worrisome alacrity, and was now passed out on the couch.

After the card game had died off, Justine had spent the remaining hours of the night taking pictures with you and uploading them to Instagram with a dizzying variety of filters, captions, and hashtags. The sun was beginning to rise over the dark outlines of the mountains by the time Rebecca and Quincey absconded to the bedroom. You were in the middle of telling Justine, at her request, about what autumn and winter were like in Ohio when she lunged at you and locked her lips upon yours. She threw her body with enough force to drive you onto your back. Gently nudging your lips open, she snaked her tongue into your mouth and ran its tip along the backs of your teeth. She tasted of alcohol and nicotine and weed, though the concoction wasn't wholly disagreeable.

Pulling back and straddling you, Justine looked at Mara and said, "So, like, can I fuck your cousin?"

You looked over at Mara, too, meeting her eyes. Something passed between the two of you, something you couldn't identify, and then she said, "Yeah, whatever, I already told you that you could. Do you want me to go in the other room?"

Justine deliberated, then shook her head and peeled off her shirt. The swell of her breasts pushed enticingly against the cups of her lacy bra, and you felt yourself begin to harden in spite of your reluctance to pursue the venture with which you'd been presented. "No," Justine said, "I want you to stay. It's kind of hot."

You looked at Mara again, but she had resumed perusing her Timeline, her foot flicking with absent intermittence.

Justine dismounted and pulled you to your feet, whereupon she led you to the armchair and shoved you down into it. Getting on her knees, she unfastened your belt and pulled your pants down around your ankles. You gasped when she took you into her mouth. Her lips and teeth lightly grated over the taut skin of your stiff cock as she worked it around in her mouth, running her tongue teasingly over its head and applying suction. You gripped the arms of the chair with white-knuckled hands.

Despite your willful attempts not to do so, you found your eyes drifting back to Mara. She still wasn't paying attention, so you closed your eyes and imagined that she was. More than that, you imagined that *she* was the one going down on you. You replaced Justine's raven-haired head with Mara's fire-streaked one, pretending that the mouth currently enveloping your erect member was the same one from which had emerged all of the soulfully sweet words that had claimed your heart and brought you down into the dark throes of lovesick longing.

There it was. The L-word. Yes, you knew then that you were, indeed, in love with your cousin. As the ditzy little social-me-dia-*savant* rigorously sucked you off, you finally allowed yourself to fully acknowledge the truth. You loved Mara, and there was no going back from that. The damage had been done.

Or, at least, so you'd thought.

When Justine gradually began to increase the tempo of her movements, you felt yourself slip outside your body and float back to the afternoon by the pool. The scent of the suntan lotion filled your nostrils like a phantom odor accompanying the onset of a seizure. Your hands fell to Justine's head and burrowed into her sleek black tresses, but it was Mara's skin you felt against your palms, not Justine's hair. In your fantasy version of the memory, you didn't run upstairs at the end. Instead, Mara stood and turned around, her hands falling to her sides, revealing the ripe fullness of her breasts as if she were presenting you with some kind of sacred offering. Then she pulled you onto the chaise lounge and sat astride you, her hand cupping the back of your neck and guiding your mouth to...

Justine suddenly made a gagging sound and pulled back. You were dimly aware that you were groaning through clenched teeth. A thick white trickle oozed from between her lips, and she coughed. She started to say something, but then another stream of ejaculate shot out of you and hit her in the chin. The next struck the hollow of her neck and dripped down between the slopes of her breasts. The final burst was weaker and its trajectory faltered midair, landing on the floor at Justine's knees.

Standing up, Justine retrieved her shirt and used it to wipe her face and chest while you sat there gasping raggedly. "*Well*," she said. "*That* was fast. I was just getting started."

Mara was laughing. "Cut him some slack," she told Justine. "He's a virgin."

Justine gaped at you. "You're a *virgin?* Holy shit, I didn't think those even existed at our age anymore. Was that the first time you've gotten head?"

You gave a short, sheepish nod.

Justine looked at Mara and said, "*Girl*. I literally just gave a blowjob to a unicorn." To you, she said, "For real, virgins in LA are less common than, like, free parking."

Shrugging, you said, "There's lots of free parking where I'm from."

They both laughed at that. "Listen," Justine said, "this isn't over. I've never taken a dude's virginity. I'm gonna claim that dick with a big ole Justine flag one of these days, like Lance fucking Armstrong."

"Neil," Mara corrected her. "*Neil* fucking Armstrong."

Justine cocked an eyebrow at her. "Are you sure? I thought Neil Armstrong was the guy whose arm is on the baking soda box."

Mara blinked. Before she could respond, Quincey and Rebecca emerged from the dark hallway. Quincey was holding up a Ziploc bag filled near-to-bursting with white powder. "Check out what I found in my parents' dresser," he said with a proud grin.

And Mara said, "That better not be fucking baking soda."

CHAPTER 14
– TUCK AND
ROLL

1

MARA WASN'T AROUND MUCH the following week, leaving you alone at the house with your solitary pining. You spent most of your time lying around and fretting about where she might be and whom she might be with, always inevitably arriving at the conclusion that she must certainly be out fucking some guy that wasn't you. Whenever you were able to rouse yourself from those bleak spirals into ever-worsening depression, you would frustratedly masturbate into a pair of her panties that you'd stolen from her dresser. Within forty-eight hours they'd already become starchy and putrid, but you slept every night with them clutched tightly to your chest. In between the frenzied masturbatory sessions and the seemingly endless hours of jealous woolgathering, you would wander aimlessly around the big empty house, slowly going mad from the silence. You were never quite sure where your aunt and uncle were, and you didn't think Mara knew, either.

On Saturday, however, after nearly a week of being MIA, Mara appeared in your bedroom doorway. She didn't bother knocking that time. You thanked whatever lucky stars you may have had left for the timing of her arrival, which was mercifully before you'd graduated from lustful fantasies to hysterical masturbation.

"Get up," she said. "We're going to a party."

You sat up and asked, "What kind of party?" It was a trivial inquiry, because there was no question of your going. You couldn't possibly refuse an invitation from her, and you suspected she knew that.

Crossing her arms over her chest and tilting her head to the side, Mara said, "It's the Fourth of July, stupid. What kind of party do you think?"

You honestly hadn't realized the date. You had, at that point, stopped counting days of the month and started counting "Days Since You Last Saw Mara."

"Put on something nice," she said. "It's a little more high-brow of an affair than Quincey's '*soiree*' last weekend." She herself was wearing a sequined black dress that came down to a point on her thigh that was somewhere in the gray area between modest and indecent. Her white pumps had weapon-like heels, and she wore a string of pearls around her throat.

"I'll wait downstairs so you can change," she said.

You came dangerously close to telling her that she didn't have to, that she could stay, that she could *help* you change, but you caught yourself and responded only with a weak nod. She closed the door behind her.

You constructed your outfit with as-of-then-unworn articles of clothing purchased for you by your aunt's personal shopper. When you stood in front of the full-length mirror garbed in a white polo shirt and beige slacks, you frowned with disapproval. You looked like a kid headed to Sunday school, replete with tasseled brown loafers and a too-large gold Rolex. You started to take the watch off, but you couldn't figure out the mechanism to release the catch. When Mara impatiently called your name from downstairs, you gave up and went down to meet her.

As you descended the stairway, Mara smiled up at you with wry amusement. "Well, don't you look cute. Justine would just about jump your bones if she saw you right now."

Instead of saying, *I would prefer that* you *jump my bones*, you said, "Is Justine going to be there?"

"I think so, but I'm not sure. I know Quincey will be there, and probably Ianthe, but not Rebecca. She's doing something with her boyfriend."

"Rebecca has a boyfriend? But...what about her and Quincey?"

Shrugging, she said, "What about them?" You shrugged in turn, and then followed her outside and got in the passenger seat of her yellow Corvette Stingray. The top was rolled down, and the warm air buffeted your face and hair as she drove down Silver Lake Boulevard and turned north onto the 101, merging into place among the maze of cars like a Tetris block. The ambient music coming from the stereo, coupled with the hypnotic accordioning of traffic, put you in a light trance. You occasionally sneaked glances at Mara, her eyes shielded from the setting sun by a pair of Wayfarers. Being there, next to her at last, the lonesome week spent in her absence quickly dissolved into obscurity like a rapidly fading nightmare. Now that you were with her again, the world was as close to how it should be as it was ever apt to get.

As traffic slowly chugged north, you asked Mara, "Where is this party?"

"Up in the Hills," she said, abruptly changing lanes and sliding into a rapidly closing gap between a braking Tesla and an accelerating Mercedes. You looked over your shoulder to see the guy in the Mercedes seething over his steering wheel, waving his middle finger and laying on his horn. Mara paid no attention. She lit a cigarette and turned the music up louder. You felt your face break into an admiring smile, and she looked at you quizzically. "What's so funny?" she asked.

You shook your head, but you couldn't mop away the goofy grin. "Nothing," you said. "I...I just...I lo..." Your throat hitched before your mouth could form the rest of the treacherous word, making you cough. You felt your temples dampen with burgeoning sweat. How were you supposed to go on like this, constantly at the mercy of a tongue that seemed steadfastly determined to betray you? It was like some Nicholas Sparks version of Tourette's.

As you took a deep, sputtering breath and choked down the congealed saliva in your throat, Mara's lips curled into a cool half-smirk. "You okay, cowboy?"

"Yeah," you managed to reply. "What I was going to ask was, um, could I...have a cigarette?"

2

The party was at a gigantic house on Mulholland. It had what you deemed to be far too many windows, all of them tinted and featuring mechanical blinds that could shut out the outside world with the touch of a button. You couldn't determine whether the helipad on the wide, flat roof was for legitimate purposes or just a gimmick. When Mara edged the car through the gate, she was immediately accosted by a valet in a red tuxedo. He opened the door for her to let her out, signaling you to do the same. Then he got in the car and drove it to the lift that led down to the underground parking structure beneath the house. As you and Mara stood watching him and the Corvette disappear beneath the earth, you asked her, "What does this guy do, anyway? The owner of this house, I mean."

"His name is Arthur Seward," Mara said as she led the way up to the house. "He's some sort of business magnate. Owns all sorts of huge corporations. A movie studio, a publishing house, even a propane company, of all things. He used to be a doctor. Then he got sick of that and became a lawyer. Then he got sick of *that* and just started buying up everything he could get his hands on. They call him Doctor Law."

"How do you know him?"

"Um. Mutual friends." There was something in her face that suggested there was more to the story, but you didn't press the issue.

A butler, who looked identical to the valet, opened the door for the two of you and gestured you inside with a low bow.

The instant explosion of wealth that erupted before your eyes made you immediately uncomfortable. Everything seemed to be carved from gold and silver, pewter and polished brass. The furniture was constructed from high-quality leather. All of the party guests were preternaturally beautiful, nipped and tucked into plastic perfection. The very buttons upon their clothes were probably worth more than the median yearly income back in Ohio.

Mara took your wrist and led you straight to the bar. She ordered two martinis and then whispered in your ear, "If anyone asks, you're twenty-two."

You looked dubiously at her. Passing yourself off as sixteen to Mara's friends...now *your* friends, as well, you supposed...was reaching enough, but twenty-two seemed ludicrous. You looked very much your age, as it was, and you felt like the church boy outfit only made it worse.

"No one is going to ask," Mara reassured, sensing your doubt.

The bartender handed Mara the drinks. She gave one to you and raised her glass, saying, "Here's to America, or whatever."

You clinked your own glass to hers and then took a sip, resisting the urge to grimace when the astringent alcohol lit upon your tongue and scorched your trachea. The sip Mara took of hers was at least double the amount you'd ingested. She didn't so much as flinch. Instead, she frowned down at the drink and said, "Huh. He made this awfully weak."

"Totally," you agreed, looking away so she wouldn't see your watering eyes.

Quincey appeared from an adjacent room carrying a cocktail, and the slackened muscles in his face suggested it wasn't his first. There was a man next to him who appeared to be in his late twenties, tall and tan and with blond highlights in his brown hair. He wore a simple black suit and the tortured expression of a child who'd just found out Santa isn't real. There was a perspiring bottle of Evian water in his hand and a pin on the lapel of his jacket that read "UNITED PROPANE" in bold red letters.

"Ohio Boy!" Quincey exclaimed, fist-bumping you. "Check it out, this guy is from Cleveland, too." He turned to the guy with the water bottle and said, "Shit, man, what did you say your name was, again?"

"Jack Monroe," the man said, shaking your hand. "You're from Cleveland?"

You nodded.

"Well, isn't that a shame."

You laughed awkwardly, then abruptly stopped when Jack didn't reciprocate. You took a nervous sip of your drink and looked around, sticking your free hand in your pocket and pretending to be fascinated by a Jackson Pollock painting on the wall.

"Where are the others?" Mara asked Quincey, not really paying attention to Jack.

Quincey shrugged. "Around. Ianthe was out on the deck flirting with Russel Brand the last time I saw her. I think Justine is upstairs getting stoned with some comedians."

An elated voice from across the room called, "Mara, my *love!*" You looked in its direction to see a tall man with bedazzled white sunglasses come striding over, holding his arms wide. He had silver hair brushed back over his head and a half-smoked cigar tucked behind his ear. He bent to kiss Mara's hand, an action that stirred up a sharp gust of jealousy within your chest.

Now it was Mara who looked uncomfortable, but she bore it with a smile. When she introduced the two of you, he shook your hand so firmly that you thought the birdlike bones of your fingers might snap. "Just call me Doctor Law, yeah?" Seward said. "Everyone else does." To Mara, he asked, "How was the drive? Did you take the 5 to the 134?"

Mara made a face. "*Fuck* no. We never would have gotten here if we'd done that. We just took the 101 and hopped off on Barham."

Seward was no longer paying attention. He'd turned to Jack and said, "I beg your pardon, young man, but have we met?"

Jack squared his stooped shoulders and extended his own hand for Seward to shake. "Mr. Seward...um...Doctor Law, it's a pleasure to finally meet you. I'm Jack Monroe."

Seward studied Jack hard for a few seconds, apparently trying to place the name. When he got it, he clapped his hands and said, "Ah, *yes*, Jack Monroe! You run the Data Review department at our corporate office in Ohio, yeah?"

"Yes, sir."

"I've heard great things about you, young man. You could really go places in my company." Seward looked at you and explained, "United Propane is the biggest propane provider in the country. Jack here is ultimately responsible for the verification of data integrity on *all* of our customers' accounts."

You nodded, trying to look interested. You glanced at Mara and saw that she appeared to be just as bored as you were with the conversation.

"Well, yes, that's true," Jack said, "but I'm also a writer. Fiction, mostly. And I thought maybe the editors at your publishing company could..."

"Sure, sure, of course," said Seward noncommittally. "Just have your people call my people and have them sort something out, yeah?"

Jack looked crestfallen. You suspected he didn't have any "people." He ran a hand through his hair and forced an uneasy smile. "Right, yeah, sure," he said.

Seward gestured at his Evian and said, "Now, what the hell are you drinking *that* for? Come on, let's get you a real drink, yeah?"

Jack looked down at his water and said mournfully, "I don't drink."

"Well, I'm terribly sorry to hear *that*. Tell you what. I'll have one for the both of us, yeah? Anyway, keep up the good work, kid." He clapped Jack on the shoulder and floated away to the bar.

Jack watched him go and then looked down at his shoes. "Enjoy the party, guys," he said to the three of you, and then skulked off.

You had hoped Seward was done with you, but he came back from the bar holding a Cosmopolitan in his manicured hand. He was looking at Mara, who wasn't returning his gaze. He started to say something to her, but Quincey cut him off and said, "So, I hear you can get stuff. Like, *any* stuff. *All* the stuff."

"Jesus Christ, Quincey," said Mara, rubbing her eyes with her thumb and forefinger and shaking her head.

Seward folded his arms over his chest and stared at Quincey with an expression you couldn't decipher. "Officially," he said, "I'm morally and legally obligated to dispute that."

Quincey became serious and businesslike. He straightened his posture, cocking back his shoulders and lifting his head. "Off the record. Completely *un*official." He pantomimed zipping his lips and tossing an invisible key over his shoulder.

Seward studied Quincey for what felt like a very long time, and then he sipped his drink and asked, "What, exactly, are you looking to get?"

Quincey edged closer to Seward and whispered something in his ear. He had to stand on tiptoe to do so, as Seward was at least six or seven inches taller. You didn't hear what he said, but you didn't have to.

Seward's face darkened. "Are you out of your fucking *mind?*" he hissed. "Fuck, I really hope you're not dicking around with that shit." He looked at Mara, worried and disapproving. "*Please*, Mara, tell me you're not caught up in that."

Mara rolled her eyes and sucked down what was left of her drink. "Lay off it, Arthur," she told him with calm sternness. She plucked the olive from the bottom of the glass and plopped it into her mouth, chewing it slowly and holding Seward's stare with smooth passivity.

Seward sighed and softened his tone. "Look, just stay away from that bullshit, yeah? Trust me, it's grimy stuff. I'd be more inclined to sell you Mexican black tar heroin than that weird purple demon dust. I'm telling you, it'll fuck you up. *Bad*. Just...stay away from it, yeah?"

At that, a woman on the other side of the room called his name and waved him over. Seward took one last look at Mara, told her again to "stay away from that shit," and then put on a flashy PR smile so he could go greet the woman.

When he was well out of earshot, Quincey looked from you to Mara and then shrugged. "Goddamn. What a fuckin square, huh?"

3

After the interchange with Doctor Law, Quincey led you and Mara upstairs to a room that made you think of Victorian opium dens. People were lounging everywhere...on the floor, on the furniture, on each other...smoking from all manner of paraphernalia. Your eyes watered and your throat burned from the oppressive gray-green clouds hanging in purgatorial suspension above the heads of the drugged-out stoners. The main scents you detected were pot and tobacco, but there were others you weren't able to identify. Judging from the looks of some of the incapacitated partygoers, you figured there were things much stronger than weed getting passed around.

Your mind drifted to thoughts of Captain Howdy, but you pushed them from your head.

Quincey spotted Justine sitting on the floor, and the three of you took up spaces beside her among the litter of raggedly-breathing bodies. She was sitting next to a fifty-ish guy and telling him, in exhaustive detail, about her most recent photoshoot in Milan. The guy, whom Justine introduced as Danvers, purported to be a "semi-famous" standup comedian. He looked like what would happen if David Carradine and Steve Buscemi had a lovechild together and then shot it up with felonious amounts of THC. His eyes were affixed in a perpetual squint and he had a crooked-toothed smile that bore all the clueless joy of a kid with Down's syndrome.

When you told him your name and reached to shake his hand, he just held up a peace sign and said with a grin, "Tuck and roll, baby, tuck and roll."

You blinked at him. "Huh?" you asked, feeling stupid and wondering if you'd already caught a contact high that was altering your perception of reality.

Danvers cackled and jerked a thumb at you, looking at Justine and saying, "Listen to this kid, will ya? 'Huh?' Shit, that's great. *Mmmotherfucker.*"

Justine laughed, and so did Quincey. You and Mara did not.

"Tuck and roll, baby, tuck and roll."

You were about to tell Mara that maybe you needed another drink, after all, and that you should go back downstairs, but then someone handed you a colossally fat blunt. You held it between your fingers for a second, then shrugged and took a hit. Then you took another.

Over the course of the next hour, an endless barrage of drugs passed through your hands and, subsequently, your lungs. Every time you'd finished sucking from a bong or dragging from a joint, some other form of smokable intoxicant took its place. Eventually, you emerged from a vague fugue and found yourself lying on the floor next to Justine, your arms and legs touching.

When you felt her roll over on her side, you turned your head to look at her. The details of her visage were blurry and unformed, as if she'd emerged from the womb too early for her face to develop completely. You tried to say something to her, but your intended words flew away before you could catch them. You needn't have said anything, anyway; with disorienting suddenness, she planted a hard kiss on your mouth, trailing her fingers up your chest. You tried to kiss her back because you were still cognizant enough to know that that was what you were supposed to do when a pretty girl kissed you, but you couldn't make your mouth work properly. You figured the drugs were partly responsible for this, but there was also the problem of Mara, who was sitting unseen...but surely *seeing*...somewhere in the green fog. Kissing Justine felt like a betrayal, no matter how ridiculous such a notion was when examined beneath the lens of logic.

"You look *so* stoned," Justine said when she pulled back, smiling the way a person smiles at a litter of puppies.

You tried to tell her that you *were* so stoned, but all that came out was an embarrassing "*Glkk*" sound.

"Tuck and roll, baby, tuck and roll," came Danvers' voice from some other planet.

You felt yourself sliding back beneath the blanket of unconsciousness. Your hands drifted up into the air and made grabbing motions, trying to cling to a nonexistent ledge that might keep you from passing out again.

"*Glkk*," you said helplessly to Justine, who only laughed and patted your leg. You sensed her sitting up. There was the sound of a bubbling bong, and then she was leaning over your face and exhaling pot smoke into your mouth. You sucked it in with an easy grace that surprised you. Justine lay back down and entwined her legs with yours, kissing your neck and nibbling your ear.

Now it was Quincey's voice that emerged from the fog, saying, "Oh yeah, *get* it, Casanova."

You weren't getting anything, in spite of Quincey's encouragement. Even if Mara hadn't been part of the equation, you were too fucked up to get fucked.

"Yeah, Casanova, get it," came Danvers' disembodied voice, followed by a crackly laugh. "Ha, 'Casanova.' That's good, I approve, I approve. *Mmmotherfucker!*"

You could still feel Justine's lips on you, but you were no longer able to discern where. Your neck, your face, your mouth...any or all or none of the above. You experienced the falling sensation again. A wave of dizziness rippled through you, and you once more reached out for something to hold onto. It landed upon something soft and round, and you were able to deduce that it was Justine's breast when she giggled into your ear. You tried to withdraw it, but she caught your wrist and kept it pressed there. Someone...probably Quincey, or maybe Danvers...started clapping.

"Ohhh, *shit!* Tuck and *ROLL*, baby! *Mmmotherfucker!*"

Justine blew more smoke into your mouth. You gulped it down as vigorously as before, feeling the synapses in your brain spark and pop and shrivel up. You were slipping faster. You were beyond any misconceptions that you could fight it, and even farther beyond caring. The voices and laughter around you faded, and Justine's touch became imperceptible. You might have uttered one final "*Gllk*" before checking out, but you couldn't be sure.

The last thing you saw prior to the claiming of your consciousness was Mara's face. Whether the image was real or imagined was irrelevant. The grin you wore as you fell out *was* real; that much you knew to be true. It wasn't quite as wide as the Grinning Man's grin, but it was close.

It was much too close.

CHAPTER 15
– PART OF
LIVING

1

You woke up in the passenger seat of Mara's car, the wind playing with your hair and whispering sweet, unintelligible nothings in your ears. Mazzy Star was on the radio. The sky seemed too low; it seemed as if it had grown weary of its sovereignty in the high heavens and was allowing itself to fall from its long-established grace.

Mara drove with a distracted kind of calm, the expression on her face one of distant serenity. The wind teased her hair with the same spirited mischief that it did yours, blowing red and gold wisps around her face as if gently stoking a quiet flame. Your heart overflowed with longing and sorrow. Such beauty, you thought, should not be permitted to exist in a world so ugly.

Mara looked over at you, catching you watching her before you could pretend to still be asleep. She smiled and said, "I'm surprised you're awake. With as much trouble as we had getting you out to the car, I thought it would have taken an act of God to wake you." Her eyes twinkled.

The details of your departure from Doctor Law's mansion were fuzzy, but you had fleeting remembrances of Quincey and Mara struggling to keep you upright and lead you down the stairs and out of the house. Flashes of you falling down and bumping into walls flickered behind your eyes. "I'm sorry," you said abashedly. "I shouldn't have smoked that much. I hope I didn't...embarrass you, or anything."

Mara snorted. "Oh, stop. You had a good time. We've all been there, and we're better for it. It's part of life. It's part of *living*."

Your shame was such that her soothing assurances did little to abate it. Figuring a change of subject was in order, you looked out at the night and asked, "Where are we?" The Corvette was cruising smoothly along a winding road that might have been Mulholland, but it was difficult to say for sure. Whatever street it was, it was oddly bereft of other cars. You'd seen not a single pair of headlights since you'd wakened, neither ahead nor behind you.

"I'm taking you somewhere," Mara said. Your altitude was steadily increasing as the road snaked up an ever-steepening incline. She took each treacherously tight turn with the tranquility of a sage. "I'm going to show you something."

You could think of many things you wanted her to show you, but you doubted there was any overlap between your ideas and hers.

Turning up the music and lighting a cigarette, Mara began to sing softly along to the music, her voice carrying out mellifluous intonations about strangers and dust. It was enough to melt you, to break you.

For the rest of the drive, you fell helplessly beneath a roaring flood of confused emotions. You wanted her, *needed* her, but hated yourself for it. Being within her proximity filled you with conflicting feelings of contentment and torment. The totality of her beauty, and the comforting sense of ease she unwittingly provided, made you want to weep with something between dejection and joy.

"Almost there," Mara said, coasting around another sharp turn with the casual ease of a limousine driver. The Corvette's big tires kissed the yellow line in a manner not unlike lip-locked Parisian lovers embracing in a shadowy alley just outside the red glow of scandalous paper lamps. "How are you feeling?"

There were all kinds of applicable answers to that question, but none of them were appropriate. You settled for a pitifully meek thumbs-up and a toddler's entertained grin. You instantly felt foolish and pathetic.

Continuing up the winding hill, you thought you could hear faint popping noises, like the uncorking of champagne bottles. It filled you with a mild panic, making you wonder if it was the sound of your drug-fried brain cells exploding. "Do you hear that?" you cautiously asked Mara, worried she might think you were going crazy. Or, worse...that you couldn't handle your drugs.

But Mara just smiled knowingly and nodded. "Yes," she said, "I hear it."

"What is it?"

"You're about to see."

2

After rounding one final steep turn, Mara pulled onto a gravel-paved outcropping that jutted out from whatever great hill you'd just ascended. The view overlooked the city far below, with downtown serving as the twinkling epicenter of a gold-glinting orchard of night-defying light. The surrounding towns, districts, and boroughs beneath the skyscraping towers of blazing yellow electricity were spread endlessly across the landscape like a blanket of wildfire embers.

It wasn't the cityscape that first caught your eye, though. No, your attention was instantly arrested by what you recognized as the source of the popping noises. Dappled all across the black sky were exploding fireworks. The rockets shot up from innumerable launch points for as far as you could see, all of them belonging to their own individual shows but joining together into a conglomerated spectacle reserved singly for you and Mara. Down there, the people saw only what was immediately above them. Up on that hill, you saw it all.

"I'm hard to impress," Mara said, turning the music down a couple of notches, "but *this* is pretty cool."

You swallowed and nodded, transfixed by the fizzling eruptions of fire and sparks spangled across the night. A broad spectrum of multihued flashes danced before your eyes; there were splashes of red, yellow, blue, white, orange, green…and purple, a seemingly atypical amount of purple. A bizarre image appeared in your mind, one of the Grinning Man throwing packets of Captain Howdy into the air and making them explode with a snap of his fingers.

"You don't see this kind of thing in Cleveland, do you?" Mara asked, making the intrusive thought evaporate with welcome efficiency.

You looked at her, and in doing so forgot all about the fireworks. You drank in the sight of her sitting there with her face lit up by the sporadically blinking lights of the rockets. The way the silver sequins on her dress shimmered and glistened made it look like she'd stolen all the stars out of the sky and sprinkled them over herself like party glitter. "No," you said. "No, I never saw anything this beautiful in Cleveland."

When she turned her head to meet your gaze, something happened. You didn't know how or why, and you still don't, to this day. What you *did* know, the very second that she looked at you, was that the fuse she'd lit that afternoon by the pool had finally burned down to its detonator. The resultant explosion was infinitely more brilliant than any of the fireworks in the distant foreground. With that simple look, you knew that she'd found in your eyes whatever it was she'd been searching for in those few intimate moments you'd shared before that point.

There were a million things you wanted to tell her in that instant, but you had the words for none of them. All you could do was sit frozen and deer-like in the paralyzing path of the halogen-blue headlights beaming out of her irises.

It was she who moved on you, but when she leaned forward, the action had a magnetic effect that pulled your body to hers, so she didn't have to lean far. You met halfway, your mouths finding each other and interlocking above the car's center console. You both raised to your knees on the seats, your bodies moving in such perfectly-coordinated harmony that you could have been each other's mirrored reflection. Your torsos melded together and her hands went into your hair, her acrylic tombstone nails delicately scraping your scalp. The sensation, so heavenly you could hardly bear it, sent a pleasing chill deep into the marrow of your bones. She tasted not of chemical inebriants, as one could have expected given the events of the evening, but instead of cherries and peppermint. You felt your hands, which had quickly found her hips, move down past the hem of her short dress. Your palms and fingertips tingled when they left the sequin-studded silk of her dress and graduated to the pliant flesh of her thighs. Acting in a fashion that was largely beyond your conscious control, they grabbed the hem of her dress and began to pull it upward.

At this, she broke away, and you thought you'd gone too far. But then she yanked the lever on the side of her seat, making it swing down and flatten. You blinked, and then did the same with your own seat. You joined her again in another torrid kiss that soon sent the two of you rolling to the back of the car, with you lying laterally on the leather and her sitting astride you with her hands on your chest. She kissed you again, and then it was *she* who grabbed the hem of her dress, her arms crossing across the front of her body and then pulling it over her head.

Lucero's "Night's Like These" came on the radio, and the sad poignancy of it contrasted sweetly with the ecstatic radiance that was building in your chest and igniting your veins.

Your hands ran up her stomach and took hold of her breasts as she undid your belt and unbuttoned your pants. Your fingers went to the clasp of her bra, situated in the front between each swollen cup. You fumbled at it with clumsy futility, and she gave you a patiently amused smile and gently moved your hands away so she could do it for you.

This is happening, you thought, trying to keep a wave of anticipatory nervous shakes at bay. *Fuck, fuck, FUCK, this is really happening.*

While you maladroitly wriggled from the confines of your shirt, Mara tried to shift into a position that would allow her to slide out of her panties. The arrangement of your bodies would not permit her to do so, leading her to improvise by taking up two firm handfuls of the flimsy fabric and tearing them free. She pitched the ruined garment over her shoulder, whereupon it was swallowed up by the hungry night.

When she mounted herself upon your erection, she gave a tiny gasp. With that soft intake of breath, she took with it every tangible quality you had ascribed to life itself. The corporeal foundation of reality blurred, trembled, and then shattered completely. The universe became a hallucinatory caricature of the one you thought you knew. There, in the back seat of the Corvette, you mused, *The world outside is not my own. I know nothing of life or its infinite meanings. I have been wrong about everything.*

Something inside of you...perhaps some unquantifiable manifestation of your soul...escaped your body via the portal of your gasping mouth. It drifted from your body and lifted into the air like evaporating rainwater following a long drought. Through its eyes, you saw the earth below shrink and disappear. You soared with the spirit over the palm trees and valleys and traffic-jammed streets until you were somewhere above the city. The fireworks exploded all around you...*within* you, their technicolored eruptions serving as the cellular framework of the wraithlike essence with which you were conjoined. The black clouds of night parted to reveal Mara's face, painted upon the sky with all of the enormity and airbrushed faultlessness of a billboard model. A pair of brightly gleaming stars acted as the ever-present twinkle in her eyes, and it was the sheer intensity of their white-blue glint that sucked you back down into the car with her, grounding you and rendering you a material entity once again. As a pleasure beyond bounds seized possession of you, you became faintly aware of a noise coming from your throat. It originated in your stomach, took form in your chest, and emerged as something borne more of a primitive animal than a civilized man. Mara shouted forth a similar noise, though hers was far less crude; the composure of its choral tonality was a melodious siren song that opened rippling fissures across the surface of your soul. The pleasure centers in your brain became erratic and overwhelmed, unable to keep up with the unlimited surge of dopamine crowding into their receptors. And then there was sweet release unlike anything you'd ever thought possible. Each individual atom in your body split into halves, setting off a trillion seismic Hiroshima blasts all throughout your insides. Your spirit had returned to you, but in that climactic moment of heightened sensation, both physical and emotional, it liquified into shimmering ectoplasm that flooded from you in a triumphant exodus, shooting out of you and into Mara. Its melted formlessness melded with her soul, binding the two of you together in an unbreakable chain-link unity. It was then that you fully became a part of her, and she of you. Not even the most catastrophic act of force majeure could sever that blood-bound contract. You may have known nothing of life, but that much you knew to be true.

If nothing else, there would always be Mara.

You were certain of that.

So tragically, naively certain.

3

When it was over, she let herself fall onto you, the beaded sweat on her naked torso gluing her skin to yours. Your hearts beat in rhythmic tandem, wildly at first, and then gradually slowing to a shared murmur.

"Well," Mara said, her cheek resting against your shoulder, "I *did* say I could take care of the virginity thing for you. This really hadn't been what I'd meant at the time, *buuut...*"

You responded with a little laugh and started to ask, "Did you know..."

"What? That you wanted to fuck me?"

"Yeah."

"Of *course* I knew, dodo bird. The googly eyes are hard to miss."

All of the blood that had been in your groin rushed up to your face. "You...um...you weren't, like, weirded out?"

"Because we're cousins? Nah, I don't put a whole lot of stock in social constructs. It's not like we're brother and sister. *That* would be weird. But people used to fuck their cousins all the time."

Her lack of guilt or shame did wonders to alleviate your own. Not that you'd felt much of either in that moment. You felt too good to be burdened by such moral trivialities. If society said you weren't supposed to feel like that just because of who your parents had been in relation to Mara's, then society could go fuck itself.

4

On the way home, you were sitting at the stoplight at the corner of Sunset and Hyperion when you saw the Grinning Man. He was sitting on a bench outside the Black Cat, holding another one of his cardboard signs. This one read, "HAPPY SHALL HE BE, THAT TAKETH AND DASHETH THY LITTLE ONES AGAINST THE STONES (Psalm 137:9)." When your eyes met, he stood and gave you a Princess Diana wave.

Mara saw this and smirked. "Friend of yours?" she asked.

"No," you said, lighting a nervous cigarette. "I've never seen him before in my life."

"He's kind of hot for a hobo."

"If you say so."

The light turned green. It was only when Mara looked away from him and accelerated forward that the Grinning Man's mouth spread into a giant, face-consuming smile.

CHAPTER 16 – BRIGHT DAYS, DARK NIGHTS

1

THE FOLLOWING MONTHS WERE, in spite of the tragic circumstances surrounding your being in LA in the first place, the best of your life. Looking back, it seems impossible that someone in your shoes could have been so tremendously content, but you were.

The remaining days of summer were spent, more often than not, with Mara and her friends. You quickly fell into their blithely decadent lifestyle. It was at first jarring to your simple Midwestern sensibilities, but it didn't take long for you to become accustomed to limousines and valets, dinner at Spago followed by private screenings at the Arclight, and parties in the Hills with movie stars who talked incessantly about their gluten-free vegan diets while casually sucking thousands of dollars of Peruvian marching powder up their noses.

There were countless nights at the Roxy, the Viper Room, the Troubadour. Bottle service at Lure and Ohm and the Argyle,

Avalon and Skybar and the Medusa Lounge. You hung out with Al Jourgensen backstage at the Whisky a Go Go, who "went way back" with Quincey's parents. Rebecca's father, a record producer, threw regular parties at which the brightest unit-shifting iTunes stars were always in attendance. Ianthe frequently brought Adonis-like teen actors with her when she met up with you and the others, often arriving late and muttering empty apologies about traffic and brunches with her agent who "just didn't know when to shut *up*."

The first few nights out on the town, your hands shook when you presented the bouncers with the fake ID Justine had procured for you, and you shrank under the skeptical stares of the terrifyingly broad-shouldered and black-suited men. After the fourth or fifth night, you were flashing it with the same aplomb as your more experienced friends.

At the Rainbow Room one night, in a tiny dark alcove above the stage, you and your five friends got drunk and stoned while a deathrock band called the Nameless Narrators sang-shouted hateful ballads about necrophilia and cannibalism. Before entering the little room, Quincey had pointed out a plaque over the stairs with a list of names, the only three of which you recognized were Alice Cooper, John Lennon, and Ringo Starr. "John Lennon was notorious for getting blowjobs from groupies in here," he explained. You made a face as you sat down at the cramped table, looking warily around as if you might see the ghosts of these trysts smeared along the wooden surfaces. Quincey laughed at this and said, "Just be glad we don't have a blacklight." Later, when Mara, Quincey, Ianthe, and Rebecca went downstairs to watch the band, Justine held you back and, "for the sake of tradition," went down on you while the Nameless Narrators played a slashingly boisterous cover of "Whole Lotta Love." Afterward, she took a felt-tipped marker from her purse and penned your name upon the plaque, just below Mickey Dolenz. She substituted your given name with

"Casanova" and misspelled your surname, then took a picture of her handiwork and posted it to Instagram. Filter: Clarendon.

Most of the days and nights that you and Mara didn't spend with the others were spent alone together. There were many a Sunday when she took you out to the desert and gave you driving lessens, first in empty parking lots and sleepy villas in Joshua Tree and Riverside, and then along flat stretches of highway cutting through the Mojave. One Friday night, after leaving an inordinately bland party in Brentwood, the two of you drove to Vegas. You took turns behind the wheel, with her taking over whenever traffic started to get too heavy. After twelve-plus hours of gambling away exorbitant amounts of her parent's money and getting wasted on on-the-house cocktails, you and Mara checked into an Executive Parlor Suite at the Bellagio, where you smoked stupefying amounts of weed and had sex on the billiards table before raiding the wet bar and blacking out just as a pink dusk was beginning to descend upon the neon-gold city. You woke late the next morning, hung over but about as happy as any orphan kid could ever hope to be.

The next time you did Captain Howdy was right before school started. You were wracked with anxiety as the six of you drove up to Topanga in Ianthe's Range Rover. The horrific imagery of your friends' monstrous transformations was still imprinted on your brain like screen burn on an overused iPad. You masked your fear with an artifice of indifference, but Mara saw through it. When you arrived at Quincey's cabin, she hung back with you while the others eagerly hurried inside. "We don't have to do this," she said. "I'm serious. You better not be doing it just because you think it's going to please me."

"I'm not," you swore to her in what was really only a half-lie. Yes, part of the reason you'd agreed to a second round in the ring with the demon dust was based on your knowledge that *she* wanted to do it. The other reason was a little more complex. You wanted to prove to yourself that you could handle it, that your ability to enjoy all of the things your friends did wasn't hampered by trauma or immaturity or whatever it was that had initiated the fucked-up hallucinations the first time around. You wanted to prove to yourself that you could be normal.

Once the lines had been chopped out, you volunteered to go first in the interest of giving your scaredy-cat inner child a defiant middle finger. Just as had been the case the first time, you experienced an intense euphoria as soon as you snorted it, and then promptly fell out. *Unlike* the first time, your blackout was mercifully unplagued by any nightmarish hallucinations. You woke later that night with that familiar sense of cumbersome headiness, but according to your friends, you hadn't been incapacitated the entire time. Ianthe informed you with a haughty sneer that you'd "acted like a *complete* and *utter* fool," dancing and singing to Queen and Guns 'N' Roses. When you fiercely denied this allegation, Justine provided you with video-recorded evidence that validated Ianthe's claims. The others laughed gusty gales of delight while you watched the video with a horror not too far removed from that which you'd felt when you'd seen your friends turn into demonic abominations.

Not too far removed, no, but *enough* removed that your fear of the drug subsided a great deal. If doing it came down to either demonic visions or embarrassing behavior, you'd gladly take the latter. And by the time the embarrassment had mostly worn off, you felt confident that your "bad trip" had been nothing more than exactly that, and thus there was no real reason to see Captain Howdy as anything more than a gimmicky party drug. You were, by then, quite versed in the subject of party drugs, and had experienced things infinitely more horrible than anything they could conjure up.

Of that, you were almost certain.

Almost.

2

When the summer ended, you were pleased to find that the Grinning Man's foreboding words about high school were largely unfounded. Mara introduced you to all manner of

friends and acquaintances in the halls of William Marshal. Just
about everyone was affable and laid-back. And while there
was an undeniable air of superficiality about many of them, it
rarely manifested in ways that could have been considered cruel
or judgmental. Even the worst ones were too concerned with
themselves to bother inflicting the kind of schoolyard sadism
that you understood to be more common Back East. You had
never faced too much of it firsthand (not yet, at least), but as
a whole you recalled the Ohioan youth as possessing a much
higher degree of callous aggression than their Californian counterparts.

In the autumnal months, your home life largely remained
as picturesque as it had been over the summer. Your aunt and
uncle were in town even less than they had been when you'd first
moved there, so you and Mara often had the house to yourselves.
This greatly benefitted your mushrooming adolescent sexuality,
something Mara had not only awakened but continued to stoke
with more carnal gluttony than even the most concupiscent
of Harlequin heroines. She took to calling you her "secret sex
Padawan," teaching you things of which you'd only glimpsed
fractions in grainy online videos. Her insatiability was such
that even the uncommon presence of your guardians was rarely
enough to quell her rambunctious lust; if they happened to be
in the house, it wasn't unusual for her to sneak into your room
late at night and assault you with her body, her only precau-
tionary act being to force a hand over your mouth to stifle your
involuntary cries, or to sink her teeth in your shoulder to stifle
her own.

The secrecy was the only piece of the equation that truly wore
on you. You'd more or less gotten past the guilt and shame surrounding that filthy i-word, but you couldn't shake the nagging
fear that the two of you would be discovered. Irrespective of
how you and Mara viewed the relationship, others would not
be so accepting. Your friends would surely scorn and shun you,
for you doubted their compassion would extend far enough

for them to look past your West Virginia romance. Your aunt and uncle would send you back to Ohio in a cardboard box, probably pulling some strings to have you locked up in the Midian Mental Institution for the Criminally Insane. Mara's reputation would be shot; she said Hollywood was "the biggest small town in America," and word travelled fast. If news got out that two of the most powerful people in the industry had a cousin-fucker for a daughter, Mara's future would be ruined, and she would rightfully blame you. The thought of Mara ever harboring ill feelings toward you was soul-crushing.

But for every day that ended with you safely enclosed in your cousin's arms, undiscovered by would-be witch hunters, the dread steadily lessened. It never went away completely, but it was bearable. Your La La Land love story was too potent to be diluted with fear of an uncertain (and, it seemed, increasingly unlikely) future.

Being now graced with the archetypal 20/20 visual acuity that comes with hindsight, it distresses you that you were unable to see just how *overly* idyllic your life was. You were existing in a pornographic fantasyland of fairytale happy endings. So many things had fallen into your lap. You had the perfect lover, an unwavering support group of compassionate friends, more materialistic opulence than you could dream of, and limitless freedom from supervision and traditional responsibility.

Real life, you now know, doesn't work like that.

Maybe it was all the sun. Maybe it was the drugs, or the sex. Maybe you were just so desperate to escape the horror show of reality that you subconsciously chose to blithely ignore all of the omens that indicated the coming darkness.

Because there *were* omens, and plenty of them.

Not the least of which was the Grinning Man, whose ubiquitous presence never failed to unnerve you anytime you saw him. He tended to haunt Silver Lake with preferential regularity, usually standing around Floyd's or smoking cigarettes in the alley behind Café Tropical, but he showed up in other places, too. You'd see him ambling down the Strip on Friday nights, or standing on street corners holding up his darkly biblical cardboard signs. There was a night when you, Mara, and Justine were drinking smoothies at the Galleria in Sherman Oaks and he strolled right by, pushing his shopping cart and whistling a Rolling Stones tune. He grinned at you when he walked past. He always grinned at you.

Mara noticed him as soon as you did. She gave you a meaningful look but didn't say anything.

Still, for as much as he creeped you out, you proved to be highly effective at compartmentalizing it. For the most part, you could keep him out of your mind when he wasn't in your immediate sight. Not always, but usually.

Another red flag started cropping up not long after school started. Though Mara was around *most* of the time, the stretches of time she spent with you were bookended by periodic interludes of mysterious absence. There were weekends when she'd disappear altogether, only to flippantly return without so much as even offhandedly acknowledging that she'd been away. Sometimes there were days during the week when she would be gone upon your wakening, which was always frustrating because you had to rush to catch the bus since the two of you usually drove to school together every morning. These days were always filled with fretful worry that bordered on panic, but then you'd get home in the afternoon to find her lying by the pool or sipping champagne and watching Netflix.

You never dared ask her where she went. If you did, she might answer with reticent vagueness, and that would only magnify your suspicion. Worse, she might actually tell you, and it might be something you didn't want to hear.

It was after one of her vanishing acts that you encountered the most foreboding omen of all. Late on a Sunday night toward the end of September, you woke alone in your bed to the sound of music coming from down the hall. Your bedroom door was open, which was ominous in and of itself; you always closed your door when you went to bed, whether Mara was there or not.

Your head was still fuzzy with sleep, so it took you a few seconds to recognize the song. When it hit you, it did so with the crushing weight of a cartoon anvil dropped from the sky. The ghostly chill of icy, crackling static that passed through you made your hair stand on end, as if you'd been rubbed all over with a balloon.

It was *the humming*.

The humming that you'd heard the first time you did Captain Howdy.

What you should have done was lock yourself in your room and wait for the purifying light of morning. That had honestly been your intention when you got up and went to your door, but instead of closing it, you walked out into the hallway and turned toward the direction of the music.

It was coming from Mara's room. Her door was closed, but emanating from the crack beneath it was a slice of near-blinding purple light.

You groped for the light switch on the wall and jammed it upward. The bulb burst into life and then promptly blinked out.

This is a dream, you failingly tried to convince yourself as your legs carried you forward. *This isn't happening. I'm still asleep.* You recited those three sentences like a religious mantra, but they brought you no comfort. The humming turned to singing...that eerie not-quite-other-language melody that you had, until that night, managed to stuff into the mental lockbox along with your fear of the Grinning Man. By the time you arrived at Mara's door, the arcane words had grown deafening.

Please be locked, you prayed to nothing in particular as you reached for the doorknob, though you couldn't hear the thought over the sound of the song. *Please, please be locked.*

It wasn't locked.

Once unlatched, it slowly swung open without your having to apply any pressure. The hinges creaked as if you were on the set of a horror movie, but you couldn't hear that, either. There was only the music.

Mara's bedroom lights were off, but the purple glow waltzed across every object between all four walls. You couldn't see any source of its origin, but you hadn't expected one because it wasn't really light, at all. Not in the traditional sense. It was more of a *presence*, something that needn't depend on anything in the physical world, neither natural nor artificial, in order to maintain its existence. It was just *there*.

Mara herself was standing naked in the middle of the room, facing away from you. Her arms were stretched perpendicular to her body. She was swaying back and forth in a way that could almost be called dancing, but she was out of synch with the rhythm of the music.

When the door stood fully open, she became still. The music stopped. Her arms dropped to her sides, her palms slapping against the bare flesh of her thighs. For what seemed like minutes, but was probably only two or three seconds at the most, she just stood there.

And then she started to turn her head.

That was when you ran.

You hadn't even made it halfway down the hall when you heard her behind you. Her footfalls boomed like cannon fire. It sounded like you were being chased by a gorilla, not a skinny sixteen-year-old girl.

You made it into your bedroom and slammed the door behind you. Locking it with tremulous hands and then backing up against the wall, you watched the doorknob and expected it to start shaking, but it didn't. The crashing footsteps went silent, and the only sound became your hammering heart.

Until Mara started to pound on the door.

It rocked in its frame, quaking under the force of her blows. A lightning-shaped crack rippled down its center, widening with each successive strike until a chunk of wood flew off and grazed your cheek. From the other side, a glowing purple eye stared at you through the jagged hole.

Not knowing what else to do, you tore across the room and dove under the bed. No sooner than you'd obscured yourself with a downward tug of the bed skirt did you hear the splitting sound of the door flying off its hinges and smashing into the wall where you'd stood just seconds prior. Mara's thunderous footsteps entered the room, and you could hear her sniffing the air like a bloodhound. A primitive growl rumbled up from her throat.

A dream. A dream. A dream. Not real. Not real. Not real.

And maybe it *wasn't* real, but the tears spilling from your eyes were real. They burned too much to be anything else. They were silent, but they were real.

You listened to her clomp around the room. You heard her throw open the closet and storm inside it, rummaging around and shrieking in frustration when she came up empty-handed. She pulled out all of your dresser drawers as if she might find you there, and you winced at the sound of each one hitting the wall when she flung them across the room.

Next, she went into your bathroom, and you heard her ripping down the shower curtain rod and tossing toiletries around with irritated haphazardness.

Finally, she came over to the bed.

There was a sliver of space between the floor and the bottom of the bed skirt, and you could see her feet just inches from your face. You'd half-expected them to be equipped with long black claws. They weren't, but her toenails...which you'd never known her to polish...were painted purple.

You couldn't explain how she didn't find you. She did, after all, look in your dresser, so looking under the bed would have been consistent with that kind of box-checking thoroughness. But instead of getting down and lifting the bed skirt so she could pull you out of your hiding place and eat your face (or whatever it was she'd had planned), she just stood there for several eternally-long moments before stomping out of the bedroom. It was only when you heard her bedroom door slam shut that you realized you'd been holding your breath, and you let it out in tandem with a choked sob. That turned into full-fledged weeping, which carried on uncontrollably until exhaustion triumphed over fear, and you fell asleep.

3

The next morning, you woke up in your bed, not under it. Buckets of sweat had soaked through the sheets and leaked into the mattress.

When you turned on the light, you weren't greeted by an avalanche of destruction as you'd thought you'd be. The bedroom door was undamaged and still anchored to its hinges, and all of your dresser drawers were firmly in place. You could see the inside of your bathroom from your bed, and everything appeared to be as it was supposed to be; the shower curtain hung undisturbed, the drawers and cabinets were all closed, and the counter was clean and uncluttered. There was nothing to indicate that anything more than a bad dream had occurred the night before.

A dream. A dream. A dream. Not real. Not real. Not real.

When you went into the bathroom to get ready for school, the nightmare was already beginning to fade into blurry obscurity. But as you were about to turn on the shower, you caught your reflection in the periphery of your vision and froze.

On your cheek, crusted with a thin layer of dried blood, was a small cut.

You stared at it for a long time, the images from the nightmare resurfacing with sharpened clarity and sucking you down into a hellish rabbit hole as you fought to convince yourself that it had, indeed, been nothing more than a dream.

"Hurry up, kiddo, we're gonna be late."

You turned to see Mara standing in bathroom doorway, leaning against its frame. All Mara and no monster. "What happened to your face?" she asked, coming over and gingerly touching the cut on your cheek.

You looked back at the mirror. There was a pause between her question and your answer that lasted a few seconds too long. When you finally did reply, you were speaking more to your reflection than to Mara.

"Cut myself shaving."

CHAPTER 17 – PIPE DREAMS

1

EARLY ONE FRIDAY MORNING in the middle of October, Mara nudged you awake. You squinted at the clock. It was four AM, and she was already dressed. Afraid something was wrong, you sat straight up and searched her face for something that might indicate a problem, but she just smiled and said, "Get up. I don't feel like going to school today, so we're gonna go to the beach, instead. They're calling for record-high temperatures."

Relieved, you rubbed your eyes and yawned. "It's four in the morning. Can't we sleep a little longer?"

"You can sleep in the car, if you want. I want to get on the road before traffic gets retarded."

"Which beach? Santa Monica?"

"*Fuck* no," she scoffed. "I wouldn't be caught *dead* at that beach. Everyone who goes there is either a tourist or an asshole. Or both. No, we're going up to Mandalay."

"Isn't that in Vegas?"

"That's Mandalay *Bay*, which is a casino. We're going to Mandalay *Beach*. It's in Oxnard. It's maybe an hour north, or so. *If* we beat traffic, so *get up*." She hauled you to your feet and then watched as you groggily dressed yourself.

You kept nodding off on the drive down Sunset, so Mara gave you a cigarette and had you take a swig from a travel-size bottle of Jack Daniel's that she produced from the center console. The nicotine cleared the drowsy fog from your head, and the liquor wakened your body. By the time you hit Pacific Coast Highway, you were bright-eyed and enlivened.

The sky was still dark as you cruised up the coast, and the early-morning air coming off the ocean was chilled and biting. Mara switched on the heat and then turned up the volume dial on the stereo. A dreary Lucero song segued into the Kinks' "Lola." Mara sang along with carefree merriment, replacing the eponymous name with her own. She swayed her head and moved her shoulders with the rhythm, taking drags from her cigarette in between verses. You watched her with an ever-expanding heart that nearly brought tears to your eyes. A goofy smile broke out upon your face and you knew you looked ridiculous, but you didn't care.

Never having been someone who sings along to music, you surprised yourself by taking up the next verse, belting out the words with an easy confidence that sharply contrasted with everything you knew about yourself.

"Well I'm not the world's most passionate guy,
But when I looked in her eyes I almost fell for my Mara
Ma-Ma-Ma-Ma-Mara."

Mara's ensuing laugh was full of delighted surprise. She rolled up next to a portly old man in a BMW sitting at a red light, and you looked him in the eyes and sang out the next verse, raising your voice over the sound of the music.

"Well I'd left home just a week before
And I'd never ever kissed a woman before.
Mara smiled and took me by the hand.
She said, 'Little boy, I'm gonna make you a man.'"

Mara sang the last line with you, and then pulled your face to hers and kissed you with such forceful eroticism that your head lightened and you thought you might faint. The old man grimaced and looked away, punching the gas when the light turned green. Mara kept kissing you for a few seconds more, only pulling away when a car behind her honked and shot around her. You both laughed, and if there was a single god-damn thing in the world to fret over, you didn't know what it was.

2

The sun was just starting to come up when you reached Ventura County. You had breakfast at a small restaurant on the bay, and then spent an hour walking around the harbor, getting stoned and watching the sea lions jockey for position on the docks. Once the sun had burned away the last of the morning chill, Mara drove the rest of the way to the beach. She stripped down to her highlighter-green bikini in the parking lot, leaving her shirt and jeans in the car. She went to the trunk and took out a red beach towel with a yellow hammer-and-sickle logo emblazoned upon it, wrapping it around her waist like a long skirt. Then she took your hand and led you between a pair of low dunes and out onto the white sand.

The only other people you could see were two formless specks a few hundred yards down the shore. An eerie thought entered your mind, and you wondered if the couple was actually a pair of doppelgangers, alien versions of you and Mara, existing in a future so near that it had come dangerously close to overlapping with the present.

The absurd notion flickered away when you reached the wa-ter's edge and the frigid sea slithered up the sodden sand to caress your feet with its phantom fingers. Mara squealed at the sensation but did not recoil. Instead she pulled you in front of her and kissed you, throwing her arms around your neck and pressing against you. You kissed her back, and then she pulled you down into the sand. Your bodies entwined in a writhing pretzel of limbs as oceanwater washed over you. Mara's towel came undone and was greedily pulled away by the tide. You looked up and around, scanning the beach for voyeurs, but there were none. Even the imagined doppelgangers had vanished. You and Mara may well have been the last people on earth, for all either of you knew. And so, with the rest of the world being unaccounted for, all that really mattered was that the two of you were alone.

At a party a couple of weeks prior, Ianthe had served you a cocktail she called "Sex on the Beach." It had been dreadful, and you'd not finished it.

That morning with Mara at Mandalay, though, had tasted of all the exquisitely tangy sweetness that you had expected from the drink before you had brought it disappointingly to your lips.

And you both finished.

3

After, covered in salt and sand and sitting upon the towel that Mara had managed to retrieve from the ocean, you said, "It should always be like this."

Lighting two cigarettes and handing you one of them, Mara said, "What should always be like what?"

You took a long, meditative drag from the cigarette and looked off at the huge blue shadows of the mountains looming in the distance. "It should be easy like this. Without all the secretive shit."

Mara laughed good naturedly. "Aw, it's not so bad. You don't think the forbidden *Romeo and Juliet* element is kind of fun?"

You thought of the Grinning Man and whatever it was he'd said about Shakespeare. "I just want things to be easy," you said.

The expression with which Mara regarded you was filled with infinitely more sympathy and patience than you felt you deserved. "*Everyone* wants life to be easy, but it's not. You just have to play the cards you're dealt. Every hand is a winning one if you do it right. And *our* hand really isn't all that bad, when you think about it. I mean, fuck, we've pretty much *always* got that house to ourselves. That *definitely* wasn't something Romeo and Juliet had going for them."

"I never read it."

"Neither did I. SparkNotes for the win. But anyway, the point is that we have a pretty solid gig going, when it comes down to it. I think the pool boy might be suspicious, but he doesn't speak a lick of English. He can't say anything to anyone no matter *how* bitter and jealous he is that I'm the one fucking you, and not him."

"We should just run away."

Her next laugh was a bit more caustic, and the look she gave you was similar to the one Agatha Clerval had given you in second grade when you tried to reason with her that babies came from storks. "Come on, kiddo. What is it with you always wanting to act out the plots of stupid movies? Where are we gonna go? Ohio, on some Bonnie and Clyde mission to catch the Mudhoney McFuckwit?" She bit her lip as soon as she said it, realizing it may have been too much.

"No," you said. "That's not what I meant." It had been a long time since you and Mara had talked about McPleasant because it had been even longer since you'd so much as *thought* about him. You couldn't remember the last time you'd had one of the nightmares, nor could you recall having felt that constrictive clench of unshakable hatred in your chest in recent memory. Unbeknown to either of you, it seemed that Mara had exorcised the ghosts from your head.

"I'm sorry," Mara said, looking away. "I didn't mean..."

"It's okay. I'm not upset. McPleasant isn't a concern of mine right now. Not anymore."

Mara's eyes flicked back to you. You felt her probing your mind, and you didn't resist. There was nothing in there you needed to hide from her. "It wasn't that long ago that he was your *only* concern," she said. "What changed?"

"A lot of things." You thought about it for a moment and then amended, "One thing. One thing changed."

Mara's face remained solemn for a spell longer as she continued to search your eyes, but then the hard line of her mouth
eased into a crooked grin. "Don't get too sappy on me, kiddo.
You're starting to sound like the dudes in the movies my *mom*
makes, now, and *her* movies are even worse than my dad's."

"Do you think she'll give me a producer credit if I pitch the
idea to her in twenty-five words or less?"

Mara threw her head back and laughed. "Oh, *for sure*. 'An
orphan kid finds a new purpose in life after fucking his cousin.'
That's some romcom gold, right there."

Now it was you who laughed, and the sound and feeling
of it startled you. Hearty, genuine laughter like that had, you
thought, been left behind in the days prior to your parents'
murder. It was something you associated with a life that seemed
so far in the past that it no longer felt like it even belonged
to you. You had thought that laughter...true, unadulterated
laughter...was a luxury well outside of your emotional capacity.
Trying to find room for it within your damaged soul would have
been as nonsensical as a Jack in the Box cashier attempting to
clear space in his garage for a Bentley.

Nevertheless, you were laughing all the same.

Maybe that Bentley wasn't such a preposterous pipe dream,
after all.

4

In bed on a Saturday morning a couple of weeks later, Mara
asked you when your birthday was. When you told her, she sat
up and looked at the calendar on her iPhone. "November *sixth*?
Jesus, that's next Friday. When were you planning to tell me?"

You hadn't planned to tell her at all, actually. Your previous
birthdays were fondly-remembered affairs that you associated,
naturally, with your parents. Being that you were trying not
to think about them, you would have been more than happy
to never celebrate another birthday again. Some things, you
figured, ought to remain in your Old Life. Birthdays were one
of them.

"I really don't want to make a big thing out of it," you told Mara. You took her pack of cigarettes off the nightstand and lit one, using a mostly-empty can of warm Diet Coke as an ashtray.

"It doesn't have to be a *big* thing, but it should be *some*thing. Birthdays are the one day where everything is about you. Where you get to let other people make you feel special."

"You already make me feel special. Every day."

She snickered and took the cigarette from you, taking a drag and blowing smoke up at the ceiling fan. "You have *no* idea how gay you just sounded. Either way, I'm throwing you a party, so you..."

"You really don't need..."

"It's happening, get over it. Seriously, you'll have fun, I promise. I throw some pretty mean parties. I'll keep it kinda low key, don't worry. But trust me, it'll be a *hell* of a night."

CHAPTER 18
– THE BAD
BATCH

1

By NINE O' CLOCK the following Friday, the party was in full swing. You'd figured Mara would only invite a handful of people...the usual group, and maybe a few of your classmates...but that turned out not to be the case. Once seven o'clock had rolled around, there were almost twenty people there. That number nearly doubled by eight, and at nine you estimated the headcount to be well over sixty. Most of them were people you didn't know. You recognized some of the faces from school, but the majority of the crowd was composed of complete strangers.

They all, however, seemed to know who *you* were. All night, people had been coming up to you and wishing you happy birthday, showering you in hugs and air-kisses, and drinking to your health and success.

The walls of the house reverberated with music and exultant conversation. There were at least four stereos blasting music from strategic positions in the house, and twice as many cell phones rolling through Spotify playlists with the volume turned all the way up. There was an old man you didn't recognize seated at the grand piano in the parlor playing jubilant showtunes, his fingers dancing across the keys with extravagant, disembodied grace.

When it started to become too much, you ducked into the bathroom cradling a red plastic cup filled to the brim with foamy beer. You sat down on the edge of the tub and nursed it gingerly, yearning for a cigarette. Ten minutes passed, maybe fifteen. You were just beginning to gather the courage to rejoin the festivities when the doorknob turned. As the door started to open, you took a deep breath and struggled to construct an embarrassed apology to whatever drunken fornicators were about to enter.

It was Mara who entered, instead. The sight of her made you release a relieved breath and brought a smile to your face. You'd seen little of her that night; she'd been busy whisking around from one guest to the next and offering them refreshments and warm welcomes, ever the Hollywood hostess.

Mara hastily shut the door again and thumbed the lock. She came over and pulled you to your feet, kissing you hard upon the mouth. Your half-empty beer splashed to the floor, sending frothy green rivulets trickling through the cracks between the linoleum tiles. You put your hands on her waist and pulled her close to you as she locked her arms around your neck. A soft moan escaped your lips.

She smiled when she pulled away, brushing a lock of hair out of your eye. "Sorry there are so many people," she said. "I know crowds aren't your thing. I honestly hadn't expected this many to come. I invited, like, forty people because I figured maybe half of them would show, but it looks like they *all* came. *And* brought friends."

You put a finger to her lips and kissed the tip of her nose. It was a gesture that made you feel older than you were, like you were a grownup, like you had the whole world figured out and you weren't just a clueless kid who was in love with his cousin. "Don't be sorry," you told her. "Everything is perfect."

"I wanted to invite your hobo pal, but I haven't seen him around."

A sickly chill washed over you, rousing goosebumps upon your arms and sending a spidery shiver down your back. "He's not my pal," you said.

Mara gave you one of her playful nudges. "I'm kidding, relax. I would *never* let some homeless dude in my parents' house, no matter *how* hot he is." Her smirk was light and teasing, but her words unnerved you. "Seriously, though," she went on, "Are you sure you're okay with all of this? The people and the noise and whatnot?"

"Really. It's all very nice. I feel very...loved."

She kissed you again with breathless fervor and then stepped back and ruffled your hair. "I *do* love you, kiddo. You know that, right?"

Your heart did a stumbling somersault. She'd never actually said it before. The l-word. You didn't know if she meant it in the same way you felt it, but it didn't matter. In that moment, it was enough.

You started to say something...you didn't know what, but *something*...but then she looked down at the spilt beer and said, "Go get yourself another drink. I'll clean this one up."

You opened your mouth to protest, but she silenced you with one final kiss. It was long and tenderly amorous, filled more with maturity and affectionate devotion than with the lasciviousness of sex-crazed adolescence. It was not the kind of kiss shared between a boy and a girl, but the kind shared between two wizened lovers whose passion has stood constant and eternal through countless years of adversity and tribulation. It was the kind of kiss ruminated about in fairytales and cheesy romcoms. It was the kind of kiss a person would die for.

"Now go," Mara said when she broke away. She took a roll of paper towels from under the sink and got on her knees to clean up the beer. "It's your birthday, and you're not nearly drunk enough."

2

You bumped into Justine in the kitchen. She squealed and leapt upon you, throwing her arms around your neck and wrapping her legs around your waist and then covering your face with kisses. When she got down, she rummaged in her purse and procured a small white package with a plastic purple bow glued to its lid. "Don't open it now," she instructed. "Wait till later, after everyone has left."

You nodded and thanked her, putting the box in your pocket and kissing her cheek.

"So, you're...what, sixteen, now?"

"No. Fifteen."

"I remember *my* fifteenth birthday," she said wistfully, much in the same way an old woman reminisces about when gas was thirty cents and children respected their elders.

"Um, when was it?"

"Like, two and a half years ago. I lied, I really don't remember it. That whole weekend was just one long blackout. Mara has videos, but she won't show me. Where *is* Mara, by the way?"

You shrugged.

"Well, I'm gonna go try and find her. Quincey just got here, too, by the way. I think he's out by the pool." She pointed at your pocket and said, "I'm serious, don't open it until *everyone* is gone."

Promising her you wouldn't and thanking her once more, you went to look for Quincey. You cut through the dining room, where a girl in a red one-piece bathing suit wielding a silver triangular cake knife was slicing the enormous birthday cake into modest little squares. She handed them out to the greedy guests on tiny plates from a tall stack of chinaware. You didn't recognize her, but she blew you a kiss as you walked past.

3

Out back, people were sitting around smoking joints and cigarettes and talking too loudly. The November night was unusually warm. Someone had set up a beer pong table, around which was a cheering crowd of guys in football jerseys. A quartet of girls were skinny dipping in the pool, their discarded clothes strewn across the ground like the forgotten carcasses of small mammals on the side of a desert road. You felt the weight of all the boisterous frivolity starting to encumber you again, and you wished you'd followed Mara's instructions and gotten a drink before going outside.

Quincey wasn't out there, but Rebecca and Ianthe were. Both of them hugged you and bade you happy birthday, each of them kissing one of your cheeks at the same time as the other. A heavy alcoholic odor wafted from Ianthe, and you wondered with a kind of apathetic curiosity what sort of stomach-scorching concoction she had in her cup.

Rebecca lit a cigarette and then handed it to you before lighting her own. You accepted it graciously, holding the smoke in your lungs and savoring the sensation of the chemicals diving into your bloodstream and shooting up to your brain. "Where's Quincey?" you asked, your head pleasantly swimming from the nicotine rush. "Justine said he was out here."

"What, *we're* not good enough for you?" Ianthe said, swaying a little on her feet. You looked at her coldly, and after a moment her sneer dissolved into laughter. "Oh, chill*ax*, I'm only *teasing*. You literally *just* missed him, though. He went inside to find you and Mara."

Regarding Ianthe with both concern and amusement, Rebecca said, "Did you just say 'chillax?'"

Ianthe blinked dumbly at her. "Um. Yeah? What it is, is basically a cross between 'chill' and 'relax.'"

"Got it," Rebecca said, exchanging a glance with you.

Ianthe seemed to have already exited the conversation, for she was studying one of the football players at the beer pong table with lecherous scrutiny. "I think I'd like to have sex with that boy," she said with disarming insouciance, and then started walking over to him in a zombie-like trance.

"Goddammit," Rebecca cursed under her breath, pursuing her friend and looking back over her shoulder at you with an apologetic frown.

"Casa*nova!*" came a voice from behind you. You turned around to see Quincey strut over to you, beaming a sloppy grin. He grabbed your hand and pumped it vigorously. "Happy motherfuckin birthday, my man. How old are you now? Eighteen, right?"

"Fifteen, actually."

"Christ, you're a *baby*." He ruffled your hair. "Do you feel older? Ha, just kidding. It's so retarded when people ask that. Like, how do you *feel* older, right?" He was talking fast. His jaw was worrying a piece of chewing gum, his breath scented strongly with the aroma of watermelon. You suspected he'd paid a visit to one of the numerous coke-peppered tables inside.

You took a drag from the cigarette and looked over at the naked girls, laughing and wrestling with each other in the pool. "Yeah," you said. "So retarded."

Quincey took your arm and pulled you toward the far end of the yard that bore the lowest proximity to the other partygoers. Once he'd ascertained that the two of you were out of earshot of anyone else, he said, "Dude, I got some."

You felt an uncomfortable tingling at the base of your spine. "Got some what?" you asked, even though you already knew.

"*Captain Howdy*," he whispered. "I wanted to hook us up so the six of us could do it tonight in honor of your birthday. The problem was that I couldn't fucking *find* any. Everyone was out. A couple of my dudes told me that their supply was permanently dried up. That the government put the crackdown on it and managed to totally wipe it off the streets. But then something *totally fucking nuts* happened."

Your palms were sweating. You sucked the cigarette nervously, goading him with your eyes to continue but wishing he wouldn't at the same time.

"So, I'm walking over here tonight, right? And I'm all bummed out because I failed, I fuckin *failed*, I let my friends down because I told them I could get it by tonight and we could surprise you with it, but I couldn't deliver on my promise, and I was feeling really down on myself, you know?"

"Okay. And?"

"And when I was maybe, like, a quarter mile away, this homeless dude steps right in my path and is like, 'Hey, you want to get fucked up?' So, naturally, I'm like, 'Fuck no, you're a homeless dude,' right? But then he reaches into his jacket and pulls out a fuckin *eighth* of good ole Captain Howdy. I mean, what are the *odds* of that shit? And to top it all off, he only wanted *five bucks* for it. Can you *believe* that shit?"

Your knees were starting to quaver. You could feel the perspiration on your back bonding your skin to the fabric of your polo shirt. "Quincey," you said, "what did this guy look like?"

"Oh, man, don't even worry, he wasn't grimy or anything. I probably wouldn't have bought it if he looked *too* scuzzy, but he didn't. Like, his clothes had seen better days, but other than that I'd say he was probably the cleanest homeless man I've ever seen."

"Quincey. What did he look like." You could barely hear your voice over the sound of your thundering heart.

"Well, uh, he was really pale. Like, *really* pale. And he had, um, brown hair, I think, and really dark eyes. Uh, what else...um, his fingers were kind of weird. Like, they were too long, you know? Like an alien's fingers. And he had a shopping cart with a purple sheet over it."

Your cigarette fell from between your lips. Your legs threatened to give out at any second.

"Oh, and he had this really funky grin."

You couldn't breathe. Something huge and invisible was sitting on your chest, and your lungs were collapsing in on themselves. "Where is it. The Captain Howdy. Where is it."

Quincey laughed. "Whoa, dude, chill. I came out here to get you and Rebecca and Ianthe so we can all do a line. You can even go first. It's *your* birthday, after all."

"Give it to me. Right now. I need you to give it to me *right fucking now.*"

Quincey was starting to look wary. The brusqueness of your demands was clearly making him uneasy, but you didn't care. You repeated yourself, consciously attempting to sound less stern but knowing immediately that you hadn't succeeded.

"I don't have it, man. I left it inside with Mara. She's getting it ready right now, as we speak."

You bolted for the house.

The door flung open just as you were reaching for the knob, your hand closing on empty air. Someone staggered out before you could see who it was, bumping past you and shambling toward the pool. When you looked down, there was a warm, wet smear of scarlet on your shirt. With tentative hesitance, you touched two fingers to the stain and held them up to your face. Your heart and stomach swapped positions in a roiling wave of nausea.

You spun around. The figure had reached the edge of the pool. When she turned, it was Justine's face that looked back at you.

Her big eyes were submerged in silver seas of sodden tears. There was a hideous cut running diagonally across her cheek. A flap of skin hung down, exposing pink gums and pain-clenched teeth. Her hands were pressed against her stomach in an ineffective attempt to cover the dozen or so stab wounds perforating her torso. Blood seeped between her fingers and dripped onto the concrete.

She mouthed your name, extending a tremor-wrought hand out to you. A weak cough made a freshet of blood surge up her throat and dribble over her trembling lower lip. You took several shuffling steps toward her, stretching your own arm out. Cold, salty grief spilled from your eyes.

You had almost reached her when she doubled over in a spasm of more blood-spewing coughs. Clutching her stomach, she looked up at you with such agonizing desolation that you were nearly brought to your knees. Then she straightened, rasped something unintelligible, and flopped backward into the pool. Murky red clouds bloomed beneath her.

By that point, everyone had lapsed into horrified silence as they watched the scene unfold with fatalistic fascination. Even the music had stopped. The naked girls in the pool were frozen in shock, noiselessly treading water and watching the blood clouds ebb closer to them, too stunned or stupid to move.

The quiet was broken when Rebecca let out a throat-searing shriek. She was pointing back at the house, her face an uneven topography of fear.

You turned around.

4

The silhouetted figure standing in the doorway was enshrouded in shadow, backlit from the bright interior of the house. The only part of her countenance that was visible was her eyes; they glowed with a vivid magenta light, two purple spheres staring out from a face that was otherwise obscured by darkness. You didn't need to see her, though, to know who it was. You could feel the essence of her presence. You would have known it anywhere. Vision was unnecessary, little more than a convenience affording you the pleasing sight of her beauty. You could have been struck blind by God or the devil or the Grinning Man (or perhaps they were all one and the same), and you would have been able to identify her just as easily as you could with the aid of physical sensation.

There was something else, though...something different. It wasn't just *her* presence you sensed; it was coupled with another, one birthed in darkness and groomed in hellfire. You could feel it trying to smother the core of its host's soul, snuffing out the flame that had drawn your mothlike heart into its hot, mesmerizing light. You could feel it trying to destroy her.

And you could feel it winning.

When Mara stepped into the light of the outside lamps, more people started to scream. She was holding the cake knife, its trowel-like blade tinged pink with white frosting and a red substance that could only be blood because you were pretty sure the cake had been vanilla. The thin fabric of her white lace blouse was dotted with spots of soggy, congealed gore, and there was a bloody handprint on her white miniskirt. Streaks of it ran up her forearms and down her thighs and calves. A glittery plum-colored mixture of blood and Captain Howdy leaked from her nostrils and ears.

Beneath her shining purple eyes, her face was painted with a huge, malevolent grin.

She started toward you.

"Mara," you whispered, holding up your hands and taking a step back. "Mara, don't. Don't do this. It's me. It's *me*." The tears were coming with all the torrential intensity of a pre-hurricane rainstorm. Your breath snagged in the tangled sobs deep within your chest. "Please, Mara."

You caught a blur of movement in the periphery of your vision, and then Quincey was barreling out of the darkness, screaming Mara's name. It looked as though he meant to tackle her. Mara, her violet eyes never leaving yours, casually swung her arm around and backhanded him across the face. The force of the strike was paranormally superhuman. It made the sound of a dropped egg smashing on a kitchen floor. Quincey's spectacles exploded in a shower of glass and plastic. His face caved in, and his body went soaring into the air. He landed hard on his side, fifteen feet away. He did not stir.

With enraged yowls, two of the football players charged Mara. There was a flash of silver, and one of them went reeling back with his hands clapped to a deep, bleeding trench carved into his forehead. He looked around, his eyes stupid with dazed confusion, and then he collapsed. Mara grabbed the other football player, who was a solid foot taller than she was and outweighed her by at least 100 pounds, and lifted him clear off the ground. His feet kicked and he struggled to pry the delicate fingers from his throat, to no avail. Mara looked up at him, widened her grin, and then hurled him forward with incredible ease. He landed all the way on the other side of the pool, his head cracking audibly on the concrete.

Mara walked toward you with calculated slowness, placing one deliberate foot in front of the other. When she was close enough for you to see the thin veins webbed across the whites of the eyes that no longer belonged to her, she swung the knife in an upward arc, slicing a vertical line through your shirt and cutting a deep incision down the center of your chest. Before the blood had even begun to flow, she slashed at you again, horizontally this time. You felt the skin split open, the second gash crossing over the first. You instinctively brought your hands to your chest to impede the bleeding, but then Mara lunged at you and knocked you onto your back. Sitting astride you, she let the knife fall from her grip so she could place both hands around your neck. The pressure she applied was something far beyond the kind of strength even the fittest of sixteen-year-old girls could have possibly possessed, but if Quincey and the football players had proved anything, it was that you were no longer dealing with a sixteen-year-old girl.

It wasn't until the corners of your vision began fading to black that you finally reconciled to yourself that she meant to kill you. As you looked up into the face grinning down at you with sinister joy, the last threads tethering you to fantasies of happily-ever-after started to snap. There was no good way it could end. Even if you or someone else managed to disengage her from you, and you both lived, there would still be no turning back. She'd killed one person and savagely injured three others. You suspected that the chances of any or all of the three boys' survival were mortally grim. Even if you could detain her, nothing would take back what she'd already done.

It seemed queerly just, then, that this was how things were to end. If your life was to be taken from you, better it be Mara to complete the transaction.

Being that death had assumed such a profound and formative role in your life, it suddenly struck you as odd that you'd never given all that much thought to your own demise. Before your parents' murder, of course, there had been no reason to think about it. You had been a happy and content child, whose understanding of the world was blissfully limited. After Sterling McPleasant had come along and turned all of that on its head, the paradigm shift had been sudden and drastic. Death became a primal component of your being. You were defined not only by the murder of your parents, but by the all-encompassing urge to avenge them and reign down a special brand of death all your own.

And as you lay there getting strangled by Mara, that urge suddenly returned to you with blazing renewal. It had left you for a while, chased away by your affection for Mara and your desire to construct your life with her as the sole foundation. Your new friends had been a welcome distraction from your bleakly hateful and murderous obsession. They had shown you a lightness of being that you had written off as unattainable the very moment you discovered your parents' mutilated bodies.

They had shown you how to feel without suffering.

She had shown you that there was more to life than anger and vengeful resentment.

But that was all over.

Just as you were ready to surrender yourself over to the welcoming arms of the Reaper, you realized that you *couldn't* die, not yet. You still had something to live for, even if such a *raison d'etre* was far less cozy and appealing than Mara. Yes, it was only when your cousin was crushing the life out of you that you realized you could live without her. That you *had* to, because your quest was not yet complete.

Your slowing heartbeat steadily began to quicken as your chest filled with ironclad resolve. As you felt along the ground for Mara's forgotten knife, you were only partly aware that you were crying harder than ever, your wailing sobs violent and uncontrollable. When your fingers found the knife's handle, a billion images whirled through your head like a Kodak Carousel gone haywire, starting with that first day by the pool and continuing all the way up until that final kiss in the bathroom.

You closed your eyes and saw Mara reclining on the chaise lounge, pulling you toward a proverbial precipice, and daring you with her eyes to jump. You saw her in the driver's seat of the Corvette, one hand holding a cigarette and the other draped over the top of the steering wheel, the sun glinting off her Wayfarers. You saw her making love to you high above the city, her moans intermingled with the faraway pops of the exploding fireworks. You saw her in your bed, nestled in your arms when you weren't nestled in hers, her naked skin providing you with all of the warmth and comfort of a child's security blanket. You saw her kissing you on Mandalay Beach while the tide crashed against your ankles and the pelicans dove into the rolling waves. You saw her with her tan legs clinched around your waist, grabbing handfuls of your hair and stifling her cries in your neck. You saw her sipping a cocktail and smiling her forever-wry smile, amused and bored and ecstatic all at the same time. You saw her stroking your hair and whispering you to sleep, ushering you down into shared dreams where you could be together without fear of discovery, ridicule, or forced separation.

You saw her alive, teaching you how to live.

A billion images, all condensed into a fraction of a second. A million smiles, a thousand laughs, a hundred orgasms, and fuck knows how many furtively sneaked glances heavy and pregnant with everything that never needed to be said. It made sense, because they say your life flashes before your eyes when you die. And while you weren't going to die in the traditional sense, there was a very big part of you that was not going to survive what you intended to do next. It was only rational that the life associated with that part of you, tragically short as it had been, would sing out its swan song in the form of a whirring slideshow of five months' worth of picture-book-perfect memories that may as well have occurred over the span of an endless lifetime.

When the flickering projector in your mind ran out of slides and its bulb blinked off, you opened your tear-saturated eyes and drove the cake knife into the soft flesh of Mara's side, burying the blade inside her all the way up to the hilt.

For a second, her grinning face twisted into one of hellacious outrage. There was nothing of Mara in that face. It belonged purely to whatever frenzied evil had claimed ownership of her. It was the face of a monster.

As quickly as it had appeared, though, it dissolved and vanished. The fiery purple glow in her eyes dimmed and went out, once more becoming their natural cool-blue hue. The anger in her expression softened and was replaced by a terrible sorrow. She looked down at you with a twinkle of recognition and whispered your name. She stroked your face with the blood-stained backs of her fingers, and then her eyes widened when she noticed the red marks around your neck and the wounds in your chest, as if it had been someone else who'd inflicted them. Which, you supposed, it had.

Shutting her eyes, she took a deep, uneven breath and said your name one final time before collapsing off of you.

You sat up, your bones aching from the shuddering sobs that just wouldn't stop. Then you gathered up Mara's head in your lap and sat there crying and bleeding, unaware of the timidly advancing partygoers or the rapidly approaching sirens in the distance.

You were aware only of one thing.

When are you going to do it? When do you plan on going back? I don't know, you'd said to her. *I'll know when it's time.*

It was time.

CHAPTER 19 – UNTIL EVERYONE IS GONE

1

SHE DIDN'T DIE.

Not at first.

You insisted on riding in the same ambulance that she did. You held her limp hand and watched one of the paramedics tend to her injury while the other one fussed over yours. A convoy of three additional ambulances followed, their bleating sirens tearing the night apart with impudent indifference. Quincey was in one of the ambulances, and the two football players were in another. The last one held the cake-cutting girl in the bathing suit, whom Mara had apparently stabbed in the neck upon taking the knife from her.

Mara's right hand...the hand you weren't holding...was cuffed to the gurney. Sitting across from you on the other side of the ambulance was a scrawny police officer with his cap pulled low over his eyes and a shotgun lying across his lap.

During the course of the entire drive to Cedars-Sinai, no one said a word.

Once you reached the hospital, you and Mara were separated in spite of your tearful protests. You watched them wheel her off down the long white hallway, unable to shake the fear that you'd never see her again.

They took you to a small private room and had you change out of your bloodstained clothes and into a stiff cotton gown, whereupon the cuts on your chest were cleaned and stitched and dressed up in bandages by a pretty blonde nurse named Wendy. She was polite and gentle but spoke to you like a child. You'd never felt less like a child than you did that night.

A parade of policemen began filing in and out of your room for the rest of the night. They all had identical faces and asked identical questions in a frustrating barrage of meaningless circles that started and ended at the same point. They'd already interviewed all of the twenty-plus witnesses who'd been outside when the violence had occurred, and their testimonies corroborated your innocence. As a result, they had little interest in your involvement with the night's events; they seemed much more curious about what information you might possess of the mysterious drug that had been the cause of it all. Naturally, you responded to all of their questions by steadfastly feigning ignorance. You told them nothing of your own experiences with Captain Howdy, and claimed not to have any knowledge of how Mara had gotten it.

You made no mention of the Grinning Man.

It wasn't until dawn that they gave up and the steady stream of cops finally trickled to a halt.

Only then did you sleep.

2

When you woke late in the afternoon, Rebecca and Ianthe were occupying the chairs beside your bed. Both of their faces were drawn, and their eyes were puffy from too much crying. The sight of them there, looking at you with grave concern, made you want to cry, yourself, but you didn't think you had any tears left.

"How is Mara?" was the first thing you asked.

The two girls looked at each other and then looked back you. "They won't let us see her," Rebecca said, idly twirling the drawstring of her pink Victoria's Secret hoodie around her index finger. When you inquired after Quincey, her eyes welled up and she said, "It doesn't look good. *He* doesn't look good. There's nothing left of his face. The doctor said even Jennifer Aniston's plastic surgeon wouldn't be able to fix it. And if he pulls through, he'll probably never walk again. They don't know exactly how bad the brain trauma is yet, but they said it's...extensive."

You looked out the window. The sun was slinking toward the horizon, its waning rays winking on the windshields of the sprawling ocean of cars in the parking lot below. "What about the others?" you asked. "The two guys, and the girl that Mara...that she...um..." You trailed off, unable to make yourself say it.

"The guys will be okay," Rebecca answered. "The one who got his face cut is never going to be Mr. America, and the other guy will have to shit into a bag for a while, but he'll pull through. But the girl..." She paused and looked down at her lap. She started to say something, but broke down and wept quietly to herself.

Ianthe put a hand on Rebecca's shoulder and looked at you. "The girl didn't make it," she said.

Rebecca regained her composure and wiped her eyes and nose with the sleeve of her sweatshirt. "Listen," she said, "are *you* okay? I mean, um...you know what I mean."

You didn't know how to respond to that, so you just looked back out the window.

"It wasn't your fault," Ianthe said. You sensed her getting up, and then she took your hand in both of hers and squeezed it with a compassion you'd not seen in her before. "There was nothing you could have done. It wasn't your fault."

"It wasn't *her* fault, either," you grumbled.

"It wasn't *anyone's* fault," said Rebecca.

You disagreed on that count. You pictured the Grinning Man's carefree face smiling through a cloud of cigarette smoke, holding up a baggie filled with glowing purple powder.

There was a long stretch of time where no one said anything. Ianthe returned to her chair and she and Rebecca intermittently checked their phones in between abbreviated crying spells. When you could stand the silence no longer, you blurted, "I love you guys. I really, really love you guys."

They got up and hugged you, curling up next to you on the narrow bed, and it turned out you had some tears left, after all.

3

You woke sweating from a fuzzy, unremembered nightmare late that night, sitting straight up in the bed and gasping wheezily. Rebecca and Ianthe were gone, but they'd left a note promising to be back in the morning. Sighing and looking out at the eerie Cheshire grin of the crescent moon, you knew that you wouldn't be there to receive them. You knew you would never see them again.

Stripping out of the hospital gown, you went into the bathroom to wash your face and take a few swallows of water from the faucet. Grimacing at your reflection in the mirror, you peeled off the bandages on your chest and examined the stitched-up wound.

Mara's work with the knife had been clean and neat, with all the precision of a master surgeon. The vertical cut was about nine inches long. It was bisected by the horizontal one, which was roughly three inches long, a couple of inches beneath the first cut's halfway point. The result was an upside-down lower-case *t*.

Or, more appropriately, an inverted cross.

The staff had disposed of your ruined shirt, but your jeans and socks were folded beneath your sneakers on a little table in the corner. Rebecca had forgotten her hoodie on the chair, so you pulled it over your head and carefully straightened it over your torso, trying not to stretch the skin on your chest. Then you stepped into your jeans, pulled on your socks, and hurriedly tied your shoes.

You weren't sure how far you could get before being caught, or how you were going to go about trying to find Mara's room, but you had to try. When you opened the door and stepped out into the hall, though, you were shocked to find it silent and empty. No doctors, no nurses, no janitors or orderlies...not even the incessant chirping of machines or the tortured groans of the infirm, sounds you'd thought were synonymous with hospitals. Your first thought was that you were still dreaming, but you quickly dismissed that notion. If it had been a dream, there would have been blood and corpses and monsters.

You wandered the empty halls with what you initially assumed was aimlessness, but then you realized you were following the quivering needle of some internal compass you hadn't known you had. Your legs carried you with a surety not shared with your mind. You were just starting to think that you should abandon the venture altogether when you found yourself standing before a door with the numeral 15 printed on the wall beside it. Before you had the opportunity to second-guess yourself any further, you turned the handle and walked inside, shutting the door behind you and flipping the light switch.

And there she was.

Her bed was larger than yours had been, and she looked small and atrophied beneath the crisp, unwrinkled sheets. There was nothing peaceful about her slumber. Her face was that of a child trapped within a nightmare from which the prospect of waking was a paralyzing impossibility.

Her hair had been brushed and her face cleaned up, but she was a wasted husk of the girl you knew. It was as if something had come in through the window and drained her of all vitality. Her skin was washed out and papery, like her tan had been scrubbed off with steel wool. There was a bluish, hypothermic tint to her slightly parted lips and the skin beneath her translucent fingernails. She was hooked up to a number of machines, and a clear IV tube snaked out of her left arm. A pair of long-chained silver handcuffs secured her right wrist to the bed's railing.

You turned the light back off.

Going over to sit in a chair beside her bed, you ran a hand through your hair and studied the dark shape before you. Her restless face was partially illuminated by the various machines' yellow-green LED monitors, and you tried to transpose upon her your memories of how she'd looked the previous night before everything had gone to hell, when she'd belonged to you and not the raging monster that had inhabited her via Captain Howdy's Trojan horse. It was a fruitless endeavor. Mara was no longer inside of the girl in the bed. You didn't suspect anything was. You were looking at an empty shell that was rapidly fading to dust.

You sat there for a long time, your eyes shimmering with unwept tears. A poisonous sorrow coursed through your blood, a sorrow that was as excruciating and deadly as any high-dosed drug of origins unknown or otherwise. When your waking self could no longer endure it, you fell into a sleep that was no more restful than Mara's.

4

You jerked awake a couple of hours later, your body stiff and aching from the uncomfortable sitting position. Mara was just as she'd been before you'd lost consciousness, appearing to have moved not at all in the lapsed time frame.

Something, however, was different.

Not with her, but in respect to the atmosphere of the room. It was colder, the air thin and pressurized like the cabin of an aircraft. You could feel a foreign but familiar presence looming somewhere in the dark. Even before your eyes adjusted to the sparse lighting and you saw the tall figure standing by the wall beside the door, you knew who it was.

The planes of his face were veiled by the darkness, but his grin was as white and bright as the sliver of moon still visible from the window.

"Shit, kid. Isn't *this* a bit of bad luck, right here?"

You were on your feet and upon him before you knew what you were doing, your body taking initiative lest your brain fail to do so. You took the lapels of his dirty jacket in your fists and slammed him against the wall. He had at least a couple of inches on you, but you snarled up into his face with all the rabidity of a mad dog.

"Whoa, whoa, *whoa*," he said, raising his hands in faux helplessness. His grin never faltered. "Seriously, kid, *chill*. Think about what you're doing. I am not your enemy. Trust and believe that you do *not* want that to change."

Undaunted, you growled, "You did this. This is *your* fault. All of it. All that blood is on *your* hands."

"*Well*, if that isn't the most good-golly-goddamned ri*diculous* thing I've *ever* heard. That shit ranks right up there with Leviticus and Amanda Bynes' Twitter account."

You tightened your grip on his lapels and pressed him harder against the wall. You could feel his breath on your face, but it was strangely cold and odorless. In fact, *no* part of his body seemed to emit any scent at all. There was nothing akin to the smell of garbage and filth and shit that, as a general rule, was as unifying a trait among the homeless as hunger and penniless pockets.

Nor was there anything akin to the innumerable fragrances of human life to suggest that he was even a person, at all.

"Cut the shit," you seethed. "I know you sold the Captain Howdy to Quincey. You gave him a bad batch and you knew it. You knew what would happen. You know everything."

"Except calculus," he reminded you, holding up his finger.

"I'm going to kill you. I don't care what the fuck you are. *I'm going to fucking kill you.*"

"You'll do no such thing, actually, but you sure do sound *awfully* convincing. Look at you, all grown up."

You tried to say something back, but all that came out was a low, guttural growl.

"Fuck, kid, sit down before you make a fool of yourself. Like I said, I'm *not* your enemy. So, yeah, I sold your friend some shitty drugs. But riddle me this: If Mara had died, say, by drunkenly crashing her car into a palm tree, or something, would you blame the sales guy her daddy bought the car from? No. You wouldn't. You're just looking for a convenient scapegoat because you can't come to terms with the fact that your beloved cousin is a fucking idiot who did way too much of a very bad thing. I didn't *make* Quincey buy that shit, and I didn't *make* Mara snort it. That was all them. Even *I* would never put that garbage in my body. Their actions were completely of their own accord. If I could make people do whatever I wanted, the world would be a *very* different place. Now, *sit down.*"

Contradicting his assertion of relative powerlessness, you suddenly felt compelled to obey his command, even though you had no real desire to do so. You released him from your grip and let your feet carry you backward to sit down on the edge of Mara's bed.

"Good boy." He looked over your shoulder at Mara. "You know, I think she looks quite beautiful right about now. Better than ever, actually. I happen to be of the opinion that death brings out the very best in people."

You looked down at her, not sharing in his sentiment. She was beautiful, yes, but only as beautiful as a person can be in a faded black-and-white Polaroid photograph. There was nothing material about her anymore. Only the steadiness of her breathing and the chirping heart rate monitor suggested there was any life left within her.

Looking back at the Grinning Man, you asked, "Is there any chance she'll live?" All of the gravelly rage had fled from your vocal cords. Now, you just sounded like a defeated child.

The Grinning Man cackled, slapping his knee. "Aw *shit*, that's a *good* one. Look at her, man. What do *you* think?" He lit a cigarette with a snap of his fingers. "You sure do ask a lot of stupid questions. You ought to work on that."

The only thing you could think to say was, "I don't think you can smoke in here."

"*I* can do whatever *I* want. What *you* need to do is get the fuck outta Dodge, as you well know. I'd step to it, if I were you."

"No. Not yet. I can't leave her yet." What you didn't add was, "*Not until she's dead,*" but it didn't need to be said to be understood.

The Grinning Man pointed at the vital machines, gesturing for you to look. You didn't know what most of them were for, but you didn't think the numbers on their screens were supposed to be plummeting the way that they were. And you'd seen enough movies to know what it meant when the spikes of the heart rate monitor dipped closer and closer to the flat line at the bottom.

You stood up, clutching Mara's hand with a tightness that surely would have pained her if she'd been conscious. Her eyelids were fluttering, her toes twitching slightly beneath the sheets as you whispered, "*No, no, no, no,*" over and over again, tears spilling down your cheeks. The tempo of the machines' shrill beeps had quickened to an alarm-like rapidity, piercing your ears and drowning out your thoughts.

"Better get going, Casanova," the Grinning Man persisted. His use of Quincey's nickname for you should have made you bristle, but you weren't present enough to really register it. "They'll be in here any second."

As soon as he'd said that last part, the numbers hit zero, the heart rate flatlined, and the beeps leveled out into a continuous high-pitched whine.

"It's over, kid. She's gone."

And it was. She was.

You stood there for a moment longer, looking down at her through a bleary pall of tears, and then bent to kiss her. Just before your lips touched hers, though, you stopped. You thought of that last kiss the night of your birthday, by then already feeling like a long-ago memory from a different life. You thought of how it had felt to have her mouth pressed to yours, warm and alive, and you realized that you wanted to remember her like that. You did not want your final kiss with her to be cold and dead.

Straightening, you turned around and looked at the Grinning Man. He was no longer grinning. The corners of his mouth were turned down, and you felt an inexplicable and wildly out-of-character sympathy radiating from him. In that moment, he almost seemed kind.

In that moment, you almost didn't hate him.

"Go," he said, his voice soft and no longer barbed with his usual cruel humor. "There's a cab waiting for you out front. The driver has been paid. He knows where to take you."

You gave a curt nod but didn't have the voice to thank him, so you wordlessly went to the door and made to leave. When your hand closed around the handle, the Grinning Man said, "Oh, one last thing."

You looked back at him. His grin had returned. Dropping his cigarette to the floor and grinding it out with the toe of his boot, he winked and said, "Nice shirt."

5

Mere seconds after exiting Mara's room and starting briskly down the hallway, a team of doctors and nurses rounded the corner and jogged past you, none of them paying you any mind.

You didn't look back at them as you continued on. You knew where they were going. You knew it was in vain.

The hospital had become itself again sometime between then and when you'd first sneaked out of your room. The halls were busy with all forms of medical staff in scrubs and white coats, but you went by all of them with the invisibility you had thought belonged only to ghostly apparitions. An unattended teenaged boy meandering through an ICU in a Victoria's Secret hoodie should have provoked some degree of suspicion, but no one so much as looked in your direction.

As promised, a blue and white taxi was idling at the curb when you walked out. You didn't address the driver, nor did he you. His eyes very briefly met yours in the rearview mirror, and then he put the car in drive and punched the accelerator.

Shifting in your seat, you felt something in the pocket of your jeans. Bemused, you withdrew the alien object and held it up to light of the streetlamps cascading in through the car window.

It was Justine's gift. The little bow-tied square box. The ribbon was the exact same color Mara's eyes had been when she'd nearly strangled the life out of you. The color they'd been when you stabbed her.

Don't open it until everyone is gone.

Everyone was indeed gone.

Holding your breath, you removed the lid and peeled back the tissue paper inside.

You stared at the item resting within it for a long time, and then you began to weep.

CHAPTER 20 – WRECKAGE OF THE PAST

1

YOU HAD THE CAB driver drop you off at the corner of Sunset and Occidental, not wanting anyone to see you pull up to the house in the back seat of a taxi. You didn't want anyone to see you at all.

As you walked up the hill for the last time, you tried to smother thoughts of all the times you'd made that same walk with Mara. Despite your efforts, you could feel her beside you, could smell her perfume and hear the peals of her laughter. At one point, you even reached out for her hand, and for a second you almost felt the warmth of her palm and the gentle tightness of her grip. But then it was gone, and you were alone.

When you reached the top of the hill, you ducked under the yellow police tape and punched in the code to enter the gate. You kept your eyes trained on the ground, because you weren't sure you could handle seeing Mara's Corvette and all of the memories that existed within it.

You breathed a relieved sigh when you found the front door unlocked, because you didn't have your keys. As you walked inside, you froze mid-step, your heart lurching into your throat. There was music coming from somewhere in the house. All of the stereos had been turned off save for one. The song playing upon your entry was "Nights Like These." You hadn't heard it since the night Mara took your virginity, but now it was playing with such clear purity that it transported you back to that fateful Fourth of July.

"It's nights like these...that make you feel so far away."

You closed your eyes and found yourself on the overlook, the fireworks decorating the sky all across the city down below. You felt Mara moving against you, felt that overwhelming sensation that nothing else mattered and you had found somewhere you belonged, with some*one* who could save you.

"It's nights like these...when nothing is for sure."

When you opened your tear-stinging eyes, you took in the disaster that had been left in the wake of the ruinous birthday party. Cups and tumblers and empty bottles were scattered everywhere. Crumpled snack bags and crumb-sprinkled plates littered the floor. Bongs, pipes, half-smoked joints, and rolled-up twenties were cluttered across every conceivable surface. Broken glass crunched under your shoes as you proceeded through the living room and into the dining room. Flies buzzed around what remained of the cake. There was a smattering of blood over the melted frosting, obscuring your name and the word "birthday." In a cosmic display of sad irony, the word "happy" was oddly untarnished.

You found the wreckage out back to be much the same as what was inside, with a wide assortment of trash strewn across the lawn and the concrete around the pool. The pool itself had been drained, but there remained a dark stain on the ground where Justine had uttered her indecipherable last words. Near it was another stain, the one consisting of both Mara's blood and yours. The one that had been created when you'd sat with her head in your lap, the two of you bleeding together. Dying together.

"It's nights like these...the sad songs don't help."

Wiping your eyes with the back of your hand, you walked over to the spot where Justine had died and knelt down before the dark splotch. "Everyone is gone, Justine," you said, taking the box from your pocket and setting it down in the center of the stain. You kissed the tips of your fingers and then touched them gingerly to the darkened cement, swallowing a sob.

"It's nights like these...your heart's with someone else."

You turned and crawled over to the other spot on the ground. Mara's spot. *Your* spot. Lying down and curling into a ball beside it, you let the tears come.

You wept for Mara, for all of the love gained and lost. You wept for Justine, whose unsullied, childlike glee had so many times kept your demons at bay with kindness and laughter. For Quincey and Rebecca and Ianthe, who had been more like family to you than perhaps even your own dead parents, and who had, in many ways, brought you closer to Mara than you would have become without the stanchion of their friendship. You wept for futures that would never be realized and lives that would never be lived. For wasted time and time well-spent. For unions of body and blood, of shared experience and treasured individuality. For truth, for lies, for hatred, and for indifference. For life. For death.

Most of all, you wept for yourself. So much had been stolen from you, and you could identify no reasonable cause for any of it. Up until then, your attitude toward the injustices inflicted upon you had been one of bitterness and resentment. But as you lay there by the pool where you had first found love and where you had lost it, where your beatific romance had started and where it had ended, all you could do was feel sorry for yourself.

"'Cause nights like these tear me apart."

You wept for a long time, until there truly was nothing left. As the night sky ebbed into dawn, the well of your sorrow dried up, leaving only a dark, mildewed cavern of hollow emptiness. The final cessation of your tears was one of eternal permanence. After that last time, you never cried again. You got to your feet and walked back to the house, and by the time you reached the door and went inside, you were as barren and vacant as the drained pool you had just left behind.

You had to wade through more heartrending nostalgia when you went up to your room, but you endured it with hardened tenacity. You changed into a fresh outfit and threw some clothes into a duffle bag, careful to only select articles you'd not before worn lest you carry any cognitive associations with you on the journey that lay ahead. You wanted to leave behind everything meaningful, anything that bore the potential to incite melancholic reminiscences of the last five months. Such ruminations would be inevitable, but that didn't mean you had to invite them. You took one last look at the crumpled pink hoodie on the floor, the smear of Rebecca's snot and tears still on the sleeve, and then you shouldered your bag and went downstairs. You locked the door behind you, and you did not look back.

The sun was beginning to rise as you descended the hill. When you got to the bottom, you looked west toward Floyd's. The Grinning Man was not there.

Taking a deep breath, you turned and headed east.

Toward the sun.

Toward Ohio.

Toward McPleasant.

Toward revenge.

Toward home.

CHAPTER 21 – THE BATMAN

1

YOU HAD A GOOD run.

A fifteen-year-old boy hitchhiking from California to Ohio is bound to get picked up by a pedophiliac rapist at one point or another. You made it all the way to Illinois before your luck finally ran out.

It was the fourth or fifth night since you'd fled Los Angeles. You were on a flat, lonely stretch of road somewhere outside of Chicago. You could see the lights of the city in the distance. The clumped concrete forest of tall buildings was etched into the black horizon as if it had been carved there with an X-acto knife.

Up until that point, your journey had been graciously un-eventful. The strangers who picked you up tended to be kindly old men and red-eyed, tobacco-chewing truckers. They would usually drive you a couple hundred miles before dropping you off at a rest stop or twenty-four-hour diner when their own travels required them to veer from your eastward course. They almost always would buy you a meal or hand you a fistful of crumpled dollars before going about their way.

When your well of good fortune dried up, however, it did so in spectacular fashion.

Your last driver had dropped you off at a tiny rest stop with a single unisex bathroom stall and an out-of-order vending machine. From there, you set off on foot, and you hadn't seen a single motorist since then. As you ambled alongside the road with your hands in your pockets, you began to feel more and more as though you were traversing some barren, purgatorial wasteland that existed somewhere outside the restrictive bounds of earthly reality. The heavy, surreal quality of the quiet nightscape was beginning to unnerve you.

You had endured almost two hours of this forlorn trek when someone finally came along. Your body flooded with relief when you felt the white-yellow beams of the headlamps hot on your back. You heard the engine slow to a grumble, and the tires crunch over the weedy gravel as it pulled onto the shoulder. When you turned around, the vehicle had nudged up so close to you that you could reach out and touch the bumper. Squinting, you raised your arm over your face to shield your eyes from the piercing headlights. You heard a door open, and the lights flicked off.

You lowered your hand, blinking away the painful splotches seared into your retinas. The vehicle was a dusty white mini-van with Michigan vanity plates that read, "TEAMSTR". The hood was streaked with the smeared corpses of innumerable ill-fated insects. You could make out the silhouette of a figure in the passenger seat, and the driver had come around the open door to lean against the left fender with his arms folded across his chest, smiling amiably.

"You lookin for a ride?" the driver asked. He was a heavyset man of stocky stature and pasty complexion, with thick-framed glasses and a dense growth of coarse stubble on his round face. He wore a wrinkled gray work shirt and muddy steel-toed boots.

"Yeah," you said, hoping the desperation wasn't evident in your voice. "I'm headed for Cleveland."

The man nodded. "Cool, we're on our way back home to Detroit, so we can probably get you most of the way there before we have to shoot up north." His voice was high and squeaky in such a way that was almost laughably comical, as if he'd been huffing helium.

You looked him up and down, figuring he appeared harmless enough. "Okay," you said. "Thank you."

He smiled and gestured for you to get in, and then he resumed his place behind the steering wheel.

You walked over and slid open the rear door to find two Hispanic men sitting in the back seat, regarding you with cold, unsmiling expressions. The one nearest you was tall and broad-shouldered, with crude tattoos snaking up his arms. He had a Detroit Red Wings baseball cap cocked to the side. The other one was short and diminutive, with a marsupial face and the neatly-trimmed pencil mustache of an amateur pornographer. The overhead dome light made his bald brown head shine like amber.

They scooted over to make room for you, and you climbed in.

The figure in the passenger seat turned around to appraise you, and the sight of her was so startling that you twitched, as if her countenance was an actual affront to your body's physical homeostasis. She was jowly and obese, with skin so pale and haggard that she bore uncanny resemblance to a bloated, waterlogged corpse. Her gray-blonde hair was stringy and slickened with shiny grease. Her witch-like nose hooked sharply downward, and when she smiled at you, her chapped lips parted to reveal yellowing teeth that appeared to be in the early stages of rot.

You averted your gaze, shutting the door and buckling your seatbelt. The dome light flicked off.

"The name is Grainer, by the way," the driver said in his ridiculous voice, turning the headlights back on and pulling onto the road. "This here lady is my wife, Ursula."

Ursula didn't say anything. She just kept staring at you with her beady eyes, the flesh beneath them dark and shriveled. Her filthy smile made your stomach tighten and flip over.

The tall man in the baseball cap sitting directly beside you held out his hand and said, "'Sup, bro. I'm Lorenzo. This little guy next to me is Tito."

You shook Lorenzo's extended hand, which was hard and callused. Tito nodded at you but said nothing.

You waited for one of them to ask the tired, obligatory questions. *What's in Cleveland? Why are you traveling alone? How old are you? Where's your family?*

No one asked any of these things. In fact, no one said anything at all. After the introductions had been made, the ugly quartet had sunk into silence. Ursula continued to stare at you for several long, uncomfortable minutes, and then she turned away and switched on the radio to a twangy country music station.

2

You'd been on the eerily empty road less than twenty minutes when Lorenzo suddenly leaned forward and nudged Grainer, pointing up ahead to where a narrow dirt road peeled away from the highway and led to an old, derelict gas station. The pumps had been removed and the windows were slatted with graffitied boards.

"There, bro, there," Lorenzo said. "That place is *perfect*, bro."

Grainer nodded, turning off onto the dirt road and driving around to the rear of the small building, obscuring the vehicle from the deserted highway. He threw the van in park and killed the ignition. The headlights went dark.

"What are we doing?" you said, barely able to hear yourself over the palpitating of your heart. Ursula had turned back around to grin at you again, and then so did Grainer. Lorenzo and Tito remained passive, but their eyes crawled over you like spindly-legged beetles.

"That's a pretty retarded question," said Ursula. "Are you a retard? You don't *look* like a retard, but you did just allow yourself to get picked up by four strangers in the middle of the night. And now you're all surprised that we're not a bunch of good Samaritans."

"That's some pretty retarded shit, bro," Lorenzo agreed.

"*Si*," chimed Tito, nodding. "Retarded shit."

You saw Lorenzo's arm cock back. He drove his fist forward before you had time to brace yourself, and you felt the impact explode against your temple. You went limp in your seat, your eyes fluttering as you tried to stay conscious. A cold stream of drool escaped your lips and pooled in your lap.

You heard a door open, and someone got out. The side door from which you'd entered was pulled open, and then your seatbelt was unfastened and you were dragged from the van and dropped on the ground. You tried to sit up, but someone hit you again, this time on your other temple, and you flattened back down with your arms spread out beside you.

"Let my hubby go first," you heard Ursula say. "He's been doing all the driving."

"Yeah, me first," Grainer squeaked. The other two men grumbled noncommittal protests. You heard a belt unbuckle and a fly unzip.

You heard footsteps coming toward you, heels dragging on the gravelly pavement.

You heard Ursula let out a long, tinny cackle.

And then you heard another car.

Not from the road...you doubted you'd be able to hear a car passing by on the highway from back here. No, this car was close. Very close. You could hear the purr of the motor, the slow approach of the tires. You could even hear the sound of a radio, though you couldn't make out the song. Something angry and loud, with a manic guitar and a sludgy, droning bass. Early nineties grunge, maybe.

"The fuck?" you heard Lorenzo say. Ursula's laughter hitched and then caught in her throat.

You managed to prop yourself up on your elbows and force one eye open. Your captors were standing in a wide semicircle around you, but none of them was looking at you. They were all looking at the blue BMW that had pulled into the lot, idling near their van. The windows were tinted. It had Ohio plates.

The car's engine shut off, and the driver's door opened.

3

The man who emerged from the BMW was very blond and very tan. He was young, probably in his mid-twenties, and dressed in stonewashed jeans and a white button-down Izod shirt with the sleeves rolled up to his elbows. He had the kind of face you'd seen on countless billboards and movie posters up and down Sunset Boulevard. His delicate features were cast in a cold expression of passive indifference. He lit a cigarette with a dexterous snap of his Zippo, his wrist flicking with such graceful speed that the movement was almost imperceptible. You thought of the Grinning Man.

The others waited expectantly for him to speak, but he didn't. He just stood there, smoking his cigarette and looking at them with docile disinterest.

When it became clear he wasn't going to initiate the exchange, Lorenzo spoke up and said, "Get lost, bro. I'd hate to have to mess up that pretty face of yours."

"*Sí*," Tito said, smiling and nodding. "Mess up his face."

The driver of the BMW still said nothing.

"Seriously, we'll fuck your shit up, motherfucker," Grainer said. He suddenly remembered that his small, shriveled dick was exposed, so he hastily tucked it back into his pants.

Without answering, the blond man walked to the rear of his car and opened the trunk, from which he removed a wide-barreled aluminum softball bat. Cigarette dangling from his mouth, he walked with languid deliberation toward his opponents, absently twirling the bat in one hand like a baton. He came to a stop about five yards away, leaning the bat casually against his shoulder. He took one last drag from the cigarette and then dropped it into the dirt, crushing it beneath the toe of his brown leather boat shoe.

Ursula started laughing again. "What's this, you gonna play Batman and try to be a hero? Wave your toy around and hope you can scare us off?"

Tito snickered and said, "*Si*, Batman."

The man shook his head slowly. "No," he said. "I'm not going to try to scare you off. I'm going to kill you. All four of you."

Lorenzo joined in Ursula's laughter, saying, "*Ay,* you're funny, *cabron*. One pretty-boy bitch against all of us? Just how are you planning to do that?"

The stranger pointed the bat at Ursula and said, "I'm going to start with you, just because you're so goddamn ugly." Ursula turned tomato-red, her thin lips curling into a sneer and her meaty hands clenching into fists.

"Then I'll kill you, next," said the stranger, pointing at Tito, "because I don't think it'll take much more than a tap to knock your little head right off your shoulders." He then pointed at Grainer and said, "You'll be third, because I want to save homeboy here for last." He nodded at Lorenzo. "Something about you just rubs me the wrong way, so I'm going to savor beating your face in."

"Oh, I'll rub you the wrong way, all right," Lorenzo said with a leering grin. He started to say something else, but the stranger had already sprung his assault. He was upon Ursula with impossible speed, whipping the weapon around in a whistling arc. Her beak-like nose disconnected from her spongy face in a shower of blood and landed on the hood of the minivan. She shrieked and thrust her hands up at the gushing wound, and her assailant drove the bat's handle into her forehead. She fell backward, sitting down hard upon her bouncing buttocks. The man then brought the bat straight down onto her head with two successive strikes, the first one causing her skull to bend inward, the second making it split open. She fell onto her back with pink and black goo leaking and squirting from her cavernous injury.

Lorenzo ran up behind the stranger, swinging his huge fist, but the man ducked and spun on his heel into a crouch. He jabbed the end of the bat into Lorenzo's kneecap with a quick stabbing motion, pulverizing the bone with an audibly wet crunch. Lorenzo collapsed onto his side, howling and clutching his ruined leg.

Now Grainer lumbered forward in a waddling charge, his head down and his shoulders hunched. The stranger casually sidestepped him, and Grainer tripped over his shoelaces. He tried to throw his arms up to break his fall, but he was too slow and landed on his face.

The stranger looked now to Tito, who was watching all of this with paralyzed horror. A line of saliva trickled from the corner of his open mouth. When he saw the man coming toward him, he attempted to turn and run. Before he could complete even half a step toward the minivan, the softball bat smashed into the right side of his bald cranium. The force of the blow broke his neck and lifted him from his feet. He pitched hard to the left and landed in a small heap, the huge dent in his head making it look like a deflated basketball.

Lorenzo was still writhing in the dirt, but Grainer was getting shakily to his feet. He pulled off his shattered spectacles and tossed them aside. His gravel-pocked face was streaming with blood and snot and tears. Fat lips quivering, he beseeched the man with blubbering pleas to spare his life. The ruination of his glasses had rendered him almost completely blind against the dark of the night, and he strained his squinting eyes to try and make out the shape of the killer among the blurry black shadows. He was still pleading when the softball bat, thrown from its owner's hand with expert precision, pinwheeled through the air and struck him between the eyes. He uttered a small whimper as he was knocked off of his feet. His extremities twitched for a few moments as he lay there on the pavement. Foamy spittle collected on his chin and cheeks and bubbled in the back of his gargling throat. After one last shuddering convulsion wracked the fleshy bulk of his body, he became silent and still.

The stranger walked over to pick up the bloodied bat, and then stood looking down at Lorenzo, who returned his gaze with doleful, tear-brimmed eyes. "Please, bro, don't kill me. I'm sorry, I'm sorry, please just don't kill me. Come on, bro, *please*. You don't have to kill me."

"My boss says otherwise," the stranger said.

"Who's your boss?" Lorenzo asked, trying to drag himself away from the stranger. "Is it Carlito? Is this about the bust? Tell him I can get it all back, all of it and more. I can't do that if I'm dead, bro. Let me live and I'll fix everything."

The stranger regarded Lorenzo with a puzzled expression for a moment, and then smiled, shaking his head. "No, I don't know any Carlito. My employer isn't interested in you. He's interested in the kid. You just happened to get in the way. Nothing about this is personal."

"Then let me go! Take the kid and let me live! Come on, bro, I..."

The stranger didn't let him finish. He swung the bat around and hit Lorenzo in the face, shattering his jaw. Bloody teeth spewed from his mouth and clicked onto the pavement. The next strike hit him in the same place, as did the third. The fourth caused the bottom half of his face to tear off completely. The gnarled clump of flesh and bone and cartilage went soaring into a patch of jagged-leafed dandelions sprouting up from the cracks in the asphalt. The fifth blow, delivered to the temple, was probably what killed him, but the stranger brought the bat down a sixth and final time in the center of what was left of his face. It made the remains of his visage pucker inward, like a dimple on a golf ball.

You flinched and tensed up when the stranger turned and walked in your direction, though you knew he wasn't going to kill you. As he approached, you flicked through your mental

Rolodex and tried to think of who in your life would send this dark harbinger of death to your aid, but you could think of no one. No one who would give enough of a shit about you, much less have access to a man like this one.

Holding his hand out to you, the stranger said, "I'm Derek. I was sent here to rescue you."

You reached up and took his hand, and he hoisted you to your feet with cool, effortless strength. The motion caused the pain in your head to sharpen, and you almost fell down again. Derek caught you and stooped down a little so he could sling your arm over his shoulders. As he helped you to the car, you asked groggily, "Who sent you?"

Gently easing you into the passenger seat, Derek said, "I'm not supposed to tell you that." He shut the door and went around to the rear of the car. You heard the trunk open, followed by a rustling as its contents were moved around. Then it shut again and Derek got behind the wheel, sans softball bat and now wearing a black polo shirt in place of the bloodstained button-down. He reached under his seat and pulled out a bottle of Johnnie Walker, which he uncapped and then handed to you. "Drink some of that," he said. "It'll help with the pain. Just don't drink too much because I don't want you to throw up in my car."

You took a swig from the bottle, fighting back a cough as the alcohol galloped down your throat and left a trail of tingling, fiery heat in its wake. The second swig went down smoother, and you relished the spreading warmth.

Derek lit a cigarette and offered one to you, which you took. He turned the ignition and rolled the windows down. Mark Lanegan's voice leapt from the speakers, crooning throatily of pain and misery and sweet oblivion. As the car wheeled out of the lot and onto the highway, racing along with smooth, hypnotic grace, you shut your eyes and let your head fall back against the seat. The whipping torrent of the wind was refreshing on your face. You finished your cigarette in silence and then tossed it out the window, watching the shower of sparks in the side mirror. Then you rolled the window up and looked over at Derek, your eyes heavy. "Where are you taking me?" you asked.

"Home," he answered. The tone of his voice suggested that this should have been obvious. "Villa Vida, Ohio, right?"

You nodded, unsurprised at his knowledge of this.

"That's where I live, too," Derek said.

That didn't surprise you, either.

"You should get some sleep. You look like shit."

You nodded again, taking one last, long swallow of whisky before handing the bottle back to Derek. He took a swig, himself, and then screwed the cap back on and restored it to its place beneath his seat. "We're maybe six hours out, give or take," he said. "I'll wake you when we're close."

"Am I going to meet your boss?" Your words were distant, underwater. Your eyes had swung shut of their own accord, and you were drifting fast.

"No," Derek said. "Not tonight."

"When?" Farther away, now. Almost inaudible.

If Derek answered, you didn't hear him.

CHAPTER 22 – HOME OF THE BULLDOGS

1

DEREK WOKE YOU WITH a soft nudge on the shoulder just as he pulled off 90 at the Villa Vista exit and turned south toward Villa Vida. "Almost there, kid," he said, lighting a cigarette.

You rubbed sleep from your eyes and squinted at the bright green numbers on the dashboard. It was 4:38 AM. The sky was still dark, but a faint pre-dawn glow was visible in the east. You yawned and stretched, your joints creaking. The pain in your head had returned. When you asked for the scotch, Derek shook his head but offered you a cigarette in its place. You declined and looked out the window. Up ahead you could see the familiar sign proclaiming, "WELCOME TO VILLA VIDA, HOME OF THE BULLDOGS!"

Yawning again, you asked Derek, "Is there any way I can shower at your place? I haven't showered in days. After that I'll get out of your hair." You almost added "Unless your boss has other plans," but thought better of it.

Derek didn't say anything.

Shifting uneasily in your seat and fidgeting a little, you said, "Or, um, you can just drop me off wherever. I can take it from here." In truth, you didn't know what you were going to do next, or where you were going to go. You hadn't planned that far ahead. When you left California, your goal had been to first Get Home and then Find Your Parents' Killer. Upon completing the first objective, which now seemed surreally miraculous in and of itself, you had no idea how to proceed toward the second phase of the mission.

Still, Derek said nothing. He turned right onto Main Street, and then right again into the parking lot of the Villa Vida police station. He edged up the curb toward the entrance, where two officers stood waiting alongside the flagpole.

It was too late to run. You doubted you would have been able to, anyway. Your head was heavy from the remnants of liquor and the blows you'd taken, and all of the strength had left your legs upon the realization that you'd been betrayed. You looked at Derek, feeling the wounded anger scrawl itself over your face. "What the fuck?" you croaked, sweat beginning to collect at your aching temples. He'd brought the car to a stop, and the officers were approaching. "What the fuck? Why?"

Avoiding your gaze, Derek said, "I'm supposed to tell you that this will all make sense very soon. That's all I know. I'm just the messenger."

The cops were standing outside the car, now. Lowering your voice and narrowing your eyes, you said, "I could tell them what you did, you know. I could rat you out."

Derek was unmoved by this. He just nodded and said, "Yeah, I know. But you won't." The first spikes of sunlight had begun to shoot up from the horizon, and Derek took a pair of Wayfarers from his center console and put them on. Then, unlocking the doors, he motioned his assent to the cops outside. One of them reached forward and yanked the handle, pulling your door open.

"This the runaway?" he asked. He braced one arm on the roof of the car and placed his other hand on your shoulder, his grip firm and unfriendly.

Derek nodded. "Yeah, this is him."

Leaning toward him, you whispered hatefully to Derek, "I won't forget this, asshole. This isn't the last you'll see of me."

Then Derek did look at you, and he smiled coldly. "I know," he replied. "But it will all make sense very soon. I was told to make sure you know that. It will all make sense. Much sooner than you think."

The officer unbuckled your seatbelt and hauled you unceremoniously from the car. Derek gave a curt nod, though whether it was directed to you or the cops, you couldn't be certain. He then reached across the seat and pulled the door shut before driving off with a screech of his tires.

Your head bowed, you placidly allowed the officers to lead you up toward the station's tinted glass doors. In that moment, so full of bubbling, frustrated rage, your failure felt profoundly absurd. To make it 2,300 miles only to be foiled at the very last moment...the whole thing reeked of random, cosmic indifference. Derek's assurance that it would eventually make sense seemed flat and empty. The idea that any meaning could ever be derived from this soul-crushing turn of events was beyond implausible.

And yet, you believed him.

The nature of his sudden insertion into your life was of such bizarre coincidence that it could only be described as supernatural. For as devastating as this setback was, you could not make yourself deny the feeling that something of grand scale was at work beyond the peripherals of your understanding.

Maybe, you reasoned, that was for the best.

Your own machinations had led you across the country and landed you in the lap of suburban law enforcement.

You were out of ideas.

Maybe it was time for someone else to start calling the shots.

After all, it was beginning to feel like someone else already was.

2

They didn't handcuff you, but they did lock you in a cold, gray interrogation room. You had expected they would do the former, not the latter. Sitting alone in the plain little room, your hands folded on your lap beneath the table and your back stiff against the straight-backed metal chair that was bolted to the floor, you felt more like a criminal than you would have if they'd slapped cuffs on you and locked you in a jail cell.

After sitting by yourself for the better part of an hour, your head still thrumming faintly from the mild hangover, one of the officers who'd taken you in entered the room and shut the door behind him. The heavy *clang* of the latch made you jump.

The cop had a bad spray tan and the bulging, unnatural muscles of a juiced-up gym rat. You could almost hear the threads on the sleeves of his uniform crying out in agony as they clung desperately to each other in a dire struggle to remain intact. His freshly-cropped crewcut was straight out of a discount salon likely specializing in children's haircuts and not much else.

If ever there existed a living stereotype of a douchebag cop, it was that asshole.

"I'm Officer Walpole," he said gruffly, flicking on the short lamp on the table and pointing its hooded bulb directly in your face. He grabbed the chair on the other side of the table (which was apparently *not* bolted to the floor as yours was) and whirled it around so he could straddle it and sit with his huge arms folded atop its back. He was working a fat wad of chewing gum with his rear teeth. You could smell the biting scent of spearmint riding the waves of his hot breath.

Resisting the urge to laugh at his over-the-top tough guy act, you lifted your hand to shield your eyes from the searing white light of the lamp. As soon as you did so, Walpole slammed his fist on the table and barked, "Put your goddamn hand down! I need to see your face. I need to see your *eyes*. It's how I'll know if you're lying."

You swallowed down a smart response, instead raising your chin and glaring at him. "I didn't do anything wrong," you said evenly. "I'm not a criminal."

"False statement, shithead. You're a runaway. You know what runaways are? They're criminals. You know why? Because it's *against the fuckin law for a kid to run away from home*. And you know what *else*? I've *also* been informed you're a killer. That's right. A cold-blooded killer."

You flinched, gritting your teeth and imagining yourself pummeling the cop's face in.

"Yup. Yessiree. Word is you killed your cousin. What kind of fucked up little shit kills his own goddamn cousin?"

"It was self-defense."

He nodded slowly, the gum smacking loudly in his cheek. "Yeah, I saw that. 'Self-defense.'" He used the middle and index fingers of both hands to put air quotes around the term. "That's what the report says, at least. Case closed. But that's according to *California*, and I know about those *Californians*. Bunch of pansy-ass fuckin pussies. Give you a smack on the wrist 'cause they don't want to offend anybody for this or that or the other. Well, we do things a little different here. And the way I see it, you're a fuckin murderer."

You weren't exactly up to date on murder statutes, but you were pretty sure the law didn't work like that. Still, you didn't think it was a good idea to argue.

Walpole leaned leeringly across the table. The aroma of his gum stung your nostrils. "I want you to listen to me *real* close," he said in a voice that fell somewhere between a whisper and a growl. "I'm gonna see to it that you spend a *long* time in..."

Before he could finish, the door flew open. Standing there was an attractive blonde woman with black-framed Gucci glasses and a stack of files under her arm. Her cheeks were flushed. She was wearing a peculiarly-constructed outfit comprised of a dark blue cashmere sweater, gray sweatpants, and worn Reebok sneakers. Her unbrushed yellow hair was pulled back in a hastily-tied ponytail.

Walpole looked up at her, and a strange electrical current passed between them, so saturated with a confusing mixture of hatred and sexual tension that you could almost hear the crackling of television static. He narrowed his eyes, and she in turn narrowed hers.

"Lance," she acknowledged him, her tone cold and remote.

"April." Walpole's face had become unreadable. The bulldog disposition had given way to something both bitter and forlorn, and maybe even a little tender. It was as though his head was trying to process more emotions than his simple mind was accustomed, and he was short circuiting.

The woman looked at you, and her face softened. "Lance, what the fuck is going on here? Why do you have a fucking light shining in his face? What is this, *LA Confidential?*"

Walpole's forehead turned an ugly shade of burgundy, though you didn't know whether it was from embarrassment or anger. "He's...a murderer," the cop said, lacking conviction now that he was faced with whatever authority this woman had over him.

"He's not, actually," said the woman, whisking over to the table and turning the lamp off. "I read his file. I'm taking over his case. You can go, now. Your services are no longer required."

Now he *was* angry, without doubt. He glowered up at her, his nostrils flaring, but reluctantly relinquished his seat when she made a shooing motion with her hand. He gave you one last murderous look, started to say something, then just shook his head and stormed out, slamming the door behind him.

The woman took a deep breath and brushed a stray lock of hair away from her face, tucking it behind her ear. The smile she offered you was an odd one; it was kind and sympathetic, but also distant and possibly even a little rehearsed. You suspected she'd worn that smile many times before, for many different people, in many different circumstances. It wasn't exactly fake, nor was it entirely genuine.

In any case, you didn't smile back.

"I'm sorry about that," she said, laying her files out in front of her and leafing through them. "Lance can be...difficult."

You didn't respond.

Meeting your gaze, the woman said, "My name is Dr. April Diver. You can call me April. I would prefer it if you did, actually. I'm a psychiatrist."

"I don't need a psychiatrist. I didn't do anything wrong."

She nodded with the same kind of put-on sympathy that had been present in her smile. "I know you didn't. I read the reports. I'm very sorry about what happened to your cousin. Were you close with her?"

You thought about lying and playing it down, but figured there was no real point in that, so you simply said, "I loved her. She was my best friend." Saying it aloud required you to suppress a surge of memories that threatened to rear up and trample you carelessly underfoot.

April reached across the table and took your hand. You didn't pull away, mostly because you didn't have the energy but also because the small gesture of kindness afforded you a small degree of comfort.

"Why did the cops send for a psychiatrist?" you asked, desperate to change the subject. You kept your voice to a whisper, because the exertion of speaking any louder would certainly have made you pass out.

"They didn't," April answered. "My brother told me you were here. I have a vested interest in the McPleasant killings, so I have a vested interest in *you*. Derek called me and told me he'd found you hitchhiking on the side of the road, and that he knew I'd want to talk to you."

The cogs of your mind, still sluggish from the intoxicants you'd imbibed the night before, cranked laboriously as you tried to piece together what she was saying. "Wait," you said. "That Derek guy is your brother?"

April nodded solemnly.

"He's a fuckin dick."

After coughing out a short laugh, April put a hand to her mouth and said, "Excuse me, I'm sorry, I shouldn't laugh. He *can* be a dick, yes, for sure. But this time I think his heart was in the right place, for once."

You doubted that.

This will all make sense very soon.

"Why did you come back here?" she asked. "Why come all this way from California, back to a place that holds such terrible memories?"

"There was nothing left for me in Los Angeles."

"What's left for you here?"

You didn't answer. You had one thing left here, and one thing only, and you wouldn't leave again until you made sure it was gone, too. Gone like everything else.

But you couldn't tell April that.

Hoping to divert her from her curiosity regarding the motives surrounding your return, you asked, "What's going to happen to me now?"

April considered before responding. When she did, she spoke slowly and cautiously, selecting her words with the care of an antique collector perusing an estate sale.

"First, we'll need to contact your aunt and uncle. If they request that we return you to their custody, we will do so. If..."

"They won't. They're not going to want me back."

The look in April's eyes suggested that she understood this, but she didn't acknowledge it. Instead, she continued by saying, "If they elect to surrender custody of you back to the state, the next step will be to find a guardian in the form of a foster family."

You'd figured that was coming, but the thought of it was still enough to make you shudder. "Why can't you just let me go?" As soon as the question was out, you heard how stupid it sounded and you wished you could take it back, if only for dignity's sake.

April's smile was patient. "Where would you go?" she asked softly, her voice measured and meticulously devoid of anything that could be interpreted as patronizing, though such a tone would have been warranted. When you didn't answer, she said, "You're lucky you didn't get caught in another state. At least here you'll be able to go back to school with all of the people you knew before you went to California. I don't know if you believe in fate, or destiny, but it wouldn't be out of the question to attribute your circumstances to one or both of those...phenomena."

"Do *you* believe in them?"

Her lips parted, ready to regurgitate whatever tried-and-true textbook line was applicable for such a question, but then she surprised you. She closed her mouth, took off her glasses, and folded them on top of her sheaves of paperwork. Clasping her hands on the table, she looked you dead in the eyes. There was something in her gaze that was profoundly tragic. It was the look of someone who has seen too much darkness, or maybe not enough light.

"No," she said. "I don't."

CHAPTER 23 – THE BREAKFAST CLUB

1

THINGS MOVED VERY FAST following your return to Ohio. After being expedited through the foster care process and placed under the custody of a stuffy tax accountant and his nasal-voiced paralegal wife, you were re-enrolled as a Villa Vida "bulldog," and by the third week of November you were stepping off the bus onto what you would come to silently refer to as "the prison grounds."

Your first day back to school was very telling of the months to come. You'd gone in with an attitude that couldn't quite be described as a chipped shoulder, but it was somewhere in that vicinity. You had no interest in befriending anyone or applying yourself to your studies any more than was necessary to get by. Derek-induced setback or not, your mission remained the same.

Hands in your pockets, shoulders stooped, and eyes trained on the ground, you resolved to make yourself an embodiment of the wraith you felt you'd become.

It was because of the downturned eyes that this plan backfired when you accidentally bumped into Felix Clerval before home-room on the Monday of your not-so-triumphant return. Felix had been something of a friendly acquaintance throughout your childhood; the two of you had never been tremendously close, but there'd never been anything approaching animosity between you, either. The same could not be said for his twin sister, Agatha, who'd always had a mean streak, but nothing that had ever escalated above stuck-up snobbery and the occasional jeer.

Even though it had only been a little over six months since you'd last seen Felix, he was nothing like you'd remembered him. Gone was the scrawny kid with braces and square-lensed glasses. In his place stood a broad-shouldered, mountainous man-child with an undercut pompadour and no glasses or braces to speak of. When you collided with him, his Starbucks latte flew from his oversized hand and exploded across the sneaker-scuffed tile floor.

Reflexively shoving you into a locker, Felix said, "Watch the fuck where you're going, you fucking..." He stopped short of finishing the insult and scrutinized you with squinted eyes. When the wires in his brain aligned properly, his eyes widened and he said, "Holy shit, no *way*. I heard rumors you were coming back, but I didn't think..." Trailing off, he looked over his shoulder and barked, "Hey, guys, come check out who's rolled into town."

From the swarming masses of students cramming the halls emerged a trio who, along with Felix, would thereupon become your devoted tormentors. Leading them was Agatha who, shaped like a stalk of asparagus and sporting an awful poodle-perm, had changed not at all since the previous spring. With her was Walton De Lacey, a preppy elitist kid who had, for as long as you could remember, dressed exclusively in Lacoste polo shirts and pleated slacks. Skulking behind them was a greasy kid named Bill Beaufort who, by sixth grade, was notorious for being an underachieving pothead with a disturbing affinity for huffing gasoline and Dust-Off.

Seeing them standing there before you...the jock, the burnout, the prep, and whatever the hell Agatha was...you had to suppress a laugh. California might be known for its stereotypes, but Ohio had its share of them, too. You would eventually start referring to them as "the Breakfast Club," though only to yourself and never to their faces.

"Felix," you said, straightening. "Great to see you, too."

The other three were still trying to figure out who you were, which was surprising; aside from a sun-lightened tint to your hair and an already-fading tan, you didn't think you looked much different. Oddly, Bill was struck with realization before Agatha or Walton. His face lit up with recognition, though his eyes remained unchangingly void and washed out. "Well, fuck me runnin," he said. "I thought you ran away to become a movie star after your parents got all hacked up, and shit. What happened? Tinseltown too big for ya?"

That sparked the *aha* moment for both Agatha and Walton. "Oh, fuck, that's *right*," said Agatha. "It *is* him. I was *just* reading a HuffPost article about him the other day, actually."

"Yeah, I remember him, now," said Walton. "Took me a sec. What did the article say about him, Ag? Are they still talking about his dead parents? I thought that shit was old news."

Agatha shook her head, her poofy hair shifting back and forth like a windblown topiary animal. "No, this shit is *new* news. Juicy as fuck, too. Get this...the little fucker *killed* his *cousin*."

"Holy fuckin *shit*," said Bill, his red eyes widening. "And they just let him go?"

"Apparently it was self-defense. I guess she was some druggy cunt who got fucked up on some weird acid shit and went totally nutso."

You came very close to hitting her when she said that. You still wish you had.

"I don't know," said Felix. "Seems pretty coincidental, don't you think? First his parents end up dead, then his cousin? Looks like a pattern, to me. Come on, Hollywood, you can tell us. Did you kill them? Was it you? Are *you* the Mudhoney Monster?"

"Fuck off," you grumbled, trying to squeeze past them. Felix blocked your path and pushed you back into the locker, harder this time. The back of your head slammed into the metal, making fireworks

...purple fireworks over Los Angeles, "Nights Like These," Mara and her Corvette and the Grinning Man and...

dance before your eyes. Blinking them away, you said, "I'm not going to fight you. Just leave me alone."

"Or what?" taunted Bill. "You'll *keeeel* us like you killed your family?"

Yes, you thought. *I will. I'll kill all of you, and I'll fucking get off on it.* An image appeared in your head with startling clarity: the four of them lying dead on a muddy playground beneath a rain-bleeding night sky. You blinked that away, too, somewhat shaken. Taking pains to ensure your voice remained level and assured, you said, "Get out of my way. All of you. Right. Now."

The Breakfast Club broke into a chorus of titters. "'Wah, wah, get out of my way,'" goaded Bill in a high-pitched voice. "'All of you, right now, wah, wah, wah.'"

"I'm not fucking around. Get out of..."

Before you could finish, Agatha stepped forward, grabbed your crotch, and squeezed. *Really* squeezed...not the way a lover would, the way Mara *did*, but the way someone would if they wanted to inflict the kind of indescribable pain that Agatha succeeded in delivering. You saw the purple fireworks again, but this time Mara wasn't among them. Your face drained of color and a shaky whimper escaped your throat. When she let go, you slid down the locker and put your head back, closing your eyes against the hot tears and breathing erratically.

"You should have stayed in Cali, Hollywood," said Felix. He kicked you in the stomach, making you slump over onto your side, but the pain in your groin was too great for you to really feel his attack.

"Better yet," said Agatha, "you should have just killed your cunting *self*. No one wants you back here. Whether you killed your parents, or not, you've got death crawling all over you. Like cunting leprosy. We are *not* into that shit."

"Cool," you croaked, rubbing your throbbing crotch. "Just leave me alone and you won't have to worry about catching my cunting leprosy."

"Don't get smart with us, fuckweasel," said Walton, kicking you in the ribs. You shrunk into a ball.

Bill kicked you in the shin and said, "Yeah, fuckweasel, don't get smart. We'll fuckin leprosy *you*."

Gritting your teeth as you tried to will your pain receptors into magically closing, you said, "Leprosy isn't a verb."

"I swear to fuckin God, you little fuckin..."

The bell rang, and the other students in the hall dispersed into their respective classrooms like rats into holes. Bill spat on you. The other three did the same.

"You're so fuckin leprosy, you don't even know it," said Bill.

"It's not an adjective, either."

Bill started toward you, but Felix stopped him and said, "We'll get him, buddy, don't worry. We've got the whole rest of the year to get him. And then we'll *keep* getting him." He spat on you again and said, "See you soon, Hollywood. See you *very* soon."

When they were gone, you struggled to your feet and shuffle-limped to your first class.

The teacher gave you a detention for being late.

2

Your life outside of school was no better. The problems started with Dr. April Diver, who was a nice enough woman but who had way too much faith in the powers of Western pharmaceuticals. From the start, she was convinced that you were suffering from severe depression. She said that this was, "Perfectly reasonable, given your circumstances, and nothing to be ashamed of." You told her you weren't ashamed of anything, but you didn't want to be put on drugs. She ignored you and prescribed you three antidepressants.

You hadn't intended to take them. Had, in fact, intended to flush them with extreme prejudice. Your foster parents, however, had a different agenda, saying "We will not live under the same roof as an unmedicated psychopath, no matter *how* much money the state is paying us." Because of this, both of them insisted upon watching you swallow the pills every night. They even checked your mouth with a flashlight to make sure you weren't holding them under your tongue.

Having lost that particular battle, you set out to convince April to take you off of the medication. During your weekly, court-mandated appointments with her, you employed a wide range of tactics to accomplish this goal, but all of them were foiled. First, you tried telling her that the drugs made you nauseous and gave you headaches. In turn, she prescribed two additional medications to counteract each fabricated side effect. When you told her the following week that the new pills failed to provide any relief from the ailments incurred by the antidepressants, she discontinued said new pills and replaced them with three different ones. Ironically, one, some, or all of those three additional drugs actually *did* make you suffer from nausea and headaches. You came clean and admitted that you'd lied the first time but were now telling the truth, but she didn't believe you and subsequently increased the dosage on all six of the medications.

After three months of this, you became resigned to the notion that you weren't going to get off of them. Wanting at least for her to stop jacking up the doses, you told her you were feeling great and that she should just leave the meds as they were. Delighted that your "depression" had been solved, she said it was time to hone in on your "anxiety" and started you off on three antianxiety medications.

You gave up fighting.

By the end of 2015, you were on eleven different drugs, all of them FDA-approved. You became paralyzingly docile and vegetative. Time not spent getting harassed and jumped at school was slept away in your door-less bedroom. It was difficult to pinpoint how responsible the medications were for your misery, because much of it could surely be attributed to your environmental situation. Before your first week of school had drawn to a close, everyone knew what had happened to Mara. Or, more accurately, *thought* they knew. As a result, you faced an endless barrage of scorn, ridicule, and violence at the hands of your classmates.

Worst of all, your hopes of finding McPleasant began to steadily wane until they disintegrated completely. Even if you'd had the energy to pursue your quest, your foster parents kept you so firmly beneath their thumbs that it would have been impossible, regardless. You had no access to any electronic devices more complex than a toaster, and you were forbidden to leave the house. You tried to escape numerous times, but quickly realized that it was a doomed venture due to your foster parents' high-tech custom security system that was designed for the sole purpose of keeping you prisoner. You had no idea how it worked, but if you even *approached* the front door after a certain time, an alarm on both of their Apple Watches would go off and they'd be out of bed and down the stairs, apprehending you before you could so much as utter the words, "What the fuck?"

Nor was there any possibility of escaping from school. Having been labeled what April called a "flight risk," you were under strict supervision while on school grounds. Every morning, a teacher would be waiting outside to escort you into the building as soon as the bus (which picked you up right from the house) arrived at the high school. A similar procedure was in place for the end of the day to ensure that you got on the bus, and one or both of your foster parents would be waiting on the porch when you got home.

In spite of the ever-watchful gaze of the school administration, the faculty always seemed to be struck temporarily blind whenever Felix and his cronies (or anyone else who felt like roughing you up) backed you into a helpless corner. On many occasions, teachers had stood and watched with folded arms and stern-but-approving faces as you got the shit kicked out of you.

Thoughts of suicide came to you constantly. The only thing that prevented you from throwing yourself in front of the school bus was the fear that the Grinning Man would be waiting for you on the other side. But as time went on, the desire for release started to ebb closer and closer to winning out over that fear. With your dreams of vengeance unrealized and out-of-reach, your new dreams consisted only of a visit from the Angel of Death to take you away from this hell on earth.

No such angel came, but on the one-year anniversary of your parents' death, you were visited by someone else.

It was a Tuesday afternoon, and you had just finished staring disinterestedly at your untouched lunch tray. You got up from the otherwise-empty table, dumped the tray's contents in the trash, and went into the bathroom. Turning on the faucet and cranking the left lever as far as it would go, you put your hands under the steaming water and breathed a relieved sigh. Shortly after returning to Ohio, you developed a problem in which your hands were always cold. You didn't know if it was nerves, the weather, or the drugs (one, some, or all of them), but holding your hands under hot water became one of a select few things in life that could provide you with a modicum of pleasure.

You were just beginning to nod off (falling asleep standing up was a new problem, too) when you heard the door bang behind you, jolting you into semi-alertness. You looked down to see that the scalding water was spilling over the edges of the sink with your pruned and reddened hands lying submerged in the basin like dead things. Hurriedly twisting the faucet off, you turned around to see the Breakfast Club sneering at you. Walton was twisting the lock.

"Happy Dead Mom-and-Dad Day," said Felix, rousing laughter from his friends even though you didn't think it was all that clever. "*The Plain Dealer* ran a piece on the Mudhoney Monster this morning. Said it's been a year to the day since his last killing. What do you think of that?"

"Nothing. I don't care."

Agatha finished checking her face in her compact mirror and then lit a cigarette. "I don't think it's been that long at all," she said. "*I* think he killed a certain druggy cunt in Cali last fall. Funny how they didn't mention anything about that in the article. They mentioned *you*, but not your cunty dead cousin."

"Go to hell," you said in a voice that lacked clear conviction. You *felt* angry and hateful, but you couldn't make yourself *sound* it.

"You know what pisses me off more than anything else, Hollywood?" Felix asked. "I mean, more than *anything* else. You want to know? Okay, okay, I'll tell you. What pisses me off more than anything else is when assholes like you do something fucked up and get away with it. Here you are, Villa Vida's own resident murderer, and you're walking around free as the rest of us. That shit is fucked, man. *Fucked*."

As you stared at him passively, you realized something that hadn't occurred to you until that very afternoon: Felix didn't *really* think you were a murderer. Maybe even Agatha didn't. Fuck, maybe *none* of them believed it. They probably didn't care one way or another. It was just a convenient excuse to terrorize you. Maybe they needed to *pretend* to believe it to justify their actions to themselves, but probably not. It likely wasn't that deep. *They* weren't that deep.

Were they?

Like a clicking Super-8 reel, a memory from long ago bubbled up in your mind. It was in first grade, or maybe second. School had just let out for the day, and you were walking toward where your mother's car was idling in the pickup/drop-off lane along the side of VVPS. The side door on a minivan a few cars behind your mother's slid open, and a raggedy-haired border collie came bounding out onto the lawn and beelined past you. You turned to see Felix rush to meet it, bending down and welcoming it into his arms. The squeals of his high-pitched laughter mixed with the dog's excited barks as it lapped at his face. Agatha joined them, and the dog rolled over in the grass as its two humans showered it with affectionate petting.

"Hell*ooo?* Anybody in there, Hollywood?" said Felix, smacking his chewing gum.

You blinked yourself back into the present. "Huh?"

"He *asked* you," said Agatha, "if you fucked your cousin before you killed her. Or did you wait till after, when she wouldn't struggle?"

That did it. The damp fuse within you that wouldn't light finally caught fire, and you ran at her with a raised fist.

Felix and Walton caught you with no visible exertion of effort. They each took one of your arms and dragged you toward one of the stalls, kicking it open and shoving you down on your knees in front of the toilet. Its bowl was filled with yellow-brown urine.

"Were you really gonna hit a fucking *girl?*" said Felix. "That is fucked *up.* I guess that's your style, though, huh, Cousin Killer? Walton, let's show him what we do to twats who hit girls."

You opened your mouth to beg for mercy right before they dunked your head into the piss-filled toilet. The acrid fluid poured down your throat and shot up your sinuses. You flopped your arms, your eyes and throat burning. All attempts to break free were easily thwarted. You felt yourself losing the battle to remain conscious. The edges of your thoughts crinkled and darkened like smoldering paper. You were just about to let yourself go when they hauled you up and shoved you out of the stall, sending you sliding across the floor. You sat up, choking on sour coughs and trying to rub the fire from your eyes.

You looked up just in time to catch a fist in your face.

You never found out whose it was.

It didn't matter.

They were all the same.

3

Nothing out of the ordinary happened on the night you finally decided to kill yourself. There was no specific catalyst, and the decision wasn't preceded by any mournful contemplation. You weren't listening to Hawthorne Heights. It was just another humid August night like any other; you'd spent the day cooped up in your room, as you had done all summer, passing intermittently from partial waking into half-sleeping, the intervals between which were irregular and unmeasured.

You stirred from a fitful doze around midnight, wakened by music from outside. Dragging yourself out of bed, you shuffled to your open window. The neighbors were having a bonfire, blasting "Zombie" by the Cranberries. You could see the silhouettes of several shadow couples swaying together in the grass on alcohol-unsteadied feet.

You shut your eyes and swayed with them. A balmy gust of wind swept the curtains around you. You gripped the windowsill and breathed it in.

The thought that flared in your mind when you opened your eyes was, *Fuck it.*

Fuck it.

After a final glance at the shadow people, you left your room and tiptoed down the hall, listening for your foster parents. They were still awake, and you could hear them talking downstairs. Their voices were loud and jolly with drink; they imbibed only on Friday nights, but when they did, it didn't take much for them to get tipsy. For a short second you thought about making a run for it, but then again thought, *fuck it.* It wasn't worth the disappointment of failure.

After retrieving a jug of Drano from the utility closet, you slunk back into your bedroom, took a tall plastic cup from your nightstand, and filled it nearly to the brim.

"Fuck it," you said aloud, and lifted the cup toward your mouth.

The lip of the cup was perhaps a centimeter away from the point of no return when you heard an explosion of shattering glass from downstairs.

You spun around, dropping the cup and staining the carpet blue. You had enough time to briefly muse on how your guardians might punish you for the stain, and then the loud sounds of a combative struggle began to emanate up from the living room. Things were being knocked over. Your foster mother screamed. A second later, so did her husband.

You were frightened, but there was something else, too. Another feeling. Something you hadn't felt since before Mara's death.

Excitement.

You couldn't explain it...there was no reason you should be excited by what sounded like a violent burglary, but you were excited nonetheless. It wasn't anything approaching giddiness or elation, but it was *something*. Maybe it was the prospect of potential death at the hands of whatever criminals had just broken into your home. Maybe you were simply glad that *something* was happening, because *nothing* of note had happened in what felt like a very long time.

Or maybe it was something more.

Something you knew, had perhaps *always* known, but couldn't yet define.

You waited. More screams from downstairs...both the woman and the man at the same time, now. And then...laughter. Yes, definitely laughter. Not from your foster parents, but from whoever had broken in. Whoever was making them scream.

PART III – THE DEAD OF NIGHT

CHAPTER 24 – ONE OF US

1

YOU WAKE TO FIND Erzsebet sitting in the armchair by the window, sucking on a lollipop and reading a worn paperback copy of *The Memnoch the Devil*. When you sit up and yawn, she closes the book on her lap and folds her hands on its cover.

"It's time," she says, taking the sucker out of her mouth. Her voice is grave. Her lips are candied purple.

"Time for what?"

"For you to prove that you're one of us. I believe you are. Varney and Mircalla do, too. But you still have to prove it. We all did."

"I have to kill someone, right?"

Erzsebet doesn't answer with her voice, but with her eyes. Their green fire, hot and radiant in the scant light of the bedroom, tells you everything you need to know.

"Who?" you ask.

She shrugs. "None of us know. Ambrosio told Varney where we need to go, but he didn't tell him who would be there." After a heavy pause, she asks, "Can you do it? *Will* you do it?"

Instead of replying, you get out of bed and get dressed.

2

Varney and Mircalla are waiting in the foyer when you and Erzsebet come downstairs. Their smiles, though genuine enough, can't mask their apparent anxiety. They're jittery and preoccupied. Varney is leaning on his cane and sucking hard on a cigarette, and Mircalla is fidgeting with the various pockets on his black satin romper.

"Big night, kid," Mircalla says, clapping you on the back and beaming a big nervous smile. "You ready for this shit?"

"He's ready," Erzsebet says in a staid tone. "Let's go."

Varney drives in relative silence. The music is turned down to a murmur, and the only other sounds are that of exhaled smoke and the timid night rushing by outside. Occasionally, the distant rumble of a rolling thunderclap will resonate from the rain-threatening sky.

"Where are we going?" you ask Varney. Wherever it is, you don't want to get there. Erzsebet is huddled close to you in the back seat, and you want only to remain here for as long as possible. If eternal life is a possibility, then let it only be this.

"Where Ambrosio told me to go," Varney answers cryptically. "That's all I can say. It will all make sense very soon."

3

When Varney turns into the dark, nearly-empty parking lot of the Villa Vida Primary School, your joints lock up and your mouth goes dry. This is a place that belongs in your past, not your present. It belongs to a life before Mara, before McPleasant, before the orphaning catastrophe that had befallen you just over a year ago. It belongs to someone else.

Varney parks the Phantom diagonally across three lanes and kills the ignition. "We're here!" he announces in a cheery singsong voice. "Come, my brethren, let us make haste. The night beckons us forth." The only other car in the parking lot is a white Volvo that looks mildly familiar, but you can't place it.

You all get out of the car and follow Varney onto the school's newly-tended lawn and around the corner of the long brick building. There's a playground in the back, and that's where he leads you. As you draw closer to it, you can make out four figures in the darkness, their drunken laughter cutting into the still night air.

A thunderclap sounds from overhead, closer than it had been earlier. You can smell the mildewy scent of impending rain in the air. A cool gust of pre-storm wind blows over the flat terrain, and you pull your hood up.

When you reach the edge of the playground, Varney holds up a hand, signaling the rest of you to stop. You push your sunglasses down the bridge of your nose so you can peer over the lenses and see if you're able to recognize any of the four shadows.

After a moment, you recognize all of them.

The first one you notice is Agatha Clerval. She's sitting on one of the swings, the chains whining as she sways forward and back. The toes of her sneakers drag audibly in the dirt and wood shavings.

Her brother, Felix, is reclining in the sandbox. A cigarette hangs from his upper lip, and a bottle of Miller Lite rests between his legs.

Bill Beaufort is sitting at the top of the slide, transfixed by something on his phone screen. The blue light casts his slovenly face in an unflattering manner.

Walton De Lacey is perched atop the monkey bars, trying to light a joint with a dying Bic.

"I surmise that you know these blokes?" Varney asks you, his gaze cycling through the four sadistic teenagers.

"Yeah," you respond after swallowing a mouthful of cold, thick saliva. "I do."

"Well I'll be god-*fuckin*-damned," says Felix, standing up. "If it isn't Mr. Hollywood. To what do we owe *this* pleasure? Couldn't wait till school starts back up to see us again?"

You feel your hands close into fists, thinking of the last time you'd seen the Breakfast Club. They'd stuffed you in a garbage can in the cafeteria during finals week. You'd had to take your Algebra exam covered in pizza toppings and yogurt.

Felix looks at your companions. "You finally make some friends, Cousin Killer? That's cute. They could use some help in the wardrobe department, though." He gestures at Mircalla. "Is that dude wearing a fucking *romper?*"

"It's unisex," Mircalla says.

Felix and his friends burst into laughter. Walton falls off the monkey bars.

"And what's with *your* outfit, Hollywood?" Felix says to you. He kills his cigarette and then drops it into the sandbox. "Who are you supposed to be, the Unabomber?"

Your fists tighten. Your teeth clench.

"Wow," Varney says, stroking the head of his cane. "These guys are assholes."

"Says the fag dressed like Charles Dickens," heckles Bill from atop the slide, inciting more laughter from the group of bullies.

With a taunting smirk, Varney points his cane at Bill and challenges, "Name *one* book that Dickens wrote."

Bill grins confidently. "Easy. *For Whom the Bell Tolls.*"

Now it's your group's turn to laugh. Even you find yourself chuckling a little; you can't remember who wrote *For Whom the Bell Tolls*, but you know it wasn't Dickens. Despite the darkness, you can see Bill's nose and cheeks turn the color of cranberries.

A jagged shaft of lightning splits the sky apart, and you feel raindrops begin to patter on your shoulders and the hood of your sweatshirt.

Agatha gets up off the swing and goes to stand by her brother. "Let's get out of here," she says to him. "The rain is going to fuck up my hair."

Erzsebet cocks an eyebrow and says, "Honey, what's there to fuck up? What did that godawful perm cost you, anyway? Ten bucks at Best Cuts? If you paid any more than that, darling, you were *robbed*."

Agatha's pinched, rat-like face folds into a horrid scowl. "Ex-*cuse* me? You better watch your cunting tongue, Cruella De Vil, before I..."

"Before you *what?* Douse me with hairspray?"

Agatha snarls and starts toward Erzsebet, but Felix holds her back. He pulls from his beer and then points at you. "Listen here, you Cali libtard fuck. I don't know what kind of trouble you're looking for, but this is *not* the place you want to find it. If you don't believe me, *try* me. We'll squash you and your candyass friends like the little bitches you are."

Varney sniggers. "You're quite wrong about *that*, my good man," he says. "For it is *you* who shall be squashed this night. Your comrade's incorrectly-attributed book title was actually rather prophetic, because tonight, the bell tolls for *thee*."

"Sounds like fightin words, to me," Walton says, standing up and brushing wood shavings off his person.

Bill slides down the slide and chimes, "Fuckin-A right. These assclowns are obviously lookin to get taught a lesson, or two. And since school don't start for another week, it's our moral subjugation to teach 'em, don't ya think?"

"*Obligation*," Varney corrects him. "It's your moral *obligation*."

Bill cracks his knuckles. "Okay, Felix, for real. I've had it with this fuckin douche. Say the word and I'll rip him wide open."

The rain is falling harder. Its heavy steel-gray sheets pelt the earth in a fretful torrent. Another flare of lightning flashes across the charcoal sky.

"Last chance, Hollywood," Felix warns. "Back off now, and we'll settle this when we're not getting our asses soaked."

Your companions look to you, and you realize they're waiting for your go-ahead. This is *your* show, *your* test. How they proceed with this particular fight is entirely dependent upon you. This is your make-or-break moment. What you do right now will determine your entire future, or lack thereof. Should you choose to engage your tormentors in battle, you're guaranteed a seat among your friends' immortal ranks. Provided, of course, you survive said battle. If you turn a pacifist's cheek, however...well, that will almost certainly ensure the end of everything.

If you're being completely honest with yourself, you really aren't sure which option is more appealing.

Looking upon the rain-dripping faces of those vicious schoolyard tyrants, though, something happens inside of you. Logic and reason sloughs away like a layer of necrotic flesh, making way for pure, unbridled emotion. You think of every damaging word Felix and his cohorts ever uttered against you. You think of every beating, every blow. All of the malicious rumors and the jeering insults. You think of how they so callously mocked your suffering, turning such sensitive subjects as Mara's death and your parents' murder into nothing more than a string of cruel jokes.

Standing there, contemplating homicide, you aren't thinking of the future. You aren't thinking of what will happen if you do this, or if you don't. You aren't thinking about living forever, nor are you thinking about dying. All you're thinking about is the past, and what the past has done to you.

And if there exists any better personification of your past than these four pricks, you don't know what it is.

You look at Erzsebet. At Mircalla. At Varney.

This has already happened, you think to yourself with a jolt of déjà vu. *It's already going to happen. I couldn't stop it even if I wanted to. And I don't want to stop it.*

When you speak, you don't recognize your voice. It is not the voice of a fifteen-year-old orphan boy. It's not the voice of a boy, at all. It's an evil voice, full of hate and suffering and anguish. It's the voice of resentment, of lies, of rage.

It is the voice of Death.

"Kill them all."

And then, you charge.

Everyone charges.

You go straight for Felix, and he for you. Beside you, Erzsebet and Agatha rush at each other. Mircalla pairs with Walton, and Varney with Bill.

All four duos collide in unison to the accompanying clamor of a thunderclap.

Felix may be bigger than you, but his footing falters at the last second when your shoulder connects with his chest, sending him sprawling backward in an explosion of mud and wood-chips. You fall astride him and manage to deliver three quick punches to his face before he recovers and hurls you off of him. He smashes the beer bottle on the side of the sandbox, creating a makeshift knife for himself. For the first time, it occurs to you that you're unarmed.

You risk a quick glance to your right. Erzsebet has drawn her dagger, but Agatha has gotten on top of her and has one hand around her throat and the other pinning Erzsebet's knife-wielding arm to the ground. Erzsebet uses her own free hand to claw at Agatha's face, her deadly nails raking bleeding lines across her opponent's forehead and cheeks. Agatha wails in pain but doesn't relinquish her grip.

Mircalla and Walton are both on their feet. Mircalla has drawn his dagger, as well, but Walton has, in turn, produced a mean-looking pocket knife with serrated edges. The two of them circle each other, slashing wildly, the blades missing one another by hair-width fractions of space.

Varney's knife is still sheathed on his belt. He's swinging his cane at Bill like a baseball bat, but Bill is proving to be surprisingly deft in his evasive movements, ducking and weaving with an ease that renders Varney red-faced and exasperated.

You redirect your attention back to Felix in time to see him lunge at you with the broken bottle. You roll out of the way and the sharp end of the bottle sinks into the ground where your heart had been a tenth of a second ago. Felix yanks it free as you scramble to your feet. He comes at you again, swinging the weapon in wide, sweeping arcs. You start to feel yourself travel back to the night of your fifteenth birthday, when Mara had attacked you in much the same fashion, but you shake away the memory and focus on the present. You need to remain rooted here on this rainy playground, wholly engaged with the current threat. If you allow yourself to slip backward into a different time, a different universe, the real one will eat you alive.

Felix's next swing is high, so you go low. You crouch down and then spring frog-like into his abdomen, driving your shoulder into his stomach. He doubles over with a loud *oof*, landing on his side in the mud. The bottle rolls from his hand and out of his reach.

Erzsebet and Agatha are still wrestling on the ground, clawing and striking at each other in such a mad flurry that it's impossible to determine who has the upper hand. Erzsebet is no longer pinned down, but the knife has been knocked from her hand. She's keeping her face pressed close to Agatha's body to shield it from her blows, but that prevents her from getting in any solid strikes of her own. Both of them are covered in woodchips and marinated in a dark glaze of mud.

Felix is clutching his stomach and groaning. You bend down to pick up the broken bottle, advancing toward him with your face set in a murderous scowl and your rain-soaked hair hanging over the lenses of your sunglasses.

Varney's cane finally connects with Bill's forehead, but Bill doesn't go down. He staggers sideways, but instead of falling, he delivers a surprise kick to Varney's ankle. Varney *does* go down, his hat toppling off and his cane flying into the mud. He lands on the slide, its aluminum frame quivering with a metallic thrum.

You get on top of Felix, brandishing the bottle and putting your knee on his chest.

Mircalla thrusts his dagger at Walton's face, who dodges in time to avoid losing his eye, but not quickly enough to prevent the tip of the blade from slicing off the top of his ear. Walton yowls, dropping his knife. He slaps one hand to his bleeding ear, and with the other hand he makes a fist that he slams into Mircalla's kidney. Mircalla cries out and retreats two steps before losing his balance and falling onto his back.

You grab a handful of Felix's hair and tilt his head to the sky. Raindrops plink into his lolling eyes, collecting there and then spilling down the sides of his face like tears.

Walton takes his bloodied hand from his ear and holds it up to his face, blinking at it in disbelief. "That's it," he growls down at Mircalla, stopping to pick up his pocket knife. "*Now* I'm *really* going to fucking kill you."

Mircalla gathers himself to his feet, shaking woodchips out of his hair. Then, to Walton's visible surprise, he laughs.

"The *fuck* is so funny, romper boy?"

"Dude," Mircalla says, "you *can't* kill me. You can't kill *any* of us."

"Oh yeah? Why's that, fuckface?"

"Because, dude. We're fuckin immortal." At that, Mircalla lunges forward and plants his dagger in Walton's chest. Walton's face goes slack, and he looks at Mircalla the way a baby looks at an adult who's snatched away its favorite toy. Mircalla returns the look with an evil grin, and then pulls the knife out of Walton's chest so he can swipe its blade across his throat.

For a second, it's as though Mircalla hasn't done anything at all because Walton's neck appears undamaged. But then a thin line appears, one that seems to rapidly darken and thicken until a sudden fountain of blood sprays out. It makes the loud hiss of a shaken soda bottle that's been opened before its carbonated contents have had the chance to settle.

At the same moment that the blood explodes onto Mircalla's face, Varney leaps off the slide and tackles Bill, forcing him to the ground and jabbing his thumbs into his eye sockets. Bill's shriek is short-lived, because Varney quickly draws his dagger, lifts it over his head with both hands, and plunges it down into the center of the blinded boy's forehead.

And at the same moment that Bill's scream is silenced by Varney's hack-job lobotomy, Erzsebet wrangles out of Agatha's grasp and slashes the side of her neck with her stiletto nails, rending open her adversary's jugular.

And at the same moment that Agatha's lifeblood begins to squirt from the ragged wound in her throat, you're just about to plunge the broken bottle into the exact same place on her brother's neck when you think of the dog.

The vision is every bit as clear as it had been the day in the bathroom earlier this year. Felix, running to greet his dog and laughing as it assailed his face with slobbery kisses. The dog had no idea what that giggling boy in grade school would grow up to be. To the dog, Felix was just an object of adoration and a source of safety and comfort. Right now, it's probably sleeping by the door and waiting for him to come home. It will know nothing of its master's transgressions. Felix will walk inside, and the dog will...

No, you think. *Fuck that shit. The dog is probably dead by now, anyway.*

You stab the bottle into your enemy's throat.

But when the glass pierces Felix's skin, it *isn't* glass, and it *isn't* Felix. The bottle is a cake knife, and Felix is Mara. In spite of your dire attempts to remain in the moment, you're helplessly transported back to that night by the pool with Mara on top of you and the knife in her side, inserted there by your own hand. The playground vanishes, and you're surrounded by horrified party guests. Your senses sharpen to superhuman levels. You can smell Justine's coppery blood as the gently-sloshing pool water laps at her floating corpse. You can hear Quincey's belabored heartbeat as he lies broken in the grass. You can feel the sweaty, sticky fear coming off Ianthe and Rebecca in roiling waves as they watch in wide-eyed terror. You can taste the cherries and peppermint that Mara's final kiss had left upon your lips, just as all of her kisses had. Most of all, you can see the light leaving your cousin's eyes...first the terrible purple glow that was not hers, and then the ocean-blue shimmer that was. You can see the light leave her, taking with it all of the light she had sparked within you.

You blink.

The party disappears again, and all of the nightmares that came with it. You're back on the playground, looking not into Mara's eyes but Felix's. The light is fading from them, too, but it had been a dim light and it had meant nothing to you.

Beneath the sound of the rain, you can hear a trickling noise. The kind of noise made when a person urinates into a toilet. You look around dumbly, and then realize that it's the sound of Felix's blood swirling into the dark green half-cylinder of the busted beer bottle. You pull the bottle out of his neck and stand up, looking down at him as the ground around his head darkens into a ghastly maroon halo.

Erzsebet comes over and takes your hand. You start to say something to her, but then you hear a small sound come from Agatha. She's writhing weakly, her hands pressed against her neck. You stalk over to her with a hard grimace. Forcing her mouth open, you shove the broken bottle into it as far as it will go. It makes a satisfying *crunch* when you kick her in the jaw. Her dying eyes fill with tears as she turns her head to the side and tries to cough out splintered shards of glass and teeth.

"That's for calling my cousin a druggy cunt," you say. You kick her again, and the glass breaks further. Then you hunker down, holding her mouth closed with one hand and pinching shut her nostrils with the other. She squirms, the broken glass tinkling against her ruined teeth. After a few moments of struggle, she does what you'd hoped she would do.

She swallows.

Her throat moves in accordance with the action, causing a fresh squirt of blood to shoot from between her fingers. Her face, more like a rodent's than ever, warps into a mask of agony that no decent person should ever have to endure.

But this is no decent person.

The first swallow is followed by an accidental second, and then a reflexive third as her throat attempts to clear the harmful obstructions collecting within it. When you remove your hands, thick streams of blood gush from her mouth and nose. She gasps pitifully and tries to scream, but all that does is make her swallow a fourth time. Tinges of blue creep into her cheeks, deepening to the point of absurdity until she stops moving and whatever light had been in her eyes is gone, too.

You stand and turn around. Your friends, all of them covered in mud and blood and wood shavings, are standing stock-still and looking at you with something approaching veneration. Varney had re-adorned his hat after killing Bill, but now he removes it again and falls to one knee. Bowing his head, he says reverentially, "He is one of us."

"One of us," Mircalla echoes with an equal amount of solemn admiration, also getting on one knee and bowing his head.

Erzsebet smiles at you and takes off her sunglasses, her emerald stare piercing your soul. She drops to both knees, bows her head even lower than the others, and repeats, "One of us."

One of us.

You look up at the black sky.

The rain has stopped.

CHAPTER 25 – ROYAL FLUSH

1

"GO ALL THE WAY up to the top of the stairs. It'll be the first door on the left."

These are the instructions Varney gives you when you get back to the mansion. The four of you are standing in the foyer, still wet and filthy like bedraggled coyotes.

"Is it going to hurt?" you ask. "Dying, I mean. Will it hurt?"

You'd thought they might laugh, but they don't. Their smiles are mirthless. Erzsebet says, "No, it's not going to hurt. There will be no pain at all. It won't feel at all like dying, really. Your body doesn't shut down, or anything. It's like...it's like it gets kicked into overdrive. Your heart won't even stop."

"On the contrary," says Varney, "it'll go on beating forever."

"Unless someone puts a stake through it," says Mircalla.

"That won't happen," says Erzsebet. "I mean, like, who even uses wooden stakes anymore, anyway?"

You look at the stairs, your anxiety building. "How does it..."

"No more questions," Varney says. "Ambrosio will tell you everything you need to know. Now go."

With a heavy sigh, you start toward the stairs. You look once more back at Erzsebet, and the smile she gives you fills you with the necessary courage to begin to climb.

2

Upon entering the wide chamber behind the heavy wooden door at the top of the staircase, the first thing you notice is the women. There's an entire harem of them, all of them beautiful and young and in various stages of undress. They lounge about on the numerous sofas and loveseats and armchairs, and a tangle of them is engaged in a writhing orgy within the sheets of the enormous bed. Their blood-flushed flesh glows in the amber light cast from the countless candelabras and wall-mounted torches.

Your attention is then struck by the perplexing presence of Derek Diver, the Batman who had come to your rescue last year when you'd been so sure you were going to meet your doom under the lonely sky of that fateful Illinois night. He's reclining in a plush leather armchair with a cigarette in one hand and a highball in the other. A topless girl with crow-feather hair and implausibly long lashes is sitting in his lap, lightly stroking his tan face. He acknowledges you only with an impersonal stare, saying nothing.

A figure emerges from the shadowy far corner of the room, and every molecule in your body seizes up with confounding dread and disbelief. Your heart clangs and sputters like the rusty engine of a dying car, grinding to a brief and silent stop before lurching forward into a hammering, anticipatory drumroll.

You should have known.

You really should have known, and the perturbed astonishment in your stomach is accompanied by deep-seated shame for not having guessed that this was how things would turn out.

The man from the shadows comes to stand in the center of the room, grinning his unbearable grin and holding his arms out wide as if he were welcoming an old friend. Which, perhaps, he is.

He's eschewed his tattered street clothes in favor of a lavish costume of elegant apparel and gaudy accessories. His white, creaseless dress shirt has lace ruffles down the front and at the cuffs of the sleeves. He still has the ivory cowboy boots, but the torn jeans in which you'd last seen him have been replaced by cerulean velvet trousers. A long black cape hangs over his shoulders, fastened by a length of thick golden twine.

Everything else about him is the same. The stylishly swept-back hair, the smooth white skin, the burning black eyes sparkling in the firelight. The too-long fingers. The *grin*.

"My *dear* boy," he says warmly, "what an *exquisite* pleasure it is to have you as a guest in my home." He clasps his hands in a prayer-like gesture and bows his head in a show of gentlemanly deference.

Sweat breaks out behind your ears and in the crooks of your arms. "You're..."

"Ambrosio Cotard," he finishes for you, "at your service. And have I not, indeed, *always* been at your service?"

"I...don't understand," you say, but you aren't sure if the words are audible because your throat is painfully scratchy and dry.

"Oh, come on, kid. This isn't exactly a plot twist."

You try to retort with something mildly clever, but all that comes out is an ugly hacking noise, like a cat coughing up a hairball.

Ambrosio frowns a little, his expression one of dutiful concern. He signals to one of the girls and says, "You, get the poor kid a drink, will you? The poor lad can barely talk."

With expedient compliance, the girl brings you a finger of whiskey in a crystal tumbler. She drops to her bare knees and holds it up to you like an offering to a god. You take it from her and knock it back like they do in the movies. Coughing, your eyes burning, you thank her hoarsely. She scurries away, and you look back at Ambrosio. "What is going on?" you ask him, your voice husky from the liquor. "What are you doing here?"

Wagging his long index finger back and forth, Ambrosio says, "Now, now, don't start launching into your usual torrent of stupid questions. You're a smart kid. Don't get bogged down by practicality. After all, let's face it...you can't *really* be *that* surprised by this turn of events."

"What about *him?*" you ask, shooting a pointed glare at Derek. "What's *he* doing here?"

Ambrosio sighs. "I guess that's a *halfway*-fair question. Derek is sort of my...*assistant*, I suppose. He does my bidding and unwaveringly responds to my every whim without even the faintest hesitation. Like, say, when I sent him to rescue you from those rapey scoundrels last year. He's basically my Renfield, if you will. Though, mercifully, he doesn't eat flies or spiders or anything like that."

You don't catch the reference, and from the puzzled look on Derek's face, he doesn't, either, but you don't ask for elaboration.

Ambrosio then waves to another one of the girls, and she wheels over a luxurious leather desk chair. He sits down and crosses his legs, grinning over his steepled fingers. "Now," he says, "let's get to the fun stuff. Your friends speak very highly of you. All three of them have assured me that you would be a welcome addition to the legions of the night."

"You make it sound like it's a treehouse club."

Running a hand through his hair and sighing again, Ambrosio answers impatiently, "Whatever. Call it what you like. The point is, they are adamant that you are quite worthy of the immortality that I can bequeath you. I tend to agree, even in spite of your habit of asking abhorrently dumb questions. I've always thought you were fated for greatness. That's why I pulled so many strings to get you here. And, you must admit, all of that string-pulling was pretty impressive, am I right? Look at how everything lined up so intricately and landed you here before me tonight. That's some grade-A predestination shit, if I may say so myself."

You nod slowly. "Yeah. I guess so. But I don't know what you see in me. Or what they do. I haven't done anything."

Without having to be summoned, one of the girls brings Ambrosio a pack of Dunhills, putting one in his mouth and lighting it for him. He compensates her with a kiss upon the back of her hand. His black eyes never leave yours during this brief transaction.

Taking a long drag, Ambrosio says, "Look, I could feed you some line of inflated bullshit about how I 'care about *all* my children', or whatever, but that kind of indulgent placation really isn't my jam. No, what it really comes down to is this: I like to be entertained. Your juvenile quest for vengeance is superbly entertaining to me, and I want to give you the tools you need in order for you to perpetuate it."

"This isn't some game. It's my life."

Ambrosio responds with an exaggerated, eye-rolling shrug. "Semantics. Now, do you want my help, or not?"

You shift from one foot to the other, casting a nervous glance over your shoulder at the door from whence you'd come. You could leave right now and be done with all of it. Yes, the thought of ditching your eternally-welcoming friends is an unpleasant one, but you think you could do it. Have, in fact, done it before. You could go back downstairs and walk out the door and forever leave behind the Grinning Man and his murderous band of pranksters. It wouldn't be easy, but you could do it.

But...could you, though?

If nothing else, the Grinning Man has proven that he's about as easy to get rid of as an AIDS infection. He'd followed you to Cleveland all the way from California, and had carefully orchestrated the events in your life to ensure you'd end up here before him tonight. You very much doubt that you can shirk yourself of his presence just by walking away.

And then there's the issue of McPleasant. Before Varney & Friends had showed up, you'd resigned yourself to the notion that vengeance would never be yours. Now that it's being offered so freely to you...it *seems* free, at least...how can you turn it down?

Lastly, there's Erzsebet. She's not Mara, but there's something indisputably special about her, in her own right. You'll never love anyone the way you loved your cousin, but the thought of Erzsebet's glowing green eyes and the feeling of her sharp acrylic nails on your skin makes you think that she just might be able to provide the salve needed to mend your broken heart.

"You've got it pretty bad for the girl, don't you?" Ambrosio asks, sinking further into his chair and blowing a succession of smoke rings into the air. "First your cousin, now a blood-drinking runaway. You sure do know how to pick 'em."

"Leave Mara out of this." After a moment's consideration, you add, "And Erzsebet. Leave her out of it, too. This isn't about either of them."

Ambrosio raises his eyebrows and leans forward. "Kid, be-*lieve* me, it's about *both* of them in more ways than you can imagine."

You're about to ask him to clarify, but decide you don't want to run the risk of irritating him with more of your "stupid questions." Taking another direction, you ask, "How does it work? Do you have to...are you going to bite me?" The thought of the Grinning Man's teeth on your throat makes you want to shiver, but you suppress it.

Ambrosio laughs, his black eyes twinkling. "Fuck, kid. Haven't you been tooling around with your little undead pals long enough to realize that most of the shit you see in the movies is nonsense? No, I'm not going to bite you, for fuck's sake."

"What, then?"

"Oh, it's a very simple procedure, really. You just let the blood in."

You blink at him, not understanding but not willing to open yourself up to ridicule by asking what he means. Perhaps pleased by this, he explains without your having to inquire. "It's a Hemingway reference," he says. "Well, sort of. I changed it a little, but the essence remains the same."

"I never read any Hemingway."

"Are you for *real?* No Shakespeare, no Hemingway...have you read *anything?*"

You think for a second and then shrug. "*Where the Red Fern Grows*. And, like, some Dr. Seuss, I guess."

Ambrosio laughs again. "You kill me, kid, I swear. Anyway, listen...it really *is* very simple. All you have to do is drink some of my blood. Drink from me and live forever."

"That *is* from a movie."

He shrugs. "So what. It's fitting."

"You said the shit from the movies is nonsense."

"I said *most* of it is nonsense. With as many movies as there are, a handful of them were bound to get a thing or two right. Speaking of which, Varney *did* explain the rules, yes? You know not to go sunbathing or impaling yourself on any wooden stakes, right?"

"You know he did. You know everything."

"Except calculus."

"Fuck you."

Ambrosio pretends to be offended, letting out a long whistle. "Well, *shucks*. I'm offering you the dark gift of immortality, and all I get is a 'fuck you'? *That* isn't very nice *at all.*"

"I didn't accept your 'dark gift,' yet."

Rolling his eyes again, Ambrosio says, "Jeepers *creepers*, kid, do you want to consult a Magic 8-Ball, or something? Maybe sift through some tea leaves? Seriously, what the fuck is there to consider? This is a no-brainer. It's what you're *meant* to do. It's what you were *always* meant to do. You've spent your life sitting there with a royal flush in your hand while everyone around you is playing Go Fish. It's high time you came to the grownups' table."

You bite the inside of your cheek and look back at the door again. Last chance. If you don't leave, your fate will be eternally bound to the Grinning Man and all of his malevolent whims. You will belong to him forever. If you don't get off this hell-bound ride right the fuck now, you never will.

Then again, you probably never would, either way.

You probably already belong to him.

You take a step forward, and Ambrosio smilingly rises to his feet. He signals to another girl, and she brings over an ornate dagger upon a velvet red pillow. The weapon is almost identical to the ones carried by your bloodsucking friends, but the jewels in its handle are purple, not silver.

When Ambrosio lifts the knife from the pillow, its narrow blade shining in the orange firelight, he says, "Isn't this just so *exciting*? It's *all* been leading to this. When you first met me that night in LA last year, did you think you'd be standing here now, about to be turned into an eternally-young creature of darkness? Don't answer that, it's a rhetorical question." He touches the tip of the dagger's blade to a pulsing vein in his wrist. A spot of blood wells up on his white skin, growing in size and then trickling down to the floor.

You take another step forward. All of the girls, as well as Derek, are watching in rapt silence.

In a moment of last-minute reverie, you consider the idea of an endless lifetime without sun. You find yourself drifting back to all of those bright California days spent with Mara. The sun was an omnipresent force in your relationship, and you've come to equate it with her. The way it made her hair shine like hellfire, how it bronzed her skin and lit up the canary paint job of her Corvette...without it, there would have *been* no Mara. And now that she's gone, the sun has lost its purpose. You've been living in eternal night for a long time.

You take another step forward.

There's the prospect of killing, too...lots and lots of killing. In drinking Ambrosio's blood, you'll be thrust into a life of ceaseless, bloodthirsty (literally) murder. For a second, a shadow of doubt passes through you, and you wonder if it's possible for you to fashion yourself into that kind of monster. That doubt dissipates as quickly as it had come, though, when you remember that you're *already* that kind of monster. You've already killed three people, and only the first one had been difficult. If you could kill the love of your life, you can kill anything.

Including...*especially*...Sterling McPleasant.

You remind yourself that *he* is the reason for all of this. Ambrosio's "gift" is just a means to an end, really. And if his gift gets you to that end in as efficient of a manner as he purports, then it's more than worth any other repercussions that may ensue as a result.

You take one last step forward, and then you take Ambrosio's bleeding wrist. With -hardened eyes, you look up at his grinning face. His smile has taken on that cartoonish enormity it sometimes has a way of doing, but you are unperturbed.

"Welcome home, Casanova," he says.

"Whatever."

You press his wrist to your lips.

3

The sensation is instantaneous. You can feel each individual nerve-ending in your body explode in rapid-fire succession. It induces a euphoria more potent than any of the uncountable drugs you did in LA. Not even the brief-but-monumental bliss brought on by that first snort of Captain Howdy can compare.

And then there's the *taste*. Ambrosio's blood possesses the flavor of a thousand things at once, all of them wonderful. It's like chocolate ice cream on a hot childhood day. A breath of cigarette smoke after going too long without one. A gulp of ice water following a muscle-frying jog.

It's like Mara's cherry-and-peppermint kisses.

Ambrosio is saying something, but you can't hear it. *Won't* hear it; any distraction from this is wholly unwelcome, and so you shut out the world around you so you can focus only on the taste of the Grinning Man's immortalizing blood. You can feel your mind slipping from reality and edging into unconsciousness, but you struggle against it. You don't want it to be over. Not yet. It's just too damn good.

Despite your efforts, each successive swallow pulls you farther down into yourself. The last thing you see before letting go is Mara's cherry-peppermint lips leaning in to kiss you.

CHAPTER 26 – FROM THE DUST

1

SOMETIME IN THE COLD darkness of early morning, the sunrise still several hours away, you rouse with a start. You're alone in the bed...the one in the spare bedroom, not the one you'd shared with Varney, Mircalla, and Erzsebet the night before. The sheets are awash with sweat. There's a feeling deep in the far recesses of your body, an empty feeling that isn't quite hunger and isn't quite thirst, but something in that family. It isn't familiar to you, but you know what it is.

This is it, you think. *I'm dead. I'm* un*dead. I'm one of them.*

"Well, this is a pretty interesting turn of events, huh, kiddo?"

The voice makes a fresh coat of perspiration break out on your skin. Your heart (*"It'll go on beating forever...unless someone puts a stake through it."*) wheezes like a dying locomotive and you feel as though it *will* stop, stake or no stake. When it doesn't, and you remain bolt-upright in bed with terror screaming through your brain, you spy a flash of movement in the farthest, darkest corner of the room. A dimly flickering candelabra appears at first to be floating in midair, until its bearer steps forward and is given shape by the sconces along the wall.

She is exactly as she'd been the night of your fifteenth birthday. The night of the bad batch. The night you stabbed her. Dressed entirely in white, she possesses none of the grotesqueries that Quincey or Justine had exhibited when they'd appeared to you. She's still tan and beautiful, lively as she ever had been in life. The only disfiguring mark is the red splotch on the side of her blouse where the knife had gone in.

"*Mara*," you try to say, but you can only mouth her name; your voice refuses to adhere to your will. This is frustrating, because there are so many things you need to tell her. Above all, you want to apologize. Not just for killing her, but also (and perhaps more importantly) for everything afterward. You can't help but wonder just how disappointed she must be in what you've let your life become. You don't know what she might have wanted for you, but you doubt it was a life (*un*life?) of bloodsucking murder. And there's the matter of Erzsebet, too...how are you supposed to explain *that?*

"You don't have to explain anything, and you don't have to apologize, either," Mara says, setting the candle on the nightstand and sitting down on the edge of the bed. She's close enough for you to reach out and touch her, but you don't dare. If your fingers passed through her, like a hand over a projector light, you wouldn't be able to stand it. "I'm not, like, your babysitter, or whatever. I'm dead. I don't get to pass judgment on anything you do. And as far as the chick goes, I wouldn't expect you to take a vow of celibacy just because of what happened with us. You can fuck whoever you want. *Love* whoever you want. I mean, sure, I guess I'm a little jealous, but the dead really aren't allowed to be jealous any more than they're allowed to pass judgment."

You try your voice again, and are surprised to find it in working order. "This isn't what I wanted. Not really. *You* are all I ever wanted. This thing with Ambrosio and Erzsebet, and Varney and Mircalla...it's just the only thing that seems to make any sense right now. But I'd trade it all to have you back. All of it. I'd give up immortality for just one more day with you."

The smile Mara gives you is sad and wistful, but something about it almost feels somewhat patronizing. "Oh, stop that. Don't be ridiculous. We never would have lasted, anyway. It was doomed from the start."

"No. That's not true. We could have..."

"It *is* true, and you're smart enough to know it. You don't want to admit it, and I understand. But deep down, you know it. What we had was nice, but it was always going to end. You were always going to end up back here, because this is where you're supposed to be. You're supposed to kill Sterling Mc-Fuckwagon. If you had to become Barnabas Collins to do that, then so be it."

You really don't want to talk about McPleasant, or even think about him. Not now, at least. *Mara* is *here*, and the last thing you want to do is spend your precious time with her discussing that asshole.

"I know," she says, "but we have to. You might be strong enough to kill him now that you're all Draculafied and shit, but you have to *find* him, first. And do you even know where to look? No, of course you don't, so I'm going to show you." She holds out her hand, gesturing with her eyes for you to take it. You look down at it uncertainly, still afraid she won't be there when you try to touch her. Ultimately, her imploring eyes convince you, just as they'd always been able to convince you of anything.

And then, with heart-surging elation, you *do* feel her. Her hand is warm and soft and smooth, exactly as you remembered it. It is not cold or ethereal or sticky with goopy ectoplasm. It is only Mara, and it is beautiful.

When she closes her hand on yours and squeezes, Ambrosio's mansion disappears, and you're standing beside her outside of a huge gothic cathedral, looking up at the menacing spires shooting into the heavy black sky. You immediately recognize it as the church of St. Dominic Savio, Villa Vida's one-stop shop for all of the town's Sunday-best Catholics, devout or otherwise. Neither your real parents nor your pretend ones had been churchgoing folk, so you'd never been inside, but it's one of the most identifiable structures in Mudhoney County. Its sheer size always struck you as more than a little obnoxious, considering Villa Vida's otherwise small-town aesthetic.

"What are we doing here?" you ask Mara. You're aware that you're holding her hand too tightly, but the sensation of *feeling* her again is too good to resist, and she doesn't seem to mind.

Because she's not real. Because she's not even really here.

As if on cue, the dull color saturation of your surroundings seems to shift and melt. You blink, and for a frantically terrifying moment you're back in bed at the mansion, cold and alone. Mara...or your dream manifestation of her, whatever...is gone. The room is dark, and when you exhale, your breath comes out in a smoky gray fog.

"Still with me, kiddo?" The warm light of her voice comes from somewhere inside you, and you shut your eyes to go search for it. Your mind skulks along the caverns within your chilled bones but finds no respite there. Exasperated, you open your eyes again and find yourself inside the church, with Mara once more beside you and her hand in yours. You're standing next to the altar, which is set upon a stage-like surface with a purple velvet curtain behind it. Mara parts it and steps through to the other side, motioning for you to follow.

"Don't leave me again," you say as you go to her, your voice approaching a whimper.

"I never did," she says.

The area behind the curtain looks to serve mainly as a storage room, with casks of communion wine and endless stacks of bibles and psalm books. Mara leads you past the clutter to a door at the back. There's a gold nameplate on it that reads, "FATHER ALEISTER BENWAY."

The door opens on a dark stairwell. Mara indicates for you to go first, so you grab the railing and walk down the steps, mindful of your footing. At the bottom of the stairs is a short hallway dead-ending at another door. You look over your shoulder at Mara, and she nods.

You open the door.

The priest's quarters are cramped and drably undecorated, little more than a cheap studio apartment with all of the necessary trappings and nothing by the way of extraneous creature comforts. There's a man sitting on the edge of the small bed. You take this to be Father Aleister Benway of the nameplate fame. He's a small man, probably in his mid-fifties, with receding salt-and-pepper hair and silver half-moon spectacles. His delicate hands fidget on his lap as he cautiously watches the other man in the room pace back and forth.

The second man is brutish and giant, with the broad stature of a lumberjack and a height that has to be close to six-five or six-six. His unruly red-orange hair reaches down past his shoulders and sticks out in every direction, as if he's been fucking around with electrical sockets. The hair on his face is like a mutated hybrid-clone of the tangled mop on his head. He's muttering what sounds like an incantation of nonsensically-strung-together curse words. Each time his pale, vacant gray eyes point in your direction in the course of his pacing, they go right through you.

Because this isn't real. Because I'm not even really here.

"McPleasant," you breathe.

You sense Mara nodding her head from behind you. "Yes," she says. "Sterling McDouchefuck."

You resist the urge to charge at him and flay open his throat with your teeth. It is a powerful urge, but you're cognizant enough of the situation to know you would only pass through him just as his eyes pass through you.

Because this isn't real. Because I'm not even really here.

The room's colors begin to morph, and you will your eyes to remain open lest you slip again from Mara's presence.

When Benway clears his throat and begins to speak, his voice is nervous and unsteady. "Sterling...Mr. McPleasant...you can't, ah...well, I'm afraid you can't s-stay here much l-longer. It isn't safe for...f-for *either* of us. I'm...I'm s-sorry, but you need to l-leave. T-tonight, preferably. R-r-right now, as a m-matter of f-fact."

McPleasant stops mid-pace and swivels on his heel to glower down at Benway. The little priest cringes, his body folding inward and making him even smaller. It looks like McPleasant is going to strike him, but after a long and tenuous silence, he resumes his pacing and grumbles, "Something wrong. Fucked. All cunted up. Cuntcuntcunt. Looking. Found. Found. Fuckcuntfuck."

You'd expected a bit more sophistication from your nemesis, as opposed to this disjointed and profane babble. But...there's *something* behind those eyes of his, isn't there? Yes...it's an unconventional intelligence, a kind of disorganized-but-calculated scheming. He's no Lex Luthor, but those eyes intimate that there's more to the Monster than bestial force and badly-paired expletives.

You feel Mara take your hand again. When you look at her, she says, "It's time to leave. You know where to go, now."

Your first instinct is to protest, though you don't know why; there's nothing you can accomplish here, not in this form. But before you could come up with an excuse to justify prolonging your presence in the church basement, either to Mara or to yourself, you're back in bed at Ambrosio's mansion. There's no dramatic *whoosh* of lightspeed travel, nor any sensory indicator to accompany the change in environment. You blink rapidly, trying to shake the disorientation this causes.

Mara is sitting on the bed as she had been before she'd transported you to the church, but she's no longer holding your hand. She's about to say something, but you interrupt her and plead, "Don't go. Not yet. Don't go."

Her smile is sad and strained. "You know that's not how this works, kiddo."

"Then take me with you."

"It doesn't work like that, either."

"No, please, you can't..."

"You'll be okay. I promise." She leans down and softly brushes her cherry-peppermint lips against yours. "Sweet dreams, Casanova."

As your eyes swing shut of their own accord, you blindly reach out once more for her hand.

This time, there's nothing there.

2

It's just past seven PM when you wake again. You open your eyes to see Varney sitting by the window, his feet propped up on its sill. When he realizes you're awake, he gets up and says, "My boy, my boy, my *boy!* I bid you formal welcome to our ranks among the legion of darkness." He bows low at the waist and then takes a scroll of parchment from inside his long sport jacket. There's a jovial spring in his steps when he waltzes over and hands it to you.

You sit up and unroll the long sheet of brittle paper, your eyes scanning its contents. There are six long columns of alphabetically-listed names scrawled in a tiny, old-fashioned font so ornate and heavily inundated with serifs that they're almost illegible. Squinting, you read aloud, "Armand, Aro, Arra Sails, Arrow, Ash Redfern...Brad Moreau, Bree Tanner, *Bunnicula?* What is this?"

Beaming, Varney says, "As a creature of the night, you must shed your previous identity and select one more befitting of your new, immortal self. We all did, and now it's your turn."

"This is stupid. I murdered two people to prove that I'm one of you. I shouldn't have to start calling myself something like

Count fucking Orlok or..." You look back down at the paper, shaking your head. "'Thuringwethil.'"

Varney's smile reverses itself. "You could do a lot worse than Thuringwethil. That's Tolkien, you know. Look, this is *tradition*, one as old as our kind."

Somehow, you doubt that others of your kind had, centuries ago, changed their names to things like "Blade" or "Quackula." You're about to say this when a name in the first column jumps out at you and makes your skin go cold. You put your finger to it and say, "What's this from?"

Varney comes over and looks at the name beside your fingertip. "Ah," he says. "That's a character played by Annabella Sciorra in Abel Ferrara's film, *The Addiction*. I want to say it was...oh, I think '95 or '96 that it came out. It's one of Erzsebet's favorites. I'll have her show it to you."

"It's a girl character?"

"Well, yes, but that's not important. Mircalla's namesake is a female, as well. As we've told you, gender isn't..."

"I'll take it. That's the one. That's my name."

Varney's good-natured smile returns. "Very well, then. From this night and forever onward, you shall..."

Mircalla and Erzsebet enter the room before he can finish. Erzsebet rushes over to you, taking your shoulders in her hands and saying, "Is it...? Did he...?"

"It is, and he did," Varney says, his chest puffed out like a proud sparrow. "Erzsebet, Mircalla, it is with great pleasure that I introduce you to our newest companion of night."

"How does he call himself?" Mircalla asks, attempting to imitate Varney's flourishing dialect.

"His name," Varney says, "is Casanova."

CHAPTER 27 – LET IT BLEED

1

As the Rolls-Royce barrels past the Villa Vida welcome sign, Mircalla turns around in his seat to ask, "So, of all the people you could choose for your first meal, why a priest? You get diddled as an altar boy, or something?"

You blink at him blandly from behind your sunglasses. "No. I was never an altar boy. And no one ever diddled me."

"*I* diddled you a couple nights ago," Erzsebet says, unwrapping a Blow Pop and putting it in her mouth.

Mircalla grins and nods. "Dude, same."

"And you can add me to that number, as well," says Varney, pushing down his Aviators so he can wink at you in the rearview mirror.

You blush and look out the window. "It's about my parents," you say quietly. "This priest knows where their killer is. He might even be with him."

The three of them utter the same "*whoooaaa*" that they had when you'd first told them about your parents' murder. It's Erzsebet who asks the question you'd known was inevitable but had still hoped might go unspoken: "How do you know that he knows?"

My dead cousin came to me in a dream and showed me.

Deciding simplification might be best, you shorten this to, "I...had a dream." It's still not the best explanation, but for a group of bloodsucking monsters who'd be more at home in a horror novel than in real life, you figure they'd be apt to buy into the concept of precognitive premonitions.

"Martin Luther King had a dream," says Mircalla. "Look how *that* shit worked out."

The others murmur in somber agreement.

"Maybe it's nothing," you say. "But I have to know for sure. The dream...it was, um, very real. I mean, it *felt* very real."

Mircalla takes off his sunglasses and looks at you with his brows knitted in comically funereal seriousness. "Dude, even if it's nothing, it's *not* nothing. You feel me? You have to trust that shit, man. It was the right thing to do, coming here."

"He's right, you know," says Varney, maneuvering into the church parking lot and sliding into a patch of shadow beneath an overhanging willow tree, where the lawn gives way to asphalt. He switches off the lights and turns around, also taking off his sunglasses. The expression with which he regards you matches the severity of Mircalla's. "You belong to a different race, now. A different race with a different set of rules. And obeying those *new* rules sometimes means breaking the old ones. This actually applies to a *myriad* of different contexts, but tonight I'm specifically referring to the abandonment of learned logic. You see, we..."

"Uh, Varney?" Mircalla nudges him, looking out the windshield at something you can't see because Varney's face is blocking your field of vision.

"Hold on, I'm on a roll. Anyway, Casanova, *learned logic* teaches us that dreams are irrational and not to be trusted. Just random images whipped into semi-life by our overactive imaginations, right? Well, as a creature of the night, this sentiment needs to be resolutely eschewed. Your dreams are..."

"*Varney*," Mircalla whines, nudging him again.

Turning around with an irritated grunt, Varney says, "Dammit, Mircalla, *what* could *possibly* be so...oh. Well, fuck." He strokes his chin. "I'll be honest with you, I definitely didn't foresee *that* development."

You and Erzsebet lean forward between the front two seats to get a look, both of you removing your sunglasses and squinting against the dark. It comes into focus for each of you at the same time, and you gasp in unison.

A white Lincoln Continental has pulled up alongside the church's side-entry door, and a short man in black is helping two children out of the car's trunk. Both of the children have plastic Walgreens bags tied over their heads, and their wrists are bound with what appears to be some sort of wire. As the man hurries them inside, a ray of starlight flashes upon the clerical collar around his neck.

"Interesting," says Varney, still stroking his chin.

"I'm pretty sure," says Mircalla, "there's a great joke about a Catholic priest that would go perfect with this, but I can't remember how it goes."

"The one with the nun who has Down's syndrome?" Erzsebet offers. "Or the one about the archbishop's three-legged dog?"

"No, it wasn't either of those," Mircalla says, shaking his head. He snickers to himself. "The one with the dog *is* pretty fuckin great, though."

You're growing impatient. You care little for whatever appropriately-inappropriate joke might exist at the heart of this matter, and you care littler still for the captive children who brought it to mind. You just want to go in there and do what you came to do.

Perhaps sensing this in your tense demeanor, Erzsebet opens her door and says, "Come on, let's go. We're here for a reason."

And then, winking at you as she gets out of the car, she adds, "We're here for Casanova."

As your dark quartet trots up toward the church, Erzsebet stops and bends over to cough with her hands on her knees and her hair hanging in her face. You and the other boys stop, as well, watching her. You start timidly in her direction, but she shakes her head and holds up her hand. After several agonizing moments of this, she stands and collects her breath. Straightening her sunglasses and pushing back her hair, she says, "It's fine, I'm okay, let's go."

Varney shrugs and resumes toward the church, and then Mircalla does the same. You follow their advance, but you do not shrug.

2

The side door through which Benway had disappeared with the children (and which he had also left unlocked) opens into a narrow hallway that leads into the lobby, which you are unsurprised to find looks exactly as it had in your dream.

Because it was *real. Because I* was *really there.*

And if that's the case, as it certainly seems to be, then both of those conclusions can be made about Mara, as well.

Can't think about that right now. Focus.

You signal for the others to follow you, and then you lead them through the chapel, up to the altar, and behind the purple curtain where you're even less surprised to find the door marked "FATHER ALEISTER BENWAY." This time, though, the door is already open and you can hear loud music coming from the little apartment down below. You tilt your head, listening. It's the Stones' "Gimme Shelter."

"I thought priests were supposed to hate rock 'n' roll," Mircalla whispers.

Varney says something you can't hear, and then Erzsebet giggles and says, "Savage." You shake away a creeping chill of *déjà vu.*

You descend the stairs two steps at a time, feeling them creak beneath your shoes but unable to hear the actual noise over the sound of the music.

"Rape, murder.

It's just a shot away."

As you walk toward the partially-ajar door, you find yourself absurdly annoyed with Father Benway for all the wrong reasons. Never mind the fact that, if Mara and your dream are to be trusted, he's been providing asylum to your parents' killer; that's bad enough, but it isn't what has you pissed off. No, what pisses you off is the piece about the kids. Principally, you don't give a damn about their fate, but it's Benway's embrace of the stereotype that irks you more than anything. A pedophiliac priest? *Really?* Why is it, you wonder, that people are so compelled to unoriginality and caricature-conformation? At the end of the day, Benway may as well be just another member of the Breakfast Club, and that makes you want to kill him more than anything.

You kick the door open, drawing your dagger as you do so.

Benway has stripped to his underwear. The two boys are on the bed. The shopping bags have been removed, but their wrists are still bound with what you can now see are cell phone chargers. They're identical twins, of fair skin and hair, and can't be much older than eleven or twelve. Their passive, slack-jawed expressions lead you to believe they've been drugged.

Benway had been pulling at one of the boy's pants when you'd entered, but as soon as he hears the door thunder open, he jumps to his feet and spins around with the "oh fuck" look of a child who's been caught stealing from the cookie jar.

Erzsebet appears at your side, and Varney and Mircalla file in after her. "And here I'd thought the pedo-priest thing was just a punchline," she says.

"Stereotypes exist because the world is one enormous cliché," says Varney, clucking his tongue.

Benway tries to run for the tiny bathroom, but Varney and Mircalla apprehend him, holding their knives to his throat. You tell them not to kill him, not yet, so they tie his arms behind his back with his discarded pants and then force him down into a ratty armchair that's bleeding white stuffing from numerous tears in its upholstery. You approach him, your eyes flicking around the room for signs that McPleasant might still be here, but you know he isn't. You'd known as soon as you entered the church, really. You would have felt him.

"*Where is he?*" you growl at the priest, poking his bobbing Adam's apple with the tip of your knife.

"W-where's w-who? I d-don't kn-know what you're t-talking..."

"Don't bullshit me," you snarl, backhanding him across the face and sending his glasses flying across the room. "McPleasant. I know he was here. *Why* was he here, and *where* is he now?"

The priest blinks but doesn't answer.

You touch the point of the dagger to his scrawny bicep and start applying pressure. It pierces his milky, translucent skin, making blood slide down his arm. He begins to cry and squirm, and then he says, "Please, he'll kill me, okay? He'll k-kill me if he f-finds out I told you anything!"

"*I'll* kill you if you *don't.*"

Benway bites his lip and looks behind you at your friends, whom you imagine are probably grinning at him. You suspect it's those evil grins that persuade him to talk more than anything. When he speaks, his voice is an uneven whisper. "He was only here for a c-couple of weeks. I d-don't know why he came here. One day after m-mass, he was d-down here waiting for me. S-said he needed to l-lay l-low. S-s-said he'd kill me if I didn't let him. I p-p-prayed about it, and..."

"Stop stuttering. It's an act and it isn't winning you any sympathy."

The meek terror in Benway's eyes turns into hateful rage. The transformation flares like a mushroom cloud in his pupils. He grits his teeth, cracks his neck, and then continues evenly, "I prayed about it and God told me to let him stay, so I did."

"God told you to provide room and board to a serial murderer and rapist."

It's just a shot away.

"Yes. I am not one to question the will of God."

"Where is he now?"

"I don't know."

You dig the knife deeper into his arm, and he howls.

"I really *don't* know," he insists. Pained, angry tears leak from his beady eyes.

"Take a guess. You hung out with the fucker for two weeks. You can't tell me you have no idea where might go."

"H-he m-m-m-might have g-gone to..."

"*I TOLD YOU TO STOP STUTTERING.*" You push the knife even deeper, and the fire in the priest's eyes becomes a blaze.

"Trainyards," he blurts, panting. "That's where he spends most of his time. Among the tramps at the trainyards. He smuggles himself onto cargo trains to get around. I swear to you, in *Jesus' name*, that's all I know. He didn't tell me anything else. He's too clever to go around divulging all his secrets. It's why he's lasted so long. Now, *please*, can you please let me *go?*"

You feel the ghost of a smile alight upon your face. "No. I'm not going to let you go. I'm going to..."

"Actually, you *are* going to let him go."

The voice is like a slippery green tentacle tickling the inside of your ear. You spin around. The others do, too. Ambrosio is standing in the apartment doorway, dressed in a long black robe. His face is obscured by the shadow cast from its hood, but his bright white grin glows like a lighthouse beacon.

"I'm *terribly* sorry to interrupt your festivities," Ambrosio says, "but I'm afraid I cannot permit you to kill the priest."

"But...he's a *pedophile*," protests Mircalla.

"Oh, I know *that*. And trust me, that's not even the *least* of his transgressions. Aleister is, in just about *every* imaginable sense, a *loathsome* human being. I would love nothing more than to see him bled like the pig that he is. But even the worst of humans have their purpose, and his has not yet been realized. I need him alive."

"Why?" Mircalla persists. "What purpose could he *possibly* serve?"

Ambrosio's smile vanishes, rendering his hooded countenance more Reaper-esque than ever. "Question *not* my will, youngling. Aleister Benway's tale has not reached its conclusion, and it will overlap with another that is of some importance to me. It is, however, of *no* importance to you, so I advise you to *mind your tongue*."

Mircalla's head droops and he mumbles an embarrassed apology.

"Now," says Ambrosio, "Casanova, I believe the priest has given you the information for which you came, yes?"

You nod grudgingly. You still want to kill Benway.

"He hasn't had his first meal, though," Varney broaches with uncharacteristic timidity in his voice. "He...*thirsts*."

That unpleasant twist of empty yearning in your stomach seems to raise its head at its mention.

Ambrosio points two terrible fingers at the twin boys drooling on the bed. "Have you forgotten *them?*"

Every set of eyes in the room lands upon the twins.

"Take them upstairs and have your fill," Ambrosio says mildly. "The good father and I have some things to discuss."

"*Wait*," says Benway, wide-eyed and wriggling against his restraints. All eyes shift from the twins to him. You notice with revulsion that he has an erection. He licks his lips and then asks, "Can I watch?"

3

Staggering back out into the night, you brace yourself against the bumper of Benway's Lincoln and bend over to release a rush of bloodpuke. The coppery burn scalds your throat and nostrils. It hadn't tasted as you'd thought it would. You'd expected it to be a similar experience to when you drank Ambrosio's blood, but this was not so. It had been overly metallic and potent, and extremely thick, like tomato soup.

When Varney finishes puking up his share, he comes over to stand beside you, patting you on the back. Erzsebet and Mircalla are still in the throes of it. "There, there," Varney says. "It's always a trifle bit unpleasant the first time or few, but you'll get used to it. You'll come to *cherish* it."

When you're sure everything that's going to come up has done so, you stand shakily and take off your sunglasses so you can wipe at your watering eyes. "Why wasn't it like the first time? When I drank Ambrosio's blood, it was..."

Varney throws his head back and laughs. "Oh, my good man, nothing is ever as good as the first time. Ambrosio's blood is the elixir of divine immortality. Comparing a human meal to *him* is hardly fair. There's also the unlucky fact that those two boys were virgins. Such blood is a delicacy of sorts for me, Mircalla, and Erzsebet, since our palates are a tad more developed. For a fledgling such as yourself, however, virginal blood is going to go down kind of harsh. Your young tongue is still sensitive." He pauses. "Ironically, had we been gotten here just a *few* minutes later, Father Kiddie-diddler would have had time to deflower those kids, and your first blood-drinking experience may have been vastly different."

You put a hand to your mouth to stifle a belch. With it comes the lingering tang of oily pennies, and you have to bend down to puke some more.

"Don't worry, Cap'n," says Mircalla with a pink smile as he and Erzsebet walk over to you and Varney. "You'll get your sea legs in no time."

When this second bout of vomiting has reached its conclusion, you stand and ask Erzsebet for a cigarette. She gives one to you and says, "At least it's gone, right?"

You light the cigarette and put your sunglasses back on. "What's gone?"

"The *thirst*."

You absently place your hand on your stomach, as though you'll actually feel the gray presence of the worm-like *thirst* coiled there. But she's right. That gnawing emptiness has departed, leaving in its place a sense of satisfied fulfillment. "Yeah," you say. "It is."

"It'll be back," grins Varney. "With a vengeance. Thankfully, we live in America, and there's no shortage of sustenance."

You nod again and look down at the bumper of the priest's car. There's a sticker right next to your dusty handprint that says, "JESUS SAVES" in big purple letters.

Picking a piece of skin from between his teeth and examining it idly, Mircalla says, "I'm starving. Who's thinkin Arby's?"

CHAPTER 28 – DARK BOY

1

ALL THROUGH SEPTEMBER AND well into October, you take to your new night life with ever-increasing gusto. You feel yourself becoming stronger, both mentally and physically, with each passing phase of the moon. By the end of September, your wits are sharper than piano wire and your stride is just as confident and defined as those of your companions. You can also run faster, jump higher, and lift with ease objects that once would have required great expenditures of effort. Your life has become the wettest dream of every comic book nerd who ever jacked off to the idea of getting bitten by a radioactive spider.

You start sleeping full-time in the bedroom on the fifth floor, with your friends. The sex is constant, and eternally titillating. It's different from the sex you had with Mara; there's less emotion and more primal carnality, which you don't mind. With Mara, much of the pleasure had been in the way she tuned you into your body and the life that inhabited it. With Erzsebet and the boys, it's more of a tuning *out*, and there's great pleasure to be had in that, as well.

In that vein, you and Erzsebet begin to grow deliciously close, though perhaps not as much as you'd prefer. There are plenty of nights you spend only with her, including a particularly good one in which she treats you to a private screening of *The Addiction*. You find the movie itself to be vaguely pretentious and drab, full of heavy-handed philosophical monologues that go way over your head. The *real* treat comes afterward, when she makes love to you in one of the reclining chairs while the credits flash across the screen. It's not as magical as the night with the fireworks, but it's enough.

Well, *almost* enough.

Because the fact remains that she isn't yours, not in the self-proclaimed "socialist" dynamic of your group, where nothing belongs to anyone and everything belongs to everyone. You had always thought that was more akin with communism, actually, but then again, you'd never paid much attention in history class, so you can't be certain.

Either way, whatever it's called, she isn't yours. Just when you think you've formed some sort of uniquely private connection with her after a night alone at the house, Varney and Mircalla will waltz in and she'll throw herself upon them with an alacrity that equals (and sometimes, at least in your mind, surpasses) that which she exhibits when it's just the two of you. It rouses confusing feelings of jealousy in you, specifically toward Varney. Varney, who seems inimitably groomed for immortality in a way you aren't certain you'll ever be, in spite of the rapidity with which you've already taken to it. He has a cool untouchability to his demeanor that is impossible to emulate. Even that brief occasion when it had cracked ever so slightly that night at Ellis Lake feels like something that, for all its trivial insignificance, might not have happened at all. Your inability to match his refined poise is enough to breed stirrings of dull resentment deep in your stomach.

Still, you love him.

Not in the same way you think you might be falling in love
with Erzsebet, and *certainly* not anywhere near as much as you'd
loved Mara, but it's a very similar kind of love to what you felt
for Quincey, Justine, Rebecca, and Ianthe.

And that, at the very least, is an awful lot.

2

Most of the nights over that first month and a half are spent
with your fellow immortals in some capacity or another, but not
all of them.

You haven't forgotten your True North.

Two or three nights of each week, you strike out on your
own. You take Ambrosio's glossy black Audi and hit up one
trainyard after another, inquiring after the whereabouts of the
Mudhoney Monster. Your main targets for interrogation are the
homeless men and women who haunt the musky boxcars or sit
around their putrid trashcan fires. Mostly, you come up empty.

The first of these interrogations had been a disastrously
unwieldy affair. You'd come upon a homeless man sleeping
half-under a train car, covered in a bug-infested blanket constructed from folds of newspaper glued together with mud.
Once you'd kicked him awake, you shouted a slew of questions
at him, threatening him with your dagger and demanding to
know where Sterling McPleasant was hiding. The man had cried
at first, then broken into laughter, and then had finally launched
into a discombobulated story about a rubber duck that had lost
its mother, who happened to be a mechanical kangaroo. You
killed him in a red rage of frustrated fury and sped back to the
house.

Each effort after that had gone progressively smoother, if not
any more fruitful. You became surer of yourself, more in command of your power. After just two weeks of these solo excursions, you're a natural; you stalk the trainyards like a prowling
panther, ruthlessly questioning your targets and then killing
and drinking them when they fail to yield any information.
Their blood tastes of trash and sewage going down, and even

worse coming back up, but it at least quells the uncomfortable knot of thirst.

It's in the first week of October that you learn you've garnered a reputation.

You pull into a trainyard in Green River, blasting "Honky Tonk Women" and feeling pretty good. Getting out of the car, you pull up your hood, put on your sunglasses, and hop the fence. After skulking around in the shadows with your head down and your hands in your pockets, you spot a target and close in.

She's sitting Indian-style by a burning trashcan, her eyes closed and her expression serene. Her gnarled wasp's nest of hair is prickly with twigs and dead leaves. On her wrinkly white forehead is the shape of a cross in smeared black mud. When you walk up to her with your knife held at your side, she opens her eyes and smiles up at you, revealing rotted gums embedded with teeth as yellow as Mara's Corvette.

"You's come," she says. "I knowed you would."

You raise an eyebrow at her and say nothing.

"Oh, you's got yourself a reppertation. A bad one. A *dark* one. Thass why's they call you's the Dark Boy."

"How clever."

The woman titters, her dark eyes catching the dancing light of the fire. The sound of her laughter is like that of a puking cat. "You's best be *real* careful, Dark Boy. He knows you's lookin for him, and he ain't wantin to be found. Sooners or laters, he's gonna find *you*. 'Cause if he thinks someone's gonna find him, he *always* makes sure he finds 'em first. He always makes *real* sure of that, Dark Boy."

"I'll take my chances," you say, secretly pleased that word of your inquest has spread but also a little concerned that you've lost the element of surprise. "Why don't you tell me where he is, and I'll save him the trouble of having to look for me?"

The woman titters again. "Oh, Dark Boy, he is *everywheres* and he is *nowheres*. You can't never find him. He's too *bad*. He's more bad than *you's* is. More bad even than that devil-man you's hangin 'round with. The one at the tippy top of that castle."

Your preternatural blood undergoes an arctic transformation into frigid slush. You try to tell yourself that she's just a batty old hag whose ramblings have struck upon a lucky coincidence, but...

Ambrosio doesn't deal in coincidences.

"I don't know how you know about Ambrosio, you disgusting fleabag, but let me make two things clear. *No one* is worse than he is, and he's on *my* side." You're pretty confident in the first part of that statement, at least.

"Oh *my*, you's a *silly* Dark Boy, ain't you's? That man ain't on *nobody's* side but his *owns*."

"Shut up. You don't know what you're talking about. Tell me where McPleasant is."

With her jittery, claw-like hand, the woman points behind you.

Your heart drops. The hair at your temples dampens. The dagger loosens in your sweat-laxed grip.

You turn around.

And there's nothing there.

The woman howls her witch-like cackle from behind you, and then you feel her hurl her body into yours. You go sprawling into the dirt with her on your back, and the dagger slips from your grasp.

"*I GOTS THE DARK BOY! I GOTS THE DARK BOY! JEEZY, MARIA, AND JOSEPHINE, I GOTS THE DARK BOY!*"

She starts pelting the back of your head with her tiny fists, and you think back to Mircalla's story of how he'd met Ambrosio. You roll out from under her and nimbly spring to your feet, scooping up your dagger in the same motion. When you grab her by her hair and jerk her head back, she grins up at you and says, "That devil-man ain't on you's side, Dark Boy. You's shoulda just let me kill you's."

"You can't kill me, bitch," you say as you open her throat. "I'm fuckin immortal."

CHAPTER 29 – CONVENIENCE AND OPPORTUNITY

1

THE HONEYMOON PHASE DRAWS to a close shortly after the encounter with the "Jeezy, Maria, and Josephine" lady. You can't pinpoint exactly how or why it ended; a number of contributing factors are evident, but you don't know which, if any, were the primary catalyst. Probably none of them alone, if you're being honest. But added together, these things quickly become troubling enough to cast an unpleasant shadow over the lustrous wonderment of immortal life.

The first is your growing frustration over your inability to find McPleasant. You've spent the better part of two months traipsing around trainyards and leaving a trail of dead hobos in your wake, and you've come up with exactly zero leads in respect to the Mudhoney Monster's whereabouts.

The second is Erzsebet. Not only does she seem distant in a way she hadn't been during those delicious first weeks, but there also seems to be something physically wrong with her. Her cough has steadily grown worse, her energy levels are uncharacteristically low, and you're pretty sure she's been losing weight. You raised the subject to Varney, but he essentially blew you off and insisted you were "imagining things."

Third, Varney keeps displaying signs of incompetent recklessness in his role as your group's de facto leader. The victims (ahem, *meals*) he selects increasingly begin to fall in a vague gray area between the "worms" afforded you by "convenience and opportunity" and the individuals whom are deemed unworthy of life on the basis of moral high ground. Too often, he'll randomly decide to kill someone because he or she is wearing white after Labor Day or is sporting a haircut that he reasons is "an affront to everything that was ever in good taste." You're far enough removed from your own humanity...a process that started long before you actually stopped being human...to not get bogged down by pity or guilt over the deaths of these expendable bags of blood, so the morality of the issue *isn't* what's the issue. No, the *issue* is that Varney often makes these selections with little-to-no planning, and sometimes even in profoundly risky locations where there exists a high potential for witnesses. Immortal or not, you still have to be smart.

Lastly, you still haven't taken to the taste of blood the way the others have. You don't *hate* it, and there is an undeniable sense of satiated relief when you drink from a victim or meal or worm or whatever, but you don't particularly enjoy the act itself. Yes, you've more or less gotten used to it, and no, it's not as overpowering as it had been the first time at the church. But no matter how much you try to make yourself *relish* in it the way your companions do, you just aren't there yet, and it's beyond frustrating.

All of that aside, you're still a fuck-ton happier than you had been before Varney & Friends had come along. Every night, as you're drifting to sleep after a sweaty bout of lovemaking, you remind yourself of exactly that. You'd been ready to say "bottoms-up" to a glass of Drano not two months ago.

Mara hasn't come to you since that first night after Ambrosio turned you, but you assure yourself that this is what she would want for your life.

And if that comes at the expense of some frustration and the odd wave of existential malaise every now and again, then so be it.

Drinking blood, after all, sure as hell beats drinking Drano.

2

The late-October air is cool as the four of you walk down Jubilee Street. The night is alive with the guffawing gabble of Millhaven's drunken denizens. Men stand clustered outside of dive bars and nightclubs, eying the droves of scantily-clad women stumbling stupefied along the filthy sidewalk, their eyes lecherous over the stale glow of their Mavericks and Newports and Dorals.

It seems, however, that you and your trio of companions are somehow immune to the attention of the townspeople. No one appears to pay you any mind, or so much as glances in your direction, though the conspicuous aesthetic ascribed to your group should ostensibly arouse curiosity.

Varney is adorned in his traditional gentleman's attire, the tails of his coat trailing behind him as he swings his luxurious cane, the heels of his boots clacking on the pavement and his pale face obscured by the shadow cast from the brim of his top hat.

Mircalla is garbed entirely in black leather, from his combat boots to his tight pants to his zipper-laden motorcycle jacket. His long wisps of hair are held back by a black bandanna upon which the words "FUCK YOU" are printed in a dozen different fonts.

Erzsebet still looks ill; her skin is too pale and there's a dogged weariness about her that is concerning. When she'd woken you earlier that evening, you thought you'd seen the faint traces of purple veins beneath the soft skin of her face, but it might have been a trick of the light. In spite of all this, though, the commanding presence of her beauty remains intact. In her too-short black cocktail dress and knee-high stiletto boots, she is far more alluring than any of the tottering floozies upon whom the blue-balled men are inexplicably fixated. How she can float so effortlessly beneath their testosterone-powered radar is beyond your comprehension.

Then there's your youth, on top of everything else. You're all so *young*, and surely *someone* must think it's odd that four kids visibly beneath drinking age are confidently strolling this booze-soaked boulevard of debauchery.

Oh, and the sunglasses. Can't forget the sunglasses. Wearing them makes you feel ridiculous, but as long as the others insist upon wearing them, you'll dutifully follow suit no matter how silly it looks. Still, not even the cheesy Cory Hart affectation appears to draw any attention. The four of you might as well be utterly invisible; nary even the most fleeting of a sideways glance is cast in your direction.

Not, of course, that you have any complaints regarding this apparent invisibility. Being as you are...*what* you are...it goes without saying that the mysterious anonymity afforded you and your friends is a comfort you do not take for granted. Whether it's luck or some touch of Ambrosio's magic is difficult to determine, but it makes you think of how you'd passed unseen through the hospital the night of Mara's death, so you suspect the Grinning Man has more to do with it than you'd like.

Varney suddenly stops and holds up his hand to signal the rest of you to do the same. He's looking down a dark alley between a burger joint called Fat Manuelo's and a strip club called the Wild Rose. You have to lift the deeply tinted lenses of your sunglasses to make out whatever it is he's looking at.

The others, their vision apparently better suited for the night than yours, see it right away and smile hungrily.

Silhouetted in the dark is a pair of figures pressed up against the grimy brick wall beside an overflowing Dumpster. They're engaged in a fervid kiss, the kind that brings with it a blissful oblivion that blots out the rest of the world's distracting trivialities. They caress one another's body with ravenous sexuality.

Varney looks at Mircalla, who looks at Erzsebet, who looks at you. You don't like it...anyone could turn down that alley at any time...but from the looks on your friends' faces, no argument you present is going to dissuade them.

"Convenience and opportunity," Varney says.

"Worms," Mircalla agrees.

Varney enters the alley first, and the rest of you follow in a single-file line

As you draw closer, their features come into focus. The male is tall and sinewy with lean muscle, looking to be in his late twenties or early thirties. The girl is younger, maybe twenty-two or twenty-three. She has wavy black hair and a fading spray-tan. Her jeans sit low on her narrow hips, and her tank top is pulled up to expose her midriff.

"Mircalla and I will take the girl," Varney says. "Erzsebet, you've got Loverboy." He looks at you and says, "And you can feel free to jump in wherever."

At the sound of Varney's voice, the two lovers abruptly pull apart, staring at the four of you with confused, wide-eyed outrage. The man starts to say something, but Erzsebet puts a finger to his lips and gently pushes him farther back into the shadows. Varney and Mircalla pull the girl into an embrace and begin to cover her with tongue-lapping kisses on her face and throat and arms. As if hypnotized, the fear in her face melts away and she moans at the touch of the two boys.

Erzsebet unceremoniously shoves the man against the Dumpster and then drops to her knees. Her nimble white fingers unclasp his belt and unbutton his jeans with a flurry of expert motion. She yanks his pants down to his ankles, exposing an exclamatory erection, which she takes immediately into her mouth.

Your stomach seizes with a sour sting of jealousy, which you realize is absurd given the ill-fated climax in which this scene will ultimately culminate. Taking a half step back and lighting a cigarette, you try not to watch, but are unable to look away. Erzsebet's head moves with salacious rhythm as she runs her clawed fingers up and down the man's hairy thighs. He lets out a groan and buries his own hands in the tumbling white-and-gold locks of Erzsebet's hair, his shoulders shuddering.

Varney has one gloved hand on the girl's breast and the other around her throat, his lips locked with hers, their tongues ensnared in a tangled, writhing dance. She's been freed from her jeans, and Mircalla is on his knees with his face buried in her bare groin.

You look back over at the man, whose face has contorted into a clenched pre-orgasm expression. "Oh, *fuck*," he says through his gritted teeth, leaning his head back. "Oh fuck, I'm gonna come."

It is at the utterance of those words that Erzsebet pulls away, releasing him from her mouth with a goofy-sounding *plop*. He looks down just in time to see the flash of the dagger. The head of his penis vanishes, and a geyser of blood and semen explodes onto Erzsebet's face. She greedily stuffs his ruined cock back into her mouth and sucks noisily from it, her throat working as she swallows. The man opens his mouth to scream, so you drop your cigarette and throw yourself at him, clapping your hand over his parted lips. He thrashes his head and tries to wriggle free, but you're stronger than he is.

The girl is startled out of her ecstatic reverie by the commotion. She tries to cry out when she sees what has become of her lover, but Varney takes up his cane and presses it horizontally against her throat, pinning her to the wall and cutting off her air passages. She noiselessly gags and chokes, squirming futilely. Mircalla takes his dagger from his jacket and stabs it upward into her vagina, twisting the blade around inside of her. When he pulls it back out, a torrent of blood gushes out from between her labial lips. With a horrible, childlike grin, he reattaches his mouth to her cunt and drinks deeply. Varney releases her from the vise-grip of his cane, but her crushed windpipe renders silent her attempts at screaming. He then draws his own dagger and thrusts its tip into a bulging vein in her neck, clamping his jaws around the resultant blood fountain.

Erzsebet's victim has stopped struggling. The color has drained from his stricken face, his hazy eyes fluttering as Erzsebet continues to suck him dry. You're no longer restraining him as much as you're simply holding him up so she can finish her meal.

When his body slackens and your muscles give out against the force of his dead weight, you let him fall to the ground where he lands on his side in a lifeless heap. Erzsebet continues to suckle him for a few moments longer, merely shifting her position to accommodate his collapse. You look over at Varney and Mircalla, who have let their victim fall to the ground, as well. Varney is wiping his face and sunglasses with an embroidered handkerchief, which he then passes to Mircalla, who repeats the action. Erzsebet does the same, but with a strip of fabric cut from the dead man's shirt. As she stands there polishing the smeared lenses of her Wayfarers, her eyes meet yours. Their green-gold glow isn't as bright as you're used to it being, but it still sets something within you alight and you have to remind yourself to breathe.

"You didn't want any?" she asks, putting the sunglasses back on.

You reach out and brush a smudge of blood from her cheek that she'd missed, willing your tentative hand not to tremble. "I'm still full from last night," you answer, thinking of the foul homeless man you'd drank while the others had been at the Bad Seed. In truth, you really just don't feel like throwing up, which Varney and Mircalla are already doing. Varney is hunched over a tin trashcan next to the Dumpster, the regurgitated blood splashing around inside with a metallic clamor. Mircalla is on his hands and knees, retching up a surge of dark blood-bile onto the dead girl's face in a final act of unholy desecration.

Erzsebet's white cheeks are starting to take on a sickly greenish hue, so you grab her hand and lead her farther down the alley to another trash can. You remove the lid and kick it over, spilling its reeking contents onto the ground. "Come on," you say, righting the can and pulling her over to it. "I'll hold your hair back."

CHAPTER 30 – TELEKINESIS SHIT

1

SITTING IN THE NEAR-EMPTY Denny's an hour later, your companions' spirits are high. The ill-begotten blood itself may have been violently expelled from their bodies, but the vital essence of the young lives they'd stolen is fresh in their veins.

Something, however, is wrong with Erzsebet. She's sitting beside you in the booth, and you keep stealing troubled glances at her. Despite her jovial demeanor and the ease with which she lapses into the others' good-natured laughter, her condition seems to have worsened after the episode in the alley. Her vomiting had been violent and torrential, and the color of it had been wrong. It was too dark, almost black. She'd puked for nearly ten minutes before she'd been able to tear herself from the trashcan, and even then, she'd had to sit for a little while so she could catch her breath.

Back at the house, among the long shadows and dim fire-light, it had been easy enough to downplay the apparent severity of her condition. Here, in the harsh blaze of the restaurant's crackling fluorescents, it is irrefutable. The sharply intricate beauty of her features is shrouded in a veil of somatic malaise. Her skin, normally as pure and white as fresh December snow, is encased in a glistening sheen of oily perspiration and now bears closer semblance to age-soured mayonnaise. Her hair, after forfeiting its voluminous buoyancy over the course of the last couple of hours, is heavy and matted. There's a cloying scent of fever-stricken infirmity wafting up through the mask of her perfume.

If the others notice Erzsebet's afflicted appearance, they make no show of it. Mircalla is attacking a stack of greasy strawberry pancakes with a gusto that would be impressive even for someone who *hadn't* just puked up a few pints of freshly-ingested blood only an hour prior. After every few bites, he pauses to add more syrup and whipped cream. The sugar-drenched plate is offset by three adjacent coffee mugs...all of them his and all of them empty...as well as a half-drunk chocolate milkshake.

Varney hasn't touched the plate of French toast in front of him. He sits quiet and pensive, sipping his own coffee and studying a group of stoned high school kids a few tables away with a look of bemused disgust. His top hat lies on the seat between him and Mircalla, and a long lock of dark hair has fallen out of place and now hangs over one lens of his sunglasses.

You're not eating, either, nor is Erzsebet. She'd taken one bite of her omelet, grimaced, and then pushed the plate away after swallowing with visible difficulty. She's watching Mircalla vacuum up his food, and she says with teasingly feigned horror, "My *god*, how can you *eat* like that and stay so *thin?*"

Mircalla looks up at her, his mouth full. A brownish-pink concoction of syrup and strawberries and whipped cream leaks from between his lips and dribbles down his chin. He chews with dramatic slowness, swallows audibly, and then replies, "Dude. I'm fuckin immortal."

Varney wrenches his gaze from the stoners and looks imploringly at you and Erzsebet, gesturing at the kids with a subtle flick of his head. "Look at them," he says, his voice lowered. "They're probably our age, right? How sad it must be, being them. Here they are on a Friday night, hanging out at Denny's because they have nowhere else to go. Not tonight, not ever."

"Varney," you say, "we're hanging out at Denny's, too."

He waves a dismissive hand as if that detail were irrelevant. "There's a difference between us and them."

"Yeah, 'cause we're fuckin immortal," Mircalla says through a mouthful of food. Producing the *f* sound causes him to involuntarily spew flakes of pancake onto the table.

"It's more than that," says Varney. "We're *going* places. We've *been* places. We have a future far more interesting than any they could hope for. Their lot in life is one doomed to mediocrity. A dead-end job, an ugly wife and uglier kids, progressive weight gain and seasonal depression and an ever-growing sense of ennui...*that's* what those clowns have to look forward to."

Sloppily wiping his face with a crumpled napkin and then slurping noisily from the milkshake, Mircalla asks, "What's ennui? Is that, like, an STD, or something?"

Erzsebet giggles at this, but her laughter quickly turns into a coughing fit. You look at her with your face scrunched up in concern. Neither Varney nor Mircalla pay her any mind.

One of the stoned kids has realized that Varney is staring at them. He's tall and broad-shouldered, with an enormous stomach and legs like rolled-up bread dough. His face is round and soft, with babyish features that stand in comical contrast to his bulky stature. Atop his egg-shaped head is a crown of wispy white-blond hair fashioned in an atrocious bowl-cut. Varney grins at him and flutters his fingers in a coquettish wave.

"What are you lookin at, faggot?" the boy asks, too loudly. His poorly-executed attempt at machismo is betrayed by the childlike pitch of his voice.

Varney says nothing. He just keeps smiling and staring, with bold indifference to the looming threat of conflict. The other kids at the table...two boys and two girls, all overweight and affixed with the dull, sloping faces of inbred trailer trash...have turned to look at the four of you.

The blond boy clenches his fists on the table and says to his companions, "Look at those fags, they look so gay." Then, to Varney, "You guys think you're cool with your sunglasses and fag outfits?"

"As a matter of fact," Varney says with an aristocratic flourish to his voice, "Yes, we do think we're cool. We *are* cool."

"Whatever, fag," the boy answers, shaking his head. He stands up and says to his friends, "One of you get the waitress and pay the bill while I go take a piss. I want to get out of here, these fags are creeping me out."

"Your liberal use of that particular pejorative is suggestive of a latent struggle with your own sexual identity," Varney says.

His face a map of confusion and outrage, the boy half-shouts, "What the fuck does that even mean? Are you trying to call *me* a fag?"

Casually sitting back in his seat and running a hand through his hair, Varney replies, "Well, I wouldn't use that word, no, because I am a man of class and civility. I am, however, implying that you may indeed harbor some repressed homosexual urges."

With an enraged growl, the kid starts toward your table, but one of the other boys jumps up and holds him back. "Come on, man," he says to Varney's adversary. "He's not worth it."

The tall boy stands there seething for a moment, his teeth clenched and his wide, pillowy chest rising and falling rapidly. The haggard old waitress has emerged from the kitchen and stands on the opposite side of the room, leaning against the wall and watching the juvenile standoff with bland passivity. After another few long moments, the boy shakes his head again and stalks off to the bathroom, muttering under his breath.

Varney and Mircalla exchange a darkly mischievous glance.

"Guys," you say uneasily, "you literally *just* fed."

His pale face painted with a madman's wild grin, Varney says, "Oh, I don't want to eat him. My standards are far too high for me to drink from that oafish buffoon. But I *do* want to kill him."

"Yeah," Mircalla agrees emphatically. "His homophobic language was really offensive. That word is a total trigger for me."

"This isn't the time or place. Let's just get out of here." You look to Erzsebet for support, but she doesn't even appear to be registering what's happening. Her face is drawn in strained fatigue. "Look at Erzsebet," you persist. "She looks sick. We should really get her home."

Erzsebet snaps out of her stupor and forces a wan smile. "Huh? No, no, I'm fine, I'm not sick. I'm fine."

"See?" Mircalla says. "She's fine. We're fuckin immortal, dude. We don't *get* sick." He gets to his feet and pushes his sunglasses up his nose in what you suppose is a gesture of defiant determination. "Seriously, let's go fuck that douchebag up."

Varney stands, as well, placing his hat upon his head and straightening his bowtie. Erzsebet rises, next, and then the three of them are looking at you with expectant impatience.

With a heavy sigh, refusing to meet any of their gazes, you get up and follow them into the bathroom with your head hung low and your heart roaring in your chest.

2

The bathroom is empty save for the boy, who stands gripping the sides of the sink and admiring his reflection in the murky mirror, turning his head this way and that and flashing confident smiles at himself. One of the urinals is emitting its post-flush gurgle, with gray water still running down into its basin and washing over the spongy blue cake, which does nothing to hide the fresh odor of the boy's piss.

When he hears the door clatter shut, he spins clumsily on his heel to face the four of you and nearly loses his footing. Suddenly bereft of favorable odds now that he's alone and can no longer fall back on the support of his friends, the boy's cocksure bravado is nowhere to be found.

"Listen, guys," he says, holding up his hands and taking a faltering step backward. "I don't want any trouble, okay? Forget what I said. I don't want trouble."

Varney gives you a look and nods his head. You turn the deadbolt on the bathroom door, wincing behind your sunglasses at the resonant *click*. In doing so, you're reminded of the day Felix and his minions had cornered you in the high school bathroom. It had been uncannily similar. Four cool kids against one loser.

Part of you feels bad for the fat kid. The other part of you is just happy you're on the other side this time.

Varney draws his dagger from his belt and starts to advance upon the boy, but Mircalla puts a hand on his shoulder and says, "Hold up, I got this shit." Then, raising his arm toward the boy, he opens his fist and twists it into a claw-like shape. His brow furrows in concentration.

Everyone is silent.

When nothing happens, Varney says to Mircalla, "What, pray tell, in the ever-loving *fuck* are you doing?"

"Shh," Mircalla says, his eyes narrowing and his forehead creasing. "I'm doing some telekinesis shit, here."

"And since when can you perform telekinesis?"

"*Shh*," Mircalla hushes him again. "I've almost got it."

Erzsebet leans back against the wall and lights a cigarette, looking bored. "It's not going to work," she says. "You don't have telekinetic powers."

"Ambrosio can do it, so why shouldn't I be able to?"

"Because, idiot, Ambrosio is, like, a *zillion* years old."

"Enough nonsense," Varney says, pushing Mircalla's hand down and starting toward the boy again. "I want to paint the walls with this kid's blood."

The boy starts to cry.

"Varney," you say, absently wiping your sweating palms on your jeans. "Don't. This is a thousand kinds of stupid. You can't just leave a dead kid in a Denny's bathroom." You really don't give a shit whether the kid lives or dies, in truth. When you think about it, he probably would have merrily joined your tormentors if he'd known you in high school, so the world would probably be just fine without him. Irrespective of whether or not he deserves to live, though, he certainly isn't worth the risk of getting fucked by the cops.

"R*elax*," Varney drawls. "Ambrosio will take care of it. He always does."

"This is different. It's too high-profile. We're in a public restaurant and a dozen people have seen us."

"Shut *up*," he snaps, his cool temperament slipping. "I want this fucker *dead*." He shoves the boy up against the moldy tile wall and seizes his throat, holding the point of the dagger just below his chin. A line of perspiration is trickling from the boy's temple down over the swell of his plump pink cheek. Varney leans in close and licks the sweat away in a slow, protracted motion. Smacking his lips, he smiles and says, "Ah, yes, how I *love* the taste of fear. It is the nectar of the darkest flowers that ever bloomed in the shadow of the valley of death."

"Good line, dude," Mircalla says. Apparently resigned to his psychic inability, he's drawn his own dagger. He glides across the bathroom in several quick, long strides, sidling up on the other side of the boy. He lightly pokes the tip of the blade at his corpulent stomach

"Guys, *seriously*, we need to *go*," you insist. "Erzsebet, tell them we need to go. You *know* this is stupid."

But Erzsebet is lost in some other world that is not your own. Her face is tired and listless. She smokes the cigarette with perfunctory detachment, as if her arm and fingers and lips and lungs are a mere machine programmed solely for that single function.

There comes a sudden thunderous banging on the door, making you jump so sharply that your feet almost leave the floor. "*Mark?*" calls a voice from the other side. "*Mark, are you in there?*" More banging. Your heart is pumping so furiously that you're sure it's going to explode.

At the sound of his friend's voice, the boy lets out a shrill, shrieking, "*Heeeeellllp!*" Varney curses and tightens his grip on the boy's throat, cutting off his scream, but the damage is done. The rapping on the door becomes heavier and more frantic. The handle rattles.

"*Mark! Fuck, Mark, what's going on in there?*" The door starts to shudder as the owner of the voice begins hurling himself against it.

"Guys, *NOW*," you growl urgently. "It's *over*, we need to get the fuck *out* of here."

Varney frowns as he deliberates. Mircalla's resolve has faded; he's backed away from the boy and is standing with the dagger at his side, looking anxiously at the shaking door.

"*Mark, let me in! MARK!*"

The last dregs of your patience have finally dried up. You stomp forward and grab both Varney and Mircalla by their collars and haul them back with a strength you didn't know you had. The boy's legs give out and he slides down the wall and curls up in a blubbering ball. You tug on your friends' collars once more and then turn to the door, no longer sure that you care if they follow or not. You unlatch the door and throw it open.

The kid on the other side had been in mid-lunge, so he comes stumbling into the bathroom. His sneakers skid on the linoleum and he almost goes down, but he recovers his balance and wheels on the four of you with sweating fury.

Before he can do or say anything, Erzsebet languidly walks over to him and curls her arm around his neck and pulls him close to her before kissing him hard on the mouth. When she disengages from him, she stabs the burning end of her cigarette into his shock-widened eye. It makes a sizzling hiss like a match dropped into a cup of water. The sound of it makes the hair on your arms and the back of your neck stand on end.

With the howl of a gut-shot dog, the kid claps his hand over his ruined eye and staggers backward. His heel slips and he bowls over, cracking his head on one of the urinals, mercifully extinguishing his anguished cry.

"Aw, shit," Erzsebet says drily. "I think I might have killed him."

You grumble something incoherent to her and grab her arm, pulling her toward the door. Her skin is alarmingly cool to the touch. When you release your grip, your hand is damp and sticky with her sweat.

CHAPTER 31 – FUCKIN IMMORTAL

1

No one says anything as you all jog briskly across the parking lot and pile into the car. It's not until Varney pulls onto the freeway and opens up the engine that he finally shouts a string of expletives and pounds his fist repeatedly into the center of the steering wheel, the horn barking out a staccato rhythm of high blasts in tune with his strikes.

When his outburst reaches its panting conclusion, he glares at you in the rearview mirror and says darkly, "You should have let me kill him."

Your muscles tighten as you prepare to fire back a line of argumentative reasoning, but you quickly realize the futility of such a venture so you just let yourself wordlessly sink farther into your seat. You look over at Erzsebet, who has fallen asleep with her head against the window and her sunglasses askance.

Mircalla, who appears hypnotized by the flashing lights on the whirring fidget spinner between his thumb and forefinger, says, "Yeah, I mean, *Erzsebet* probably killed that other kid, and you didn't freak out on *her*."

"I think Erzsebet is sick," is all you can say.

No one says anything to that.

Varney gets off the freeway at the Chatterley exit and cuts through Ballard Heights, a sprawling neighborhood of upper-class housing. The big car rolls sleek and silent through the dark, the grotesqueries of the gaudily plain homes flashing by on the other side of the vehicle's tinted windows. You're still studying Erzsebet with dour consternation when Varney slams on the brakes, jolting you half off your seat and jostling Erzsebet awake. Her sunglasses fly off and she looks around confusedly. The sight of her eyes makes you take a sharp intake of breath, though not for the usual reason; their glowing chartreuse color has faded to a dull grass-green, and the bloodshot whites resemble poached egg yolks laced with embryonic chicken blood.

"What's going on?" she asks in a thick, swollen-tongued voice. "Are we home?"

Varney shifts into reverse and guns the car backward. The tires squeal as you and Erzsebet pitch forward again.

"We're making a pit stop," Varney says as he pulls into the driveway of a wide Tudor-style house with a white picket fence lining its meticulously-tended lawn. The saccharine cheer has returned to his voice. As soon as you start to speak, he throws the car in park and whirls around in his seat to look at you with an angry, almost hateful grin. Pointing his finger at you, he says, "*No*, you are to *shut the fuck up*. I want to kill something. I want more blood. The girl in the alley wasn't satisfying. I need *more*."

"Dude, same," Mircalla says.

Taking a deep breath and trying to keep your voice as level as possible, you say to Varney, "That shit at Denny's was way too close of a call. The cops might even be looking for us, already. And dawn is coming, anyway. Don't be stupid."

"It's not up for debate. If you choose to remain here, it is of no consequence to me. But *I'm* going in there." At that, he yanks the keys from the ignition, gets out of the car, and slams the door shut.

"I'm joining him," Mircalla says, getting out, as well.

You look to Erzsebet, your eyes pleading. She simply shrugs and retrieves her sunglasses from the floor, putting them back on and clambering awkwardly out the door after struggling with its handle.

Naturally, you follow her.

2

As the four of you ascend the slight incline of the driveway and then follow the brick path leading to the front door, you ask, "Can you at least tell me why you chose this house?"

Varney points at a blue sign sticking up from the lawn. You lift your sunglasses so you can read it. "Trump-Pence? So?"

Mircalla gasps. "What the fuck do you mean, 'so?' These are *Trump supporters*, dude. That means they're racist, homophobic, misogynists."

"I've never paid attention to politics."

"Man, all you need to know is that Trump is a piece of shit, and anyone who likes him is a piece of shit, too. Tell him, Varney."

Varney nods gravely. "Indeed. What we're doing here is a service to society. By killing whomever lives within this house, *we're* the ones making America great again. Any person who puts a sign like that in their yard deserves to die."

You find their sensationalistic generalizations to be a bit reaching, but you know better than to challenge them, so you just nod and murmur your assent.

Dropping to one knee, Mircalla takes a lockpick from one of his jacket's countless zippers and goes to work on the door. Varney lights a cigarette, his face flushed with excited anticipation. Erzsebet is swaying unsteadily on her stiletto heels, all of her characteristic elegance and light-footed grace having departed her body, chased away by whatever sickness is festering inside of her. She leans against you for support, clutching your arm and putting her head on your shoulder. You wish desperately to remain like that, feeling her against you, the tangibility of her existence as raw and rich as it ever was or could ever be. But then the lock clicks and the door swings open, reminding you with the clarity of a hypnotist's trance-breaking bell that such things are not meant to be.

Not for you.

Varney crushes his cigarette beneath the toe of his shoe and then leads the way inside, his sinister grin so like Ambrosio's that for a brief moment you almost wonder if they're the same person.

The house is quiet, clean, and dark. You take your sunglasses off and tuck them into the inside-pocket of your jacket. Erzsebet stays close to you, her hands wound tightly around your arm. Varney and Mircalla have both drawn their knives, and you can hear one or both of them attempting to choke back gleeful, stifled giggles.

The four of you make your way up a wide staircase to the second floor. Tiptoeing down the hallway, you pass a bathroom, a study, and what appears to be a teenaged girl's bedroom decorated with posters of boy bands and a vast assortment of stuffed animals, though the bed is unoccupied. This fills you with a desperate hope that no one is home, and you can feel Varney and Mircalla's unspoken dread that they may have picked the wrong house. The final door at the end of the hall is closed, however, and somehow you know that the two of them will find exactly what they're looking for on the other side of it.

You aren't wrong.

The door opens silently into a master bedroom, at the center of which is a four-poster bed with two sleeping figures nestled beneath its covers. On the far side of the room, a glass pair of double doors leads out onto a balcony. The transparency of the doors ushers in a swath of orange moonlight that illuminates the shapes in the bed with a sort of saintly holiness.

Varney and Mircalla grin at one another with boiling excitement. Erzsebet pulls away from you, drawing her dagger from her boot and smiling through whatever pain her mysterious illness must certainly be inflicting upon her.

Knowing it's of no use but unable to stop yourself, you attempt to make one final entreaty. Your voice a low, harsh whisper, you say, "Guys, really, I..."

You don't have a chance to say anything more than that. Your three companions spring onto the bed with cackling howls, their knives rising and falling in a dazzling blur of silver and red. Their victims scream and kick and try to shield themselves with their hands, only to see their palms punctured and their fingers hacked away like afterthoughts. The killers take turns pressing their lips to bleeding wounds and then kissing each other with ferocious passion, their tongues swishing stolen blood from one greedy mouth to the other.

Erzsebet pulls her dress over her head and casts it casually aside so she can run handfuls of gore over her exposed flesh.

Varney suckles the bleeding throat of the woman and then spits her blood into the screaming mouth of her husband before letting out a shrill noise that's somewhere between a laugh and a scream.

Mircalla wrangles himself out of his jeans, tears away the woman's shredded nightgown, and then begins to violently thrust into her while belting out the words to "Singin' in the Rain."

The man almost gets out from under Varney, fixing to get at Mircalla, but Erzsebet jumps on him and she and Varney wrestle him off the bed. They bite and claw at him, rending flesh from bone and kissing and fondling each other all the while, until they tumble off him into a thrashing knot. Erzsebet gropes wildly at Varney's belt and frees him from his pants, wrapping her bare legs around his waist and letting out an animal cry as she pulls him into her.

Mircalla is still hammering away at the woman, who has stopped moving, bellowing the lyrics to the song in an atrociously out-of-tune voice, so unlike the one he had exhibited onstage at the Bad Seed.

"*What a glooooorious feeling...*"

Varney's hips pump with superhuman speed, his coattails flapping as Erzsebet shrieks his name.

His name. Would it be yours if you'd joined them, just now? If you had partaken in their blood-circus sideshow act, would it be *you* fucking her beside the hacked-up man on the floor?

"*I'm HAAAAPPY again!*"

Erzsebet's sunglasses have come off, and for a second her eyes meet yours. Even in the dark, the sickness within them is apparent. There's something else in them, too, though, but you aren't sure what, exactly. An apology, maybe? Yes, for a very short moment, her eyes seem to be apologizing to you, though for what, you'll never be certain. But then her eyes roll back in her head as her body is wracked with a back-arching orgasm, and whatever she might have been attempting to communicate to you is lost forever beneath the chords of her ecstatic scream.

Mircalla's coupling seems to be reaching its conclusion, as well, and the next line of the song becomes an unintelligible burst of grunts and groans that overlap with similar noises emitting from Varney's throat.

Standing there and watching your three friends achieve simultaneous orgasm, you can take it no more. You stomp across the room and throw open the glass doors, bursting onto the balcony with your chest heaving and your veins glowing with rage.

It wasn't supposed to be like this. Reckless murder and senseless cruelty interwoven with crippling jealousy...that's not what you'd signed up for. You don't know exactly what you were expecting, but it hadn't been this. And what about McPleasant? Hadn't *he* been the driving force behind your embrace of this life of darkness and death and endless night? Ambrosio had promised you the power to find and kill him, but you feel no closer to doing so than you did when you were in LA. And Erzsebet...she'd been a factor in that final decision, too, had she not? Had the prospect of getting closer to her not been almost as tantalizing as the idea of finding the monster that you put your life on this terrible trajectory in the first place?

But if tonight proves anything, it is that you are no closer to her than you are to finding your parents' killer.

You attempt to light a cigarette with quavering hands, but upon striking the wheel of the Bic, it flies from your hand and plummets from the balcony, bouncing off the pointed tip of a fencepost and disappearing in the dark grass. You're left standing there with the cigarette dangling stupidly from your lips, one hand still cupped around its end and the other frozen around the shape of the empty space where the lighter had been an eyeblink ago.

The sound of the doors opening behind you makes you spin around. Your mouth drops open at the sight of them, the unlit cigarette falling cold and forgotten to your feet. They are the image of personified death and incarnate suffering, drenched in blood and viscera, with scraps of torn flesh sticking to their skin and their clothes. Erzsebet is the worst, with her mottled eyes staring out from her blood-smeared face and her soaked hair hanging in tangled clumps. She's put her dress back on, but the way its sodden fabric clings to her body makes you realize how frail she looks.

All three of them, though...even Erzsebet...are grinning.

"Fuck, you missed some good shit," Mircalla says, stretching and yawning. "I feel *so* much better." He lights a cigarette. Erzsebet and Varney do the same, but you leave yours on the ground. You feel like you should speak but you can't think of anything to say.

Erzsebet walks over and kisses your cheek. You resist the urge to flinch away from the syrupy smell of death wafting from her gore-clogged pores. She grabs your crotch and squeezes gently, whispering, "We missed you in there."

Sitting down on the dark wood, Varney sighs contentedly and takes a drag from his cigarette. "My friends," he says, "I've never loved anything more than I love you in this moment."

With catlike grace, Mircalla leaps onto the railing and puts his hands on his hips, looking down at you and Varney and Erzsebet with his cigarette clenched between his grinning teeth. "My dudes, my lady, life is fuckin *good*." Then, taking the cigarette from his mouth with his thumb and forefinger, he spreads his arms wide and tosses his head back, letting out a long howl before shouting, "*WE'RE FUCKIN IMMORTAL!*"

3

You're the first person to see the man appear in the doorway. When Erzsebet takes note of your stricken face, she turns and sees him, too. Then Varney sees him.

Mircalla never sees him.

The man is leaning against the doorjamb, slouched and grimacing in pain. His hair hangs over his silently weeping eyes, the tears running white tracks through the caked blood on his face. His clothes are in ragged tatters, revealing a dozen gaping wounds. A coiled loop of intestine sags from a deep gash in his stomach, leaking steaming green bile onto his shredded pants.

He shouldn't be alive, much less be able to stand there brandishing a long double-barreled shotgun.

His grip on the gun is awkward and feeble. If someone moves fast enough, it could easily be knocked from his hands. The twin barrels are resting lightly atop his holey left palm; all five of the fingers on that hand have been sliced off. He has the stock cradled in his right armpit, and his right middle finger...the sole remaining finger he has left...is curled around the trigger.

No, it wouldn't take much at all to disarm the man if someone would just move fast enough.

But no one moves fast enough.

Mircalla's head is still cocked back, the word "immortal" not yet dead upon his lips, when the man with the gun growls, "Suck my Second Amendment, you commie fuck."

He pulls the trigger, and the end of the gun explodes in a flash of light that rips the waning remnants of the night apart with a godlike crash. The blast hits Mircalla squarely in the chest and propels him off of the railing in a shower of blood and splintered ribs. You feel some of it spray onto your cheek. His cigarette bounces onto the balcony and rolls across the wood, coming to a stop at the toe of Erzsebet's bloodstained boot. The smoke curls up into the air and mingles with the heavy blue-gray plumes of sulfurous smog pouring from the barrels of the shotgun.

For several long moments, no one moves. Everyone just stares at the cigarette, its white filter dyed red with the gunman's wife's blood.

Then, all three of you are upon him.

You don't remember drawing your dagger, but all at once it's in your hand and you and Erzsebet and Varney are atop the shooter, plunging your weapons into him over and over again with blinding, manic rapidity. The sounds of the blades entering and exiting his body are like hot-breathed secrets uttered between clandestine lovers under the forbidden shroud of night. The sounds go on long after the man's breathing has stopped, until the three of you collapse onto the floor, your burning lungs gasping for air.

Once the fiery red craze has lifted from you, leaving you exhausted but clearheaded, you sit up and wipe a smattering of blood from your face with the sleeve of your jacket. "Fuck," you say quietly. "He got Mircalla. He fucking got him."

Now Varney sits up, looking at you with a befuddled expression. Then he begins to laugh. Erzsebet sits up and laughs, too, though her laughter is more that of a delirious old woman in the dark throes of dementia. It's fetid and squelchy, like the bubbling of swampy pondwater.

"He didn't *get* anyone," Varney says, standing up and running his sticky hands through his blood-dampened hair. "I *told* you, we're not that easy to kill. Sunlight, stake through the heart, decapitation...*that* shit will kill us. But a gunshot? That's a mere flesh wound, at worst. The immortal equivalent of a papercut. By the time we get outside, Mircalla will be right as rain."

You think of the way Mircalla's chest had caved in and the way his blood had felt on your face, but you don't say anything. You just nod and follow Varney and Erzsebet out of the house and into the yard.

4

When you turn the corner to go around the side of the house to fetch Mircalla, the three of you freeze.

Mircalla is not, as Varney had so confidently claimed, *right as rain*. He is not gathering himself to his feet and brushing himself off, his wounds knitting themselves back together like they do in the movies. He's not even on the ground.

He's impaled on a fencepost, its wooden point sticking up through his concave chest. Blood and bits of his pierced heart coat the wood like a child's gloopy finger-painting. As you and your companions warily approach the corpse with wide eyes and open mouths, you think you can make out tiny ventricles and individual arteries slowly sliding down the post as though longing to return to the vessel from which they had emerged.

When you're a few feet away from Mircalla's body, Varney doubles over and pukes out all the blood he'd ingested upstairs. Erzsebet coughs, gags, and does the same. While they're vomiting, you spot your lost lighter in the grass. You don't pick it up.

When the two of them are done throwing up, you whirl around and punch Varney in the face, shattering the left lens of his Aviators. The blow knocks him off his feet and he falls flat on his back. He just lies there for a few seconds, not moving, his breathing slow and tapered. When he pushes himself up on his elbows and looks at you, the one eye that's visible through the empty frame of his crooked sunglasses is brimming with tears.

"You got Mircalla killed," you say down to him. "This is your fault. This is on *you*." Your voice is deep and menacing, full of power and condescending disapproval. It frightens you, for it sounds more like Ambrosio's voice than your own.

Varney gets unsteadily to his feet, swaying a little on his heels. For a second it looks like he's going to be sick again, but he swallows down whatever was about to come up and looks back over at Mircalla's body. "We can't leave him here. We have to get him down."

Your eyes lift to the lightening sky overhead. It feels like it had been night-black when you were on the balcony just minutes ago, but now it's glowing faintly, pregnant with the impending dawn. The once-orange moon has dulled to a pale, dusty amber disk that's quickly receding with the waning darkness.

"No," you tell Varney. "We need to go. Dawn is coming. And the gunshot..."

As if adding declarative punctuation to your unfinished sentence, the bleating cry of a distant siren rises up from somewhere to the east.

"They're coming," you say. "There's no time. We have to leave him."

"We can't," Varney says, on the verge of a sob. He starts towards Mircalla again, but your arm shoots out and you grab him by the collar just as you had in the Denny's bathroom earlier that night, so long ago.

"*No*," you say in that horrible voice that's far too much like Ambrosio's. It makes Varney whip his head around, his one visible eye wide with submissive terror. "You're not calling the shots anymore, Varney. No more bullshit. I'm telling you we need to go, so *we're going*."

His posture slackens and he looks at the ground. He nods sullenly and says something imperceptible that you don't ask him to repeat. He spies Mircalla's sunglasses lying in the grass and snatches them up, storing them in the inside pocket of his jacket.

You turn to Erzsebet, who is leaning against the fence and weeping silently. "Let's go," you tell her. Your tone is softer with her, but still infused with your newfound authority. She doesn't say anything, but when you and Varney start running back to the car, she follows.

When Varney reaches for the driver's door handle, you snatch his wrist and growl, "No. I'm driving."

"No one drives this car but me. No one."

"I. Said. I'm. Driving." You can feel the fire blazing in your eyes, and Varney must see it, too, because he hands over the keys without another word of contest. The siren is drawing nearer. No...sirens. The overlapping irregularity of the wails suggests there are more than one of them.

5

You drive with cool precision, but your eyes keep flicking from the road up to the ever-lightening sky. A sweat has broken out upon your brow. You think you can feel an unpleasantly tingling crackle alighting upon the cold surface of your skin, but it could be your imagination. You're maybe five minutes from Ambrosio's house...five minutes, and you'll be safe. You just need the sun to stay put for five more minutes.

Varney and Erzsebet are both in the back seat, huddled close together and looking out at the sky with visible anxiety. "Hurry," one of them whispers, though you can't make out which one. Your knuckles are white as you grip the steering wheel with painfully strained tension so your sweat-slimed palms don't slip and send you careening off the road to certain death. The slightest delay will leave you fatally vulnerable to the explosion of sunlight creeping just beneath the horizon like a shark preparing to strike, the pink sky acting as its menacing dorsal fin. You look at the speedometer, the needle floating timidly at eight miles per hour over the posted limit. Intermittently, your foot will ease off the pedal when you think about the ruinously scorching destruction you and your friends will face if you pass a surreptitiously-parked cruiser, and then almost immediately press back down when you consider the probable notion that the difference between life and death (death and *un*death?) may come down to a matter of seconds.

"*Hurry*," comes the voice again, still unidentifiable. It might be both of them in unison. It might be in your head.

You can definitely feel your skin prickling, now. You're almost certain of it.

When you turn onto Ambrosio's street, you gun the gas. The Rolls jets forward without so much as a hitch. One second, you're going 32, the next you're approaching 50. The nose of the car voraciously swallows up the pavement. You slow down to go over the bump onto the driveway, and then jam the pedal again as soon as both sets of tires are upon the smooth black incline. The car races up the hill until you reach the parking plateau, at which point you punch the brake so hard that Varney and Erzsebet tumble off the seat into a heap on the floor. You crank the key counterclockwise and yank it from the ignition, and then you and your companions are stumbling out of the vehicle and sprinting for the door. You risk a glance at the horizon, which is now a smoldering, hateful ocher as the murderous sun threatens to crest above the flat dark clouds at any second. All that time spent living in the cold shadow of night has rendered your eyes sensitive and vulnerable, and the unfamiliar brightness scalds them and makes them feel as though they're boiling in their sockets.

One of Erzsebet's heels gets stuck in the dewy ground and nearly sends her sprawling into the grass, but Varney catches her and swoops her into his arms, carrying her like a baby. She buries her face in his neck, shielding herself from the encroaching light. As much as you wish it were you who was carrying her, you've never been more thankful for him.

As you near the door, you fumble with the keys and grasp the heavy black skeleton key between your thumb and forefinger, holding it out in front of you like a knife. It slams snugly home into its slot in the huge oaken door, and you twist it so violently that it's a wonder it doesn't break. Concurrently with the turning of the key, you smash your shoulder hard into the wood. The door flies open just as the others crash into your back, sending the three of you toppling inside in a flailing entanglement of limbs. The keys fly from your hand and go sliding across the foyer. You can feel scalding, terrorizing heat behind you. You wriggle free of the others and roll over onto your back, turning your head to the side and shielding your face with your arm. With a single convulsive kick, you drive your heel into the ajar door. It bangs shut, reverberating on its hinges.

Realizing you haven't been breathing, you gulp in a gluttonous gasp of air and then let it out in a slow, hissing *whoosh*.

You hear the sound of boots on the hardwood floor, approaching with slow, measured languor. "*Well*," comes Ambrosio's voice from the dark. "*That* certainly was a close call, wasn't it?" And then, with venomous disapproval, he adds, "*You fucking idiots.*"

CHAPTER 32 – LOW ODDS

1

"This is so fucking asinine," Varney grumbles as he ducks into the passenger seat of Derek's BMW. "It's Halloween. Can't you let us go out on our own, just this once?"

Derek gets behind the wheel as you and Erzsebet shut yourselves into the back seat. "No," he says. "These are the orders, and they will be followed."

Ever since Mircalla's death nearly two weeks ago, Ambrosio has stipulated that Derek act as your group's chaperone. The Phantom, he said, has been compromised; a number of eyewitnesses claimed to see a black Rolls-Royce leave the scene of the crime not long after the gunshot sounded. No one managed to get the plate number, but the car is conspicuous enough as it is. As such, it currently sleeps idly in the garage, indefinitely decommissioned. When Varney suggested that the three of you just start using the Audi, Ambrosio said that none of you could be trusted to use sound judgment when conducting your nefarious affairs, and that Derek's guardianship would be insurance against the "liabilities of your behavior."

"Fucking *asinine*," Varney says again, and then coughs into a soggy handkerchief that's stained with bloody phlegm. Not long after the night everything went to hell, he began exhibiting symptoms similar to Erzsebet's. Their severity has progressed at an alarming rate. In conjunction with the cough, he's rapidly been losing weight, and his features have become so drawn and haggard that he's taken on the look of a junkie that's a decade his senior.

Erzsebet has started wearing a small hat with a mourning veil, though you suspect its purpose has less to do with a show of respect for her dead friend than her desire to keep hidden the strange declination of her health. Without the veil, she, too, appears to have aged significantly. The purple veins and washed-out eyes are not flattering.

"We should probably head downtown," Derek says as he pulls out of the driveway. "Ambrosio says it's still not safe for you to hunt in Mudhoney. We can..."

"Whatever," Varney says, straightening his sunglasses (*Mircalla's* sunglasses, actually; he's been wearing them since you broke his Aviators). He leans his head against the window. "I have no fucks to give."

No one has had any fucks to give, lately. With Mircalla gone, nothing has been the same. The carefree lifestyle to which you'd grown familiar, imperfect as it may have been, seems a mere shadow of a memory.

When Derek trundles up to an intersection, Varney straightens and points to the BP gas station on the right. "Pull in here," he orders Derek. "I want a Four Loko."

Derek does as he's instructed, but you can see his jaw working in irritation. He parks in a space along the front of the building and looks expectantly at Varney. "Go on. Hurry up. I don't want to be out all night."

"I left my wallet at the house."

Derek takes off his Wayfarers and blinks at Varney, who shrugs innocently. After staring hatefully at him for a few moments, Derek kills the engine and starts to get out.

"Wait," says Varney, grabbing Derek's arm. "It's cold. *I'm* cold. Leave it running."

"You'll survive."

"You're *supposed* to *take care of* us. Ambrosio said so, and Ambrosio *loves* us. You wouldn't want to incur your master's wrath by mistreating his children, would you?"

Ambrosio actually never explicitly said anything about Derek "taking care of" you, but Derek didn't know that because he hadn't been privy to the original conversation. Maybe he *had* commanded Derek, in a private exchange, to accommodate to your needs, but you doubt it.

Derek jangles the keys in his hand, considering Varney with gritted teeth. "Fine," he says, at last. "Spoiled fucking brat." He jams the keys back into the ignition and twists them violently before stalking off into the gas station.

Varney turns around to face you and Erzsebet. Your reflections are warped into funhouse images on the lenses of his sunglasses. His lips, which are chapped and painted with dribbles of phlegm, peel into a shit-eating smirk.

"Don't," you say. "Varney, don't even think about it. Ambrosio will flip."

"Do it," contradicts Erzsebet, her voice a husky rasp that sounds nothing like her. "Fuck that Ken-doll douchebag. I want to have some fun. It's what Mircalla would want, too."

"Guys, we can't..." But resistance is useless. Varney is already climbing into the driver's seat. Through the window, you can see Derek at the counter. He glances over his shoulder and, failing to immediately register what's happening, starts to turn back to the cashier. Then the necessary wires connect in his brain, and he whirls around, wide-eyed and open-mouthed. Varney flashes him a peace sign, grinning like a piranha, and then slowly turns his hand around and curls down his index finger.

You and Erzsebet fasten your seatbelts.

As Derek runs for the glass door, Varney yanks the gear shift into reverse, steps on the gas pedal, and peels out of the parking lot.

2

When you ask where Varney is going, he replies, "Villa Vida. It's tradition. As a wee lad, I always did my tricking and treating there. They had the best candy. The neighborhood I grew up in, along with *all* of the neighborhoods in Chatterley, were terrible for trick-or-treating. Those health-obsessed assholes would pass out fruit platters and organic granola bars instead of candy."

He parks Derek's Beemer on the street by a gazebo, in a neighborhood not far from the one in which you'd grown up. You may have even trick-or-treated here, yourself, as a child, but you can't be sure. You tired of the concept at an early age.

As you get out of the car, Erzsebet looks around at the costumed children scurrying up and down the sidewalk and says, "We should have dressed up."

"Oh, my *dear*," Varney says, retrieving his hat from the floor in front of the passenger seat and fixing it atop his head. "We *are* dressed up."

3

From there, the night quickly devolves into hellish, hallucinatory violence. You're opposed to the entire idea of this escapade at first, but ultimately you reconcile to yourself that it's going to occur with or without your involvement. Besides, the *thirst* is awake.

It goes something like this.

House 1: An old man and woman, sitting in wicker chairs on their porch with a big popcorn bowl full of miniature Twix bars on the small glass table between them. You and your companions force them inside and cut up their soft, wrinkled faces with surgical meticulousness, lapping at the blood like cats at milk saucers.

House 2: An affable-looking fellow opens the door when Varney rings the doorbell, holding a basket of assorted snacks. His smile fades to a straight line of wary distrust when he observes the teenagers on his porch; he assumes the blood is fake, but his eyes seem to ask, *Aren't you a little old for this?* Varney shoves him backward and stabs him in the stomach. The man's wife and two small children are watching television in the living room. They scream when they realize what's happening, but not for long.

House 3: A young couple answers the door, each of them wearing ghost-shaped oven mitts and holding a platter of steaming peanut butter cookies. They're probably in their late teens or early twenties. The girl has dark red hair with blonde highlights, and the boy bears a passing resemblance to you. Or, at least, what you might have looked like if you'd lived another four or five years instead of being frozen, for better or worse, in a fifteen-year-old vessel. You push past Varney and Erzsebet and knock aside the couple's steel trays, sending cookies bouncing and skittering across the floor. You cut the girl's throat and then fall upon the boy, stabbing him in his face and then sawing off the top of his head until his brains come leaking out in a soupy, congealed lump. Varney and Erzsebet applaud as you slurp the bloody fluid squirting from his punctured eyes.

House 4: A heavyset man with a tall afro comes to the door, bearing a blue bowl with "FEEL THE BERN" painted across it beneath a grinning caricature of Bernie Sanders. You each take a handful of candy and go to the next house.

House 5: A tired-looking woman with a sleeping baby in the crook of her arm tells you that the last group of kids cleaned her out and she doesn't have anything for you. Erzsebet tells her she's wrong.

It's after midnight when you reach the fifteenth house, but by then you've stopped counting and it could be the eighth or the eightieth house for all you know. The doorbell doesn't appear to work when Varney pushes it, so he hammers on the door with his fist. When no one answers, you say, "Let's head back, Varney. I'm full, anyway." And you are. Not to mention the fact that your head is swimming and most of the cords tethering you to reality seem to have snapped.

Erzsebet nods and then pukes into a bush.

"No," says Varney with the stubborn obstinance of a petulant child. "I want one more. These blokes have their lights on. They're *in* there. I know it." He hammers on the door again.

You look over your shoulder. The neighborhood is quiet and still. The real trick-or-treaters have long since gone home to gobble their plunder. Three teenagers going door to door at this hour doesn't look good, Halloween or not. Especially when those teenagers are drenched head to toe in blood and viscera.

Halloween or not.

You start to reach for Varney's arm so you can pull him away from the house, but then he tries the door and it swings open into a brightly-lit foyer. He grins at you and says, "See? Meant to be. Let's feast."

You sigh and follow him inside. Erzsebet comes in after you, closing the door behind her.

Even before you see the nightmare in the dining room, you know something is wrong. You can feel it. It's a feeling you felt before.

First, on May 3rd, 2015, in another life.

Then, a second time only a couple of short months ago, in yet *another* life.

Varney is a few paces ahead of you, and when he turns the corner into the dining room, he stops dead in his tracks and breathes, "Sweet Mary, mother of fuck."

You join him, already knowing what you're going to see.

There's a family seated at the table. A man, a woman, a teenaged girl, and a toddler in a highchair. All of them have been gutted and decapitated. Each family member's head is on the plate in front of its respective body. Piled on a platter in the center of the table is a heaping mountain of intestines.

The left hand of each person at the table has been stripped of its fingernails.

"Who the fuck did *this* shit?" Erzsebet asks from beside you.

And then, from behind you, the stairs creak.

You turn around slowly.

You know what you're going to see this time, too.

Whom you're going to see.

Somehow, he looks even bigger than he did in your dream. His hair is wilder, redder. His limbs longer and his shoulders wider. His beard bushier.

"McPleasant," you say.

He's standing partially in shadow, but there's enough light in the dining room and the hallway for you to see his expression. There isn't, however, really anything to see; his blood-streaked expression is as bland as his faded white-and-yellow-checkered shirt. "Dark Boy," he says tonelessly. "You've been looking for me. I found you. Bad luck."

"Dark Boy?" says Varney, raising an eyebrow. "I pity the intellect of whatever lamebrain came up with that one."

"Sounds like a name you'd give a supervillain's retarded sidekick," agrees Erzsebet. "Who is this asshole, Casanova?" She looks back at the grisly scene at the dinner table. "Wait. He's not...?"

"He is," you answer flatly, keeping your eyes trained on McPleasant.

"Well, smack my ass and call me Wendy," says Varney. "What are the odds of *that?*"

"Low odds," says McPleasant. Standing there on the stairs, his posture is ramrod-straight. His deathly gaze remains linked with yours. There are maybe ten long paces between the two of you.

Your hand is wound so tightly around the handle of the dagger that you can feel the purple gemstones digging into the grooves of your palm. The black piston of your heart thumps with the rhythmic whir of boat propeller. Fog from your sweating face steams up the lenses of your sunglasses.

This is it. This is what it was all for. Everything has…

Wait.

Something is wrong.

"Go on, kill the bastard, already," Varney urges. "What are you…"

"*Quiet*," you snap, holding up a finger and cocking your head to the side. "Listen." You close your eyes and try to focus on the sound. At first, you'd thought it was your heart. That *chop-chop-chop* noise like a boat propeller. It's not, though. It isn't coming from inside you. It's coming from outside. And it's not a boat.

It's a helicopter.

Flashing red and blue lights filter into the windows from the street outside.

"*COME OUT WITH YOUR HANDS ABOVE YOUR HEAD*," commands a mechanically-amplified voice. Just like the movies. And Ambrosio had said the shit from the movies was nonsense.

But he *hadn't* actually said that, had he?

No, he'd said *most* of the shit from the movies was nonsense. Most, but not all.

Varney and Erzsebet look at each other in horror, their faces blanching beneath the coating of blood. They surely must be sharing in your line of thinking, which is that the cops are here for the three of you, but then the megaphoned voice bellows, "*WE KNOW YOU'RE IN THERE, McPLEASANT. IT'S OVER.*" Which means they must not know about *your* monstrous doings…not yet…but it doesn't provide all that much relief. Especially because the voice continues, "*WE HAVE THE PLACE SURROUNDED.*"

Straight out of a primetime police procedural. Except, of course, it *isn't*. You're a band of very real murderers trapped in the middle of a very real crime scene with a man who's on the FBI's very real most-wanted list. Their bullets might not be able to kill you (no fenceposts here), but if there are as many cops out there as you assume there to be, it's going to pose a problem regardless of your nigh-invincibility. You'd likely end up in custody, and then how long would it be before they unwittingly exposed you to the sun's annihilating rays? You've never been to jail, so you don't know what the window situation might be like, but just one is all it would take. Would Ambrosio come to your rescue in time to prevent that from happening?

Would Ambrosio come to your rescue at all?

"*IF YOU DON'T COME OUT, WE'RE GONNA COME IN, AND WE'RE GONNA COME IN SHOOTING.*"

You consider your options.

You can kill him. You know that with everything in you. You're ready, and you have Ambrosio's "dark gift" on your side. But McPleasant is *big*. You could kill him, yes, but he wouldn't make it easy for you. Even if Varney and Erzsebet help, he'd be certain to give you a run for your money before you deliver the finishing blow. That would be fine under different circumstances, but if the police come barging in while you're still tussling with him, a whole other slew of problems would open up. And if they come in shooting as the megaphone cop had said they would (and he hadn't sounded like he was teasing), you and your friends would get caught in the crossfire. If that happened, they police would want to know how three teenagers could absorb a volley of bullets and then live to chat about it. They'd probably turn you over to the government, and you'd be forced to undergo all sorts of...

"Hide," McPleasant says, cutting short your contemplations. "Hide right now."

"Excuse me?" you hear yourself say, trying to sound for-
midable but failing when your voice cracks on the second
syllable of the first word.

"Hide," McPleasant repeats. "This is my end. Get out of
my spotlight. I don't want to share." He holds up a hairy
hand when you start to retort. "You want to kill me. I know.
I don't know why. That's fine. But you can't. You need to
hide. They're coming."

The noise from the helicopter has grown louder, and it
occurs to you that there's probably more than one of them.

"*LAST CHANCE. COME OUT NOW IF YOU WANT
TO LIVE.*"

Varney and Erzsebet look to you for instruction on how
to proceed, as they had the night on the playground.

"Do as he said," you say. "This is my fight."

"Fat chance," says Erzsebet. "*Your* fight is *our* fight. We're
socialists, remember? If you're gonna go down, we're going,
too."

"Damn straight," says Varney.

In spite of everything, your heart swells. And just like
that, you realize she's right; it *isn't* your fight. Not anymore.
You've entered into something that has stripped you of the
ability to act as a solitary force. They're tied to you in such
a way that your actions affect their fate just as much as their
own. If you decide to sacrifice everything in the name of
revenge, *they're* the ones who are going to suffer, and they'll
do so gladly.

That shit will poison you, you know, Mara had once said in
respect to your resentment. But the game has changed, and if
you take that final gulp of poison tonight, you'll effectively be
killing the last two people in the world who care about you as
much as you care about them. Already, that poison has led you
to kill Mara and abandon Quincey, Ianthe, and Rebecca. If you
move on McPleasant, your desperately sought-after retribution
will come at the expense of two individuals whose only crime

(well, at least in *this* regard) was loving a fucked-up kid with a trainload of baggage and bad intentions.

In the end, it really comes down to one question.

Just how much of a selfish piece of shit are you?

The cops have gathered on the porch and are preparing to batter open the door. You don't know how you know this, but you do.

"What's it gonna be, Dark Boy?"

You look at him, your body bristling with rage and antipathy. You take a single step forward, your teeth set in wrathful tenacity. Then your fist, white with strain, loosens its grip on the knife and you slide it home into its scabbard. There's an open door halfway down the hall between you and McPleasant, leading down into a dark basement. You turn to Varney and Erzsebet, gesture to the door, and say, "There. Now."

They don't question or argue. With bounding steps, they bolt for the door and scramble down the stairs, taking them three at a time. You hang back long enough to get one final look at McPleasant. "This isn't over," you say for no explainable reason, because *of course* it's over. You know it just as well as he does.

McPleasant says nothing.

You dart into the basement, shutting the door behind you. Shutting the door on your past, as well as what had truly been your only plan for the future.

There's a crawlspace beneath the stairs, and it's here that you, Varney, and Erzsebet take refuge, obscuring its entrance with a stack of cardboard boxes once you've settled in.

Not fifteen seconds after huddling into this hiding place, and less than thirty since you made the decision to give up on your quest once and for all, you hear the front door explode open upstairs.

The gunshots come next.

CHAPTER 33 – FUCK IT

1

ALL OF YOU REMAIN awake for the remainder of the night, silently listening to the stomping commotion upstairs. You can picture police and crime scene technicians milling about, snapping photographs and shaking their heads. Only once does anyone come into the basement, and it's seemingly for a cursory routine check. A single set of footsteps descends the stairs, clomps around, and then goes back up to where the real action is.

Eventually, you doze off around dawn, once the ruckus has begun to die down. When you wake again in the late hours of morning, your neck and shoulders stiff from the cramped quarters, the house is silent. Still, none of you dares breathe a word. You take turns napping uncomfortably for what feels like days. Around seven PM, the three of you finally crawl out from the cubbyhole and cautiously proceed upstairs, your knives at the ready. No one is there. The carnage has been expertly cleaned up, and the only sign of the prior night's events is the presence of dozens of crisscrossing lines of dirty bootprints on the floor and a line of police tape sanctioning off the yard outside.

You're anxiously self-conscious of your blood-crusted appearances as you jog back to where Varney left Derek's car, but the neighborhood is mute and unnoticing. You cross paths with no one.

On the silent drive home, you pull out your phone and go to *The Plain Dealer*'s website, unsurprised to find that the top article bears the headline "MUDHONEY MONSTER'S REIGN OF TERROR COMES TO BLOODY END." There's nothing about the other murders in the neighborhood, meaning only that they either haven't been discovered yet, or you still have a friend in Ambrosio, after all.

If the latter is the case, he doesn't show it upon your homecoming. When you return to the mansion, the three of you reluctantly march up to the sixth floor and knock on his chamber door. It's Derek who answers, his eyes narrowed in contempt. "Keys, asshole," he says to Varney, holding out his hand.

Varney coughs into his handkerchief, gives Derek the keys, and says, "We want to talk to Ambrosio."

Derek makes no move to allow your entry. "Yeah. He said you would. Tough shit."

He starts to close the door, but Varney blocks it with his hand. "You don't have the right to deny us counsel with our Sire."

"Your 'Sire' is busy. He doesn't want to talk to you." With a cruel smile, he adds, "He's also given me permission to abandon my babysitting duties."

"So, we can start going out on our own again?" Varney asks, brightening a little.

"I don't give a flying fuck what you do. But you'll have to do it without a car."

The hope in Varney's face extinguishes like a snuffed match. "That's not *fair*. How are we supposed to feed?"

"Again, I don't give a fuck. Guess you'll just have to stay local. The next-door neighbor has a yappy chihuahua. I'd suggest starting there."

Varney starts to complain some more, but Derek slams the door in his face.

2

The now-customary dour mood permeates throughout the next week like a drug-resistant head cold. The three of you leave the house only twice, both times strictly to feed. The first night, you do go to the house next door, killing and drinking the old married couple that lives there. You don't kill the chihuahua.

Two nights later, you walk a few blocks east and kill a family of five. Varney selects the house based on the ugly green color of the shutters.

Excepting these excursions, you stay in the house and don't do much of anything but watch movies, play cards, and get unhappily drunk. Varney and Erzsebet are too exhausted and sick to even make love. Their coughing keeps you up, even with the aid of tranquilizers, so you go back to sleeping in the guest bedroom. You don't bother offering up an explanation, and they don't ask.

Overall, you feel very empty. Something akin to boredom sets in, coupled with an oppressive sense of purposelessness. With McPleasant's anticlimactic death at the hands of faceless lawmen, it feels like there's no longer any reason for your existence. All of a sudden, the idea of a never-ending life of perma-night seems pretty drab.

Without your resentment, you are nothing.

It begs the question of whether or not you were ever anything in the first place.

3

On November 5th, 2016, the night before your sixteenth birthday, you awaken from a dream of Mara. The details aren't clear; by the time you open your eyes, the bulk of it is all but gone. You know only that she had been there, and now she is not.

You wander around the house, looking for Varney and Erzsebet, but not really sure why, because you have little to talk about these days. It's not that you feel any differently toward them, because you don't. What's different is how you feel about yourself, and maybe that's even worse. You swear to yourself that you love them, but your mother had always said that people can't love others if they don't love themselves. You think she was wrong, but your confidence in that matter isn't as strong as it once was.

You wind up finding Erzsebet in the Savage Garden, sitting on the very bench where she'd told you the story of how she'd come into immortality. What different times those had been.

She isn't wearing her veil; she is, in fact, wearing only her bra and panties, and the sight of her would bring you to tears if you hadn't wept all of them out the night of the bad batch, almost a year ago to the day. She's shriveled into a skeletal husk of her once-shapely self, little more than a dry tangle of bone and cartilage shrink-wrapped in skin the shade of curdled milk. Her dull, dim eyes are too big for her face. Ringed red welts are polka-dotted across her body. Her greasy white hair is stringy and flat. The dark roots are starting to show along her scalp like a festering infection.

She doesn't seem to notice you as you approach. She just sits there smoking her cigarette with routine indifference. When you sit down, she says without looking at you, "I think I'm dying. I don't want to die."

"You aren't going to die. You *can't* die." Sloppily forcing a half-grin, you append this assertion with, "You're fuckin immortal."

She doesn't laugh. Your fake smile crawls away and dies. "Something is wrong," she says. "I tried to tell myself...fuck, I don't even know what I tried to tell myself. I've known for a while. I just tried *not* to know."

You mentally cycle through a list of canned responses you could apply to that, but you can't come up with anything that fits.

"Something is wrong with Varney, too," Erzsebet continues, as if this is news to you. "He's almost as sick as I am. We talked about it the other night, after you'd gone to bed. We went to go talk to Ambrosio. I'm positive that he'll have an explanation for us. Everything will be okay if we could just have an *explanation*. But Derek answered the door again, that fucking asshole. He told us to get lost and that Ambrosio would talk to us 'if and when it was necessary.'" She sniffs, and a crystalline tear wells up in the corner of her bloodshot eye and then cascades down her cheek in a straight line. "It's like we've been abandoned. I've never felt so alone before. I'm scared."

Still unable to think of something to say, you put a reassuring hand on her bare thigh. It takes a great deal of determination not to reflexively jerk it away; her skin has the cold, slimy texture of mud.

She looks at you with eyes you don't recognize, eyes so distant and lost that for a second you aren't even sure *she* recognizes *you*. "I wish you would have killed McPleasant. I know why you didn't. I know we would have probably died. But I think maybe that would have been okay. I think maybe that would have been better."

You definitely don't have a response for that one.

4

Varney is in the garage, smoking cigarettes in an aluminum folding chair and ashing into an empty Maxwell House can. He's looking at the slumbering mass of the Rolls-Royce with somber longing, occasionally wiping at his running nose with his soiled handkerchief. You sit down on the floor near him, leaning against the front tire of the haunted Plymouth.

"I have to tell you something," he says, distractedly handing you his pack of Kools.

"Okay," you say, taking a cigarette from the pack and lighting it.

Sucking in a deep breath, Varney says, "I lied. When I told my story, the one about how I met Ambrosio, I...well, I may have exaggerated some things."

"Okay?"

"The part about my family was all true. I really did kill them. All of them, and I'd do it again. But I was never one of the cool kids. I was a bookworm and a nerd. I didn't even lose my virginity until after I met Ambrosio, when he brought Erzsebet home. She was the first person I ever had sex with." He pauses to hawk a glob of red-and-green phlegm into the coffee can. "That bitch at Ellis Lake...her name was Flora Saville. Those things she said about me...how I asked her out, and that I was a loser, *et al*...she was telling the truth." He takes a long drag from the remaining stub of his cigarette before flicking it into the can. "And they really did find kiddie porn in my locker, but it really *wasn't* mine. I never did discover the identity of the asshole who put it in there, and he or she is lucky of that. Very lucky." He lights another cigarette and sighs, his breath rattling in his chest.

"Why are you telling me this?"

Varney shrugs. He opens his mouth to reply, but what comes out is a cough that produces another wad of bloodplegm. It takes him by surprise and he doesn't have time to grab his handkerchief, so the mucus lands on the dusty concrete by your feet. He frowns down at it for what feels like a long time before he speaks again. "It just seems important. Something has changed. You know it. Erzsebet knows it. I know it."

"If you're talking about your...sickness...you'll get better. Erzsebet will, too." You aren't sure why you bothered to say this. The words sound as hollow as they are. You're beyond the point of reassurances. You think of Erzsebet's clammy leg beneath your palm, and you shiver.

"I'm glad we found you, Casanova. I'm glad you're here."

For the third time tonight, you can't think of anything to say, so you don't say anything at all. The two of you just sit in smoke-filled silence for a long time, and then you go back inside, crawl into bed, and hope Mara will come to you again in your sleep.

She doesn't.

It's near dawn when you wake again, and when you sit up, you find yourself gripped with a feeling almost identical to what you'd felt the night you met Varney & Friends. This time, however, it's undeniably stronger. And this time, there isn't anyone here to stop you.

You get up and take your phone off the nightstand, pulling up Google and typing into the search bar, "time of sunrise today in Chatterley, OH."

7:06 AM.

Eleven minutes.

Just as it had been the night with the Drano, there's no melodramatic deliberation. No weighing of pros and cons. No melancholy. No Hawthorne Heights.

There are just two words, spray painted across your brain in huge purple letters.

FUCK IT.

You walk out of the bedroom, down the hall, and begin to ascend the spiral staircase. When you reach the sixth floor, you pause outside of Ambrosio's door, briefly considering one final appeal to Derek for a consultation with Ambrosio. The thought flits away almost immediately. What good, after all, would it do? What would you even say? If tonight's conversations with Varney and Erzsebet have proven anything, it's that there isn't anything *to* say.

There is only one thing, one thought that rises above all the rest.

FUCK IT.

"Yes," you say quietly to yourself. "Fuck it."

You walk past Ambrosio's door and advance down the hallway toward another door, the one at the very end.

The one that leads out onto the balcony.

The one that leads to the coming sun.

EPILOGUE

"Now *this* is what I'd call a plot twist."

You whirl around to see Ambrosio leaning against the balcony door, his legs crossed at the ankles and his arms folded across his chest. The bright yellow sunrays dance upon his white skin. You look down at your own pale self, illuminated but unharmed by the harsh morning light rising up from the east.

All you can think to say is, "What the fuck?"

Ambrosio walks up beside you and puts his hands on the banister, closing his eyes and smiling up at the sun. "Feels good, doesn't it?" he asks. "I love the feeling of sunlight in the morning."

With no small amount of hesitance, you turn back around, at first flinching away instinctively from the ferocious gold orb in the sky. When it still doesn't burn you into a smoldering pile of ashes, you look to Ambrosio and say, "I don't understand. Why aren't we burning?"

"Because, kid, sunlight doesn't make people burst into flames."

"But...I'm not a person. Me...Varney...Erzsebet...*you*...we're not people. We're monsters."

Ambrosio lights a cigarette and cocks a dubious eyebrow at you. "Be careful whom you include under that label, Casanova. *I* am *no* monster. I'm just a guy who likes to have a good time.

You and your Dracula-wannabe droogs, on the other hand, are *definitely* monsters. Some of the shit you kids have done is enough to send chills down *my* spine, and that's saying something, believe me. But it takes a great deal more than a bit of the old ultraviolet to make *real* monsters go up in smoke."

"I don't understand," you say again.

"No, I hadn't expected you would, even though it *is* pretty goddamn obvious."

You ball your hands into hateful fists. "What are you saying? That you *lied* to me? To *us?*"

"I may have bent the truth a *little*, yes. But you idiots ate up every word of it. Your generation, I *swear*. You'll believe absolutely *anything*, so long as it corroborates your own delusional fantasies." You try to protest, but he silences you with an upheld finger. "In spite of the *overwhelming* evidence that suggests none of you are, in fact, immortal, you *still* go cavorting all over town and drinking people dry."

"*Evidence?* What *evidence?*"

"Oh, for fuck's *sake*, wake *up*. How long has Erzsebet been sick? And do you *really* think it's a coincidence that *Varney* has suddenly gone under the weather? You don't think that it *might* be related to the fact that you guys run around *drinking people's fucking blood?* Shit, kid, do you know how *unsanitary* that is? Varney and Erzsebet have bloodborne pathogens crawling around inside of them that the CDC hasn't even *heard of*, yet." With a grin and a wink, he adds, "And if *they're* infected, it wouldn't be out of the question to assume that *you* might be, too, don't you think?"

You take a step back, your stomach clenching with nausea. You suddenly feel faint and chilled, and you have to grip the railing with a sweaty hand to keep from falling over.

"Furthermore," Ambrosio goes on, "how about the fact that you all puke your fucking guts out every time you 'feed'? Did *that* never strike you as a little strange? You didn't, perhaps, consider the possibility that the human body isn't *designed* for the ingestion of copious amounts of blood?"

"Varney said...he said that *you* said..."

"Oh, sure, I sold him some bogus line about how it's part of being a 'fledgling,' or whatever the fuck I called it. Honestly, I wasn't even sure he'd buy it. He came whining to me about how he couldn't keep the blood down, so I made something up on the spot. It's actually kind of a wonder that you guys can't digest blood, though, because you *can* swallow far more bullshit than I'd thought was humanly possible."

"No. No. *No.* You're lying. What about the *thirst?* I feel it, and it's real."

"Feelings aren't real, kid. I'll prove it to you. Close your eyes."

"Fuck you."

"Jeezus *pleezus*, why are you always so goddamn *hostile?* That's another thing about your generation. Always so quick to be on the defense, and *zero* respect for your elders. Now, would you *please* just *humor* me?"

You think back to the conversation you had with him in the hospital the night of Mara's death, when he'd willed you to sit down just by saying the words. It occurs to you that he could probably make you shut your eyes just as easily if you continue with your obstinance, so you do as he says and shut them of your own accord. That's what you tell yourself, at least. He may very well have put that very thought in your head, but you elect not to entertain that possibility.

"Good boy. Now, do me a favor, and picture a lemon."

"A *lemon?* What the fuck does a lemon have..."

"Settle *down*, and do as I say. Yes, a lemon. Next, I want you to imagine me taking a knife and cutting that lemon in half. Picture the juices oozing out with a little *hisss* as the blade slowly...very slowly...sinks deeper and deeper until it cuts all the way through. The lemon is now in two pieces. Picture yourself picking up one of those pieces and biting into it. Imagine your teeth puncturing its flesh, and the juice spreading across your tongue and onto the roof of your mouth. Now, open your eyes. What do you taste?"

You blink at him. "Lemons. So what?"

"Is your mouth watering?"

You swallow a mouthful of saliva. "Yeah, but again, so what?"

"Your mouth is watering, you taste lemons, but as far as *I* can see, you aren't *actually* eating a lemon. You've merely experienced a psychosomatic response to suggested stimuli. Does that answer your question about why you *think* you feel a 'thirst' for human blood?"

"No."

Ambrosio sighs. "I should have suspected as much, I suppose. Centennials. Your generation's slogan should be 'Ignorance: It's a Way of Life!'"

"Fuck you," you say again, unable to stop yourself. "It still doesn't make sense. Too many things don't add up. Ever since you made me immortal..."

"I never made you immortal. It didn't happen. You're a living, breathing, fifteen-year-old human boy. Oh, no, wait...you're *sixteen*, now, aren't you? Fuck, I totally forgot that it's your *birthday*. Gee willickers, kid, why didn't you remind me? I know this day *does* have a bit of a shadow over it because of that nasty business with your cousin, but *still*, birthdays are special."

You ignore him. "Ever since you...ever since I drank your blood, I've changed. I'm stronger. I'm smarter. I'm faster. I..."

Grinning at you from behind his cigarette, apparently having the time of his life, Ambrosio says, "Tell me, kid...were there any *other* major lifestyle changes that may, perhaps, have coincided with the sudden improvement to your health and mental wellbeing? It isn't my custom to spell things out like this in such an explicit fashion, but I'll admit, I'm *really* getting a kick out of all this. I've orchestrated my fair share of social experiments over the millennia, but dicking around with you and your bloodsucking buddies just might be in my top ten."

You try to think of what he might be talking about, attempting to piece together some missing link to his fucked-up puzzle, but your rage is preventing you from thinking clearly. "I really don't know what you're talking about," you say, frustrated both with him and yourself.

"I'll give you a hint, against my nature as it might be." He clears his throat, puffs on his cigarette, and says, "Derek's sister truly is a nice girl, and she *means* well, but...*eleven different medications?* Fuck, man, I'm surprised you could even remain upright."

The light of the sun suddenly feels very cold on your skin. *Everything* feels cold. It's like your brain has been pierced with a hundred jagged icicles.

The pills. When was the last time you even *thought* about the pills? Probably the last night you'd taken them, honestly. Out of sight, out of body, out of mind. So to speak.

"Don't beat yourself up," Ambrosio says, apparently seeing how dismayed you are at your failure to make the connection beforehand. "You've had a lot going on, lately. New friends, a reunion with the creepy hobo from LA, *loads* of cannibalistic murder...I can see how your past relationship with psychiatric medication might not have been the first thing on your mind."

Your legs feel weak, and you're afraid you're going to pass out. You put both hands on the guardrail and stare bitterly out at the sun. The sun that should be burning you alive, but isn't. "I'm so confused," you say in a softer voice, all the anger having been chased away by disorientation. "What happens now? What's going to happen to Varney and Erzsebet? What's going to happen to *me?* And what *are* you, really? How does that play into everything? What is..."

Ambrosio stops you with an upheld hand, the self-congratulatory delight no longer as evident on his face. "No more questions. I've already told you *far* more than I usually would, and you're lucky for that."

"Please," you beseech, grabbing the lapels of his jacket. Not in anger, but desperation. You're aware of how pathetic you must seem, but you don't care.

Ambrosio sighs again and gently pushes you off of him. He flicks his cigarette over the railing, lights another one, and says, "Fine. I'll make you a deal, because that's something in which I happen to specialize. If you promise to stop bleating like a toddler, I will grant you *one final question*. Just one, and *only* because it's your birthday. Ask me anything you want, and I promise to answer you truthfully. Absolutely anything. I'll tell you when you're going to die, if you'd like, or what happens *after* you die. Not both, though. I'll tell you when the world is going to end, or who's going to win the Presidential election on Tuesday. I'll tell you what's in Area 51. I'll tell you who shot Kennedy. Shit, I'll even tell you how many licks it takes to get to the center of a Tootsie Pop. Choose wisely, though, because you *only get one*." He grins his savage eel's grin and holds up a single finger. "One, and not one more."

You bow your head and shut your eyes, the black chariot of your heart beginning to pick up speed. There are so many things you want to know. You want to know where Mara is, for one, and if you'll see her when you die. You want to know if McPleasant suffered in the final moments before his death. You want to know if your parents can see you now, and if they still love you in spite of the things you've done. You want to know how you're supposed to go on from here, and whether or not it's even *worth* going on; you were, after all, ready to kill yourself just a few minutes ago, and these recent developments haven't made life any more appealing. Maybe, then, you should ask what will happen if you dive headfirst off the balcony.

There are so many things you want to ask, but in the end, the question you put forth is one you never would have expected to choose if put in this situation. From the look on Ambrosio's face when you ask it, you suspect he hadn't seen it coming, either.

Maybe it's the wrong question.

Maybe it's just another one of your "stupid questions."

Whatever it is, it's the question you choose.

And you only get one.

You raise your head, open your eyes, and meet Ambrosio's deathly black stare.

"What was in the shopping cart?"

ABOUT THE AUTHOR

Chandler Morrison is the author of seven previous books, including *#thighgap* and *Dead Inside*. His short fiction has appeared in numerous anthologies and literary journals. He lives in Los Angeles.